Just as legends and fragments of history from ancient Britain became the Arthurian tales we know—the "matter of Britain"—the story of Wyatt Earp, Doc Holliday, the Clantons, and others, told and retold in innumerable stories and dramatizations, has become a great American myth.

In the retelling you hold in your hand, some of the mystery of that brooding, puzzling tale is accounted for by the hitherto unrealized presence of magic. It is a story of power, of compulsion, and of consequences. If Roger Zelazny had written a Western, or if Susanna Clarke had reimagined the myths and legends of the American West, the results might have been something like *Territory*. But only *something* like it. Because nobody writes like Emma Bull.

PRAISE FOR *TERRITORY*

"Takes huge chances and achieves something distinctly wonderful . . . Readers will think about the story long after it ends, savoring the writing and imagining what the characters might do next."
                    —*Publishers Weekly* (starred review)

"Highly recommended!"   —*Starlog*

"You'll never see old Westerns the same way after reading *Territory*, Emma Bull's reimagining of the frontier West."   —Gavin J. Grant, *BookPage*

"Mesmerizing . . . Equal parts alternate history, fantasy, and Western. Remarkable."   —*VOYA*

"A terrific treat."   —*Rocky Mountain News*

Tor Books by Emma Bull

⇒ TERRITORY ⇐

Emma Bull

A TOM DOHERTY ASSOCIATES BOOK
NEW YORK

This is a work of fiction. All the characters, organizations, and events portrayed in this novel are either products of the author's imagination or are used fictitiously.

TERRITORY

Copyright © 2007 by Emma Bull

All rights reserved.

Edited by Patrick Nielsen Hayden

A Tor Book
Published by Tom Doherty Associates, LLC
175 Fifth Avenue
New York, NY 10010

www.tor-forge.com

Tor® is a registered trademark of Tom Doherty Associates, LLC.

ISBN-13: 978-0-8125-4836-5
ISBN-10: 0-8125-4836-1

First Edition: July 2007
First Mass Market Edition: January 2009

Printed in the United States of America

0 9 8 7 6 5 4 3 2 1

This book is dedicated to Joan Shetterly,
patron saint,
and to Bob Shetterly,
who probably still wants a cowboy book.

Acknowledgments

Many thanks to Steven K. Z. Brust, who is, without doubt, your huckleberry; John M. Ford, for handing me a copy of Paula Mitchell Marks's *And Die in the West;* Bob Boze Bell and the staff and contributing writers of *True West* magazine, who believe that history doesn't stand still; Paula Vitaris, for making sure I read Frank Manley's "Barefoot on the Barfoot Trail"; Lefty at G. F. Spangenberg's Pioneer Gun Shop, for answers to strange ammo inquiries; all the fine western history writers on all sides of the Earp-Clanton question and the Matter of Tombstone; the people of Tombstone, Arizona, particularly the staff of Old West Books on Allen Street; the Single Action Shooting Society and the Cowboy Mounted Shooting Association, whose members gave me a glimpse of what it might have been like; the Carolina Belles and the Cats of Belle Alley, for helping me immerse myself in the more decorative aspects of the late nineteenth century; the Lively Arts History Association, ditto; Cat Eldridge and the gang at *Green Man Review,* for making sure I didn't run out of soundtrack; the Reverend Rod Richards, who had the right epigram; Delia Sherman, Ellen Kushner, and Terri Windling, for sanctuary in the desert; Valerie Smith, for being all agent-y; Patrick Nielsen Hayden, who let me buck the tiger until I won; and of course, Will Shetterly, who makes almost all things possible.

Uncommon thanks are overdue to Dr. Donald Drake, Dr. Robert Chandler, Arlene Nieves and her staff, and

Robin DeRose and the gang at The Hand Center, for restoration of the author. They make me glad I live in the twenty-first century. I'm grateful also to Betsy Stemple, Geri Sullivan, and Lorraine Garland, for kindness that knows no century.

On the Horse Taming Depicted in this Book

John Solomon Rarey's techniques for gentling and training horses were revolutionary in their day, far more humane and successful than the methods they replaced. They've been replaced in their turn by modern trainers' understanding of horse psychology, which has led to better, safer training for both horse and rider. Like so many attitudes in a historical novel, the horse handling described here is a curiosity of the past. Don't try this at home; there are better ways to get the job done.

If you ever read this tale, you will likely ask yourself more questions than I should care to answer. . . . I might go on for long to justify one point and own another indefensible; it is more honest to confess at once how little I am touched by the desire of accuracy. This is no furniture for the scholar's library, but a book for the winter evening schoolroom when the tasks are over. . . .

—Robert Louis Stevenson, from
the dedication to *Kidnapped*

Nothing changes more constantly than the past; for the past that influences our lives does not consist of what actually happened, but of what [we] believed happened.

—Gerald W. Johnson

A society in crisis teaches itself to congeal into one story only, and sees reality through very narrow glasses. But there is never only one story.

—Amos Oz

☞ TERRITORY ☜

The buckskin horse walked up Allen Street just before dawn. Its head was low, its dollar-gold hide was marked with drying sweat, and its black legs were caked with dust. The man on its back was slumped forward with his face in the tangled black mane. His hat was missing, showing hair as straight and black and disarranged as his mount's. A stain spread dark on the side and skirt of his brown canvas coat.

An ore wagon thundered by, murdering sleep for newcomers who weren't accustomed to the sound. A few drowsy, half-drunk miners trudged toward the shafts that rimmed the town, clutching their coats to keep out the cold spring air. Neither the miners nor the wagon driver so much as glanced at the man on the horse. A man slumped on a horse wasn't enough to make a baby stare in Tombstone.

The horse stopped uncertainly at the edge of the street, outside a building tricked out in turned porch posts, raised moldings, and gold paint. Yellow light glowed in its window and through the open double doors. The murmur of men's voices and the clank of glass against glass reached the street.

The buckskin seemed to expect the man to rouse himself, fling the reins around the hitching rail, and clatter across the boardwalk and through the doors. When nothing of the sort occurred, it stepped forward, once, twice. A fly bit it, and it flinched. At that, the rider slid out of the saddle like an unstrapped pack, and landed hard on his back in the dust.

A man peered out the door. His face was round, blunt-nosed, and topped with a pile of sandy-red cherub curls;

a moustache, an imperial, and a scowl kept it from out-right childishness. He was red-eyed with liquor and smoke. His shirt was wrinkled, and sweat made dark half circles under his arms.

"Hell. Some damned drunk fool fell off his God-damned horse." He stepped unsteadily to the edge of the boardwalk and frowned over the still figure. "Well, shit. Milt, Billy!" he called back over his shoulder. "Give me a hand!"

Chairs scraped inside, and Milt and Billy pushed out onto the walk. Milt, the older of the two, sent an arc of tobacco juice into the street. "Just because you can't play cards worth a fart doesn't mean you can break up the game."

"Help me haul this kid."

Billy, taller than the other two, bony at the joints like an adolescent wolf, looked down at the boy in the street. His eyes grew wide. "Jesus, Ike," he said with the suggestion of a squeak. Then he seemed to recollect himself; he settled his face into an awkward sneer. "Better him than me."

"Quit yammering and take his legs."

They picked up the boy and maneuvered through the doors. They slung him, not very gently, onto the surface of the table closest to the window, scattering the components of their interrupted poker game. The bartender, nodding behind a copy of yesterday's *Epitaph*, ignored them.

There was only one player still sitting at the game. When the three men dropped their untidy burden in front of him he sighed heavily. "I believe," he said, "I am being inconvenienced."

"Sorry—Milt, go fetch Goodfellow—but the doc'll want the light." Ike jerked his thumb at the lamp shining down over the table. "Fellow's been shot, don't you see."

The bartender looked up sharply over his newspaper. "By God, Ike, if he bleeds on that table, you'll clean it up."

The seated man raised a corner of the boy's coat and extracted a glass half full of whiskey from under it. He took a swallow. "Anyone you know?"

Billy answered. "He might be Sarey Diaz's brother, up from Cananea."

"Hell, no," replied Ike, chewing his moustache. "Seen him before, though. He was riding drag with Leonard and Crane on a herd going up to Chandler's ranch."

"Is he still alive?" asked the seated man.

"Seems so."

Another heavy sigh; then the last of the whiskey went down his throat. "Yes, he would be."

Doc Holliday looked down at the wounded boy on top of his cards and tried to think of something else. He clutched at irritation over the spoiled game: now he'd never know if Milt Hicks had had anything when he raised the second time.

He wasn't drunk enough for dying boys, especially ones he wasn't responsible for. To have this one land in front of him—if he signified what Doc suspected he did—was a foul sort of practical joke.

The fever swelled in his skull, buzzed in his ears. His lungs were like hot lead bars inside his chest— lead bars you could cough up a piece at a time. He ought to be in bed, not on display in the front window of the Oriental. Damn Morgan for a perfect empty-headed, God-forsaken idiot.

He was lucky it was Frank Leslie tending the Oriental's bar. Frank did what Wyatt told him to, and Doc, in Wyatt's absence, could sometimes pass for the voice of Wyatt. He'd bullied Frank into selling him a bottle.

And the cards were good, better than medicine. He'd rather play with clever players, but he'd settle for Ike and Billy Clanton and Milt Hicks. Doc loved the cool, relentless logic of the cards. They had no pity or fear or doubt; they fell as they fell, and anyone who regretted or begged them or raged at them was a fool. Sometimes he wished he could be part of the deck. A red jack, maybe, expressionless, with two heads and no ass.

Now here was this corpse, or soon-to-be corpse, reminding him that flesh was frail and plans were made to totter and fall.

At the corner of his eye, he saw someone step through the doors. *Milt with the doctor. Goodfellow must have come in his nightshirt*, Doc thought as he looked around. But it wasn't Dr. Goodfellow.

Doc could measure and judge a man or woman at a glance; any decent card dealer could. He might choose to fly in the face of his judgment, but he always took that measure. He didn't gamble.

The man who stood framed in the doorway could be read like a book printed in three languages, none of which Doc felt he properly knew. He straightened a little in his chair.

He wanted to know how the man's eyes moved, but the newcomer wore dark spectacles like a blind man, smoky green glass in gold wire frames. His wide-brimmed, low-crowned hat deserved better treatment than it had received of late. His hair, probably brown under the dust, hung in a plait to his shoulder blades, the way some Indians and a few of the Mexicans wore theirs. Doc guessed he'd been clean-shaven a week ago.

The nap was worn off his corduroy sack coat at the sleeve hems and elbows and collar; Doc was puzzled to make out its original color. The waistcoat underneath was missing a button, and there was no collar on his shirt. The buckle of a gunbelt showed at his open coat front.

The newcomer swept his hat off and moved to slap it against his thigh, then seemed to reconsider. Good; the dust would have choked them all. The man surveyed the room and its inhabitants, and spotted the unconscious boy.

"Oh. There he is." He moved toward the table. Doc expected him to take the spectacles off then, but he didn't. It was like looking into the blank dark eyes of a locust.

"If you're a friend of this gentleman's," Doc said, "I feel I should warn you that he has a God-damned large hole in him somewhere."

The newcomer laid two fingers to the boy's pulse just below the jaw. He frowned. "No, not a friend. Have you sent for the doctor?"

"Heavens, no," said Doc, and saw Ike twitch. "We had a mind to let him bleed to death and see how long it took."

The man smiled—good white teeth—as he folded back the boy's coat and pulled up the checked shirt underneath. Doc stayed where he was. He was afraid he might sway if he stood up.

The man fumbled at his trouser pocket, but the gunbelt got in his way. His eyebrows dropped down to meet the spectacle frames. He unbuckled the belt in a single smooth motion and dropped the rig on the chair next to Doc. Doc made a point of studying it over, just to see what its owner would do, which was exactly nothing. A blued, long-nosed Colt Army with walnut grips, in worn leather.

"My name's Jesse Fox." The man pulled a handkerchief from his pocket. Unlike the rest of him, the handkerchief looked clean.

"Pleased," Doc said. "Dr. John Henry Holliday, at your service." In his own ears it sounded like an alias. Nobody called him John, and precious few called him Dr. Holliday.

"You're a doctor?" Fox's hands stopped above the boy's ribs, and his face turned to Doc.

Doc grinned. "Dentist."

"Oh. Would you pass me that whiskey, please?"

Doc looked at the bottle on the floor beside him, that he'd snatched off the table when Ike made to drop the boy on it. "Only if you intend to drink some."

"Let's pretend I am." Fox stretched his hand out for the bottle.

Doc looked up into Fox's face. No threat or plea— only the neutral, polite smile and the outstretched hand. Doc passed the bottle even as he wondered why he would do any such thing.

And of course, Fox poured it on the wound. *At least I hadn't bought the good stuff*.

Fox made a Ladies' Aid Society noise—tsk, tsk— and did something with the handkerchief and the wound. "I hope the doctor's close."

"Funny how you went right for the spot," Ike said suddenly. Doc almost jumped; he'd forgotten there were other people in the room. "Maybe you shot him."

Fox raised his face in Ike's direction. "Positively I shot him. He was stealing my horse."

That shut Ike up. And Doc, too, but he recovered quicker. "Mr. Fox, Ike Clanton. The young man with him is his brother Billy." Fox gave them each a polite and distant nod. "You appear to be wearing most of the dirt between here and Prescott. Whereabouts did it happen?"

"I was camped two hours north of here."

"And this fellow showed up on foot?"

"Maybe someone stole his horse." The face around the spectacles was perfectly expressionless.

Doc grinned and leaned back in his chair. This was as good as a play. And useful, perhaps. He stole a glance at Ike and Billy, and decided that, with a little prompting, they'd remember the conversation.

"He's got his hair braided up like a squaw," Billy said suddenly, as if it had taken him that long to recall where he'd seen it.

"Or a Chinaman," Ike said. "No, on Chinamen it's longer. You're right, Billy, it's a squaw braid."

"I hear fellas who've got the syphillis wear dark glasses. Light hurts their eyes." Billy shot a look at Ike and grinned.

A pity that Billy took his older brother for his model. And it was just like Ike to wait until a man had proved himself polite and sober, and had taken off his gun, before he poked at him.

But for all the reaction of the round green lenses, they might have spoken Russian.

"Say there, fellow," Frank broke in from behind the bar. His eyes shifted from Fox to Ike and Billy. "If you're meaning to stay in here, I'll mind that gun for you."

What's the matter, Frank? Doc thought. *Getting too old to duck?*

"Certainly. Thank you." Fox lifted the gunbelt off the chair and pushed it to Frank across the bar, as if he'd offered to take his hat and coat.

"Who says that's your horse?" Ike asked. "Might be this fella's, and you were the one doing the stealing."

"If I'd done it, my feet wouldn't hurt, and I wouldn't be standing here on them discussing it with you. I suppose you mean *trying* to do it."

Ike frowned at Fox as if he wasn't sure he'd been answered.

A crack of laughter escaped Doc before he could swallow it. "These fine distinctions are wasted on Ike," he said. Ike turned his frown on Doc. "This boy's in no condition to tell his side. Lacking that, you might want to back your claim with something."

Fox sighed. "What would you have done for fun if I hadn't shown up?"

"Won money off these boys until they quit."

Ike opened his mouth to reply, but Milt burst through the doorway with Doc Goodfellow behind him. He stopped at the sight of Fox. Goodfellow ran into Milt from behind, swore at him, and pushed past to the table. Fox stepped aside.

The doctor jerked open the wide mouth of his leather bag and began to pull things out: two brown bottles; a canvas bundle that unrolled to show the bright chrome of scissors, probes, and retractors; a wad of cotton lint; a scalpel case. Doc rose and moved away from what had become a surgery. He didn't like to linger in places where life and death were smiling at each other over their cards.

"Gunshot?" Goodfellow asked the room.

"Yes, sir," Fox replied.

Goodfellow spared him a glance before turning back to his work. "Anybody who knows how it happened should tell it to Ben Sippy."

Fox turned to Doc. "The law?"

"City marshal. But Goodfellow's a damned high stickler about these little disagreements." Doc watched Goodfellow out of the corner of his eye, and was sorry to find himself ignored.

Fox sighed. "As well now as later. Where do I find him?"

"City offices are on Fremont. North, and a block west. It'll be another hour before anyone's there."

"Then I guess I'll sit on the doorstep." Fox turned toward the door.

Ike stepped into his path. "You plan on telling him about that horse?"

Fox, from the set of his head, just stared.

Doc ambled to the end of the bar. He wanted to watch Fox's face for this. Ike must be even more drunk than he was himself.

"Well?" Ike stuck out his chin. "I'll wager you can't prove that's your horse."

Fox's voice was so soft Doc had to hold his breath to hear it. "I don't feel like taking your money."

Stand aside, Ike, Doc thought happily. *Stand aside or prepare to throw down.* The room was thick with the feeling before the lightning. But Fox's gun was behind the bar. Had he forgotten he wasn't heeled?

Fox drew his spectacles a little way down his nose. That was all: just slid them down and studied Ike over them like someone's maiden auntie might.

Fox's eyes were a penetrating light brown. The lamplight caught in the nearest one, like a glass of good bourbon with a flame shining through it.

In that suspended moment, Doc was gripped by a feeling he couldn't name. It wasn't fear. He feared only one thing, and no man could bring that down on him. But it was enough like fear to make him heedless of the weight in his lungs.

Ike stepped aside, his mouth pressed shut under his moustache. Fox pushed the spectacles up. The lightning had struck and gone, and left cold empty air behind it.

Fox walked outside. Ike, Milt, and Billy followed him, unconscious as ducklings. Doc pushed away from the bar and followed, too, as far as the doorway, where he leaned.

There was a buckskin horse of exceptional quality tied to the rail. It raised its head, nostrils flaring, as Fox reached the edge of the boardwalk.

"That's a handsome fellow," Doc said.

Fox glanced back and smiled. Then he untied the horse, laid the reins loose over the saddle, and walked away into the street.

Halfway across he stopped and whistled, three carrying notes.

The horse's ears swiveled at the sound. It lurched away from the rail and covered the ground between it and Fox in a few brisk steps. Fox looked over his shoulder at the men standing outside the Oriental and nodded. Then he turned back up Fifth Street with the horse behind him like a dog at heel.

"You forgot your iron," Doc called after him.

Fox stopped and looked back. The round green lenses flashed in the dawn.

"It'll wait for me," he replied. He, and the horse that was unquestionably his, went on up Fifth and passed out of sight.

Doc laughed.

"That son of a bitch is looking for trouble," Ike grumbled.

"I doubt it," Doc replied. "But if he is, you're not the man to bring it."

"What's that mean?"

"Not a thing, Ike. You do as you please." Doc smiled up at the morning sky. He felt pleasantly tired, sleepy even. Now he could go back to Fly's and maybe catch a few winks before he set off after the posse.

Mildred Benjamin regularly stepped out her front door braced for whatever practical joke Nature had prepared. This morning she found the best one of all: perfection.

She stood squinting and wondering like a creature let out of the Ark. The air was cool, and fragrant with sage from the foothills. Some freak breeze had laid the dust and smoke from the mines, and the Dragoon Mountains looked as close as the other end of town. The sky was blue and wide in a way she could never describe in letters to her sisters in Philadelphia. The closest she'd managed was that, out here, you understood the true circumference of the Earth, because you could see it reaching past you on every side.

Mildred thought of her riding habit in the clothespress, and the sorrel mare for hire at Crabtree's Livery. Between Tombstone and the San Pedro River lay miles of open land.

But she could almost hear Harry Woods saying, "News waits for no one," as if that were one of its chief virtues. One did not let the news down. She checked the anchorage of her hat, flicked the pleated hem of her skirt aside, and closed her front door.

"Good morning, Mrs. Benjamin!"

Mildred turned to find Lucy Austerberg coming down the street, skirts clutched up out of the dust, face shaded by a gypsy hat and a parasol. Mildred's mother had probably prayed her daughters would have skin like Lucy Austerberg's. If so, God had been busy with other things that day.

"Good morning, Mrs. Austerberg. Lovely morning." Sacrilege, to describe it as merely lovely.

"You haven't heard?" Lucy said, and pursed her little pink mouth in lieu of a frown.

"I must not have," Mildred said.

"Someone robbed the stage last night."

Mildred felt herself stiffen like a pointer dog at a bird. "Which stage? Where did it happen?"

"My goodness, I don't know. My Frederick went out with the posse, but that's as much as I've heard. Now I have to do the accounts and the ordering that he'd have done, so if I forget something, he can just blame the robbers for it, that's all. What a quick walker you are, Mrs. Benjamin!"

"Sorry, Mrs. Austerberg. I'd best get on to the office. You'll forgive me?"

"Of course, Mrs. B." As Mildred set off at an unladylike pace, Lucy called, "You let me know if you hear anything, won't you?"

Which was a polite way of saying, "Pass along anything the *Nugget* doesn't see fit to print." Mildred gave her a wave that could mean yes or no, and headed for Fourth Street.

For no reason she could name, she thought of her grandmother. Bubbe would have said that good and bad always arrive on the same horse. She would have looked out Mildred's front door that morning and commented on some omen that only she seemed to have heard of, a black bird on a white fence, or an eddy of dust, or a broken bootlace three days before.

Mildred had come west to outrun predestination, supernatural or otherwise. She wondered if Bubbe had done the same in her time.

Mildred pushed through the door of the *Nugget* office, making the bell clash. The smell wrapped around her: ink, machine oil, newsprint, and cigars. It was as far from the air of the open country as she could imagine; it was the smell of human concerns and human pride. But she felt it settle her nerves and sharpen her mind as it always did. Here rumors were sorted into facts or lies. Here the world extended beyond the reach of any one man, to San Francisco, New York, London, Vienna, Cairo, St. Petersburg, Peking. Here the random course of life could be shaped by words until it became news.

Harry Woods looked up from his typewriter and the mess on his desk, peering through his magnifying spectacles and not quite focusing on her.

"You're late, Millie."

"I'm early." She yanked the pin out of her hat and tossed it on a peg. "Just because you sleep under the press and start work at dawn doesn't mean the rest of us will."

"News doesn't wait for sunup."

"So I heard. A stage holdup?"

"Attempted holdup. Bud Philpot's dead."

It stopped her in mid-breath. Not a roughneck, not a rounder, not a rustler, but a man everyone spoke well of, who was only doing his work. "I'll set up the page. Do they know who it was?"

"If you'll quit talking and let me think, you'll get the whole story off the copy."

She took her big drill apron from the peg beside her hat and wrapped it around her. With half her mind, she thought, *Bud brought me my package of books just last week, so I wouldn't have to go to the Wells Fargo office.* The other half was thinking about the size of type for the headline announcing his death. No, "Driver killed" would be the subhead.

She caught herself and snapped, "This is no place for a lady of delicate sensibilities."

"Then thank God you're not one. Be a waste of your ability to spell." Harry yanked a sheet out of the machine, added it to a sheaf of others, and handed it to her.

"And to read your typewriting." The pages were salted with crossed-out sentences, scrambled words, and flying letters.

It was the Kinnear stage north to Benson. Bud Philpot had been driving, with Bob Paul up as guard. Somewhere between Tombstone and Contention, Philpot had gotten stomach cramps and turned the reins over to Paul. So when the stage was stopped near Drew's Station, Philpot was the one in the guard's seat. The one who drew the robbers' fire.

Paul had grabbed the dying Philpot as the horses bolted, and got the stage into Benson with the Wells Fargo strongbox untouched. An outside passenger named Roerig had been wounded, and died at Benson. Sheriff Behan, Deputy Breakenridge, and a posse of Tombstone citizens had left town in the small hours, and at last report had crossed the robbers' trail and were in pursuit.

"Doesn't tell me much," Mildred said.

"Tells you more than you knew when you walked in. If the posse finds anything, we'll know; I asked Break to tell anyone he sent back to stop here first."

"News before peacekeeping? Shame, Harry, and you the undersheriff."

"Then it's not news before peacekeeping if I hear first, is it? John Clum's only the mayor."

"If he's riding with the posse, that's the end of your exclusive."

"Read on, Mrs. Benjamin, read on."

She did. John Clum, Tombstone mayor and editor of the *Epitaph*, in company with Messrs. Parsons and Abbot, declined to join the posse, instead remaining in town to keep an eye on several persons they identified as suspicious characters.

"Oh, Lord. Oh, Harry—"

"You laugh now, you should have seen those three

skulking around as if they were in an Edgar Allan Poe story. Thank God they didn't have guns on 'em."

"I know if I'd robbed a stage on the other side of Contention, I'd ride straight back to Tombstone and linger about looking suspicious until I was sure the news had got to town."

Harry Woods grinned. "Now, you see? You keep up that kind of rational thinking and you could be mayor someday."

"I count on the *Nugget*'s endorsement." Mildred pinned the copy to her table. "Any idea how much was aboard?"

Harry smiled. "Twenty-five thousand dollars in silver."

Her hands froze over the type case. "Good God. You think they knew?"

"I think if I were robbing stages, I'd want a little more than luck and a fast horse. Say, a friend in the right place?"

Mildred turned to Harry's copy and read the last paragraph, the one she'd only skimmed. "Well, there's no libel suit here."

"Don't worry, there isn't going to be. But I'm looking forward to hearing what the posse finds."

Mildred looked out the window at her perfect day, and thought, *This is nothing. It'll dry up like water at noon, the way most things do.*

After all, when Curly Bill Brocius shot Fred White, it had turned the town into an anthill of vigilante committees that threatened never to settle. But it had. And Fred had been city marshal. Poor Bud Philpot was no one in comparison.

Here in this room, death was just another fact entered into the record. News didn't grieve. It took note, moved on. Mildred filled the composing stick with the first line of the body copy.

She was peripherally aware of reporters ducking in to deliver copy or get assignments. She heard the voice of Richard Rule, the city editor, and looked up. He and Harry were absorbed in speculation about the robbery. Reporters had time to gossip; typesetters had work to do. She smiled to think how Harry and Rule would take that.

The light from the window was bright enough to set type by. Nearly the equinox, she realized as she laid in the leading strips on the fourth paragraph. Which meant she'd been in Tombstone . . . a year? She and David had arrived in early March, and the high desert was daubed with color after a wet winter. She'd stared, awestruck, at the ocotillo: cockades of bloom so red they hurt her eyes sprouting above the inch-long spines. Like a peacock with fangs, David had suggested, laughing.

David had been dead for eight months, one and a half weeks. Their life together had taught her she was stronger even than she'd thought. His dying had been her last lesson.

Mildred squinted down at the copy and found a fearsome garble of typewriting and pencil. "Harry?" she called. "What in heaven's name did you mean by S-M-O-L-I-N?"

No answer. She looked up—into the face of a stranger.

The window light haloed the man who stood on the other side of the waist-high railing. Had she missed the bell over the door? Or had it rung at all?

She gazed a little wildly around the office. She was alone.

The stranger was as dusty and shabby as any drover at the end of a long cattle drive. But the long drives were over, except in old men's stories, and none of them had ever ended in Arizona Territory. He wore spectacles with dark lenses, as if the light of day was too much for him. She couldn't be sure, but she thought he was staring at her.

"May I help you?" Mildred said, and her voice cracked.

The stranger seemed to wake with a start. "I . . . Is this the newspaper office?"

He was real. Surely ghosts didn't stammer. She looked at the type cases, the page she was setting, the press and the folding machine hulking like bears and visible through the door to the back room. "I believe it's one of them, yes."

His eyebrows rose above the spectacles. "There's more than one?"

"Gracious, any town with only one newspaper isn't big enough for the name." She thought of some of the company mines farther north. "Or it's owned by someone."

He was still, digesting that. Mildred thought he was staring again. Where the devil was Harry? And the pressmen—shouldn't they be here by now? There was no sound from the back room.

"*Is* there something I can help you with?" Mildred asked.

The stranger ducked his head and took his spectacles off. Mildred tensed. But the eyes he raised to hers were wide and tea-colored and unmarred. His smile wasn't the toothy, confident one of a man about to call her "sweetheart" or tell her what a pretty thing she was. It was, in fact, mildly apologetic.

"I'd like to buy a copy of the paper," he said.

She hadn't expected that. *But it's a newspaper office, for heaven's sake.* "You're a tad early for today's."

"I'll settle for yesterday's. Things don't change that fast here, do they?"

"You'd be amazed." Mildred pushed through the

gate and across the aisle to the cabinet behind Harry's desk. Two copies left. She'd remind Harry to increase the run today; the holdup would sell papers.

The holdup. She felt the presence of the man behind her like a hot stove at her back. She glanced over her shoulder.

He hadn't moved. He was looking at her partly set page, his head tilted at a near-painful angle. Or perhaps he was reading Harry's copy.

What kind of temptation would twenty-five thousand dollars be to an out-at-the-elbows drifter? How dirty would a man get, waiting in the washes for a stagecoach to make its run, riding all night to avoid the posse? And what if a robber *were* brazen enough to come into town after the attempt, clever enough to realize that sensible people would expect him to be anywhere else?

She took a paper from the stack and came back to him. "Five cents."

He dropped the nickel into her palm. It seemed to burn her skin, but she closed her fingers over it anyway. "I'm new to town," he said. "My name's Jesse Fox."

Mildred ignored the hint. "I hope you have a pleasant stay."

"Meaning, you don't expect I'll be here long."

"I try not to show a rude interest in other people's business."

His eyebrows went up in mock surprise. "But this is a newspaper office."

Wary as she was, she had to laugh at his wounded look. "Oh, are you news, then?"

Fox shook his head. "I'd hoped for a mention in the social column, at least. 'Newly arrived in our fair camp is Mr. Jesse Fox, late of Durango, Colorado.'"

" 'Who has come for the benefits of our salubrious climate'?" She found herself remembering people who hadn't found the place healthful—Bud Philpot being the latest. Fox's brown eyes, clear as running water, met hers. She felt as if he were seeing all the way to the back of her skull. "*Will* you be here long?" she added quickly.

"I thought that wasn't your business?"

"You can't expect to be reported on if you won't say much." Talking to him made Mildred nervous, but *not* talking was worse.

"Are you a reporter, Miss . . ."

"No."

He looked down at the paper in his hands, then up again at Mildred. "I can find out your name, you know."

It didn't sound like a threat, but Mildred tensed, even so. "Then I needn't make you a gift of it," she said, in the voice that had warned off bankers' sons in a dozen Philadelphia ballrooms.

Either he was richer than a banker's son, or he had some more effective source of impudence. He grinned at her. "Oh, no, I wouldn't put you to the trouble."

The back door banged closed, and Mildred looked around to see Harry coming past the press into the front room. She heard the pressmen, as well; two sets of boots on the wood floor, two hoarse voices, the steel-and-cast-iron racket of setting up the press.

Harry gave Fox an unreadable stare. "Mrs. Benjamin taking care of you?" he asked mildly.

Fox blinked at Harry; then he caught Mildred's eye and lifted his eyebrows. Mildred clenched her hands together in front of her and glared at him.

"She's been a great help." Fox bowed his head gravely to Mildred. "Good day, Mrs. Benjamin." And he tucked his paper under his threadbare elbow and left.

"Who was that?" asked Harry.

"His name is Jesse Fox, he's just passing through, he's lived in Durango, and yesterday's newspaper was good enough for him."

Harry sighed. "I don't know why papers don't hire more pretty young lady reporters. People will tell 'em anything."

"Like it or not. So you've never seen him before?"

"Not that I recollect. But there are people in the world I haven't met. Isn't that column set yet?"

With Fox gone, the sun shining in the window, and Harry's dry voice in her ears, she felt foolish. The robbers would be fifty miles away by now.

"Did he say if he was putting up somewhere?" Harry asked.

"If . . . No, he didn't."

"Hm." Harry moved papers on his desk until he unearthed his humidor. He took out a cigar and nipped the end off. "Might be a good thing to know."

"So he worried you, too!"

"Millie, never talk yourself out of your instincts. So long as they don't lead you to jail or to court, you might as well see if there's anything to 'em."

"I just set type. No instinct needed."

"Hm," he said again, and struck a match on the flank of the stove. "Maybe you ought to get on with that."

She went back to her page. On the stand beside Harry's copy were six of the thin lead strips she spaced lines of type with. They teetered on their narrow edges, forming three chevrons with their points toward the door like a compass needle.

Mildred swept them back into the type case. She

wasn't sure why Harry shouldn't see them, but he was the one who said she should trust her instincts. She was certain the heat in the six strips of lead was her imagination.

≈ 3 ≈

The red paper banners flapping on a handcart made Sam jump like a cat. An old man sprang out of the way and screamed at the horse. Jesse looked down from the saddle, dazed, and the old man shifted his stream of high-pitched abuse to him.

Jesse frowned, ransacking his memory for Chinese words and inflections. When the old man slowed down, Jesse said carefully, "Sorry thousand times. Unworthy—" The noun escaped him. Or should he have already used the noun?

The old man peered up at him, snorted, and hobbled away. Jesse sighed and turned Sam's head into the flow of traffic.

It was not, strictly speaking, flowing. They'd been on the main street a moment ago, and Jesse would have sworn to a judge that he hadn't turned off it. But the passage that Sam picked his way down now would have been an alley, if alleys were ordinarily busy and crowded and loud.

On both sides, wooden buildings and canvas tents compressed the pedestrians, horses, mules, wagons, livestock, and bins of merchandise into a dense, nearly undifferentiated mass, like nougat candy. Jesse could smell incense, raw meat, cooked rice, and a faint odor of chicken coop in an oddly homely combination. Except for the old man, people seemed to dodge him without looking at him.

A grocer dragged a basket of pale green leaves out of a cart and set it with other baskets under his awning. Two middle-aged men in high-collared padded jackets met, smiled, and bowed to each other while the crowd jostled by. Two women, their hair rumpled, wrinkled silk wrappers clutched around them, stood at the flaps of a tent and scolded a man outside stirring a kettle of rice gruel. He growled, and they screamed with laughter.

In front of a squat adobe, a little boy plucked *bao* out of a steaming pan with a pair of tongs so big he had to use both hands. The sight of the rolls, the smell of steamed bread, made Jesse's stomach rumble. An apothecary stood behind a pine plank laid across two barrels. Behind him stood an antique hundred-drawer chest of polished mahogany. Jesse recognized ginseng root on the plank counter, but nothing else.

Through the door of a wooden house Jesse could see a glitter of gold and scarlet paint and the glowing tips of joss sticks burning at an altar. A handcart loaded with wooden cages of shrieking, flapping chickens made Sam throw up his head and snort.

He was in Chinatown.

Well, of course he was. But this was Tombstone's Chinatown. He realized that for the last few minutes he'd been riding through the Hoptowns of Silver City, Virginia City, Sacramento, and San Francisco, unconscious and unsurprised. It was so familiar that he felt almost at home.

And why shouldn't home be five minutes in a place you'd never seen, because a signboard or a doorway or an accent reminded you of something you took for granted long ago?

Jesse shifted his aching left arm, rolled the shoulder.

He wouldn't stop here, but he needed to find some-place soon—he should feed Sam and let him rest, get himself a bath, change the dressing on his arm. And sleep.

When he was tired, time ceased to be railroad-track linear and became like a school of fish. That was prob-ably how he'd ended up in the newspaper office. Just sleepwalking, after leaving the city marshal: get the local paper, get a feel for the place. But he wasn't stop-ping in Tombstone.

When he'd remembered that, standing in the office of the—what was it?—the *Daily Nugget*, it was like waking up. Waking up to find Mrs. Benjamin before him, deep in her work. She'd eyed him as if he were a varmint and she was trying to recall if he was the trap-ping sort, or the shooting sort.

None of that explained why he'd pretended he might stay in town. The sun through the window had turned her curling, untidy hair into a crown of fire. She'd worn the craftsman's face as she bent over the page: focused and distant at once. And when she'd raised her head, her dark eyes had seemed to pull him into her, so that those quick, tapering fingers seemed to be his, and when those eyebrows went up, he could feel them on his own forehead. That, too, was probably because he was tired.

Mrs. Benjamin. She'd been mad enough to spit when her boss had given him her name. Pretty—well, prettyish, mostly in the way her face moved. Photo-graphs probably didn't do her justice.

That was Mr. Benjamin's problem. Jesse was going to Mexico.

When the dentist, Holliday, had reminded him about his pistol, he'd answered without thinking. Al-ready sleepwalking. Well, he'd buy another damned gun. Better than turning back into the center of town, where the air seemed thick and clinging for all its dryness.

Sam stopped short. Jesse lurched forward over Sam's neck as a streak of black passed almost under his hooves. Then he heard a jangle of Chinese, and a small boy dashed under Sam's nose.

"Hey, careful!" Jesse yelled after him, and realized he'd spoken in Chinese, out of the shoals of memory. The black streak, he saw before the boy and his quarry disappeared, was a pig.

He looked up. The plaque nailed to the doorpost beside him was gilt-edged scarlet with the Chinese characters for "physician" in black. There was a notch in the bottom edge where a knot had fallen out of the wood and been painted over. The sign painter had smudged the last upright stroke of his calligraphy.

San Francisco. *"Everyone else puts his name on his sign,"* Jesse protested as he stood at the door that led up to Chow Lung's second-floor rooms.

"Perhaps everyone else needs to," Lung replied. *"My patients know my name, and those who are not yet my patients only want to know there is a doctor within."*

"So using your name would be false humility?"

"Exactly," Lung said, beaming.

"You're a madman," Jesse told him.

Sam tossed his head. Jesse realized his hands had tightened on the reins. "Sorry," he said, and stroked Sam's neck. He slid out of the saddle before he'd quite decided he would do it. Someone else might own the sign now. But at least he could ask the someone else if he knew Chow Lung, lately a physician in San Francisco.

A Chinese boy of about ten stepped out the door with a broom in his hands. He saw Jesse and stared.

Jesse tried a smile. The boy dropped the broom and ducked back through the door, shouting in Chinese too quick for Jesse to understand.

Now what did I do? He had an urge to throw himself back in the saddle and gallop off.

Then Chow Lung stuck his head out the door, squinting into the sunlight. "Ah. There you are," he said in Chinese. "You took uncommonly long to arrive."

For a moment, he doubted; this was another fish in the school. But Lung stood in the door, tall and square-shouldered as the warlords in old Chinese tapestries, his arms folded over his chest. There was something unfamiliar in the shape of his head, half-hidden by the dark doorway.

Jesse wanted to say so many things at once, he couldn't speak at all. The most pressing was, *How could I have taken uncommonly long to get to someplace I didn't know I was going?*

Lung raised his eyebrows, a silent, satirical question.

"I happiness see you?" Jesse offered in Chinese.

Lung covered his eyes with one hand, but Jesse saw the grin under it. "Oh, for the patience of the Buddha. You have forgotten everything I taught you."

"I no practice since . . . so long! San Francisco after. I—it—return." As he said it, he wondered why he had. It was like the newspaper office: the assumption that he would be here long enough for his Chinese to come back.

"It cannot do so too soon. You make my ears bleed."

Jesse bowed in the Chinese fashion, very low, and said in English, "A thousand thanks, Chow Lung, revered doctor and son of dragons."

Lung burst into laughter and English. "Go to hell, you jackass." He turned to shout back into the shop.

"Chu! Take the respected Mr. Fox's horse to the livery stable. Let no one else lay hands upon it, but tend it yourself as you would the mount of the Emperor."

Lung stepped back and the boy, Chu, popped into the street. He gazed eagerly at Sam, shyly at Jesse.

"Cool down, water . . ." Jesse's Chinese deserted him, and he asked in English, rather desperately, "Grooming? You understand?"

"Yes, sir. Brush, hoof pick, dry straw, best alfalfa hay!" Chu replied in the same language, and stroked Sam's nose reverently.

"He is not good at anything but horses, but he is very good at those," Lung said.

Chu looked sidelong at Lung and made a noise that, in a society that taught respectful behavior to its young, was disconcerting. Jesse thought Lung pretended not to hear.

"Now," said Lung, "will you come in? Or will you sit down in the street like a Hindoo cow?"

A day's ride to the border. A day's ride was the other side of the world. He was shackled by his own weariness. Jesse untied his saddlebags and handed the reins to Chu, took off his spectacles, and stepped over the threshold of Lung's house.

It was the second floor of the building in San Francisco all over again. The smell was the same: medicinal herbs, sandalwood, cedar, lamp oil. The light was the same, dim and restful, from the lamps and from the specks of sun that got through the pierced-wood shutters. Lung's black lacquer herb chest stood against one wall, drawer knobs gleaming, like a blocky warrior in studded armor. It was the only Chinese furniture. The rest was western: a square wooden table, a pair of straight-backed chairs, and incongruously, a wicker rocker. A teakettle rumbled on a black iron stove against the back wall. Beside it, a curtained doorway led to the rear of the building, and probably the stairs.

"At last I can make the tea," Lung sighed happily, taking a teapot down from a shelf.

When Lung turned away, Jesse realized what he'd seen, or hadn't seen, in the shadow of the door. "Why is there no year of the donkey in Chinese astrology?"

"If there were, I am sure you would have been born in one."

"I might have at that. What happened to your hair?"

Lung brushed a hand over his short-cropped hair, as if to make sure it was there, as if his hand made the gesture without his mind's connivance. He folded the paper back from one corner of a brick of tea and grated some into the pot, carefully, as if he could not, in fact, make tea in pitch-darkness while half asleep.

"One cannot wear the queue in prison," he said finally, with a shrug. "It is the law." Then he surveyed Jesse, a grin pinched in the corners of his mouth. "But I see you are making up my loss."

"You were in jail? Why didn't you write? I'd have come and got you out."

Lung snorted. "As if I cannot get myself out of prison."

"Well, you couldn't, could you?"

"It only took a little time. Why make a fuss and waste money if time will do everything?"

"Money exists to save time. And I like making a ruckus."

"It is past now. And the past is illusion."

"Bullshit."

Lung leaned over the pot and sniffed the steam. "Ah. I cannot imagine why I waited until you came."

"Because you didn't know I was coming?"

"I expected you days ago. But you have always been stubborn as a pig."

"What happened to 'the respected Mr. Fox'?"

"That was only to set Chu a good example. Besides, he would be disappointed if he thought you were an insignificant person, after he had been made to watch for you for days."

Jesse felt a surge of irritation. "Lung, leave off the hocus-pocus and say, 'Hello, how've you been, what a surprise to see you here.' "

Lung carried the teapot to the table in silence. Then he said, "You told me yourself about your sister."

Jesse hadn't expected that. If he'd had his guard up, it wouldn't have hurt. "My sister . . . isn't well. If I made it sound like anything else, I was probably drinking."

"We were both drinking. So?"

"So my sister is irrelevant." Jesse saw Lung frown, his gaze suddenly unfocused. He sighed and explained, "She has nothing to do with this conversation."

"Ah, thank you." Lung grinned. "Have I told you recently that you have a vile and unmusical language?"

"Not in the last three years, no. I'm sure absence was all that stopped you."

"I apologize for speaking of your sister. But she is the best proof of what you are."

Jesse's hands clenched around the porcelain cup. "What, likely to inherit the family weakness?"

Lung reached across the table and drew the spectacles from the breast pocket of Jesse's coat. "Your eyes still trouble you?"

Jesse yanked the spectacles back. "Dark lenses make people nervous. I like that."

Lung held his gaze; Jesse had to look away.

"Yes," he said. "Sometimes."

After a long silence, Lung said, "When one pours

boiling water into a pottery jar, it cracks. But a porcelain jar, that appears so frail"—Lung took the cup
from Jesse's rigid fingers and held it before him—
"will not break."

"Coefficient of thermal expansion," Jesse said, as if
each word were a flung pebble. Lung only watched
and looked patient. "All right. What the hell do you
mean?"

"That your sister is pottery. You, however, may
prove to be porcelain."

"I appear frail?" Lung only raised his eyebrows.
"Which makes the boiling water . . . ?"

"You know what it is."

Jesse's skin prickled. The flame climbed the air in
the lamp beside him, but the room grew slowly darker.
Lung's face, across the table, was fixed, frowning, his
eyes closed. Jesse fought down panic as Lung's lips
parted, as he whispered a word.

Jesse sat frozen in perfect darkness.

"Stop it," he said sharply. The room glowed around
them, as it had moments before.

Lung smiled crookedly, painfully. "You are a disaster in the making. I wish I were not a conscientious
man."

"It's rude to mesmerize your guests." His heart was
still racing.

"Drink your tea. Have you eaten?"

Jesse consulted the empty space in the middle of
himself. *Or maybe that's why the room went dark.* But
he couldn't stay.

"Wait here." Lung rose and went out the front door.
For a moment the racket from the street, the sun, the
smells, invaded the room. Then the door closed and
shut the real world out.

Or so it seemed to Jesse. Like Lung's rooms in San
Francisco, this was half temple, half fortress, and not

fully part of the city around it. The longer he stayed, the more he'd be drawn into what happened here. He shivered and swallowed tea. *I'm going to Mexico*, he reminded himself. *Nothing here has anything to do with me.*

When Lung stepped back in, carrying a basket, Jesse said, "Why are you here, Lung?"

"That can wait until we have eaten."

"I can eat and talk at the same time."

"It is bad for your stomach." Lung set the basket on the floor and unloaded it onto the table: steaming white hemispheres of *bao*, thick soup smelling of pepper and vinegar.

The pang of hunger in Jesse's stomach nearly turned it inside out. He bit deep into the *bao* to the filling of savory shredded pork.

Lung watched and nodded. "My neighbor. He makes very good barbarian food, too." He poured soup into two green-glazed bowls. "I am here because in San Francisco I went to jail, and though I was released, the embarrassment proved unexpectedly lasting." He ran his palm over his shorn hair again and grimaced.

"What were you in jail for?"

"I was accused of poisoning a white man." He said the last two words with care. Jesse would have noticed them anyway; Lung always preferred "barbarian."

"Did you?"

Lung glared. "I am offended."

"Does that mean you didn't poison him?"

"I should poison you instead. I gave him mild herbs for stiffness in his joints. Then he dined on oysters, and since the oysters he had eaten the week before were wholesome, the fault lay with me."

"The fellow didn't die, then."

"They would not have freed me if he had."

The soup burned going down. "But why Tombstone?"

"It was auspicious. At least, it should have been. That is why I summoned you."

Jesse glanced up from his spoon. "Lung, don't do that."

"What am I doing?"

"I wouldn't be here at all if some idiot hadn't stolen Sam and made me tramp all the way here to get him back."

"Sam *stolen*? Are you hurt?"

"Aren't you going to claim you arranged the whole thing?"

"I have told you, one can only press the universe a little in the direction one wishes, and hope one's goal may be achieved. You cannot believe I would wish for someone to steal your horse?"

"If I thought you had anything to do with it, I'd walk out right now. I shot the man, Lung."

Lung was very still. "Is he dead?"

"Not the last time I saw him, but he may be by now."

"Was it self-defense?"

"What does that have to do with it?"

"There is a balance—was your own blood shed?"

"Lung—"

"Tell me!"

Jesse looked at the door. But he wasn't sure where Chu had taken Sam, or how to find Chu. And he was no longer plowing ahead on willpower and novelty. "A little."

"If it is not enough, I will do what I can."

"Like what, shoot me somewhere else? Lung, this isn't a good time for . . . whatever you're talking about."

Lung studied him, eyes narrowed, and said something in Chinese that Jesse didn't recognize. "So I see. Where are you hurt?"

"It's nothing. I was up all night."

"I apologize for the urgency with which I called you."

Jesse shook his head. He was still hungry, but he hadn't the energy to finish the soup. "I'm on my way to Mexico."

Lung made a rude noise through his lips. "There is nothing in Mexico."

"There's a man who wants to give me a lot of money to train his horses."

"What, have you lost all your money? O cruel goddess of fortune!" Lung smacked the back of his hand against his forehead. Jesse wondered if there were amateur theatricals in China.

"The more he pays, the better bargain he'll think he's got. And I like training horses."

"A better reason than money. But it is not your—purpose?—to train horses."

"Hell, say 'destiny.' It won't change a thing. If I weren't so damned tired, I'd be ten miles south by now."

"Of course you would," Lung said, the way Jesse would reassure a skittish yearling. "But since you are here, you may as well bathe and sleep. And I will look at your wound."

For no clear reason, Jesse remembered the air on Allen Street, clinging, stifling. He shook his head again.

"Jesse."

He looked up, startled. Lung wasn't across the table anymore; he was at the stove, refilling the kettle.

"There is nothing but wilderness between Tombstone and the border," Lung said.

"The good people of Bisbee camp"—Jesse yawned—"would love to hear you say so."

"If you are going to fall asleep, it might as well be here."

"All right. But after that, I'm going. No offense."

"None at all," Lung agreed.

Jesse managed to stay more or less awake after that, though things seemed to happen in bursts with blank spots between, like a book with missing pages. He nodded off once in the big tin bathtub, but when the back of his head banged against the rim, he woke up.

Lung showed him to a room at the back of the house, just big enough for a cot, a scarred trunk, and space to walk between them. There was a small, shuttered window, and the daylight came in as spangles of light on the wall.

The cot creaked as he lay back. He was aware of that, but nothing beyond it.

He lay on his side, his head on one outstretched arm. His other arm was flung out before him. One knee was drawn up in front of him. The other leg . . .

It seemed to bend backward against the joint, a long, smooth curve. In fact, all of him was long, reaching out in many directions. He was unimaginably heavy.

He felt the ephemeral things move on his skin. The roots of mesquite trees shuddered in him as wind swung their branches. A mouse skittered through his dust, rushing from shade to shade. Water coursed over him, wearing a smooth trough down to his bones. At the edge of him, pressed up to his belly on the northeast, the town was a gentle, irregular scratching of activity.

A hawk took the mouse, the force of its strike like a leaf falling. Many men's boots, many horses' hooves, many wheels rolling and banging, touched him like spatters of rain. Blood soaked into the sand of him and dried, and meant less than sweat drying in a breeze.

For those were quick things. He was slow, ancient, strong. His bones defied time and animal lives, defied wind and water, defied the sunrises that warmed them, the cold nights that gnawed them with so little effect.

Even his blood was slow: dense soft threads of stone, rich and cool, thick in his veins. He felt the power in it feeding his lungs, his brain, the thousand-year pulse of his heart. He existed to contain that power. He kept it inside him, safe, alive.

A hot steel fang bit into him. It carved into his side, struck again, again.

It was carving the blood from his veins. And that blood ran in a firestorm over him, devouring the ephemeral things, cracking his invulnerable bones in a white explosion of pain—

Jesse lurched awake. His hands clenched on the mattress ticking. His lungs burned for air. He hoped he hadn't screamed.

For a long time he lay flat, staring at the ceiling. He could still feel his dream-body, the one made of stone and sand. And silver. The blow, like a pick into rock . . . and then what? Destruction. Death.

What had Lung said? That Tombstone should have been auspicious. Something was wrong, something Lung thought Jesse ought to be able to fix.

He closed his eyes and breathed deeply, and pushed the dream away. *I am going to Mexico.*

4

Mildred was right about increasing the print run. By the end of the day the shelf by Harry's desk was empty, and she was glad she'd remembered to pull a copy for herself.

"What is it about bad news that makes people buy their own papers?" Mildred asked as she cleaned ink off her fingers. "On good days, they read other people's castoffs. Bad news is just as willing to wait an hour as good."

Harry plucked a cigar out of his humidor, then closed and locked his desk. "My, you're as sour as me these days."

"As bad as that?"

"Maybe not quite. But give you a few years, and you'll be a real newspaperman."

"Thank you, Harry. I'll take that in the spirit in which it was meant."

"How do you know what I meant?"

Mildred looked across the type case at him, surprised. Harry shrugged into his coat.

"You ready to go?" he asked. "I'll lock up."

Mildred jammed her hat on her head. "Yes, boss."

Harry followed her to the front door. "You'll have to choose your ground one of these days, Millie."

She looked into his face for a hint of a joke. But he was grave. "What's this, Harry?"

"You're not a wife, or a whore, or a saint like Nellie Cashman. And you're not a girl or an old hen. I don't believe you're working here until some fellow gets down on one knee and holds out a ring. So who are you fixing to be?"

She smiled and shook her head. "I'm the eccentric Widow Benjamin."

"You're living like a prospector. Looking for Nature to make your fortune for you. And even prospectors have an answer when someone asks 'em what they do for a living."

"No one ever asks a lady what she does for a living."

"Doesn't mean she wouldn't have an answer if the question came up. What's yours?"

Mildred stared. "I set type."

Harry stood, half frowning, in the door. "Go along, then," he said at last. "There should be news worth setting by morning." He closed the door between them, and the lock clacked home.

For a moment she considered banging on the glass and demanding that Harry explain himself. But even he might not be sure what he meant. In the past months, she'd listened to him think aloud, usually on town politics. He would contradict himself, or leave conclusions half-made, until the day an editorial would land on her copy stand. Then she would see the result of the refining process she'd been listening to.

She'd let Harry take his time. So long as it didn't lead him to firing her, she refused to fret over it.

But as she walked toward Fremont, she fretted. Who was she fixing to be? Curious question; weren't people who they were, regardless of what they wanted? Shaped by parents, teachers, friends, a husband or wife, by past decisions and necessities?

She'd left Philadelphia because there was only one person she could be there: her parents' daughter, a suitable man's wife, the mother of sons who would inherit the things that passed through her hands that would never be hers. She couldn't have stayed and told her father, "I'm going to be someone else." Could she?

Her boots banged on the board sidewalk. *Walk like a lady*, their mother used to scold when she tried to copy Eli's walk. Then Eli had suggested they both learn to walk silently like Indians. It was years before she realized that he'd done it to save her from scolding.

Austerberg's stood on her left, across the street. The green-and-white striped awning was fading in the hard sun and wind-driven dust. But the windows sparkled, and "Austerberg's Dry Goods" shone on the glass in gold leaf.

If Mr. Austerberg had sent any message while trailing the would-be robbers, Lucy would be sure to relate it to Mildred. With Lucy, gossip was satisfyingly reciprocal. Now, if Mildred were a reporter, there'd be another name for it. Women gossiped; reporters collected information. She thought of Mr. Fox asking if she were a reporter. Was he joking? Or had she looked like—whatever reporters looked like?

The Austerbergs had arrived a month after Mildred and David. They'd come from Cincinnati, via Texas. Frederick had a pleasant German growl that reminded her of some of her father's friends. "Too settled-down in Texas," he'd complain, laughing. "Everybody runs a store. I want that, I can stay in Ohio!" David had called the Austerbergs commonplace, and made excuses not to accept their dinner invitations. But Mildred had gone, and never regretted it.

She paused to let a buckboard pass, nodding to the rancher who drove it. There was a black-and-white goat tied to the tail of the wagon and chewing on its tether. It rolled a milky blue eye at her as she passed behind it.

She stepped onto the sidewalk in front of Austerberg's. Some movement made her look back.

The goat stood wide-legged in the street, shaking its

head, as the buckboard went on. For a moment it seemed not to know it was free. Two horsemen rounded the corner, and the goat dodged them nimbly. The horsemen rode on.

Mildred teetered on the edge of the sidewalk. A lady didn't shout in the street . . . "Hello!" she yelled. "Sir! In the wagon!"

No use; he would be surrounded by the buckboard's noise. A man moving boxes into the shop beside Austerberg's looked at Mildred, then at the goat. He picked up another box and turned away.

The goat started back the way it had come. It would pass her in a few seconds.

Mildred looked around and sighed. Where were the ten-year-old boys of the world when one needed them? She stepped into the street.

The trick to catching a goat or a donkey was to make it think one hadn't the least interest in it until the last possible moment. *Now there's something I would never have learned in Philadelphia.* She walked into the the street, leaned over, and pretended to tie her boot.

She heard the patter of the goat's hooves. *Stay still, stay still . . .* Then she shot out her arm.

She had a fistful of frayed hemp rope with a bucking goat at the other end. She dug her boot heels into the dirt of the street as the goat threw its weight against the rope. Then it lowered its head and charged her.

She dodged and lost her balance. She flung an arm over the goat's neck as it went by, and felt it stumble. And suddenly they were both on the ground in the middle of the street, and she was sitting on the goat.

She heard whooping and clapping around her, and looked up to see the walk lined with men—mostly men—cheering. Her face went hot.

"Mighty fine wranglin'!" shouted a gray-haired drover. "Goat-fighting!" added a stout man in a suit and a gold watch chain.

Then a man was bending over the goat and grabbing its rope. "You can get up now, ma'am. I've got the bas—beast."

Mildred looked up to see the rancher from the buckboard. His face under the brim of his brown felt hat was younger than she'd first thought.

"I'm sorry I sat on your goat," she said, and immediately regretted ever opening her mouth in her entire life.

But the young rancher grinned. "I don't think much else would have worked. This fellow's an awful hard case."

He put out a hand. Mildred put hers into it. He pulled her to her feet, and she almost fell down again from the suddenness of it. "Sorry!" she said.

He steadied her. "No, no, I'm sorry. And grateful. My name's Tom McLaury. My brother and I run cattle, over in the Sulphur Spring."

"And goats."

"A few. The Mexicans pay good money for 'em. Goat cheese and *barbacoa*."

Mildred looked at the goat, who stared resentfully back. "If he's destined for barbecue, I understand why he'd run for it."

"Oh, no, ma'am. He's got plenty of good years ahead. Poquito's a first-class stud." McLaury turned cherry-red.

Mildred laughed. "So I saved him from a terrible mistake." She thrust out her hand again. "I'm Mildred Benjamin. Pleased to meet you."

McLaury was still blushing, but he shook her hand and smiled. Then he looked down at her fingers. "You've got a busted seam."

Sure enough, the thumb of her glove had pulled away from the palm, and the leather was torn.

"Ladies' gloves aren't made for ranch work, I reckon," McLaury said. "I owe you a pair."

She looked up into his smiling blue eyes, preparing to deny it. She saw the handsome lines of his long, tanned face, the sparkle of sweat in the golden brown hair at his temples, the early crow's feet and thick eyelashes. There was admiration in his gaze.

"What I'd really like," she found herself saying, "is to know what goat tastes like."

He was startled; then he grinned. "Nothing easier. Why don't I bring you some, next time we butcher a kid?"

"I'd like that," Mildred said. "I work at the *Daily Nugget*."

"Then that's where I'll find you. Good day, now." He tugged his hat brim and dragged Poquito down the street.

The street—they'd been standing in the middle of it the whole time. Mildred looked up. Her audience was dispersed, and the riders and wagons went around her without a pause. She swatted hopelessly at the dust on her skirt and straightened her hat. Had she really stood talking to that man with her hat askew?

My brother and I. Wouldn't he have mentioned a wife, if he had one? She felt her face heat up again. Mildred Benjamin, she'd called herself, not Mrs. David Benjamin. What was she thinking?

Well, there was a question that answered itself. She gave her skirts a final, irritated shake and stamped up the sidewalk to Austerberg's.

Lucy had seen the whole thing, of course. "Oh, Mrs. B, are you hurt? That was a brave thing you did."

Lucy's tone hinted that "brave" in this case meant "foolish." "Thank you, Mrs. Austerberg. I'm fine.

Awfully shabby, though." Mildred held up her hand in the torn glove and looked sheepish.

Lucy came out from behind the notions counter, clucking in genuine concern. "And your nice dress, too. That'll take a deal of cleaning."

"Think how I'd look if we'd had rain," Mildred said, laughing. Lucy smiled and shook her head, and Mildred knew she was forgiven her oddities.

"Wasn't that young Tom McLaury?" Lucy asked.

"That's what he said. Is he a longtime resident?"

"Oh, not quite on Mr. Schieffelin's heels, but long enough. He and his brother Frank had a place on the Babocomari until lately. Then they settled a ranch out south and east."

"Then I sat on the goat of a respected landowner!"

Lucy looked thoughtful. "Now that depends on who you ask. There was trouble a few months ago, about stolen government mules—"

"They stole government mules?" Mildred asked. A man could be kind and funny and still have his flaws. But stealing stock . . .

"Well, Deputy Breakenridge thought the thieves might have hidden the mules out at the McLaury ranch. So he got some men together to go see. It made for bad blood that hasn't settled yet." Lucy pulled up a stool and got comfortable. "The McLaury boys didn't think much of being accused of keeping stolen goods. But it seems some kind of burr got under Wyatt Earp's saddle, too. Frederick's dyspepsia was troubling him, and he couldn't go with Deputy Breakenridge, but he heard afterward there were words between the Earps and the McLaurys that a man doesn't forget easily. Of course, if there's a quarrel, you generally find Wyatt Earp in it somewhere."

Now that Mildred thought about it, she recalled setting a rather restrained story about William Breakenridge in pursuance of his duty, et cetera. And Harry had said, "Odds are the *Epitaph*'ll make a mountain of it, with the Earps right on top. Clum likes to put 'em on the front page."

"How did Mr. Breakenridge think the mules got there, if the McLaurys didn't steal them?"

Lucy shook her head and leaned farther over the counter. "When the deputy and the Earps went out to the McLaury ranch, there were some of those cowboys there, too—that man Brocius and his friends." Lucy nodded firmly, as if that settled where all the missing cattle, horses, and mules in Cochise County had gone.

"Mr. McLaury seemed like a nice enough young man," Mildred said, trying to sound matronly and innocuous. "Even offered to replace my glove."

"Funny how sometimes the rough-looking ones will turn out to be perfect gentlemen." Lucy nodded at her own wisdom. "While the fellows who wear nice coats and smell like lilac pomade can be mean and quarrelsome clear through."

From the other side of a shelf, crockery clattered. Lucy looked up and turned pink. A little woman in a dark cotton dress with a faded mantelet over her shoulders rounded the shelf and swept up to the counter. Her chin seemed too soft and round to be so thrust out, and her little flat nose looked out of place carried so high.

"I don't want this thread after all," she said, and smacked a spool of light blue cotton on the countertop.

Another woman came around the shelf and stood back from the counter, kneading her embroidered purse nervously between her hands. She was taller, with dark curling hair escaping her hat to brush her pale oval face.

"You won't find better anywhere in town, Mrs. Earp," Lucy warned.

"I'll pass on it just the same," said the little woman.

"Allie," the dark-haired woman said breathlessly, "you get it. It's just the color."

The short woman glanced at her companion, and her face softened. "Changed my mind. Let's go, Mattie."

Mildred watched the little woman sail out the door, with the dark-haired woman hurrying after, eyes down. The little one's firmness made her seem older than she probably was, just as the other's nervousness made her younger. They were probably of an age, and that barely twenty.

When the women were past the windows and gone, Mildred turned to Lucy. "That was Wyatt Earp's wife?"

"The short one? Oh, no. She's Virgil Earp's wife. Wyatt's is the dark, pretty one. Much good it'll do her." Lucy shook her head. "Mrs. Virgil was quick to get peppered up, wasn't she? I hope she didn't think I was talking about their menfolk when I said what I did about nice coats and lilac pomade."

Mildred studied her face. Lucy seemed convinced that Wyatt Earp was not precisely who she'd been talking about.

"Have you heard from Mr. Austerberg?" Mildred asked.

"Yes, he sent a note in. His mare went lame around midday, and he had to stop at Marsh Station. I hope they can give him his dinner. Frederick's always out of sorts without a good dinner. What about you? Mr. Woods hear more about the robbery?"

Mildred told her what the *Nugget* had printed, but nothing of Harry's speculations.

"Just as the *Epitaph* had it," Lucy said, and colored again. "Not to slight the *Nugget*."

Mildred smiled and waved it away. "No other news worth mentioning, I'm afraid," she said. Then she recalled the stranger, Mr. Fox.

"Mrs. B? Whatever you're pondering doesn't seem to please you."

I'll never make a cardplayer, Mildred thought. "I'm just trying to recall what else I need. Besides gloves."

"I've a nice gray kid right over here." Lucy flounced down the counter and ducked out of sight. "You're what, size five?"

"Six." Mildred let a breath pass, to make her next words seem idle. "Have you heard of a Jesse Fox, Mrs. Austerberg?"

Lucy straightened and laid a paper parcel on the counter. "I don't believe so. Is he from these parts?"

"He's a newcomer. He came in to buy a newspaper. I can't remember ever seeing so much trail dust on one human being." Mildred unfolded the tissue and lifted out one of the thin kid gloves. She caught the tanned leather scent and longed to hold the gloves to her nose.

"Is that so? Did he seem like one of the cow-boys?"

"He was dressed like a drover. But he sounded like a town man. He claimed he wasn't staying in Tombstone."

"Heaven's sake, where else would he stay?" Lucy said with a lifted eyebrow. "Contention's barely civilized, and Charleston's just a glorified camp. And until the railroad comes in, you can't say we're on the way to anywhere."

Mildred smoothed the gloves over her fingers and the backs of her hands. "I thought it was odd, too." Lucy would pluck the threads of her gossip-web; if there was anything to know about Fox, Lucy would be able to tell her next time she asked. "These are lovely, Mrs. Austerberg. I'll wear them home."

Mildred was startled by how low the sun was when she left the store. She bolted down Fremont and whisked into the post office with only minutes to spare. As she paused to get her breath, the door shut on the hem of her skirt. She tugged it free with a hiss of exasperation, and turned to find the clerk and his customer staring.

The customer was the smaller Mrs. Earp, Virgil's wife, who'd refused to buy the thread. Mildred felt a blush heat her face, even though she hadn't been the one to make disparaging comments.

Then she saw the periodical Mrs. Earp was trying to tuck quickly into her string bag, and recognized the title banner. *Gallagher's Illustrated Weekly.* Her eyes flew to Mrs. Earp's, and the little woman blushed, too.

Is she embarrassed because she reads it, or because her husband does?

Mildred smiled and nodded, and tried to make both as genuine as she could. Mrs. Earp looked startled. Then a cautious smile flicked across her face.

"Do you take *Gallagher's*, too?" Mildred said. She had no idea why, but suddenly she wanted to make this woman's acquaintance. "I thought 'A Fatal Woman' in last week's was splendid."

Mrs. Earp smiled wider, but still cautiously. "I did like it. But Marlena shouldn't have died at the end. Poor thing was innocent as a baby."

"But that made Lisabette so much more evil. And I love a good villain." Mildred shook her head and thrust out her hand. "I'm sorry, I haven't introduced myself. I'm Mrs. David Benjamin."

"Mrs. Virgil Earp," said the little woman, with that martial lift of her chin.

"Pleased to meet you. Perhaps, once we've both read the new issue, we might compare favorites."

Mrs. Earp narrowed her eyes and tilted her head a little, as if trying to see some part of Mildred that wasn't visible. Then she nodded, sharply, but with a grin that warmed her face. "Might be. Pleased to meet you, Mrs. Benjamin." She pulled the strings of her bag tight and hurried out the door.

Mildred watched her disappear down the street and thought, *I suppose if my husband and his brothers were at the center of so many storms, I'd be cautious, too.* She turned to the counter and the clerk. "Good afternoon. Mail for Mrs. David Benjamin?"

"Sure enough," he said, and turned to the cubbyholes of sorted mail, now mostly empty. "You're the lady typesetter at the *Nugget*, aren't you?" he added over his shoulder.

"Yes, I am."

"I wouldn't work for Harry Woods. Man never shuts up."

"He's much better at the paper. He works it all off in print." Harry's ability to talk intelligently and at length was one of the things she liked about him. But perhaps he was an acquired taste.

"Speaking of print." The clerk laid her mail, including her copy of *Gallagher's*, on the counter. "Keeping an eye on the competition?" He had a sly smile under his moustache, as if he thought Mildred might whisk the paper out of sight as Mrs. Earp had done.

She beamed at him. "Oh, we can't compete with *Gallagher's*. The *Nugget* doesn't get to make up nearly so many of its stories."

The clerk laughed and smacked the counter with his palm. "And you ought to know! Well, maybe they're writing to thank you for the kind words." He pointed to the cream-colored envelope on top of the little pile. The *Gallagher's* ornate logotype and the return address were printed in the upper corner.

Mildred's stomach jumped. "I suppose so," she managed. Was that a sensible reply? "Thank you." She scooped up her mail and smiled—she hoped it was a smile—and got out the door without running into the doorpost.

She'd reached the corner before she summoned the courage to look at the envelope again. It sat blandly on top of a few card-sized envelopes from friends in town, a bookseller's catalog. She felt as if she were cradling a cream-colored rectangular snake. More than anything, she wanted to open it . . . and she wanted never to open it. She felt cold and hot by turns, and her mouth was like a dry wash.

A lady didn't read her mail on the street corner. At least she could delay until she got home.

*The sun was a corona of fire on the peaks of the Whet-*stone Mountains when she reached her front door. For an instant she felt a different, more familiar lurch in the pit of her stomach.

It's not Friday, and it wouldn't matter if it were. Friday's sunset was no different from any other now. Mother wasn't there to say, "How could you be so late? Did you *want* to miss Sabbath?" Father didn't sit in the parlor behind his newspaper, ready to say to Mother, in front of Mildred, that it was a woman's job to teach God's law to her children.

David hadn't believed in God. There was no Sabbath with him to remember.

She hung her hat on the hook by the door and hurried through the dim parlor to the kitchen. She laid the little heap of mail on the kitchen table and stared down at it. *No, first things first.* Now, of all times, she would keep to her routines. There was religion and there was superstition, and in her case, the latter held up better under hard use.

She lit a scrap of kindling in the stove embers and carried it, sheltered by her cupped hand, to the lamp on the parlor table. She could have used a match, but she liked the symbolism of the single hearth fire, the sun of the house.

"Thank you for today, and the promise of tomorrow," she whispered, and lit the wick. When she set the chimney down over the flame, the light spread in the room like clear water. She took a deep breath, and another, and felt peace settle around her like a cloak.

The first time her brother Eli had missed the lighting of the Sabbath candles was when he was seventeen and Mildred was fourteen. He'd come home long after dark, his curly hair flattened with rain, his cheeks red with excitement, wine, and cold.

It may have been their mother's place to discipline daughters, but their father considered an adult son his responsibility. She'd heard the voices in the study, Father's deep and harsh and Eli's rising unconsciously with his feelings. She heard them even with the study doors shut, even at the top of the house.

Afterward she'd asked him, in dismay and wonder, how could he have stayed out on Friday night? Eli frowned and flushed. Of course—Father had probably started with the same question. Then his face softened, and he laughed.

"Doesn't every day belong to God, Millie Mouse? I don't think He cares which one we choose for lighting candles and wearing our best clothes."

"Did you say that to Father?" she'd asked, certain he wouldn't have.

"I did." Eli's smile took a wry turn. "He said I'd never shown any rabbinical leanings before this."

She'd laughed and let it go. But she couldn't let go of the notion that every day was, potentially, holy. After that, with the first flame she lit in the evening, she would breathe a little of the *kiddush* as the wick caught. She kept it secret even from Eli.

After Eli died, she found she couldn't speak at all when she kindled the first light of evening. She wanted to think, *All days are God's, even the dark ones*. But no prayer would come out of her mouth. The God she'd lit the candle for would not have taken her brother. So that God did not exist.

Still, she yearned toward that first light. Eventually she found herself saying, "Thank you" over the flame. But she still wasn't sure there was anyone to thank.

Then she'd married David and run away west. Mother and Father thought that God turned His face away from an undutiful daughter. So it didn't matter that her candle wasn't for her parents' God; He wasn't looking.

She lived as if she, too, no longer believed in God—except for this daily ritual. And sometimes, when the wick caught, she felt as if she'd been heard, and kindly answered. Sometimes she thought the universe might be a thinking, breathing thing, that for an instant had chosen to think about her.

The flame licked up and sent up a thread of black smoke. It shook her out of her reflections. *There,* she thought, *I've run out of delays*. She turned back to the kitchen before she could find another.

The envelope was addressed to "M. E. Benjamin." There was no sender's name in the return address; only the steel-engraved stationer's printing. Mildred squared her shoulders and tore it open.

A folded quarter-sheet fell out, with another rectangle of paper in the crease. A rectangle with an ornate border.

Mildred snatched it up. It was a draft on a New York bank for twenty-five dollars, made out to M. E. Benjamin.

She grabbed the quarter sheet and unfolded it. Under the printed Gallagher's logo, in a thick, black, looping hand, was:

Dear Mr. Benjamin,

I am pleased to tell you that we accept your story, "Stampede at Midnight," for inclusion in serial form in our publication. Payment at our regular starting rate is enclosed.

If you have anything else of this sort, I would be interested in seeing it.

Very sincerely,
Wilson H. Fraine, ed.

Mildred stared at the handwriting, waiting for it to disappear. It didn't.

Then it struck her: this was the answer to Harry's question. This was what she was fixing to be.

She felt laughter jumping in her chest. Imagine telling Father, "I'm going to write sensation stories, Papa," and watching his face change! What would Eli have said? Or David?

She had no one to share the news with. But for now, the news was enough.

Mildred clutched the letter to her breast and waltzed a few steps around the table. *Harry*, she thought, *if I've been living like a prospector, at least I've found color in the rock.* She laid the note and the bank draft on the table where she could see them, and turned to take the frying pan down from its hook. Suddenly she felt as if she could eat one of Mr. McLaury's goats all by herself.

5

Doc rode north, keeping the Rincons close on his left, until he saw the plume of dust ahead that meant he'd caught up to the posse. He nudged the hired gelding into a canter.

Soon he could pick out individual riders: Billy Breakenridge atop his big sorrel; Bat Masterson looking small as a jockey next to him on a hired horse; Morgan on his restless dark bay ranging off beside the trail, followed by—well, if it wasn't Marshall Williams, the hypocritical son of a bitch. But no fool: if the Wells Fargo agent didn't ride to avenge the honor of the Wells Fargo strongbox, it would look mighty odd.

Of course, the three men out front would be Johnny Behan, Virgil, and Wyatt. Behan, because as Cochise County sheriff this was his posse. Virgil Earp, because he was deputy U.S. marshal. And Wyatt, upright as a post on his long-tailed black horse, because Wyatt didn't trail behind anybody, least of all Johnny Behan.

Billy Breakenridge spotted Doc first. Doc heard him call out to the others, and they stopped to wait. By the time Doc rode up he'd had a chance to decide who to look at.

He smiled widely at Virgil. "I take it there's still a trail to follow."

Virgil squinted against the glare of sun above the peaks. Then a corner of his moustache twitched upward, and Doc thought, not for the first time, that Virgil knew exactly what Doc was up to. "Enough," he answered.

"Glad to see you, Holliday," Behan said. "We can use another man."

"Is that so?" Doc pretended surprise. "I would have thought you'd be wishing me in hell right now."

"Or someplace farther away," Masterson agreed, grinning as he reined his horse around.

"I've got no quarrel with you, Doc." Behan tipped his hat back and gave Doc a long, steady look. "Nor with anyone else who stays out of trouble."

Doc laughed and shook his head. "I swear, I am half inclined to vote for you next election."

Wyatt snorted. It was the first sound he'd made since Doc rode up. Doc felt it through his bones like the jolt of missing a step on the stairs.

"We're following three, maybe four men," Virgil said. "Tracks were confused at the holdup point, but it looks like they left together."

Doc met Virgil's eyes and tried to look stupid and good-natured. Virgil might believe what he'd just said, or he might not. Either way, it wouldn't do to seem too wise.

Behan wheeled his horse. "Let's go. Mountains'll cut off the light soon."

Doc waited until the group was moving before falling in at its edge. Marshall Williams seemed to want to join Doc on the posse's flank. But Doc gave him a cold stare, and Williams spurred his horse on.

It took Doc a minute to drift back naturally, until he was next to Morgan. The bay shied, and Doc waited as Morgan got him back in hand.

"Morning, Doc. Feeling better?"

"I would feel better if I knew Wyatt had cut your ears off."

Morgan put up a gloved hand to feel one. "Nope. Right where I left 'em."

"And how about the gentlemen we're tracking? Are they right where you left them?"

Morgan looked like all the Earp brothers: tall,

sandy-haired, and moustached, with narrow, bright blue eyes. Some people mistook them for each other. But you'd never do it if you knew them well. Virgil was stolid; Wyatt was cold as ice water. Neither would have so much as blinked at Doc's question.

Morgan turned red and darted his eyes away. "What are you talking about?"

"Your dear friend Williams, there, told me how concerned the two of you were about the safety of that silver. Isn't that just the hell of working for Wells Fargo?"

Morgan stared stiffly ahead. "Damnation. How'd you get it out of him?"

"Had I needed to pry, I wouldn't be so lathered up about it. He's as discreet as a fifty-cent whore. You might want to be more selective about your friends in these matters. Unless the territory has lost its charm."

Morgan took that in, his jaw working. At last he broke out a grin. "You *are* a piece of work, ain't you? Wyatt's going to comb my hair for doing it at all, and you're saying I should do a better job of it next time."

"That is because Wyatt is a wise and cautious man. You find someone who says that about me, and I'll have the pleasure of introducing you to my mother."

"You mad because I didn't let you in on it?"

"Not in my line," Doc assured him. "Certainly not with your idea of desperate *banditos*."

Morgan scowled. He might be a damned idiot, but Doc had to admit he was a loyal one. "What's wrong with 'em?"

"They didn't get the silver, did they?"

Morgan roared with laughter, and the whole posse turned to look.

Doc smiled, because it would look odd if he didn't. "Try not to get every one of these bastards over here until we figure out where you were last night."

"I was with a girl," Morgan said promptly.

"Will she say so? If she won't, then don't be a fool. Where were your brothers?"

"Playing cards at the Eagle."

"In front of God and all His creation. Hell. And if you said you were home with your wife, nobody would believe you."

"Why wasn't I with you?" Morgan suggested.

Doc felt a surge of anger. *Because you are not my damned brother, and I don't know why I am going to as much trouble as I have over you. Serve you right if I left you to Wyatt. Or the law.* But Morgan was as much of a little brother as Doc had ever had. Sometimes the boy was stupid as a rooster, but it was the sort of stupidity that Doc understood. If he was honest, which he didn't care to make a habit of, Morgan reminded him powerfully of himself.

"You were not with me," he said at last, "because at the time, I was riding hotfoot to catch you before you did it. I was too late. So I rode back to town and did what I could to make it seem as if I'd never left and hadn't a care in the world. I wish I was sure it worked."

Morgan looked at Doc as if Doc had grown a second head. "Why'd you ride after me in the first place?"

"Now why *did* I do such a thing? To keep you from hanging? To keep Wyatt from—" Then he saw the black horse's nose out of the corner of his eye.

"To keep me from what?" Wyatt said.

Doc saw the color go out of Morgan's face. He turned to Wyatt and said irritably, "To keep Wyatt from knowing every damned thing that happens to anybody. A lost cause before I started."

"I reckon," Wyatt agreed. He was smiling, but Doc knew how much that was worth. "Morg, you look as if you ate something that didn't set well."

Doc thought about answering that. No, it would only

delay the inevitable. He sighed and drew rein, and let Wyatt come up beside Morgan. Wyatt would have the whole thing out of him in five minutes. He'd also find out that Doc had known Morgan was out helping rob the damned stage and hadn't told him.

Fine day for a ride, at least. He sat back in his saddle and surveyed the wilderness of grass that lapped the feet of the Rincons, high enough in places to brush his horse's belly. It was interrupted occasionally by islands of rock, and places where, for no reason Doc could see, the grass thinned to nothing, leaving mesquite, creosote bush, catclaw, and sand.

Behan was right about losing the daylight: the single shadows of rocks and scrub and stunted trees had already stretched out to meet and coalesce. He had a sudden fancy in which evening spread like spilled ink, not in the sky, but across the land, and the sky soaked up the darkness like blotting paper until it was full of it. He enjoyed the cooling breeze on his face until Wyatt looked over his shoulder and said, "You must be mighty tired, busy as you've been."

Doc touched the gelding with his heels and rode up beside Wyatt. "Oh, not at all. I had a lovely nap before I set out." Morgan, on Wyatt's other side, rode with his eyes fixed ahead and his lips closed tight. Doc nodded at Wyatt. "Kind of you to ask, though."

"This was my business," Wyatt said. "What made you think I wouldn't want to deal with it myself?"

"Morgan is free, white, and full-grown. I would have said it was his business." Doc smiled at the mountains. "If anyone had had the gall to ask me, that is."

Wyatt's crack of laughter startled him. "Damn you, Doc, one of you's as bad as the other. How're we going to put this fire out?"

Doc shrugged. "Nothing to put out. Best I can tell,

the only ones who saw Morg on the Benson road last night were the fellows he was with. And they won't be quick to say they were there."

Wyatt stared blindly at the horizon. Doc recognized his figuring-the-odds look. At last Wyatt said, "Morgan. Who saw you after that?"

"I got back a mite after the news did. Center of town was a hornets' nest. You could've led an elephant 'round my back door and not raised a soul." Morgan grinned for the first time since Wyatt had ridden up. "So I changed horses and joined the posse like a good citizen."

"In other words, you're not sure if you were seen. Doc, how'd you spend the evening?"

"After I got back from Charleston and got a fine earful from Marshall Williams?"

"Williams isn't your problem."

"None of this is my problem," Doc said sharply. "I involved myself out of charity, and I am still waiting to hear a word of gratitude."

"Your patience does you credit. Go on."

Doc glared at him, but Wyatt showed no sign of noticing. Doc sighed. It took two to make a fight. "I hired the fastest horse I could lay hands on and rode out, but the shooting had already started. So I got the hell back to town and settled in at the Oriental to drink and play cards as if I'd never left. Hired the horse I'd ridden to Charleston and tied it up outside."

"Why?"

"Because, unlike Morgan, I don't believe that I generally go unnoticed. There is bound to be someone with a story about where I was when. I didn't want that story to point at Morgan. I had no way to wipe out my trail, so I laid three more, figuratively speaking."

Wyatt smiled. Doc wasn't sure he liked that. "Hell, it sounds like folks'll think *you* held up the damned stage."

"That's what they think about every crime in the county as it is. Why should this one be different?"

Morgan looked at Wyatt and opened his mouth. Wyatt stopped him with, "If you're not planning to tell me who your pals were, don't talk."

Suddenly Doc recalled the boy who'd stolen the stranger Fox's horse, who'd bled all over one of the Oriental's tables that morning. "He won't split on his *compadres*. Any more than I would." Doc gave Wyatt a sideways look, to say, *Any more than I tattled to you about Morgan.* Wyatt pulled his hat brim down, which Doc took for sullen acknowledgment. "But I'd venture a guess as to who they were."

Morgan whipped 'round to stare, and the bay balked. "The hell you would!"

Doc paused to let Morgan's frown reach its full potential. "One of them was a Mexican boy in a brown coat. He is an intimate of Billy Leonard and Harry Head, who are most commonly seen under the unwholesome influence of Jim Crane." He watched Morgan's eyes get big (no, neither Virgil nor Wyatt would let their faces tell so much), and grinned. "At least as unwholesome as my influence on them."

Wyatt was watching him. "Will they keep quiet?"

"Oh, hell, no. But nobody will listen to them anyway."

Doc heard a shout from the head of the posse, and looked up to see a straggle of ranch buildings and corrals in a hollow of land ahead. Breakenridge wheeled his horse and trotted back to them.

"Two riders at least came this way," he said to Wyatt. "They'd have to stop to bait the horses somewhere, so there's a chance Len and Hank Redfield saw 'em."

Wyatt nodded at the buildings. "That their spread?"

"Yep." Breakenridge's face was redder than usual, and sweat streaked the dust on his cheeks and darkened his big moustache. Doc thought some of the deputy's certainty came from wanting a rest and a feed himself.

Wyatt turned a last look on Morgan, then spurred his horse. It leaped forward with Wyatt straight in the saddle as ever.

"Thanks, Doc," Morgan said.

"I'll feel properly thanked if I never have to do it again." Doc urged his horse after Wyatt's.

The Redfield brothers were on the porch by the time the posse rode up. They'd been at their dinner; one of the brothers had forgotten to take off the napkin tucked in his shirt. Behind them in the doorway was a little Mexican woman, her white apron glowing against her dark dress.

"Good evening, Len, Hank," Behan called. "Sorry to get you up from the table."

Doc saw the smaller Redfield's shoulders relax. The larger one answered, "Evening, Sheriff. You fellows're welcome to sit down with us. There's plenty."

"You sure? We've got Billy with us."

Everyone laughed, Billy Breakenridge loudest of all. Behan swung his leg over and dismounted, and the rest of the riders followed suit.

As Doc's feet hit the ground, a wave of dizziness broke over him. A small one; he clutched his saddle and breathed as deeply as he could, and it passed. A quick look around told him no one had noticed. Cooking smells came from the open door: cornmeal tortillas, chiles, onions, seared meat. His stomach gave an unpleasant lurch, and saliva sprang in his mouth in quite the wrong way. Well, there would be that much more for Breakenridge.

The rest of the posse crowded into the house. Doc heard the rise and fall of voices, a bark of uneasy laughter, and the banging of crockery. He leaned against the wall on the porch, and watched the sunset burn the western sky. The wood at his back was warm from the afternoon sun.

He wondered why he'd come. At the time it had seemed prudent, even clever—as Morgan had said, the act of a good citizen. And sometimes Doc wanted to be one of those. But it was possible that he'd just been bored, or afraid of being bored eventually.

Kate waited for him back in Tombstone—as much as Kate waited for anyone or anything. She loved him, with the same conditions applied. Doc tried to imagine her as the wife of a good citizen, with doctors' and lawyers' and merchants' wives nodding and smiling at her on the street, or up to her chin in taffeta at a concert or a play. The vision was overlaid with another, this one real: Kate in Dodge City, folding her ruffled sleeves back to her elbow and shooting him a sly glance under her lashes before she spilled the dice across the table. They'd come up threes. She'd shrugged and knocked back her gin fix, then held up the empty glass and smiled such a smile at the bartender that Doc thought he ought to have fainted dead away.

Kate Elder was not the stuff dentists' wives were made of. And no amount of wanting would make Doc an upstanding member of the community. He was a fine dentist—he just wasn't a fine person. And he was so good at being bad that it seemed like a genuine gift. One ought not to waste one's gifts.

Wyatt stepped out onto the porch and came toward him. Morgan followed close behind.

"Redfield says a couple of boys passed through earlier, heading for New Mexico. Johnny Behan's in there playing Pinkerton, trying to find out who they were."

"And since you already know . . ."

"Hell with that. I think Redfield's lying. I think they're still here. If that's true, we'd better be the first to find 'em."

Doc looked past Wyatt to Morgan, and saw fear in his face. *He might hang yet.*

Doc's thoughts were suddenly clear as cold air, sharp as a dagger point. It was as close as he ever came to a state of grace. "Let's go," he said, and headed for the stable.

It was more shed than stable, but at least the hinges didn't shriek when he swung the door wide. The failing light picked out six narrow board stalls. There were only three horses tied in them. They all threw their heads up and whickered when the door opened, inquiring about dinner. Obviously the Redfields' nags.

Behind him, Wyatt said, "Where else—"

"Shush," Doc said. He heard it again: the muffled boom of a horse's hoof against wood. None of these horses had made the sound. He peered into the gloom. The far wall seemed closer than the end of the building. He took a few steps into the stable and let his eyes adjust.

The other end of the shed was walled off to make a room, for tack or feed, perhaps. Its door was shut, the latch slid home. "Right here," Doc murmured, and moved quietly to the door.

It occurred to him, as he pulled the latch and kicked the door wide, that anyone inside would be likely to shoot if surprised. But surprised men had uncertain aim.

Besides, the inhabitants were unarmed. Two sweat-stained horses were crowded into the space. They were too weary even to start at the opening of the door.

Wyatt frowned and shook his head when he saw them. "Put away wet. One's lame, too."

"They're not your horses. What do you care?"

Wyatt turned to Morgan, urged him forward with a jerk of his head. "Recognize 'em?"

Morgan looked, and nodded.

Doc struck a match for light and studied the rest of the stalls. "Floors are dry. No other horses in here for days." He turned back to Wyatt as he shook out the match. "So either the fellows who rode these two got their remounts out of the corral—"

"Or they're still here," Wyatt finished softly. "Come on." He pushed back through the stable doors, and Doc and Morgan followed.

The sky was the clear dark blue of twilight. The land around them was flattened by the shadowless light, and seemed almost as impossible to walk into as a painting. Wyatt appeared to have no trouble, though. He looked toward the house, then the corral, then at the outhouse and the open-sided barn. Beyond the stable was open land, ending in a line of scrub and young cottonwoods that marked the bottom of the hollow, and probably a creek.

Wyatt knelt in the dust beside the stable wall.

"You all right?" Doc asked.

Wyatt waved him to silence. He pressed both his hands to the ground, fingers splayed.

Even in the half-light, Doc could see the tension in Wyatt's arms and shoulders. Then he heard Wyatt draw breath, saw his back swell with it. His head came up, toward the barn.

"Morgan," Wyatt said softly. "Head for the south end of that barn, and when you get near, make it known who you are. Quietly, as if you didn't want 'em to hear in the house."

"How do you—" Morgan started.

"Do as I say."

Morgan moved toward the barn as Wyatt got to his feet.

"If I tried to finish Morgan's question, would I get much further than he did?" Doc said.

Wyatt gave him a look, but Doc couldn't see it,

since Wyatt's hat brim cast his eyes into darkness. It probably meant "no."

Wyatt turned back to the barn. "Once he knows Morgan's not alone, he'll try to make a break. Be ready to go after him."

Doc refused to ask who "he" was. "You go after him. I am an invalid."

That got him one of Wyatt's bared-teeth smiles. "If he gets past you, I can shoot him before he makes the creek. Without hitting you by mistake. Can you say the same?"

"Why don't you just shoot him anyway?"

"Now how the hell would that look?"

At the corner of the barn, a new silhouette joined Morgan's. Doc could read the scene without sound. The unknown man frightened, hesitating; Morgan swaggering a little too much for someone who was supposed to be afraid of getting caught. Then one of the posse's horses, tied on the other side of the house, let out a whinny over something. The unknown man started, backed away from Morgan—

"Damn," Wyatt muttered, and drew his pistol.

Doc moved to cut the man off before he remembered he'd refused to do it. But Morgan was closer, and quicker. By the time Doc reached them, Morgan had knocked the fellow down.

Doc couldn't tell who he was, or exactly what he was saying, since his face was pressed into the dirt. It sounded like begging. "Care to introduce your new friend?" Doc suggested.

Morgan pulled the man to his feet. He was younger than Doc expected, and terrified. He certainly wasn't Billy Leonard, or Head or Crane. "This is Luther King, Doc. He may not look like much, but he's an awful desperado. According to him, anyway."

"Shut up," said Wyatt. He'd come up behind Doc

through the gathering dark, his gun out. The boy, King, rolled his eyes to look at Wyatt, and Doc thought for a moment that King might faint. "Where's the rest of your gang?"

King's gaze went to Morgan. Morgan grinned at him. But Wyatt grabbed a fistful of King's hair and jerked his head up and around, and jammed the barrel of his gun under King's chin. "You don't look like a fool," Wyatt said, his voice almost gentle. "So I think it's worth my time to say this. I wager your friends are nearly to New Mexico. I, on the other hand, am right here, and nothing you can do will change that. So you think good and hard about who you want to keep happy: them, or me."

King's Adam's apple bobbed. Wyatt seemed to take that for assent, since he let go of the boy and lowered his gun. "We got split up," King told him, a squeak in his voice. "Arthur—Arthur Ortega—and me just held the horses—"

"Whose horses?" Wyatt said.

"Billy Leonard's, Harry Head's, Jim Crane's . . ." King trailed off, staring hard at Wyatt as if afraid to shift his eyes in Morgan's direction.

"And that was all?"

"Yes, sir," King whispered at last. "But I don't know where they are. When it went bust, Arthur and I lost 'em in the dark. Then Arthur's horse stepped in a hole and threw him, and . . ."

Doc couldn't help but smile. "And you bolted with his horse, instead of sharing yours, leaving him on foot in open country. Good to have that cleared up."

Wyatt frowned at him. "I'm sure the Redfield brothers'll be surprised to learn they were hiding a criminal," Wyatt said. "Let's go up to the house."

The Redfields were profoundly surprised. The enthusiasm with which they expressed their amazement

nearly deafened the rest of the men in the Redfields'
parlor.

"Good work, Wyatt," Johnny Behan said, his smile
brittle.

"I'd have lost him in the brush along the creek if it
weren't for Morgan," Wyatt replied.

And that established Morgan's upstanding-citizen
bona fides once and for all. Pity no one else in the room
would get the joke. A few more years in the company
of the Earp family, Doc thought, and he'd be nearly
amused to death.

Doc looked around the crowded room for a chair, or
even a moderately out-of-the-way corner to lean in,
and found them all occupied. He didn't much care to
hang around, anyway. Wyatt would make sure King
told his story as rehearsed. Behan and company would
react as appropriate. He could have stayed to watch
Marshall Williams sweat, but it wasn't as much fun
when he was expecting it. He shrugged and turned toward the kitchen.

The little Mexican woman was cleaning up after the
impromptu dinner party, scraping and stacking plates.
She eyed Doc suspiciously when he came in. She was
older than he'd first thought; he'd missed the gray at
her temples and the frown lines on her forehead.

"Excuse me, *señora*," he said. "But there isn't room
out there to stand with your coat unbuttoned. I hope
I'm not in your way."

She studied him for long enough that he wondered
if she spoke English. Then she said, "You were not
here with the others."

"No, ma'am. Crowds make me nervous."

She raised a heavy black eyebrow at that. "You look
hungry."

"I do?"

She nodded. "I will fix you something."

"I don't want to put you to any trouble—"

Suddenly she smiled. "That is why I do it."

This time the smell, when she set the plate before him, woke a coyote in his stomach. A starving one. He swallowed a tender morsel of *chile colorado* and nodded at the woman. "My compliments, *señora*. I would have ridden all the way from Tombstone for this dinner."

Unexpectedly, she blushed and giggled. Gracious, didn't those two bastards ever say thank you?

He was mopping the plate with a tortilla when Behan came in. He sat down across from Doc and smoothed the thin hair back from his high forehead with both hands. With his hat off, he looked as if he ought to be selling haberdashery in Boston, not trying to keep order in a county that didn't much want it.

"Slim chance that we'll catch up with the rest of the gang, but now at least we know who they are." He leaned forward and gazed earnestly at Doc. "Wyatt wasn't quick to give you credit for this, but you should know that I do."

"My, you really do want my vote, don't you?"

"King wouldn't have spilled the names of his partners if Wyatt hadn't told that tale about your Kate. You put him up to that, didn't you?"

A tale about Kate. Doc studied the sheriff's face, but there was nothing in it besides the open goodwill that Behan wore so easily. "I don't often urge Wyatt to tell tales."

"Well, King was scared white as paper when Wyatt said Kate was on that stage, and was killed in the holdup by a stray shot. Until then, he was buttoned up tight."

"Was he," Doc murmured. He should have stayed in the parlor after all. He could imagine the scene: King, surrounded by unsympathetic faces and without the incentive of a gun under his chin, had turned unhelp-ful. So Wyatt had drawn a different sort of weapon. Doc's teeth clenched. "Glad I could be of use."

Behan rose. Doc looked for calculation or satisfac-tion in his face and saw nothing. "We'll stay the night. In the morning Billy and I will take King to town. Wy-att says he'll stay on the trail."

"Of course he will. You have yourself a good night, Sheriff."

Anger was like a wildfire in him, the kind that skimmed through the dry grass unnoticed until it met the trees, to explode up the trunks and leap from bough to bough. The Mexican woman picked up his plate. He raised his eyes to her face. She dropped the plate and stepped back.

"Thank you," he said, quietly, as he'd said every-thing since Behan had mentioned Kate. Then he pushed back his chair and left the kitchen.

Outside the moon was up, full and bright and low in the east. Wyatt was untying his horse from the porch rail. Doc took hold of the reins just below the bit.

"Do I bandy your wife's name about?" Doc said. The fire in his chest had grown until he could barely speak above a whisper.

Wyatt's back was to the moonlight; Doc couldn't see his face. "I don't know. Do you?"

"If I did, what would I get from you?"

"I think you know." From his voice, Wyatt was smil-ing.

"Then tell me what you deserve for lying about Kate."

A gust of cold wind rattled the scrub around them.

"You're not angry because I made use of Kate," Wyatt said calmly. "Besides, I did her no harm." He took hold of the reins below Doc's hand. Doc didn't let go.

"I don't believe you gave a damn about that."

Wyatt stepped forward. He occluded the moon, so that the black shape of him was rimmed with silver. The night wind whistled through brush and boards and every opening that might hum with it.

There was a knife hidden in Doc's sleeve. He was suddenly conscious of how short a distance lay between it and Wyatt's body. But he felt helpless, even so.

"I didn't give a damn," Wyatt answered, cold as snow. "If I have to hurt everyone in the world to protect what's mine, I will do it like a shot. Making Luther King think you were gunning for him is nothing to what I'd do."

And Doc realized Wyatt was right. Kate was only an excuse. "I am not your hired killer."

"That's because I don't need one." Wyatt drew his reins out of Doc's fingers, backed his horse, and led him off toward the corral.

Doc clutched the porch rail and stared out at the silver-and-black landscape. The air felt thin in his lungs, searing as he dragged it in. He'd thought he was the wildfire. Now he knew he was only the tree.

Missin son flavior debac

No matter how hard Mildred stared at Harry Woods's handwritten copy, that was what it said. Missing some flavor debacle? It made no sense, and had nothing to do with the story—a short color piece on Papago Indian folklore. Besides, even Harry wasn't that bad a speller.

She held the page closer to the lamp over the type

case. No help. So much for working late to get ahead of tomorrow's edition.

The back door banged, and Mildred looked up hopefully. But it was only Ernesto Pasillo, wrestling a bale of paper from the freight wagon to the storeroom.

"Ernesto! *¿Momento, por favor?*"

"*Sí, señora,*" he gasped. A thump, and he backed out of the storeroom, dusting himself and eyeing her warily. Ernesto was about sixteen, with strong Indian features that made him look older. But whenever Mildred spoke to him, she could see him regress to half that age. He must have once been under the thumb of an implacable Anglo schoolmarm.

"Ernesto, I need to go see Harry at the county jail. I'll only be a minute. Can you keep an eye on things?"

Mildred heard his sigh of relief. "Yes, *señora.*" He looked back over his shoulder. "The new paper—"

"Finish that, then sit down and take a load off your feet." She yanked off her apron. "If anyone expects the office to be open at this hour, he can start his own newspaper."

She stuffed Harry's copy in her handbag, pinned her hat on her head, and bolted out the back door into the lamplit night.

She had to wait for two ranch wagons, a gig, and a stagecoach before she could cross Fifth Street at the corner of Toughnut. The town's early arrivals claimed that in '79 the only time they had to wait to cross a street was during the Fourth of July parade. Surely, with this many residents to draw on, a man didn't have to be both a newspaper editor and undersheriff for the county? It was downright prideful. She'd tell Harry so, right after she told him if he didn't type his copy, she'd make him set it himself.

A sunburned, grim-faced man leaned against the

front wall of the jail. No one she recognized; she shortened her steps. He looked her up and down as she came into the light of the lamps.

Mildred summoned a mental image of Ernesto's schoolmarm, looked the man in the eye, and said, "Good evening." As she swept through the jailhouse door, she thought he flushed.

"Harry," she said as the door shut behind her, "I have no idea—"

Harry stood behind the jailer's desk. Something in his face stopped her voice: a stiffness of the mouth, a fixed look in the eyes. A man stood in front of the desk, his back a vista of pin-striped broadcloth.

"Hello, Mrs. Benjamin," Harry said. "You know John Dunbar?"

Dunbar turned and smiled widely at her. "Hello there, Mrs. Benjamin. I was just telling your boss he ought to be sorry he wasn't there when his prisoner was caught. That was a damned—beg pardon—a mighty fine chase."

And if Harry had been out chasing bandits, the last few days would have been as big a nuisance as this evening. Men who ran businesses ought to stay put and run them. "Were you there, Mr. Dunbar?"

Dunbar had the grace to flush. "No, ma'am. I had a mare due to foal. But I'd admire to have seen it. Wyatt and Morgan Earp and Doc Holliday flushed Luther King out smart as you please, and scared the whole story out of him. Now that we know who the murderers were who stopped that stage, the Earps'll catch 'em."

"Sheriff Behan will probably help a mite," Harry said mildly, and looked around as if to remind Dunbar whose jailhouse he was in.

"Oh, Johnny!" Dunbar laughed. "Of course he will.

I'm in business with Johnny, though, and I know him pretty well. As long as the county stays quiet, it's live and let live with Johnny."

Harry looked over Dunbar's shoulder at her. "Mrs. Benjamin, problem at the paper?"

There was something wrong in the room, in spite of Harry's mildness, Dunbar's laugh. "Nothing a minute of your time won't fix."

"Let's step in the back, then. John, if the lawyer shows up with that bill of sale, you deal with him. I'll be right back."

Harry opened the door behind the desk and beckoned Mildred. When she got there, Harry put his hand between her shoulder blades and propelled her through.

He shut the door with a thump and pulled her to the other end of the narrow hall. "Listen to me," he whispered. "If Luther King stays in this jail, he's going to be killed. I can't do anything about it with Dunbar out front. You have to get King out."

Mildred stared. This was a melodrama, with actors playing Harry and Dunbar. It had nothing to do with real life. The hanging lamp cast the wrong shadows; there ought to be footlights. "What are you talking about? Who's going to kill him? Why would—"

"Because he can tell who held up that stage and shot Philpot and Roerig."

"But he already has!"

"He's said what the Earps want him to. If he's dead, he can't be made to say more. You heard Dunbar: they scared him into telling the story they wanted."

"That's a nasty accusation." Harry had precious little use for the Earps, but could he really believe something as bad as this?

Harry shook his head. "Witnesses saw Holliday ride like hell out of town the night of the holdup, carrying a

Henry rifle. If Holliday helped stop that stage, the Earps'll lose ground. So will people who've sided with them."

"Ground"—political office, elected and appointed; money; influence. Luther King's mouth, open or closed, could affect the balance of power in Cochise County. There'd been a lot of silver on that stage, but it was nothing to the stakes on the table now.

Harry grabbed her shoulders and gave her a shake. "Mildred, please." His grip was hard enough to hurt. Harry never touched her.

"I can't possibly do that." Was that her voice? It wasn't even short of breath.

"The cells are through there." Harry nodded at a bolted door. "The keys are here on the wall. You'll have to find him a horse. . . ."

"No, I won't have to find him a horse. It's madness—"

Harry reached inside his sack coat and pulled out a revolver. He shoved it into her hands. "Take it. It's King's."

Mildred had held a pistol before. But this one lay unnaturally heavy across her palms. The weight of a life.

Give it back. Refuse to do this. She looked into Harry's pale, sweating face, saw his eyes dart to the door that led to the front room. Cocky, ironic, confident Harry.

She turned her back on him and pulled up the front of her bodice. She pushed the pistol barrel-first into the waistband of her skirt, against her petticoat, until nothing but the grip showed. She arranged the drape of her overskirt to hide the bulge of the cylinder, and tugged her bodice down over the grip. Then she turned back to Harry. Her heart hammered like some out-of-control engine.

"Go look in on your prisoner," she said. He frowned. "Go, or close your eyes, Harry." She honestly wasn't sure if she was protecting Harry or herself.

Harry turned and went through the door to the cells.

Mildred snatched the cell keys off the hook, wrapped them in her handkerchief to keep them quiet, and shoved them into her handbag. Then she hurried to the back door and unbolted it.

Harry came back in. "Have we finished our business?"

Mildred caught her breath. "Dear heaven, that's right. Dunbar may ask. I couldn't read your handwriting. There was only one line, really—" She remembered the line, and in her head, the characters shifted, reshaped themselves. "Never mind. It was Mission San Xavier del Bac, wasn't it? It makes sense in context."

"The White Dove of the Desert. I expect it was."

"Dunbar has one of his hands waiting outside the front door."

"Then you don't want to disappoint him, Mrs. Benjamin. After you." He opened the door to the office.

She sailed through, wondering if her smile was as ghastly as it felt. Dunbar beamed back. It must be good enough. "Good evening, Mr. Dunbar," she said, and offered her hand.

He shook it vigorously. She felt the cell keys bounce in her handbag, and her stomach turned to ice. But they didn't clank. "Evening, Mrs. Benjamin." He held the front door for her.

Outside she passed Dunbar's man. She felt him like a cannon pointed at her back. Her knees quaked as she walked, and she listened for footsteps behind her.

All the way down the block, she was in sight of the jail. The Vizina Hoisting Works occupied most of the frontage on Toughnut Street. There was no cover there; only the relentless racket of second shift around the shaft building—workmen's shouts, the clang of metal on metal, the ground-shaking grind and scream of the hoist and the engines starting up. Each sound made her heart lurch.

Mildred crossed Fifth. She needed to continue down Toughnut if she wanted to be seen heading back to the *Nugget* office—another straight, relentless block with her back to the jail. She turned abruptly up Fifth and looked back the way she'd come. Darkness closed her trail behind her. There was no one there.

She stumbled against a hitching rail and clutched it to keep from falling. She couldn't do it. If her nerve failed just walking away, how could she walk back with a saddled horse, with a pistol. . . .

There was more broadcloth before her eyes, charcoal-gray this time. "Mrs. Benjamin? Are you well?"

She looked up past smooth frock coat lapels, a maroon silk tie, a crisp white collar. Lamplight from a window fell sideways on the clean-shaven face. She didn't recognize it until she saw the eyes, the clear ruddy brown of good tea.

"You're *not* well," said Jesse Fox. "Come sit down."

He put his hand under her elbow—and a shock went through her, like static electricity or a blow to a nerve. She cried out. He went pale under his tan, but he didn't let go.

"I'm fine," she gasped. "It's nothing—"

"Sit."

Fox's voice was like a second shock. She sank onto the bench outside the Russ House. She wanted to put her head between her knees to stop the buzzing in her ears, but the pistol against her stomach kept her upright. She leaned against the wall instead and closed her eyes. The Russ House front door and windows were open. She could hear the muted clatter of crockery and the buzz of voices from inside as the staff cleared tables and served diners.

"Do you have smelling salts?" Fox asked. She felt his hand close on her handbag.

"No!" She pressed the bag into her lap.

He looked into her eyes. His own were unfocused, as if he were seeing past her. Then he blinked and sat down beside her.

"Let me help," he said. It was less a request than an order, like the command to sit.

She took a breath and summoned a polite smile. "How kind. But there's nothing to help with."

"All right." His face settled into the expression she'd been trying for. "Pardon my presumption, Mrs. Benjamin. I realize we haven't been introduced, but you seem to be in some distress. If I may be of assistance . . ."

She wanted to laugh in spite of the commotion of her nerves. "Heavens. You're not an actor, are you?"

"Only when I have to be. Do you need one?"

"No, no. Thank you. You have helped, actually." She stood up. "Good evening, Mr. Fox." She turned away.

He said, "Do you always carry that much iron in your bag?"

It rooted her feet to the sidewalk.

His voice was quiet behind her. "You don't have to explain what you're doing with a ring of keys that size. You don't have to explain anything. Just tell me what you need done."

There were people around them—on the street, at the hoisting works, in the lodging house whose doors and windows shone out light only feet away. But Mildred felt as if she and Fox were standing just out of their reach, like angels walking among men.

"How did you know they were keys?"

His face was blank for an instant; then he smiled. "Well, that's the part *I* don't have to explain."

She looked at him properly for the first time since he'd appeared in front of her. He was beautifully dressed and freshly shaved. His brown hair was cut. "Tombstone seems to agree with you, Mr. Fox. I thought you weren't staying."

"So did I. Do you think I might get a mention in the social column after all?"

"I have to go. Good-bye, Mr. Fox."

She whisked out into the street. After a moment she felt him at her side.

"Where?"

"I beg your pardon?"

"Where do you have to go?"

"To hire a horse."

"Aha. I knew you needed help." He took her elbow again and drew her into the shadow of the buildings. "Think ahead, Mrs. Benjamin. You arrive at the livery and rent a horse. Is that your riding habit?"

It was obviously not. "What business is it of theirs?"

"None. But whoever they are will remember the woman who asked to hire a horse at a late hour and wasn't dressed to ride it. Of course," he said cheerfully as he continued in the direction she'd chosen, "that may not bother you."

Mildred stopped, which tugged her arm out from under his well-tailored one. He stopped, too.

She had the jailhouse keys in her handbag, and a stage robber's pistol under her skirt. Her good name, and Harry Woods's, and if Harry was right, Luther King's life, were being juggled like oranges in the middle of the street by a man who, for all she knew, was Lucifer himself. She had to do something.

"Mr. Fox," she said, though her tongue was dry and her chest was tight as stretched hide, "would you be so kind as to hire me a horse?"

He raised his eyes to hers and said, unsmiling, "I'd be pleased to, ma'am. Distance, or speed?"

"Both. Pioneer Livery is closest—around the corner on Toughnut Street."

"Sidesaddle?"

Her face grew hot. "No." If he'd believed the horse was for her, he wouldn't have asked.

"Where shall I bring it?"

Oh, God, she hadn't decided. She closed her eyes and tried to recall details of the block the jail was on. "On Sixth Street, between Allen and Toughnut, there's an alley . . . It runs alongside a boardinghouse. Tether the horse there. And then wait—please."

From the breast pocket of his coat, Fox took the spectacles she'd first seen him in, and put them on. It was so odd, the sight of a man in dark spectacles after dark, that Mildred could only stare. He touched his hat brim to her. Then he turned, walked back to Toughnut, and disappeared around the corner.

I've gone mad, she thought. But what choice did she have? Well, if he arrived in the alley with a horse, he was as guilty as she was.

And if he was not, in fact, Lucifer, but a considerate, overzealous, honest man? Then she was involving him in a crime without his consent.

For the first time, Mildred thought about what would happen if she were caught. The Territorial Prison in Yuma, without a doubt. She walked down Allen Street as quickly as she could without making anyone stare, to Sixth. She turned right, even as she wondered, *Why am I doing this?*

The boardinghouse she'd described to Fox was actually a brothel, but on the west side of Sixth Street the polite fictions were respected. She turned down the alley, trying to look innocent and purposeful at once.

Behind the brothel was an open lot, its dust and scrub hidden by darkness. A few little cabins, raw and unfinished-looking, dotted the space almost at random between the hoisting works and where she stood. Only one showed light through a curtained window. The ground between the brothel's back wall and the rear of the jail was empty, and faintly illuminated by light from the street. Mildred clenched her hands on her bag and darted across it.

Perhaps Harry had come to his senses. Perhaps he'd barred the back door. She turned the knob and pulled. It swung open.

The hallway was empty. She unbarred the door to the cells and opened it.

The only prisoner was a skinny young man who looked up when the door opened. His eyes were big with fear. He opened his mouth, but Mildred put her finger to her lips. When she opened her handbag, he cowered back against the wall.

"Oh, God—"

"Shush!" Mildred hissed. She pulled out the ring of keys and shook her handkerchief back into her bag. Then a horrid thought stopped her. "You *are* Luther King?"

"Yes, ma'am," he whispered.

"Thank heaven." At least she hadn't been waving the stolen keys in front of the wrong person. Though surely anyone met in the cells of the county jail was automatically wrong in one way or another. She felt a tickle of hysterical laughter, and began testing keys to drive it off.

The third key opened Luther King's cell door. "In front of the boardinghouse behind this building, you'll find a man in a dark gray coat waiting with a horse.

Oh, and here." She turned away from King and tugged his pistol out of her skirt.

He stared at it as she put it in his hands, then at her. "This is a trick."

"If it is, I'm tricked, too. Now, ride out of town and don't come back."

She went to the hall door and peeked out. Still no one there. She hurried King into the hall and to the back door. "There," she said, pointing, "on Sixth. Now, go!"

King stuffed his pistol into his waistband and scurried into the night. Mildred shut the door and leaned on it, breathing hard.

She was done. Wasn't she? No, put the keys back. She leaped to the peg on the wall by the office door. If anyone opened that door, she'd die of fright. . . . The ring dropped onto its peg, and she flew to the back door and out into the darkness.

Now she had only to walk away, back to the *Nugget* office. Instead she found herself heading toward Sixth Street. The worst thing to do, if anything had gone wrong; but she had to know if Fox had brought a horse, or the law, or hadn't come at all.

The sound of hoofbeats made her look up. A dark chestnut horse was coming down the street at a canter, with a man in the saddle.

It was Fox. He wore his dark spectacles, and the shabby corduroy coat she'd first seen him in. He spurred the horse and galloped by without a glance.

She swept up her skirts and ran toward the alley. What did it mean? Where was Luther King?

On the sidewalk ahead of her she saw the silhouette of a man in a frock coat. He appeared to be admiring the stars over the eastern hills, or the prostitutes' cribs across the street. She stumbled to a walk. It was Jesse Fox.

"My compliments, Mrs. Benjamin," he said. "The perfect spot for your business. People in this neighborhood have their minds on . . . other things."

She could speak, after all. "I just saw you ride down the street."

Fox smiled, his eyes half-closed. He looked like a cat in a patch of sun. "You might have seen someone in my old coat. I threw it out when I got this one. Oh, and I've misplaced my spectacles." He sighed, but he was still smiling. "I'll miss those."

Had she seen the coat and the dark glasses and filled in the rest? Luther King had a short, receding chin, sandy hair, and a sparse moustache. She thought the man on the horse had been clean-shaven, sharp-jawed, and brown-haired.

"It's all right," Fox said. "He's safely away. Isn't that what matters?"

She looked into his face and found him looking inquiringly into hers. "Don't you want to know who he is?"

He laughed. "For no good reason, I know where the county jail is. And everyone in town knows who's in it. Or *was* in it. Or were those the keys to somewhere else entirely?"

Fox offered his arm. Mildred laid her hand on it and tried to seem relaxed. Had she just helped Fox free a partner? Or was Jesse Fox one of the names King might have mentioned, and Fox one of the people who wanted King dead? If so, where was King, and who had she seen riding down the street?

She'd been insane. She knew nothing about this man. And now he knew a great deal too much about her.

"Given your suspicions, you were awfully quick to offer your help," Mildred said. Which, she realized, was a grown-up version of "If I'm one, you're another."

Fox nodded. "I suppose I have faith in your judgment, Mrs. Benjamin. Now that we've broken the law together, do you think we could use first names?"

They reached Allen Street. It was startling that there could still be streets full of people going about their business. "Certainly not," she said, and was glad her voice was strong and steady. "It would look suspicious."

He laughed, and two women walking past turned their heads and smiled. "You're not a newspaperwoman, you're a lawyer. I'll pick my argument more carefully next time." He looked at her from under his hat brim. "May I buy you dinner?"

"I'm afraid I'm otherwise engaged," Mildred said. Fox had power over her. If he meant to use it, she wanted to know.

"What a shame." He grinned. "I'm looking forward to a nice, leisurely supper at the Cosmopolitan Hotel. After which I'll hotfoot it down to the Pioneer Livery and tell them someone stole my hired horse. Tombstone seems like a mighty lawless place, Mrs. Benjamin."

There was not a hint of threat in his expression. "It's hardly safe to walk the streets," she agreed faintly.

The next morning she set the copy describing her first criminal act.

It was both less real on paper, and more. Other people made page one, not her, and since this was page one news it obviously had nothing to do with her. But the story made everything around her actions real. She could imagine Dunbar and lawyer Harry Jones in the front office of the jail, huddled over the bill of sale for Luther King's horse. "Under-sheriff Harry Woods" would be waiting for them to finish so he could take the document to his prisoner to sign. And all the time he would be listening for things he couldn't hear on the other side of the wall.

She imagined Dunbar saying, "Damn, Harry, you're jumpy as a bitch with one pup." After that, the discovery of the empty cell and unbarred back door.

Dunbar seemed like a simple, straightforward man, who'd expect straightforwardness from others. But he was involved in county politics; he might not be as simple as that. When he saw the empty cell, did he remember Harry stepping into the hall with his typesetter and shutting the door?

Harry's article concluded:

> A confederate on the outside had a horse in readiness for him. It was a well-planned job by outsiders to get him away. He was an important witness against Holliday.

Well, it was nice that Luther King was out of reach. Now the Earps and their friends could come after Harry.

She looked up from the copy and found Harry's eyes on her.

"I don't believe I've had a chance to thank you," he said.

"I can't very well say, 'My pleasure,' can I?"

"Maybe not now, but you'll brag to your grandchildren."

"Hush up and type."

Poppoppop-pop-pop. It came from outside, in the street. She stood frozen with the composing stick in her hand.

"Get down!" Harry screamed. He was already on the floor, but he reached up and grabbed her arm. Type scattered over the floorboards. She'd banged her elbow on something as she dropped, she realized.

She waited for the next sounds—more shots, the front windows breaking, shouting. All she heard was her own harsh breath.

Harry pushed himself half up, craned his neck to see through the door. "There's nobody there. What the hell?" He stood up.

"Harry, no—" But he'd already snatched the Navy Colt from his desk drawer and opened the door. Mildred scrambled to her feet and followed him. If someone shot Harry, she might at least be able to identify the gunman.

She watched him check one end of the street, then the other. He stepped out onto the sidewalk. "Well, I'll be damned," he said, amused, and walked into the street.

He stopped dead.

Mildred flew out the door and across the sidewalk. "Harry, what's the matter?" she asked his stiff back.

Harry turned and put his hands out, as if to hold her away. "Mildred, go back in the office."

Too late for that. She saw, past him, what he'd seen: a short string of Chinese firecrackers, exploded. They were tied around the wrist of a severed arm.

A silly noise, more squeak than scream, came out of her mouth. She whirled, pressed her fingers to her lips, and closed her eyes. But the thing in the street stayed in the dark inside her eyelids. An arm with no body, in a coat sleeve with no coat. She pressed her lips painfully against her teeth to distract her from a tide of nausea and faintness.

"Go back inside, Mildred."

"Why would anyone *do* that?" she gasped.

"I don't know. I'll fetch the marshal—"

She opened her eyes, and saw someone coming down the street. Jesse Fox, in a gray frock coat, squinting in the sun. He stopped a few yards short of her and Harry. "Mrs. Benjamin—"

Then he caught sight of the thing in the street. His face went white all at once, gray-white.

Harry ignored Fox. "The coroner may be able to tell whose . . . whose it is. Maybe someone died—"

"It's Luther King's," said Fox, in a strangled voice.

Mildred looked again. The sleeve had once been part of a threadbare corduroy coat.

Harry began, "How do you—"

"He's right," Mildred told him.

It wasn't a prank. It was a message, and the fire-crackers were to make sure they found it. She looked into Harry's face and saw him realize it, too. Was it for Harry, or for her? Or both?

Other people along Fourth Street were looking out of their offices and shops. A few were coming toward them to see what the fuss was. Harry went to meet them.

Fox crouched beside the severed arm. To his credit, it seemed difficult for him to do. She could only look at it in glances, or at the corner of her vision. He reached toward the upturned hand with its curled fingers, as if to pluck something from it.

He jerked his hand back with a hiss and cradled it against his stomach. Then he pulled a handkerchief from a pocket and used that to take an object from the dead palm.

"What? What is it?"

"I'm not sure. If I find out, I'll let you know."

"You're removing evidence!"

Fox looked up, his face closed and stiff. "Are you going to tell the marshal who this arm used to be attached to?"

Mildred opened her mouth to say "yes," and remembered why she could do no such thing.

"Then let's be model citizens together. I promise, if it turns out to be something the marshal can use, I'll give it to him." He stuffed the handkerchief and its contents back in his coat.

"Mr. Fox, what brought you here? At just the wrong time?"

He stood up and dusted his hands off. "If you're asking, did I kill Luther King, hack his arm off, and leave it in the street, no, I didn't."

Mildred shook her head. "I saw your face when you first—" She found she couldn't say it.

"And?"

"You may be an actor when you need to be, but Sarah Siddons couldn't have looked like that. So what did bring you here?"

Fox's shoulders rose and fell with a sigh. "I'll tell you later. It's turned into a bad moment for it. Good day, Mrs. Benjamin."

She watched him walk away, his stride long and quick. Harry came up beside her and followed her gaze. "What do your instincts tell you today, Mildred?"

She couldn't very well tell Harry that her instincts were being churned like butter and were no use to him, her, or anyone else. "They tell me to get in out of the sun." She gathered her skirts and headed toward the *Nugget* office.

7

The knocker on Lung's front door was a wooden Chinese dragon's head with a ball in its mouth. The carving was smoothed and the gilding worn by many hands, as if it was older than the door. Jesse didn't remember it from San Francisco.

It hadn't seemed like it at the time, but everything had been simpler in San Francisco.

The door swung inward to frame Lung, one eyebrow raised. "This cannot be good."

"What gave it away? That I knocked at the front door?"

A snort of disgust from Lung. "You know exactly how I knew. I will not assist you in the maintenance of your self-deceit."

Most times, the whole of Chinatown knew everything that happened to anyone, Chinese or not, in the interest of community safety. A less self-deceptive man, Jesse thought, would have learned to expect it.

But he *must* have expected Lung to know everything: he hadn't envisioned standing here trying to explain himself. "Lung, I think I just got a man killed."

Lung shot a look over Jesse's shoulder.

"No, I'm not on the run."

"Should you be?"

He hadn't considered the possibility. But no—King was dead, and Jesse needed to know if it was his fault. And his fault that a horrible *memento mori* had been delivered to the doorstep of the *Daily Nugget*.

"Jesse," Lung said sharply, and Jesse yanked his attention back to Lung's inquiring frown. "I said this could not be good. Can you tell me how not good it is?"

"Not yet. I . . . want your help. In your professional capacity."

"As a physician?"

"No." A deep breath. "The other thing."

"When you cannot even bring yourself to say the word?" Lung looked exasperated. "Very well. But only because I feel responsible for you." He stepped back and held the door open.

The room was unchanged from the last time Jesse'd seen it, except for the smell. There was something underneath the medicinal-herb fragrance, neither cinnamon nor alcohol but kin to both. It stirred his memory, but not enough to bring an image to the surface.

He laid the handkerchief bundle on the table. "What can you tell me about this?"

Lung eyed the handkerchief dubiously. Then he turned back the white linen folds. Jesse looked down at the braid of heavy-gauge silver wire, a single shining inch long.

Lung looked up at Jesse. "And hardly a week in town."

"I settle in pretty quickly," Jesse replied, trying not to sound alarmed. "What is it?"

"This is a warning sent from one knowledgeable man to another, to stay out of the sender's business."

" 'Knowledgeable?' "

"A sorcerer."

Lung was speaking metaphorically. If Jesse persevered, they'd get past metaphor to something real and useful. That was why he'd come. "It looks like jewelry. A watch fob, maybe."

"These are often made of the disputed materials. Bone or leather, if the quarrel is over a living creature. Wood, if a dwelling is at issue. In this case—"

"Silver," Jesse finished. "The local wealth. It can't be a warning for me. I'm not filing any claims."

Lung picked up the corners of the handkerchief and turned its burden into the light, until it looked as if there were a star burning in the cloth. Lung added, "They are customarily unpleasant to touch, in some way."

Jesse held out his right hand. "Nice to know it was just custom." The blisters on his thumb and forefinger were white and sore. Some kind of electrical charge, or a corrosive coating.

Lung eyed the blisters appreciatively. "I can give you an ointment for those."

Jesse shoved his hand in his pocket. "Quit having so God-damned much fun. If I believed this thing is what you say it is—"

Lung flipped the corners of the handkerchief back over the twisted wire and thrust the little bundle at Jesse. "If you do not, take it and go." His face was hard.

"Lung—"

"No! You know what this is, or you would not have brought it here. Do you think you are safe if you know nothing? You are like a child who breaks a bowl and denies it, and thinks that protects him from punishment."

"I take responsibility for what I do. For what someone else *says* I do—" Jesse clenched his teeth. "To hell with that."

"You mean, to hell with me."

"If you keep on with this, yes."

"Then take this and go." Lung still held out the handkerchief. His hand shook a little.

"Is this the way you doctor people?" Jesse said, too loud. "Superstition? Hocus-pocus? It won't work if I don't believe in it."

"What do you believe in, then?"

"Reality. Science. You know that."

Lung held out the handkerchief.

"This has nothing to do with me!" The blood thumped in Jesse's ears. He stood in the middle of the room, but he was in a corner all the same, with walls he didn't want to look at.

"You cannot stay in this camp unless you know the nature of what you have engaged. If you do not, you may as well load your revolver, put it to your head, and pull the trigger."

"Fine. I'll be off to the border, then." He could ride away—from the memory of Luther King's white, sweating face. Of Mrs. Benjamin trying not to look at the grisly thing in the street, her quick, tapering fingers hiding her mouth. (But not her eyes; too late for that. He'd wanted to wind time backward like a watch.)

He could go, and this would follow him. It would join the trail of things already behind him that he couldn't explain or excuse.

This explained so much. It couldn't be true, but it explained so much.

"Jesse."

Jesse sank down in the rocking chair. His mouth was dry. It took two tries before he said, "There could be something in what you say. Maybe."

Lung did nothing to break the silence. Possibly he expected more. If so, his expectations could go hang. When Jesse felt something like calm, he looked up from his hands.

Lung dropped the handkerchief back on the table. It unfolded as if offering its contents in an open hand. "This is no less a science because you have not studied it. A certain quantity of salt will dissolve completely in a certain volume of water. Science declares it is true. It remains true in the east or the west, for a wise man or a foolish one. There is more to weigh in this"—he nodded toward the handkerchief—"than a measure of salt and water. But it is as real as speaking or raising your arm."

If the twisted wire was what Lung said it was— "Who was it meant for?"

"It was not meant for you?"

"It couldn't have been."

"The blisters suggest otherwise."

The silver had shone in the slanting morning sun, sparkled like moving water. He hadn't been able to look away, couldn't resist reaching for it. It had done everything but call his name.

Lung asked, "Where did you get it?"

"From a dead man's hand." He thought of King's arm in his own familiar coat sleeve, flecked with tiny powder burns from the firecrackers. There'd been some blood on the cloth, but not much. The arm had been severed after King died. His breakfast sat a little less easy.

He looked up to find Lung staring. "You do not, as the barbarian saying goes, do a thing by half. Was this the man whose death you fear you caused?"

Jesse nodded.

"What was the dead man to you?"

Jesse told Lung the whole tale of assisting in a jail break. He didn't mention Mrs. Benjamin's name.

"You knew the man was rightfully imprisoned, yet you helped him escape?"

"It seemed like the thing to do." It had, too. And not just because Mrs. Benjamin had looked so desperate.

Lung shook his head. "You said a similar thing, I recall, about hiring the opera singer in San Francisco."

"I said it about a lot of things then. This was different."

When Jesse reached the part about giving his coat and spectacles to King, Lung's eyes widened, and he leaned forward.

"Tell me everything about the clothing."

Jesse had a sudden sinking feeling. "On my way to get the horse, I got my old coat out of the rubbish bin behind the tailor's where I'd tossed it. I thought it might come in handy. Then when I helped King into it—"

"You put it on him with your own hands?"

"His were shaking too much. When I got it on him, I thought of the spectacles, that they were the last thing anyone would expect to see on King's face."

"So you took them out of your pocket—"

"No, I took them off my nose."

Lung squeezed his eyes shut, as if absorbing bad news. "And as you did, you said . . . ?"

"Good God, I don't remember. Something like, 'Nobody will recognize you in these.'"

Lung covered his face and made a very odd noise, somewhere between a snort and a wail. "Of course. A strong, decisive pronouncement. And as you carried out these actions, you felt a peculiar sensation, like mild drunkenness."

Yes; just what he always felt when he was doing something stupid and reckless. Perhaps a little more so, this time. "I think I was humming 'The Minstrel Boy.'"

Lung looked down at the thing on the table, and a muscle sprang into relief in his jaw. "When next you feel that way, stop what you are doing, go back to your lodging, and lie down until it goes away. Any other course of action may shorten your life dramatically."

"Never mind my life. Did I help shorten Luther King's?"

"Have you never before shortened a man's life?" Lung asked.

"As far as I know, nobody ever died because I was stupid and careless. If that's changed, I want to know."

Lung folded the handkerchief around the twisted silver and handed it to Jesse. "This does not name its maker. Happily, your work is also mute. Indeed, if you blunder about in this fashion, your new enemy will not believe you a threat even if he learns it beyond all denial."

"Lung, what did I do?"

Lung smiled sweetly. "Science."

Jesse squinted at the front of the Oriental Saloon. It was before noon, and Sunday, but he didn't think that mattered in Tombstone.

He pushed through the doors into the comparative dark of the room. He missed his spectacles. He blinked and thought he saw, inside his eyelids, twisted gold frames and shattered lenses in the dust. He shook his head, and shook away the fancy.

The saloon seemed to grow out of the gloom: the mirrors and colored glass and shining carved wood of the backbar, the glittering ranks of many-colored liqueurs, the sheen of the bar top under the chandeliers. Under his feet, the carpet sprouted color and pattern. Around him the wallpaper bloomed.

The bartender nodded when he saw him. Maybe the bartender was remembering that the last time Jesse had been there he hadn't made trouble.

But he had made trouble. He hadn't made it in the saloon, but it had certainly found its way there, to bleed on the furniture.

"*Have you never before shortened a man's life?*" In fear, in anger, he'd shot at people who shot at him. He'd hit some of them. He might have killed them. How was that different from what he'd done to Luther King?

There was a man at the bar, a miner from his canvas trousers and heavy boots, and two town men at a table by the front window, reading the Tucson papers and smoking cigars. No sign of the dentist, Holliday. But it might be either too early or—based on when he'd met him—not early enough.

"Porter, please," Jesse said to the bartender; then, consulting his nerves and the recollection of what he needed to do, added, "and a Jameson's whiskey."

The braided wire was a weight in his pocket. He heard Lung again: *"You must get rid of that. The one who made it can feel it if it is near."*

"I'll throw it away."

"Certainly—that worked so well with your coat. No, it must change owners. You cannot even give it away."

The bartender slid the two glasses across the polished wood. Jesse paid him, downed the whiskey, and sighed.

The bartender said, "Makes you glad to be alive, don't it?"

It was true: Luther King wasn't going to feel that burn in his throat ever again. Jesse nodded.

If the token could draw its maker to Jesse (he couldn't quite give up that *if*), then he could keep it, and whoever had delivered King's severed arm like a telegram would come to him.

Lung's reaction to that hadn't been good. *"What then? Do you hope he will introduce himself and politely offer to fight?"*

Jesse drank off half the beer. "Where's the best place to find a game this time of day?"

"Faro?"

"Poker would suit me better."

"Then you're a lucky man." The bartender called toward the back of the room, "Say, Ringo! Got a chair for this fellow?"

Jesse craned his neck. Sure enough, in a back corner there were three men at a table, with money laid out on the green baize and drinks at their elbows.

The man holding the deck looked tall, even slumped in his chair, and coyote-thin. "Anyone I know?" the man asked without looking up.

"Are you?" the bartender asked Jesse.

"I don't think so."

"Complete stranger," the bartender called to the cardplayers, as if they hadn't heard the whole exchange.

"Let's have him, then," said the dealer. "Three-handed poker's a tedious business."

"Hey!" said the player to the dealer's left, a big man with sandy curls and a wedge of white grin.

"I was quoting you, Bill," the dealer observed, his eyebrows lifting.

"Did I say 'tedious'? Hell, I must be getting smarter in my old age."

Jesse wished he'd come with simpler motives. In this company he thought he might rather play poker than the fool.

He pulled an empty chair away from another table and waited to see where the players would open a space.

The big man, smiling still, scooted sideways and cleared the spot to the left of the dealer. He and the other two players would get to see what Jesse did with his cards before they played their own. Fair enough, and it might save him a little trouble.

Jesse slid the chair in and sat. The third player, directly across the table, frowned at Jesse. He had the slicked-down hair and fresh shave of a man who'd come from church or the barber. His coat was open over a dark brown bird's-eye waistcoat and a red neckerchief. By the money on the table, he was losing.

Jesse smiled at him. He couldn't help it. This was something he understood.

The dealer stared at the smoke-darkened ceiling as if

the news were printed on it, and none of it good. "Five-card draw, nothing wild, nothing fancy. That suit you?"

"I'm not fussy on a Sunday morning," said Jesse.

The dealer looked at him for the first time. His eyes were a cold, pale gray. " 'Remember the Sabbath day and keep it holy.' I'm John Ringo. The grinning idiot next to you—"

"Curly Bill Brocius," said the grinner, who did not look idiotic at all. He stuck out a vast hand. Jesse took it and had the bones of his palm painfully compressed.

"Frank McLaury," said the man across the table, reluctantly.

"Honored. Jesse Fox." Jesse gave a general nod all around. "What are you playing for?"

Ringo replied, "Friendly poker. Dollar-five dollar, dollar ante to make it interesting."

"Friendly poker," in just that kind of drawl, always meant, "We're playing high."

Ringo set the deck down on his right. McLaury cut the cards. All that time, Ringo's eyes never left Jesse's face.

"That'll be fine," Jesse said. With those stakes, he'd be cleaned out in no time.

"What am I supposed to do with the damned thing? No one will buy it from me."

"You were clever enough to earn the problem. Solve it as you please. But that object must be disposed of in an exchange of real value."

Jesse took a silver dollar from his pocket and laid it on the table with a click.

"Now you're talking," Brocius said, and anted. McLaury pushed a dollar in, and Ringo flipped in his, making it ring off the rest.

"Pot's right," said Ringo. He gazed off again into some invisible bleak landscape. He flicked cards to

Jesse, Brocius, McLaury, and himself, without so much as sitting up in his chair. Jesse watched his hands: callused, brown, the fingernails short and clean. They never paused or fumbled.

Jesse looked at his cards. Only habit kept him from wincing. Two queens, an ace. The other two cards, a deuce and a ten, were rags. But it was a pretty hand, a hand with money in it. If he were playing poker, he'd have a choice: draw two cards in the hope of catching a second ace, or discard the ace as well, to make it look as if the two cards he kept were paltry.

If he were playing poker. But he was playing the fool instead. He pushed another two dollars into the pot.

Brocius sighed like a melodrama heroine and shoved his cards into the middle of the table. "Drop like a dead dog in the God-damn road," he declared.

McLaury snorted. "I'll see you and raise three." He threw five dollars in the pot with a curl of his lip, as if the play were beneath him.

Jesse began to pick apart the meaning of McLaury's three-dollar raise, then remembered it didn't make a bit of difference. No, it made a difference; he didn't want his opponents to bluff him into winning. He was playing mirror-poker, playing for the low hand while everyone else at the table played for high. It made him feel a little dizzy.

"I'll follow you there," Ringo declared, and added his bet to the pot.

"So will I." Jesse slid three more dollars across the table. Then, with a feeling not unlike walking off a cliff, he pulled the two queens and the ace and dropped them facedown on top of Brocius's castoffs in the deadwood. It was the worst thing he'd ever done at a poker table. "I'll take three."

"One to spin, one to measure, and one," Ringo said as he snapped cards off the deck to land in front of Jesse, "to cut the string."

The jobs of the three Fates. Jesse looked up at Ringo, but the man's attention was on McLaury.

McLaury asked for two cards, and Ringo dealt himself three new ones. Jesse looked at his fresh hand.

He'd kept the deuce and the ten. Now he held the deuce, and another deuce, and three tens. The god of card-playing was an angry god: if Jesse chose to blaspheme, it was going to hurt while he did it.

"I'm out of this one," he said. The words half choked him. He pushed his full house into the deadwood and waited for lightning to smash through the ceiling and strike him dead.

McLaury bet five dollars on his hand. Ringo nodded and said, "Nice round number. I'll see that." Jesse saw the skin around McLaury's eyes pinch. *Silly proud bastard*. Draw poker was a bluffer's game, but that didn't mean it was more manly to bluff than to fold.

When the time came to show 'em, McLaury had a pair of eights, and no better help than a nine of diamonds. Ringo laid down three threes almost apologetically and swept up the pot.

"Care to deal the next one?" Ringo asked Jesse. "If Frank and Bill don't mind." He lifted his eyebrows at the rest of the table.

"Fine with me." McLaury shrugged, quick and precise. "Let's get on with it."

"My God, yes," Brocius said. "Deal me better ones than Johnny has. I need a drink, though. I'm dry as a granny's cunt."

"Bill," said Ringo. That was all he said, but Brocius looked sideways, like a horse at a snake, and pressed his lips closed.

Ringo lifted his head as if he barely had strength for it. "Frank!"

"What?" said McLaury as the bartender turned their way.

Ringo sighed. "Not you, damn it. Frank Leslie, at the bar. Another round, Frank."

Jesse shuffled the deck and tried to look awkward. The blisters helped. Still, he hoped no one was watching; though couldn't a fellow shuffle well and play badly?

Ringo shook his head and added, "Seems like this town is nothing but Franks, Bills, and Johns. I'm making a new rule: anybody gets shot around here for the next year, he'd better be named Frank, Bill, or John. I want the herd thinned."

"Damned shame you couldn't have said so before road agents killed Bud Philpot." McLaury's voice was low and hard, and he shot a sideways look toward the door.

"I don't believe the fellows who did it take much account of what I want." Ringo's mouth softened just enough to be called a smile. "Not everybody does."

McLaury eyed Ringo sharply, but as far as Jesse could tell, there was nothing to see.

Brocius stared thoughtfully at the ceiling moldings. "Frank, Bill, or John. Nope, can't do it, Johnny."

"You just try not to shoot *anybody* for the next year. It would do you a world of good."

Jesse set the cards down in front of Ringo to cut, and said to Brocius, "Do you make a regular practice of shooting people?"

"No, but the last one was the city marshal, and he died. It was an accident, though." Brocius beamed at him. Jesse wasn't sure if that was supposed to be reassuring.

Frank McLaury snorted.

Brocius leaned forward across the table. "It was, damn it! I didn't have one thing against Fred White."

"I expect that made White feel better," McLaury snapped.

"Gentlemen," Ringo said, and lingered over the word. "Might we get on with business?"

The bartender, unaware that his herd was to be thinned, brought the drinks. Brocius had stout, McLaury had brandy and soda. Jesse smelled absinthe, gin, and Curaçao when Ringo's glass passed. Jesse bought the round, which sweetened McLaury a little.

The next five hands went as the first had, or possibly worse. Jesse caught cards so sweet they might have been printed on maple sugar candy, and he had to play them as if they were wormwood and gall. At last, on the sixth hand, he got cards that seemed bad enough to make it safe to stay in to the end.

All the players were in after the draw. McLaury bet five. Ringo shook his head over his cards like a disappointed preacher over his congregation. "If that's how it is, somebody's got to make you ladies play poker." He pushed ten dollars into the pot.

Jesse looked down at his pair of nines. Nobody, *nobody*, would stay in the last betting round with less than a pair of jacks, let alone raise like a madman. He put ten dollars in the pot. He had three dollars left in front of him—almost done.

Brocius gave the rest of them an outraged stare. "Johnny, if you ask me to lend you money tomorrow, I'll laugh in your face. Drop." He slapped his cards down and shoved them into the deadwood with both hands. "Frank, what'll it be?"

McLaury looked pale. "I'll see it," he said, and laid down another five.

"All right then, you damned fools," Brocius said, "show 'em."

McLaury had two sevens and a queen kicker. Ringo had four cards to a straight—in other words, nothing at all. Jesse'd won the hand. He looked up, stunned. Ringo stared blandly back at him.

Only a madman—or someone willing to sacrifice ten dollars to find out what another player was up to— would raise with a handful of nothing. Ringo had literally forced him to show his hand. And Jesse had bought himself another hour of poker.

But the god of cardplayers seemed to have forgiven him. He got honestly bad hands from then on, and when he tried to make them worse, they tended to comply. Jesse even managed to maneuver McLaury into winning money from him, and it seemed to make the man almost cheerful.

At last, when Ringo raised, there was nothing left in front of Jesse. He shook his head. "I'm shy. Unless . . ."

He pulled the handkerchief out of his pocket and let it unfold on the table. The twisted silver gleamed against the white cloth. "I could throw that in," Jesse said.

To Jesse's stretched nerves, the instant went on forever: the three men staring at the bright, vicious bauble. Brocius tilted his head, curious; McLaury scowled; and Ringo's face did nothing significant, just as it had been doing since Jesse had first set eyes on it.

Ringo reached out, and Jesse held his breath.

"Should another sorcerer touch this, it will bite him, too, though not so hard as you were bitten." When Lung had said that, Jesse had half ignored him. Even if it was true, people like Lung didn't clog the streets. But he remembered the pain—

Ringo picked up the token. It might have been a toothpick. Jesse, on the other hand, felt something like a pang of hunger, seeing it in Ringo's hand.

"Pretty. Real silver—" Ringo flexed the metal

slightly, and bounced it on his palm. "And damned near pure, I'd say." Ringo looked at Jesse across the twisted silver. "Kind of Irish-looking. What is it?"

Jesse tore his eyes away from the metal. "Good-luck charm."

"Appears to have run dry," Brocius observed.

"Sometimes they pick right up after a change of owner," Ringo said absently. He bounced it again in his palm. "All right. I say it's five dollars' worth of used-up luck." He tossed it into the pot.

Jesse's insides gave a lurch. "Then I'll take two," he said, pushing two cards into the deadwood and fighting the urge to pick up the bright twist of silver.

Now he held five cards constituting not a damn thing. No way to win the token back—and the point was to *lose* it. What was wrong with him?

When the betting came 'round, Jesse laid his cards down. "Fold. I'm busted."

Ringo raised his eyebrows. But he said nothing.

Brocius hovered over his cards, and McLaury snapped, "Come on, Bill. Staring won't improve 'em."

"I thought one of those queens winked at me, is all," said Brocius. McLaury took the bait; his eyes snapped to Brocius's cards. Then Brocius smiled and tossed his bet in. "Show 'em all, boys," he ordered, and spread his in front of him. There were no queens in his hand. McLaury glowered at him.

Ringo won the hand and swept the pot toward himself.

And Jesse felt something in the small of his back, a tug and release, like a thread breaking. The token lay in the little heap of bills and coins. It was just twisted metal, and shone with nothing but the lamplight overhead.

He stretched and slid his chair back. For the first time he noticed his shoulders were sore and his shirt was damp down his back and under his arms. "Thank you, gentlemen. You're fine cardplayers and fine company."

They all got to their feet when he did. "Always glad to take a polite man's money," Brocius said as he shook Jesse's hand. "A sight better than taking Frank's—he gets so damned surly."

McLaury, surprisingly, smiled. "Poker's serious business."

"Frank!" a voice called from the front of the room, and McLaury and the bartender both looked up. A slender man with rumpled brown hair came toward the table. His blue eyes and straight nose were twin to McLaury's, but the frown sat on his features as if it were a stranger there. "I've been down at Dexter's for half an hour, you jackass!"

McLaury yanked his watch out of his pocket and snapped it open. "Hell, Tom, I'm sorry. We got going a little."

He and Brocius moved to meet the newcomer. As they did, Ringo laid a hand on Jesse's shoulder.

"Well, Mr. Fox. Nice to meet you. And if you ever hanker to play the same game as the rest of us, you come find me. Hear?"

Jesse met his eyes and tried not to look guilty. He didn't think it worked. "I'd like that."

The front door swung open again, and two men walked in. At first, with the light behind them, all Jesse could tell was that they were tall and light-haired. He saw Ringo stiffen.

Under the gas lamps the men's coats were sober black. One of the pair was maybe a hair taller and thinner than the other; he had a splendid silver-blue brocade waistcoat showing above his lapels. They both had light eyes, startling blue, but the thinner one's were the equal of Ringo's for cold. He nodded toward the cigar cabinet and spoke to the bartender. His brother—they had to be brothers, even more than McLaury and the man who'd come looking for him—stood at the bar and watched the room.

Ringo's attention was like an arrow knocked and aimed at the newcomers.

"Thank you again for the game," Jesse said.

"Oh, don't leave now." Ringo kept his eyes on the men. "If you're going to play in this town, you'd best meet these two."

The thinner one had his cigar; he lit it as he walked over to the table. "Don't tell me," he said. "You're all here for a prayer meeting, and the preacher just left."

It would have been a joke among friends. But Jesse could tell that it wasn't, and these weren't.

"Good morning, Wyatt," Ringo said. "Fine day for a stroll down Sixth Street. Or are you peacekeeping? I can't always tell."

If God and the Devil were to arrange a parley, they'd sound like this, Jesse thought. A wagon passed in the street, and something in its load, some bright surface, shot reflected light into the backbar mirror and off it into Jesse's eyes. For an instant the two men were black cutouts in a storm of light.

"I don't believe you've met my friend Mr. Fox." Ringo smiled, but not at Jesse. "Mr. Fox, this is Mr. Wyatt Earp."

Earp turned his icicle gaze full on Jesse. It was like a match held close to his face. Not cold; hot enough to burn. "Any friend of John Ringo's," Earp said, and didn't offer his hand.

"Likewise, I'm sure," Jesse said.

"What brings you to Tombstone, Mr. Fox?"

"A visit to an old friend. I stopped on my way to Sonora."

"Continuing on soon?"

Jesse pretended to hear nothing in that but the words. "My business there will keep."

"When you go," Ringo said, "don't take the stage. I hear it's dangerous hereabouts."

Earp turned back to Ringo. "What *are* you doing in my bar?"

Ringo's eyes grew large. "My gracious. I thought it was Milt Joyce's bar. I thought you just ran the gambling."

"And what were you and your friends doing?" Earp's eyes cut toward the tabletop, where the last pot lay in front of Ringo's chair.

"That's not gambling. That's poker. Well," Ringo added with a thoughtful look toward Frank McLaury at the bar, "maybe some people were gambling."

But Earp hadn't looked up from the tabletop. The twisted-wire token still topped the pile of Ringo's winnings. Earp leaned over the table and stared at it. He didn't reach for it.

Then he looked up, into Jesse's face. He frowned at Ringo, then at Brocius and the two McLaurys at the bar, who were pointedly ignoring him and the man he'd come in with.

"You boys should be careful who you play with," Earp said. "And where you do it." He turned on his heel and went back to the bar.

Ringo sighed. Jesse couldn't tell if it was out of relief, regret, or satisfaction.

"My, this is a nice, friendly place," Jesse said.

Ringo's head snapped around; he looked as if he'd forgotten Jesse was there. Then he laughed, a harsh crack of sound. "You really on your way to Mexico?"

"I was last week."

"Well, that's a nice friendly place. Even counting the *soldados*." He gathered up the money on the table and thrust it, haphazard, into his pockets. "I'd love to stay and trouble the brothers Earp, but now's not the time. You remember my invitation, Mr. Fox."

"I will."

Ringo went to the bar and slapped Curly Bill Brocius across the shoulder blades. Brocius threw a mock punch at him. The Earps raised their heads and watched, like a pair of guard dogs waiting for the command to bite. Brocius followed Ringo out. The McLaurys finished their drinks and went, too.

The room seemed uncommonly long, and the air had the spiderweb stickiness he'd felt when he'd arrived in town. One of the Earps—not Wyatt, the other one—looked up from his drink and into Jesse's face. His frown made two hard lines between his brows. Remarkably like Lung's expression, when Jesse had got up to leave.

"I do feel responsible for you. If I had known what would meet you here, I would never have called you."

"Nonsense. If I weren't in trouble here, I'd be in it somewhere else."

"That hardly needs to be said. But it might be trouble you understood and were skilled in. I did not call you here to have you killed."

Jesse nodded to the Earp brothers, picked up his hat, and went out into the painful dazzle of Allen Street at midday.

His room at Brown's Hotel looked out over Fourth Street, which made it marginally quieter than the ones in front on Allen. It also made it hot in the afternoon, when the western sun glared in for hours before it set.

Jesse opened the windows (they were always open when he left the room, and always closed when he came back), took off his coat, his waistcoat, his tie, and his collar, and unbuttoned his shirt. If a breeze came up, at least he'd feel it. Then he sat at the secretary desk, pulled a sheet of paper toward him across the blotter, and gave his pen a shake to start the ink.

On the rooftop across the street, three crows quarreled over a bit of trash. A cart passed out of sight below him, its axle screaming. There were two candles in candlesticks on the desk, unlit and waiting for dusk. The maid had replaced last night's burnt-down ones; the wicks were white and fresh. He set them side by side. One was a little shorter than the other. Or could that be the candlestick?

He stared at the blank paper and shook his head. He was a coward. But he had to write this.

March 20th, 1881
Dear Lily,
   I hope this finds you well. I can't help but think of how unwell you were when I saw you last,

Pottery, he thought, *and porcelain. And the coefficient of thermal expansion.* That was how he'd put it to Lung the morning he arrived. *My sister is not well.* It was a struggle to say it, even in so mild a form.

and I tell myself you must be better than you were then. You could probably bear worse, but I doubt I could watch you do it. I suppose that's why I put a few thousand miles between us.
   What a bad start for a letter! I remember being taught that letters should avoid unpleasantness whenever possible. But you and I have always told each other what we thought. When I think of you, you're as I saw you last, in that bare white room, frightened and hopeless. I can't deny that memory, even for the length of a paragraph.

I beg your pardon; I *haven't* always told you what
I thought. I failed once, and that was the time you
most needed to hear it. I'm writing now to remedy
that. I hope it's not too late.

It could be too late. It was an overdose of laudanum
that had put her in the private hospital. She'd wept
when she was revived—great, wailing, desolate sobs,
as if waking to life was the worst thing she could
imagine. He'd stood at the end of the white-painted
corridor outside her room and pressed his palms
against his ears until they ached, and he still heard her.

I never believed you were going mad. I had no
other theory to offer, besides yours, which I also
couldn't believe. So I kept silent in the face of so
many learned opinions (and a few unlearned, even
more loudly expressed). I couldn't believe that what
you described to me was objective reality, but I
couldn't accept that it meant you were insane.

I was angry at myself for that—I'd toss away
even common sense to keep from seeing a flaw in
you. But in my heart I knew you weren't raving.

She swore she had been attacked in broad daylight
on the street. Witnesses said she'd been alone when
she cried out and fell down unconscious. The doctor
used the word "hysteria," and suggested ice water
baths. Insanity wasn't an unreasonable diagnosis.

She'd been frightened when she realized no one believed her. She was afraid to be alone, afraid to sleep.
And she took the laudanum.

Things have happened to me in the last few years
that make me think my heart was cleverer than my
head. I denied that evidence, too. It was easier to

believe of myself what I couldn't of you—that I was going insane—as if it was Nature's revenge for my failing you.

But a friend tells me you and I have the same disease, and that you diagnosed it correctly from the start. I'm prepared to guard myself against the more extreme forms of it. I only wish I'd understood then, and been able to guard you.

If you aren't better I expect they won't let you have this letter. All of a piece with his visit, your doctors will say; it will agitate her. My visit did upset you, but I think this letter will be a comfort. I think what I've written is what you wanted to hear then.

I wish I could say it to you, rather than write it. But I have to deal with the events that caused me to write. I'll come home as soon as I can, and tell you how it turned out.

> With love,
> Jess

His shirt was sweat-soaked, but he shivered. Writing the letter had brought back the months in which Lily fell to bits, in which his family had broken into scrambled fragments without a single matching edge. The months that had separated the life he'd planned to live from the one he had now.

Lung wondered why Jesse couldn't even say the word aloud—and a word, once spoken, was gone. To confess in something as permanent as ink that Lily's poison was real, and that he, too, had swallowed it. . . .

He capped his pen and looked out over Fourth Street, over the buildings and into the hills beyond.

Was it poison? Had it always been? Lily hadn't thought so at first. But then, that's how some poisons worked. First the euphoria, then . . . whatever came next.

He looked again at the candles on the desk in front of him. Lily had slipped into his room carrying a lighted candle that night—how long ago? He'd been fourteen, so she would have been sixteen. Her expression was the one she'd worn when they'd learned that air pressure would hold a card over the mouth of a full glass of water held upside down, or when they'd seen the craters of the moon through a telescope.

"Watch, Jess," she'd said, and the candle flame went out.

"You blew it out. I'm not stupid."

In the moonlight through the window, he saw her grin, a fey, wicked look. "No, you're not. So watch again."

She'd stared at the wick, her lips thinned, her brows drawn together.

The wick had smoked, glowed—and burned again.

He'd made her do it over and over until she had a headache. She tried to explain to him what she was doing, but he couldn't do it, couldn't even put the flame out, which she said was easier.

Think your way inside the wick, she'd said. *You have to draw pressure around it, draw heat into it from the air.*

On the writing desk before him, at the tip of the clean white wick of each candle, a flame wavered and rose.

Jesse looked away, his stomach churning. Then he put out the flame. She was right; that was easier.

8

The floor rocked under his feet.

Doc staggered, and the floor shifted again, as if the room were a small boat. He stood spraddle-legged and knees bent, riding the motion until it subsided. Even then, the boards beneath him felt like a platform in a treetop, in a lull between gusts of wind.

The room had no windows, but there was plenty of light; the walls were only framing timbers with the near-regular crosshatch of wood lath between them. The lath looked as if it had never been plastered, and sunlight glared through the gaps. That meant there wasn't anything on the outside: no clapboards or shingles.

Where the hell was he? There was a door at the end of the room, with a stair landing visible through it. Doc stepped toward it—and the room swayed. When it settled, he slid his foot forward slowly, shifted his weight, and did the same with the other foot. That got him to the door.

The staircase was as much skeleton as stairs, zigzagging down inside a skeletal stairwell. Here, too, the walls were bare lath and framing, like a giant crate for chickens. There was a hole in the wall on the landing below him, cut for a window that had never been framed in. He crept down the flight of stairs, clinging to the rail and feeling the whole structure move beneath him like a rope bridge. When he reached the window, he clutched the wall for support and looked out.

The entire building was like the room he'd just escaped, unfinished and abandoned. And taller than anything he'd ever stood on that wasn't a mountain.

Far below, lath was falling away from the building like sugar off a doughnut. Then he saw the framing timbers breaking up into splinters and sawdust, and the wind carrying the dust away. The building was coming apart from the bottom up.

The wood under his hands was turning grainy as sand.

He woke with the sheets damp with sweat and tangled around his legs. But the walls were solid and papered, and the bed stayed put when he sat up. His room at Fly's Boarding House, just as it ought to be. In that case, there should also be . . .

"Bad dream?" Kate asked, peering around the open door of the armoire. It swung a little on its hinges, and he saw himself reflected in the long mirror on its front: naked, his white body looking as if it didn't belong to his tanned head and hands. The bones of a man who should have been tall and strong, but was only tall. His hair looked as if a tornado had passed through it, with a rainstorm close behind.

"Oh, not so bad," Doc replied. "But if this town doesn't cease building itself, I'll have to move out to get a night's sleep."

He found his pocket watch in its usual place on the nightstand and thumbed the catch for the cover. A hair before eleven. Six hours' sleep wasn't bad. Light sparkled on the engraving inside the cover, a text he knew by heart: *JHH from WBSE/1878.* Wyatt had a nice taste in timepieces.

Kate shut the armoire and swept over to perch on the edge of the bed. She was dressed to go out, in a green-and-copper striped walking dress. The frill of lace that filled in the neckline just made him think about what it was hiding. She smiled—a little movement that barely deepened the corners of her mouth and threatened to dimple her cheek. *They call that "roguish,"* he thought, with a happy pang. "Oh, I expect that was me," she said, "banging the door as I came in."

"You banged a sleeping man's door?"

"I wanted him to wake up."

"Damned vixen." He shot an arm around her waist and pulled her down on top of him. She laughed, a little explosion transferred from her chest to his. Her skin smelled like jasmine. Everything about her felt soft, smelled soft, looked soft. It thrilled him to think how much of her was iron-hard, and how few people knew both parts.

He pulled her face down to his, and she kissed him openmouthed. But when he tried to slide her skirt up to her thigh, she slapped his knuckles and sat up.

"No, you don't. Get up, Doc. I want to go out."

"I thought you'd been out already."

"I want to go to the Maison Doré for lunch. Come on, shift. If you're not hungry you can watch me eat."

Another woman would fuss over his appetite. He loved it that she wouldn't. *You're a grown man*, she often said. *I figure you can go to Hell by your own road.* He tried to show her the same courtesy, but it was hard, sometimes.

She pinned a little hat over the looped and twisted structure of her dark hair. Two golden-red cock feathers arched out of the puff of green netting at the hat's crown, fiery with the light shining through them.

"I need to wash," he warned her.

"Gracious, I hope so. I'll wait for you at Heintzelman's. I've gone and lost my watch somewhere."

"And I am buying you a new one?"

Kate blinked. "That's awfully sweet of you." That twitch of her mouth again, as she collected her bag and parasol. Then she was out the door; it banged behind her.

He swung his legs over and stood up. Today was

going to be one of the good days, he decided, consulting his inner works. The dream was clearing out of his head, too. Another one he wouldn't describe to Kate. She turned all gypsy when he told her his dreams, which made him feel as if Fate was crowding him. In Fort Griffin they'd had a hell of a row over it. Well, fighting and making up was what he and Kate did. He liked the making-up, especially. But he didn't tell her his dreams anymore.

He poured water in the washbasin and shaved and scrubbed himself down. Then he patted bay rum on his cheeks and chin. The sting told him he was awake, alive, and thinking. Some days, that was better than gold.

Doc left the room half an hour after Kate, but he thought she'd appreciate the results. He stepped onto Fremont Street and into the brilliance and racket of midday.

Kate might have slammed his door, but one could understand dreaming of half-finished buildings in Tombstone. At the corner of Fourth Street, the adobe walls were going up for a great barn of an opera house. He'd heard they were going to name it after Ed Schieffelin, who walked through town looking as if he wondered how his big silver strike had turned into this.

On both sides of Fremont, commercial buildings and little houses were springing up, or having second stories and balconies added to them. The air was full of the smell of cut lumber, adobe mud, and paint.

Towns were like people: they got big and slowed down. At this rate, Tombstone would get very big indeed. Doc didn't think that would suit him.

He bought himself a cigar for after lunch from the shop beside Hafford's Saloon, then crossed Allen Street to Heintzelman's. Through the window he saw the jeweler's assistant bent nearly double, holding out a tray of gold ladies' watches. Kate was studying them, seated in a straight-backed spindly chair. She looked like a queen of England, only hawk-nosed and sallow and beautiful. All the picture needed was for the assistant to be down on one knee.

She looked up as Doc came through the door, her eyes sparkling. "Come and look, Doc! I can't decide."

Meaning she had decided, but she would give him the comfort of pretending he had some say in how his money was spent. He leaned on her chair, close enough to smell jasmine. There were eight watches in the velvet-lined tray. The assistant's face had a touch of pleading in it. One way or another, Kate could always reduce a man to pleading.

Doc contemplated the selection: engraved, brilliant-cut, ornamented with relief-work. He spotted the one she wanted in a moment. Raised lilies off-center on the oval case lid, with a patterned bezel all around the edge. It looked ridiculously expensive, but very handsome and modern.

Doc pointed to the watch next to it, which looked costly, too, but more restrained. "That's pretty."

He felt Kate go still for an instant. "It is, isn't it? But the face isn't so nice." She snapped it open to show him.

It was a clock face like any other. "No, I see that. What's that one next to it like?"

Kate snapped the lily watch open quickly. It had numbers and hands. He thought about being dissatisfied, just to see how she'd talk him out of it. No, he felt too good. "Elegant," he said. "Reminds me of you."

Kate looked up with a flash of dimple. "Thank you, sir."

Doc plucked the watch from the tray and pinned it in the lace on Kate's breast. His knuckles brushed the skin under the lace for an instant, and he looked into her eyes from inches away. She met the look, wide-eyed, lips parted. If the jeweler's assistant hadn't been there, Doc would have consigned luncheon to the Devil.

He left the shop forty dollars lighter, but with Kate close beside him, her arm through his and the swell of her bosom brushing his sleeve. "Happy?" he said, and regretted it immediately. He hadn't meant to suggest that he was buying her happiness, or any other part of her.

But she was in a good mood, too. "Hungry," she replied. "I hope they have chicken cutlets."

"If not, I shall step out back and personally wring some pullet's neck."

Kate laughed, probably at the thought of him in a hen yard.

"Hold it, Holliday," someone growled behind him. But the growl was insufficient.

"Good day to you, too, Morg," Doc said as he turned.

Morgan wore his rough gear, not his town clothes: a colored shirt, twill trousers tucked into high boots, a leather vest, and a drab coat. His concession to town life was that he'd left his gunbelt at home. Gingery stubble showed on his chin and cheeks. Doc wondered if Wyatt had only now let him off chasing Leonard, Head, and Crane. "Damn," Morgan said. "How'd you know it was me?"

"Because you sounded marvelously like yourself."

Morgan tugged his hat brim and grinned at Kate. "Good morning, Miz Holliday. You look good enough to eat."

Kate shook her head, but twitched the dimple into view again. "Mr. Earp. *You* look like a saddle tramp."

"Purely temporary. Give me an hour with the barber, and I'll be so fine you won't be able to keep your eyes off me."

It was only Morgan, but even so Doc felt his hackles stir. "The sooner you start, the better you'll be, then. I'd invite you to join us for lunch, but they won't let you look in the windows of the Maison Doré in your present state."

Morgan laughed. "I'll just keep you company on your way." They stepped three abreast into the bustle of Allen Street.

A pistol fired from overhead. Doc pushed Kate back toward the jeweler's. He felt his revolver in his hand; when had he reached for it? At the corner of his eye he saw Morgan go for his, heard him swear when he brought his fist up empty.

On the second-floor balcony of the Cosmopolitan Hotel, a man stood black against the sky. Doc aimed; but the figure swayed, staggered toward the railing. In the street a woman screamed, and men shouted. Slowly, slowly, the figure collapsed across the railing and tumbled over. He landed in the street with a thump and a puff of dust not ten feet from the toes of Doc's boots.

Doc scanned the second-floor windows for the shooter. Then a noise, part gasp, part cough, drew his attention to the ground.

"Damn," said the corpse, and wheezed again. "Didn't look so far from up there."

It was Curly Bill Brocius, and there wasn't a mark on him.

For a moment the people in the street gaped, silent. Then Brocius swept them with a grin. "April Fool's."

A man at the front of the crowd began to laugh, then another. The explanation spread like running water, in talk and laughter, down Allen Street. Two men put their hands out and helped Brocius to his feet. Traffic began to move again.

That it actually was the first of April didn't make

Doc feel better. He jammed his gun back into his waistband under his coat, wishing he'd taken a shot at the silhouette on the balcony after all.

Brocius looked up from beating the dust out of his clothes. He beamed. "Why, it's Holliday and brave young Morgan Earp! What'd you think, boys? Pretty convincing, eh?"

Doc nodded. "Not bad. Try again, and I'll help you along a little."

"Hell," Morgan said, stepping close to Brocius, "I'd like to see how well you drop right here."

Damn Morgan—he had no sense of what a man would stand for. Or he did, and didn't care to use it, which was thoughtless. Shooting Brocius hadn't been one of the things Doc had planned to do this afternoon.

Brocius studied Morgan, his smile looking forgotten on his mouth. "Now, Mr. Earp. You wouldn't be proposing a quarrel between us? And you having nothing on you to bring it with."

Morgan's hands hovered at his hips, where his gunbelt wasn't. Doc stepped forward and said pleasantly, "He did bring me, however." He caught a powerful smell of alcohol. "And unlike yourself, I am painfully sober."

Brocius looked offended and jerked his head toward the hotel balcony. "You don't think a fellow can do a trick like that if he ain't dead drunk, do you?"

"I should bring you in for disturbing the peace," Morgan said.

Brocius threw his head back and laughed. Doc caught Morgan's arm as he cocked it for a punch and shoved it back to his side. "Oh, my," Brocius got out between gasps. "That's a pretty picture. The Earp brothers and their sportin' pal keepin' the town quiet, while they make it as much as a man's life is worth to ride the Benson stage!"

Morgan grabbed Brocius by the collar before Doc could stop him. "You lying sack of shit!"

Brocius kept laughing. "You haven't killed everybody who knows. What were your brothers gonna spend that money on? A brand-new whorehouse?"

Morgan shoved, and Brocius staggered backward and sat down in the dust, still whooping. Again, Morgan reached for the pistol he didn't have.

Doc pulled him away. "Try not to make a fool of yourself. At least not in public." He looked around to see who else might have heard Brocius.

Kate stood at his shoulder. Her eyes moved from Morgan to Brocius, and at last, to Doc.

He opened his mouth to tell her . . . what? To deny it? To say that Brocius was drunk, that he and the Earps had a standing quarrel? Nothing he could say would change what she knew. Her face told him as much.

Brocius got to his feet and walked unsteadily across the street, into the Alhambra Saloon.

Morgan began, "Damn it, Doc—"

"Shut up," Doc told him. He turned back to Kate.

She clenched her teeth—he could tell from the shape of her face. He took a step toward her, but it didn't seem to bring him any closer. Then she gathered her skirts, turned, and strode away up the street.

*Mildred sat at the kitchen table and drummed the pen*cil on the pile of paper in front of her. She suspected she'd got something wrong in the last few pages, but she wasn't sure; possibly she only had to think a little harder, and the words would start to fly out of her pencil again.

She turned to the previous pages, covered with her hasty writing (how jealous she was of her yesterday self, who could hardly write fast enough to keep up with her invention!). She would read the chapter from the start to remind herself where she was, and by the time she reached blank paper, she'd know what to write.

On the second page, she read:

"Hush!" Constanza pleaded, her dark eyes full of terror. "Oh, *señorita*, pray do not say such things where others may hear! Don Alfonso has his spies in every house!"

Constanza's speech caused Regina's nerves to thrill with fear, but she lifted her fair head in a semblance of disdain. "Alfonso Castillo does not rule over us, or over anyone on this *rancho*. Are you a serf, that you fear him and call him 'Don'? We are Americans now, Constanza. We bend the knee to no one."

"You have not seen, *señorita*. He beat a man, a *vaquero*, nearly to death, and the law did not stretch out its hand and touch him."

"Retribution comes even to such as he, Constanza. One day he will pay for all his crimes."

". . . her dark eyes full of terror" wasn't right. "Huge with terror"? "Ablaze with terror"? Much more stirring; but eyes didn't really blaze.

Mildred didn't like the start of the next paragraph, either. She drove her pencil through "Constanza's speech caused" and made it, "Regina's nerves thrilled with fear." "He will pay for all his crimes"—should that be "for his crimes"? No, it sounded so bald. "For his every crime"?

Now the first paragraph seem to have happened so long ago that no one could be expected to remember it. The whole beginning of the chapter, in fact, might have occurred sometime before Noah. Mildred groaned and started over.

It was no use—her blank page arrived, but her muse was still missing. She was convinced she'd taken a wrong turn with the story . . . but where?

She didn't know what she was doing, that was the problem. "Stampede at Midnight" had been a fluke. How could she have read stories all her life and still not understand how they worked? Jane Austen, Edgar Allan Poe, and Charles Dickens had taught her a great deal about humanity, but didn't seem to have helped in the matter of tale-telling. Still, writing "The Spectre of Spaniard's Mine" ought not to be as difficult as, say, *Great Expectations*. Unless *Great Expectations* had been the easiest thing in the world to write. If so, she'd jab the blasted pencil into her eye and put herself out of her misery.

That made her think of Luther King. Her whole inner self skidded away from the memory, like slipping on ice.

She stood up and looked out the kitchen window. A fine, bright day, too fine to be indoors. Perhaps that was why she was having trouble concentrating. No, she was concentrating—but there didn't seem to be any story to concentrate on.

Harry, who'd been organizing his thoughts on paper admirably for years, might shed light on the problem. But could she reveal to Harry Woods that his best, most serious-minded typesetter was writing blood-and-thunder tales for an illustrated weekly her mother wouldn't have kept in her house as fire-starter? She could never show her face in the *Nugget* office again.

Maybe fresh air and exercise would do what reason wouldn't. After all, the premise of "Stampede at Midnight" had come to her as she walked across town. It might work again.

She hurried into the bedroom, unbuttoning her apron as she went. Her dresser mirror showed her a pale, frowning woman whose hair looked as if she'd been clutching it distractedly—which was so. Mildred yanked her hairpins out, pummeled her curls with a brush, and twisted them into as smooth a coil as they would make.

She reached for her black velvet hat, but stopped in midstretch. The first of April was spring on anyone's calendar, and black velvet was for winter. She slid a cardboard hatbox off a shelf and lifted the lid.

David had bought the hat for her . . . last May? After he died, the silvery straw with the turned-up brim and the scarlet silk poppies was impossible to wear. Widowhood was her season.

She lifted the hat out of its tissue. She shouldn't wear it now—David wasn't a year gone. *We can't afford it,* she'd objected when he brought it home.

You'll get plenty of wear out of it, he'd said. *It's always summer here.*

It wasn't, of course. And they really couldn't afford it. But that only meant she mustn't let it go to waste. She pinned the hat on. The poppies cast color into her cheeks.

Mildred saw the little hip-roofed house on the corner of First Street before she remembered Mrs. Virgil Earp. She resolved to stop and leave her card. And if Mrs. Earp happened to be at home to visitors, and wanted to talk about favorite tales and characters . . . *At least I can* talk *about writing.*

She crossed the street and stepped into the shade of the porch. The front windows were open, muslin curtains shifting in the air, and Mildred could hear a whirring, a rhythmic *chuk-chuk-chuk,* and the murmur of a woman's voice. One voice, on and on.

Mildred raised her hand to the door, and stopped. The air on the porch was hot, dry, and still, as if some fire-creature stood beside her, and she was caught in the moment between its inhale and the fireball of its exhale.

A breeze tugged her skirt, and the fancy was gone. *Perhaps that's what ghosts feel like here. Not cold, but hot as a black rock in the sun.* She lifted her hand again and knocked. Then she thought, *Some would say it was the Devil passing.*

Sounds behind the door; it opened to reveal one of the prettiest women Mildred had ever seen. Her hair was shining blond, her blue eyes were wide and direct, and her skin was tanned, but smooth and fresh-looking as Lucy Austerberg's. She wore a wash dress of red printed calico. The humble fabric had been made to fit beautifully. "Yes?" she said.

Mildred had to rummage for a minute to find her voice. "I'm Mrs. Benjamin. Is this . . . the Virgil Earp residence?"

"That's right." The blond woman stood square in the partly open door, unsmiling.

"Is Mrs. Virgil Earp at home?"

That caused a flicker of surprise in the woman's face. "You want to see Allie?"

"I met her at the post office the other day. I thought . . ." *Could* one simply say, "I've come to further the acquaintance," as if Mrs. Earp had no choice in the matter?

The blond woman swung the door wide and smiled, and became prettier still. There was a red leatherette-bound book in her left hand, and she waved Mildred in with it. "Step on in. Allie! Here's Mrs. . . . ." She shot an apologetic look at Mildred.

"Benjamin," Mildred said as she stepped over the threshold. She found herself in a tiny parlor that seemed to be full of piled white canvas. The two Earp women she'd already met, Mrs. Virgil and Mrs. Wyatt, were sewing long seams in ells and ells of fabric, the former on a shiny black sewing machine. *That accounts for the sound*, Mildred realized. And the book in the blond woman's hand—of course, she'd been reading aloud while the others sewed.

Mrs. Virgil looked up, recognized her, and stared. Mildred was surprised at the change in her. Her snub-nosed, round-cheeked face was pink; her light brown hair was pinned up loosely and made her look much younger than when it was hidden under her old-fashioned bonnet.

Mrs. Virgil began, "Why, you're the lady from the post office—"

"Who also takes *Gallagher's*. You remember, I suggested we might . . . but this seems like a poor time." Mildred waved a hand at the canvas and the sewing machine.

"Pshaw!" said the pretty blond woman. "Nothing like visiting to make the work fly by. No, Allie," she said to Mrs. Virgil, who to Mildred's eye hadn't done a thing to prompt it, "I know where your tea things are. You settle your guest." And she hurried through a door at the end of the parlor.

Mrs. Virgil looked a little wildly from the door to Mildred. Mildred realized she was doing much the same. She met Mrs. Virgil's gaze—

—and the little woman began to laugh. Mildred had thought her transformed before, but it was nothing to that laugh.

"Oh, mercy! You looked just like I felt!" she crowed. "Lou's a cyclone when she sets her mind on something. Mattie, sugar, I'm fair sure there's a chair under all this."

That was addressed to Wyatt's wife, the pale, dark-haired woman Mildred had seen at Austerberg's. Until now, she'd sat quiet against the wall, as if she'd prefer to disappear into it. Now she sprang to her feet. "Under the window, most like," she said breathlessly. Then she smiled at Mildred, the shy, hopeful smile of a sheltered child.

"Let me find it," said Mildred. "I'm good at finding missing things." Suddenly she felt cheerful and giddy. The Earp women were so guarded in public. Mildred hadn't expected to find this comfortable chaos, this casual welcome.

She stepped over one pile of canvas and lifted the corner of another.

"Virge's slippers!" Mrs. Virgil cried. "I looked high and low for those this morning! Hand 'em here, Mrs. Benjamin."

Mildred scooped them up and presented them with a flourish that made Mrs. Wyatt giggle. "I told you I was good at finding things. And here's the chair." Mildred wiggled the spindle-backed chair out from under the pleats of canvas and sat in it. "Now, lend me a needle and put me to work."

"Oh, no!" Mrs. Wyatt shook her head so hard her dark curls bounced. "You're company."

"We don't get much visiting," Mrs. Virgil said, "but we ain't forgot how to treat a guest."

"If I were in your place, I wouldn't hesitate for a moment. Please do let me help." Industry might smooth over any awkward places in the conversation. "What is all this going to be?"

"Miners' tents," Mrs. Virgil said. Her voice was firm and flat, more like the one she'd used to Lucy Austerberg. Her little round chin went up, as it had then.

What did I say? Mildred wondered. "Do you sell them yourselves, or do the stores in town take them? It must be awfully comfortable to work in your own parlor. I have to tramp four blocks to work every morning, rain or shine."

Mrs. Virgil's expression softened. "Well, we have to clear it away at day's end if we're wanting a parlor to sit in after supper. It'd be awful nice to have a sewing room."

"Or a little shop in town," Mrs. Wyatt murmured. She handed Mildred a sturdy needle and a reel of heavy thread. Mildred scrambled in her purse and found her thimble and folding scissors with a surge of relief. They seemed like a badge of membership in this very womanly club.

"Then you're a working woman, Mrs. Benjamin?" Mrs. Virgil asked.

"I set type for the *Nugget*."

"I don't know as I've heard of a woman working on a newspaper."

"I spend so much time correcting reporters' spelling and complaining about their handwriting, it's almost like teaching school." It wasn't, really; Mildred would have hated teaching school.

Lou, the blond woman, came in with a stout brown teapot, four cups, and a plate of sliced molasses cake on a tin tray.

Mrs. Virgil made a little outraged noise. "Lou, those ain't the good cups!"

"The good cups are too small. What a blessing you came, Mrs. Benjamin," Lou said. "Allie works us like field hands, and I was fair parched for my tea break."

Mrs. Virgil laughed. Mrs. Wyatt smiled and shook her head. "Lou, you're an awful fibber." She took the first poured cup from Lou and gave it to Mildred.

Mildred wanted to carry on with the blond woman's joke. But there was something in this room, this family group, that she didn't yet understand. Besides, not everyone could tell when Mildred was joking. For no good reason, that made her think of Jesse Fox who, it seemed, could. The recollection made her uneasy. "Thank you, Mrs. Earp," she said.

"If you call us all 'Mrs. Earp,'" Mrs. Virgil declared as she came out from behind the sewing machine, "we'll be in the stickers in no time. Call me Allie. That's Mattie." She nodded at shy Mrs. Wyatt. "And Louisa, there, is another Mrs. Earp, of course."

"Mrs. Morgan Earp," Lou said, pouring another cup of tea. She brushed a blond curl off her forehead with the back of her wrist. "But Allie's right—call me Lou."

"And I'm Mildred," Mildred replied, with a deep sense of relief. She passed the cup to Allie.

The tea was strong, and the cake was dense and full of raisins. Not a token meal, but proper refreshment for working women. Mildred felt nearly as comfortable as she would in her own kitchen.

That reminded her of what she'd been doing at her kitchen table. "Mrs.—Allie, what did you make of the serial story in last week's *Gallagher's*?"

Allie frowned a little over a mouthful of cake. "Tell the truth, I thought it was pretty silly. Why didn't Jonathan just *tell* his brother he'd got married?"

"Oh, good, it wasn't just me!"

Lou poured more tea in Mildred's cup and said, "But the rest of the story wouldn't've happened if he'd just told him."

"Well, then he needed a good reason not to," Allie said, as if she'd like to give the characters a piece of her mind.

Mildred considered the problem. "What if he'd married a beautiful quadroon, and didn't dare say so for fear of being cast out of the family?" It sounded terribly melodramatic, but as she said it, she began to imagine the story. The dusky-skinned bride, her Paris gowns and lovely manners the outward signs of her inner quality, would come looking for her long-delayed husband. She would arrive on the doorstep and announce herself, never expecting that her husband would turn coward and deny he'd married her. "Connected we may be," he'd declare in front of his father and brother, "but not by the laws of God and Man!"

"Oh, that'd be a fine story!" Mattie breathed, her eyes sparkling, and Mildred realized she'd done her musing aloud. "Oh, Allie, don't you think that'd be good?"

"It'd be better by a long chalk," Allie agreed. "But then I'd say that if Jonathan married her, he ought to show some spine and stand by her."

At that, Mildred saw a look flash between Allie and Lou. It was gone before she could identify it. "Well, if he doesn't, it's a tragedy. And if he does own up at the last moment . . . Say she's gone to fling herself in the river, poor girl, but he realizes that he's just thrown away the dearest thing in the world to him. He tells his family that he loves his bride and they can, too, or they can go to . . ."

"Hartford," Allie said promptly, grinning.

"Exactly! And he runs after her and finds her on the cliff above the river. He flings his arm around her waist just as she's about to go in—"

"—And he pulls her to his bosom and calls her his dear," Mattie finished with deep satisfaction. "And says they'll never again be parted, in this world or in Heaven."

"Oh, good touch! I like that bit," Mildred said.

Allie laughed. "Well, that's a silly story, too, but miles better than what they printed in *Gallagher's*."

"Allie, there ain't a romantic bone in your body!" Lou scolded. "I liked it."

"Just 'cause it's silly don't mean I don't like it. Mrs. Benjamin—Mildred—it's a shame they don't have the likes of you writing for 'em."

Mildred half wanted to tell them she *had* written, and been accepted, and was doing it again. It would feel so good to have someone make a fuss—a good sort of fuss—over her. But she had an instinct to hold back. It was one thing to say that someone like Mildred should write for *Gallagher's*; it was another to say that Mildred should *be* that someone.

Perhaps when "Stampede at Midnight" appeared in print, she'd tell them that she was M. E. Benjamin. Instead she said, "Where did I put that blessed needle?"

They spent a pleasant half hour sewing; or rather, Allie, Mattie, and Lou sewed. Allie assigned Mildred the job of reading aloud once she saw the quality of Mildred's stitching. The book was *Vanity Fair*, and Mildred made her hostesses laugh by doing voices for the characters.

At last Mildred felt the effect of the tea. "I'm afraid I need a bit of a pause."

Allie looked up inquiringly, then understood. "Oh, sure! Go straight through the kitchen. It's at the end of the yard."

The kitchen was small, but fiercely clean, with a well-blacked stove and a scoured wood table. Four loaves of bread were cooling by the sink board. Outside the back door Mildred passed a fenced patch of kitchen herbs, already inclined to go to seed from the hot days, and a tiny chicken yard and coop. The outhouse was half-hidden and shaded by a thick growth of trumpet vine. Just beyond it was a corral with a shelter. Mildred could hear the lazy flicking of horses' tails from inside it.

Had Virgil Earp built the hip-roofed house, or had he bought it? She and David had been lucky to find their cabin when they'd come to Tombstone. Boomtown real estate didn't sit vacant long. And if there hadn't been anything ready-built, she reflected with a smile, she might have had to settle for a canvas tent like the ones the Earp women were sewing. David hadn't been what anyone would call handy.

As she returned to the kitchen through the back door, she heard voices from the parlor. One of them was Allie's, but the other was new to her: low, hoarse, attractive but sexless. The speaker could be a contralto woman or a tenor man. Mildred paused at the door to the parlor, reluctant to step into unknown social waters.

Allie was saying, ". . . peelin' her eyes for boys at her age. My Lord, Hattie's seventeen! But where's she gonna meet 'em? It ain't like Jim and Bessie get asked to parties, so who's gonna invite Bessie's little girl?"

The stranger laughed, brittle and unamused. "Let her meet men the way her mama did."

"What d'you mean?"

"Such a nice little sewing circle you've got here." Mildred thought the stranger—a woman, she decided—was changing the subject. "The Earp ladies, all good honest wives helping to support their households."

"And what's wrong with that?" Lou asked, scorn in her voice.

"Not a thing. A little sewing, a little egg money . . . And your sister-in-law Bessie on her back on the line, keeping Jim Earp in nice boots."

There was a moment of silence so deep and shocked it felt like the moment after a gunshot. Jim Earp—that was the oldest Earp brother, who kept the Eagle Brewery on Allen Street. He and his wife had a nearly grown daughter. . . .

"Bessie wasn't ever a whore!" That was Allie. Mildred could imagine the flush in her face, the fierce set of her jaw.

"Why not? Why shouldn't she get poisoned by the Earps like the rest of us?"

Quiet Mattie spoke up, to Mildred's surprise. "You

take that back, Kate Holliday. The Earps have done nothin' but kindness to you and your man."

So the new voice belonged to Doc Holliday's lady. Kate Holliday laughed. "Oh, that man of yours is kind, all right, if it gets him what he wants. Wyatt's the root of it! He's got his claws deep in a poor, sick man who—"

A sudden flurry of sound: a wooden bang, the clatter of falling objects. Mildred started back from the parlor door. She heard a piercing cry—Mattie? Yes, Mattie— and a scrabbling sound. "Wyatt's suitcase," Mattie whimpered, her words broken up by some physical effort. "He wouldn't like it—"

"So that's where Wyatt moved 'em to," Mrs. Holliday said, bitter satisfaction in the words. "I told him if he didn't get that suitcase out of Doc's room I'd throw his trash in the street."

"What are they?" Allie asked, barely loud enough for Mildred to hear.

"Wyatt's disguises, honey. Every con man and stage robber and two-bit tinhorn needs himself a few fake beards and masks and such from time to time."

"You're lying," Lou snapped.

"Am I? I think your Morgan was wearing one of those just lately." Under Kate Holliday's words Mildred could hear Mattie crying softly. "I wouldn't give a damn, but Wyatt's pulled Doc into it."

"Wyatt's a lawman!" Mattie sobbed out. "Your husband don't need Wyatt's help to get into trouble."

I shouldn't be hearing this conversation. How could Mildred not have thought of that until now? She'd wanted gossip about the stage robbery. She hadn't wanted to be a silent witness to the kind of pain that lay on the other side of the kitchen door.

"I think you've wore out your welcome, Kate," Allie said harshly.

"Oh, I wish I could be done with the lot of you!

You'll wish you were out of it, too, pretty soon. Wyatt left that suitcase full of trouble in *your* closet, after all. It won't be long before he's got your stupid Virgil under his thumb just like Morgan."

A chair scraped on the floor. "You can't talk about my Virge like that!" Allie shouted.

A moment of silence, in which Mildred imagined the women staring each other down. Then Kate said, "You ignorant little Mick." There was a weary pity in her voice that leached the insult from her words. "Oh, God, Mattie, get up off the floor and quit fussing with that trash. It's too late now."

After a moment Mildred heard the rustle of skirts, and the opening and shutting of the front door.

This kitchen had looked so simple and peaceful when Mildred had first walked through it, so clean and orderly and homely. The women in the parlor, busy with real, sensible work, had seemed so content. It was false, paint over rust. There was fear here, and secrets. The devil on the porch had been her first warning.

A sound behind her made her turn. Allie stood in the doorway to the parlor. When Mildred met the little woman's eyes, she saw that Allie knew she'd overheard everything.

"I'm sorry," Mildred murmured. "I didn't mean—"

But Allie's stricken look had nothing to do with Mildred.

"I'm sorry," Mildred said again, in a very different voice, and watched the tears spill over and down Allie's cheeks.

9

"Arthur Ortega died last night," Marshal Sippy said.

Jesse had half expected the words—but the other half had hoped for better. It was an instant before he grasped which news he'd heard. Then his head went unpleasantly light. "I'm sorry."

Sippy's face suggested "I'm sorry" was an unusual and possibly inappropriate response. "There's no doubt Ortega stole your horse. So there's no charge against you."

"Won't there be an inquest?" Wasn't that what happened, when a man died untimely?

Sippy shook his head. "Judge Spicer didn't see the point."

"There was a hearing?"

"My goodness, we must have forgot your invitation. I wouldn't call it a hearing. I brought the statements before the judge in chambers, he said if we had an inquest on every damned shooting in the county, court'd be in session night and day, and he threw the case out."

"Threw it out," Jesse repeated, stunned. There was a corpse where a living man had been. Equations balanced; this one came up short.

"His exact words were, 'Absence of felonious intent.' If he's wrong, you go tell him so." Sippy frowned, his hands planted palms-down on the scarred tabletop. "Now, so long as you let me get back to work, you can stay or leave Tombstone as you please."

He could stand in the marshal's office all day; nothing would change. "If there's anything else, you can find me at Brown's."

Sippy grunted and turned back to the pile of documents he was sorting.

Jesse let himself out onto Fremont Street. The sun sent needles through his eyes into his skull, and his head began to throb. Lung had sworn his eyes would return to normal, but it hadn't happened yet. He ought to replace his dark spectacles.

Ortega was dead. Lung would be unhappy over the news. But not as unhappy as Jesse.

In the high desert, in Apache country, stealing a man's horse was considered equivalent to trying to kill him, and shooting a horse thief in the act was self-defense. But when Jesse had heard Sam's whinny and the scramble of his hooves, seen him bolt into the firelight with his eyes white with fear and a stranger in the saddle silhouetted against the deep blue night, he hadn't thought of self-defense.

His pistol had been in his hand and the hammer back between one breath and the next. When the recoil rocked the grip in his palm he'd seen the man-silhouette jerk, but not fall. He'd cocked again. Sam had carried the thief out of range and into the dark. It had been a long time before he'd noticed the burning in his left arm and felt the blood on his skin. He couldn't remember seeing the muzzle flash from Ortega's pistol, or hearing the shot.

He looked up and realized he was walking toward the *Daily Nugget* office. Did he mean to share his unquiet mind with Mrs. Mildred Benjamin? She would be setting up a page of type, as she had been when he'd first seen her. He imagined her listening to him without looking up, imagined the ease with which he would say the most difficult things to that bent head.

"Stupid," he said aloud, and the picture scattered like sand. Not to her, not to anyone. One dealt with one's troubles or set them aside; they weren't to be handed off like an unsatisfactory present.

Besides, why should she listen to him? Mrs. Benjamin seemed like a woman who did plenty of thinking, and might expect to be listened to herself. She was as likely to throw her composing stick at him as to sympathize.

What he ought to do now was get a drink to strengthen his resolve, then go deliver the bad news to Lung. And submit himself to whatever strange equation-balancing Lung would insist on.

Lung had described his studies as a kind of science. Could he think of them that way? Metaphysical formulae with rules to learn and apply? It was comforting, but was it true?

In a spirit of self-flagellation he headed for Hafford's Saloon, which he disliked. The stuffed and mounted birds hung like wallpaper all over the long room troubled him. Light seemed to come and go in their glass-bead eyes, and their outstretched wings seemed to have just moved, or be about to move. It was as if time and not their lives had stopped, and at any instant it would start again and fill the room with trapped, frantic birds.

He was nearly to Allen Street when two men turned the corner and came toward him. Abreast, they occupied most of the physical sidewalk, and even more of the philosophical one. Jesse hugged the street edge.

He recognized them a moment before the gaunt one spoke. "There, now, Virge," said the dentist, Holliday. "Here's the very man, awake and standing. I'll wager he's even had his breakfast. Mr. Fox, Mr. Virgil Earp."

Something about the bland smile Holliday gave Earp suggested this was the latest installment of a running joke. Earp's raised eyebrow suggested that only Holliday found it funny.

Earp extended a hand. Jesse shook it while he made a swift inventory of his position. John Ringo had some bone to pick with the Earps, and they with him, but John Ringo seemed a poor barometer by which to predict a man's behavior. Jesse couldn't think of anything he'd done, besides play cards with Ringo, that would cause Holliday or Virgil Earp to come looking for him. Unless they objected to Ortega's death or Luther King's release.

"Mr. Fox, Doc here says you might know somewhat about horses," Earp said.

"And since *my* knowledge consists of mostly managing to stay on one," Holliday interrupted, "I shall leave you two gentlemen to become better acquainted." Earp frowned, but Holliday only touched his hat brim and winked at Jesse. Then he turned and headed back to Allen Street.

Not King or Ortega, then. At least, not yet. Virgil Earp didn't look like a man who consorted with stage robbers or murderers; but Jesse wasn't sure what such a man *would* look like. Or what one of Lung's "knowledgeable men" would look like, for that matter. Ortega died; that meant Jesse himself was both. What did he look like now?

They stood in uncomfortable silence. From the brother, Wyatt, Jesse had gotten an impression of ice and steel and a weighing of every action, though what it was measured against was impossible to guess. Virgil Earp's face was much like his brother's in bone and flesh and coloring. But it hinted that the man who wore it might have weighed life a little less and felt a great deal more.

"You were playing cards in the Oriental," Earp said, and Jesse realized that Earp had been studying him, too.

"First game I happened on." Why should he apologize, even that much, for playing with Ringo, Brocius, and McLaury?

"Win any?"

"No."

For some reason, Earp relaxed at that. "Doc tells me you have the best-schooled horse he's ever seen. You break him yourself?"

Jesse nodded. "I do it for a living."

Earp eyed him again, doubtfully. Did Jesse not look like someone who trained horses? Maybe he ought to walk with a limp. "I've got a colt bred for harness," Earp went on. "Everything fine about him—except he'll kick a rig to kindling if he's put between the shafts. I paid too much for him to give him up easy."

The colt took on immediate life in Jesse's imagination. Foolish. If he'd known a dozen horses like this one, that didn't mean he knew this one. Still—"I can school him to drive."

Earp waited, as if he expected more.

When a horse-breaker introduced himself it was generally with the claim that he could stick on anything ever foaled. If sticking were the issue, that might be worth something. "It'll cost you twenty dollars."

When Earp's eyebrows went up, Jesse added, "You'll be able to harness and drive him the next morning and every morning after with no trouble, unless you teach him bad habits."

"I don't intend to teach him bad habits," Earp drawled.

"I don't suppose you do. But a horse won't pick up his notions out of the air. Where'd he get the ones he's got?"

Earp's eyes narrowed. "How do you figure I went about teaching him to kick?" he asked, ominously mild.

In for a penny, in for a pound. "Easiest thing in the world. Horses can be smart as fence posts and brave as sparrows. Anything will scare them. They'll run away if they can, or fight 'til they can run away. Somebody hitched that colt up before he knew what was what. He felt the weight on his collar, heard the rattling at his heels, and thought the Devil was reaching for his tail. There's been nothing to disabuse him of the notion."

"Sounds like the way a hundred other horses get taught to drive." Earp's mouth pinched as if to shut off the next sentence.

Jesse could imagine that frightened colt, pursued by something he couldn't see. It made him reckless. "Then you have horse number one hundred and one. You've got three choices: give up on driving him, bully him into it and maybe ruin him for good, or let me have him for the day and see what happens."

He watched Earp's face. The man was proud, but not proud enough to make the horse suffer for it. Jesse added, a little gentler, "You'd only be out twenty dollars and a day of his use."

"You can do it in a day?"

"I can do it this afternoon."

Earp thought Jesse was pitching snake oil; he could see it in his face. "I won't pay 'til the job's done."

"Let's get it in writing, then." Jesse hoped that wasn't going too far.

Earp huffed, but his face relaxed. "Fair enough. Neither of us knows the other. And a man has to make his living." Earp thrust out his hand again and Jesse shook it. "Come up to my place, and we'll make a contract."

A man has to make his living. Jesse's public reason for remaining in town had just died, but no one would wonder at a man staying to pick up a little work. He could as well be a horse-tamer in Tombstone as in Sonora, until Lung was done with him. Oh, Lord, he'd been on his way to tell Lung about Ortega. But Earp had already set off across the street. It would have to wait.

The house at Fremont and First was a solid square cabin with a covered front porch and a scramble of corral and outbuildings behind. Earp led the way through a side gate to the kitchen door.

"Bide a minute. I'll see if Allie thinks the house is fit for company." Earp ducked in, and Jesse turned to study the corral.

Not the best place to work—a box stall and a big empty barn would be better—but the ground was soft, and the enclosure was big enough to maneuver a horse and cart in. He doubted there was a big empty barn in the territory, anyway. A lean-to at one end of the corral provided shade for two good-looking horses and a burro.

He heard voices in the house, a man's and a woman's. Words reached him as they neared the door.

". . . for twenty whole dollars!" the woman said.

Earp's voice rumbled, less clear, but sounding amused. Jesse thought he heard "worth more" and "save a bit of time."

"And when did we come to have more money than time?"

Jesse decided it would be better, when the door opened, to be out of earshot. He followed the beaten earth path to the corral.

The burro came to the fence, stuck its muzzle between the rails, and lipped at the hem of his coat. "No, I don't," Jesse told it, "and you haven't earned one, anyway." The burro settled for having its ears stroked.

The two horses stayed under the lean-to. One, a white-faced chestnut mare, stood at her ease, a hind foot cocked, ears slack even in the presence of a stranger.

The other was a long-backed bay with black legs. He stood behind the chestnut, looking across her withers at Jesse, his ears pricked forward.

That would be the colt, young enough to shelter behind his lead mare, wary of strangers. Earp was right about his make: he was the picture of a good carriage horse. A good all-around horse, he'd bet, for endurance and short bursts of speed.

The house door banged. Earp came into the yard, but his wife stayed on the stoop, her chin up, not quite frowning. She was a tiny thing next to Earp, a wren in calico and a flour-sack apron.

"Mr. Fox," Earp said, "this is my wife."

Wren-sized Mrs. Earp might be, but she was plainly not to be made to flit, by Jesse or anyone. She looked him up and down. "That what you generally wear for horse-breakin', Mr. Fox?"

Jesse looked down at his coat and waistcoat and smiled. "No, ma'am. I suppose I wasn't thinking."

"Oh. I figured that would account for the price you're charging."

Earp stiffened. But Jesse coughed with surprise and laughter and replied, "Yes, ma'am. You see, I'm so presentable you can invite the neighbors to watch me work, and charge them two bits a head. Toss in another dollar, and I'll give 'em a pretty girl in spangles to stand on your horse's back."

Mrs. Earp laughed, a whoop that made even her husband smile. "Mr. Fox, if you weren't the despair of your ma, I'm a Hindoo. And if you was always so careful of your clothes, she must've done a smart bit o' washin'. Give that paper a look, now."

Earp was holding it out to him, his mouth folded into a wry grin. He took the contract, read it quickly, and tucked it into his pocket.

He shrugged out of his coat and nodded toward the bay. "That's the colt?"

Earp nodded. "Pure-blood Morgan, bred up in Prescott. Name's Spark."

"If someone in Prescott's breeding horses like that, he must be having to hold the Apaches off with cannon. If you'll take the other horse and the burro out and hitch them out of sight, I'll get started."

"I'll put your things in the house," Mrs. Earp said sweetly. "You may as well wear that coat as lay it on the ground like you was about to."

Jesse felt his face heat up. He handed her the coat, and his waistcoat, collar, and tie. "Thank you, ma'am."

Among the harness and rope hung on the lean-to's outside wall, Jesse found what he needed. He draped the assorted bits of tack over the gatepost, climbed the fence, and dropped down to the churned earth of the corral.

The bay colt watched, ears hard forward, as he approached. "Sorry, young 'un," Jesse told him, "You'd like an excuse to fuss, but you won't get one from me." Before Spark could decide to shy off, Jesse had his left palm under the colt's nose to smell, and his right hand scratching under his muzzle, his fingers in the halter. When the colt tried to lip at his left hand, Jesse drew it back. The colt stretched his head out to follow, and Jesse pulled gently on the halter. Spark followed Jesse toward the gate. Good—he wasn't halter-shy.

Jesse fastened a length of rope to the halter and tied the colt to the fence rail, ready to free him immediately if he began to pull against the rope. But he stood quietly.

Jesse moved his hands over the colt's face, under his jaw, up around his cheeks to fondle his ears, talking all the while. He stayed close, almost pressed against the smooth red-brown hide, as he passed his hands down the colt's neck and shoulders, rubbed his foreleg and picked up his foot, set it down, reached under his belly, slid both arms over his back. Spark's ears swiveled to follow his movements, but he didn't sidle away.

Jesse had moved to Spark's right side when those ears swung forward, and the colt made a ruffling noise out his nose. Jesse turned to see Earp leaning on the fence rail.

"Mind if I watch?"

"Not a bit. Just don't do anything sudden." Jesse finished Spark's right side, lifting his hind foot and handling his tail. Then he gave him a scratch on the withers and headed for the gear slung over the gatepost.

"What was all that?" Earp asked.

"Just seeing if he's touchy about anything. Horses are short on reason but long on memory. For all they know, every time something happens, it will be exactly like the time they remember. And they always remember the worst time." Jesse grinned as he sorted out two lengths of leather rein and the harness surcingle. "Not unlike some people you know, I'll bet." Earp snorted appreciatively. Jesse hung the reins over his shoulder and added, "This fellow here doesn't seem to recall being hurt by anyone."

"I'd hope not."

Jesse tried to make his shrug apologetic. "Horse trainers tend to withhold judgment until they deal with the horse." Men lied; horses couldn't. He held up the surcingle, let the colt smell it, then rubbed it along the colt's chest and near shoulder and back, and finally fastened it around Spark's belly.

"You're awful patient," Earp said.

"Mm-hmm." But Earp was only a shadow. The colt was real: the density of him, the heat of the blood under his skin and the breath out of his nostrils, the weight of heart and lungs and bones. A boulder with legs. Next to Spark he felt as sturdy as a daisy stem.

He looped one end of the shorter rein around the colt's left foreleg just above the hoof and picked up the foot. Then he twined the other end in a loop around the upper leg and tied it, so the strap held the colt's left leg up. He heard Earp make a noise.

Jesse untied Spark from the rail, took hold of the halter rope, and drew the colt's head to the left. He could feel the colt's reluctance—one did not walk on three feet; it was bad, unsafe—but Spark's choices were limited. He could either follow or fall over. An uncertain hop with the right leg; step, step with the hind legs. Hop, step, step.

By the time he got Spark to the middle of the corral, Jesse felt the balance shift between them. The colt was still a large presence at his side. But he'd turned from a boulder to a wheel, and Jesse had only to roll him as he pleased.

He stroked and scratched the colt, and talked to him. He slid the longer piece of rein off his shoulder and gave Spark a good look at it, then rubbed it over the horse's neck and chest and forelegs. Then Jesse snubbed one end around the colt's right front foot, and threaded the loose end through the belly band.

"This is going to hurt your dignity," he told Spark, rubbing the colt's nose, "but nothing else." He stood beside Spark's left shoulder, took the halter rope in his left hand and the end of the long rein in his right. Then he pulled the colt's head to the left.

Hop, step, step. But as the colt lifted his right foot again, Jesse took up the slack in the strap that was tied to it. When Spark came down from his hop, his right foot was pulled up under him, just like the left. Jesse could almost feel the colt's shock as he slumped to his knees in the loose earth.

The colt's hindquarters bunched as he tried to rise. Jesse kept the strap tight, the colt's knees bent. Spark got his hind legs under him and reared, eyes rolling. Jesse moved to stay at his left shoulder and kept his grip on the strap. But he let the halter rope slip easily in his hand. Spark could have his head and welcome; as long as Jesse had his forelegs, he was helpless.

Spark came down again, and to his knees; reared again, staggered back on his hind legs. Jesse stayed with him. Sweat blackened the hair on the colt's neck and flanks and legs. Jesse talked to him, his voice gentle, while he kept the strap tight in his right hand.

He hated this part. He hated the fear the horse felt, the way that fear grew as the animal learned that nothing it did could win this fight. If he'd hand-raised Spark as he had Sam, this wouldn't be necessary. But Sam had been made to believe since before he'd first stood up that Jesse was stronger than he was. Spark still had to be convinced. The more of his strength he used, the more of it there was for Jesse to turn against him.

Humans expected horses to think like humans. Jesse knew better—but it troubled him that, in a horse, wisdom could grow out of fear.

At last Spark came to his knees and stayed there, sweat white on his hide. Jesse caressed his ears, stroked his neck, and sweet-talked him. Then he drew the colt's head to the left again and leaned into his shoulder. For a minute, two minutes, five, he felt the horse tense against the pressure. But leverage and exhaustion won. Spark collapsed onto his right side and lay still.

Wheels roll because they're round. Horses yield to fear and kindness because they're born to, blood and bone and breath. Jesse looked down at the colt, flanks rising and falling with each pant, and saw himself.

This thing that he had, that Lung had forced him to admit to, was his master. It was his own strength he struggled against when he fought it. He could deny it, but the power in him would only bring him to his knees again.

He'd tamed horses that required days of this work, that had gone back to fighting as soon as they got their wind back. They were the ones who'd known cruelty, mostly, the ones angry at the whole species of Man. What was his, Jesse's, excuse? Why did the thought of that unreasonable, inexplicable force make him want to strike out or run even when he knew it would win in the end?

Lily, of course. Lily weeping in a cold white room.

The light stopped stabbing his eyes and beating at his brain. The change was so sudden it was itself almost painful, like ice water on a burn. He was awash in the blaze of the Arizona sun, but no more than that.

Jesse let go of the strap in his right hand, and unbound Spark's left foot as well. He straightened the colt's front legs out on the ground and rubbed them, then worked his way up and all over the horse, caressing and talking. Spark had no vice or anger in him; Jesse knew this lesson would be enough.

Jesse lay down and pillowed his head on Spark's front hooves. It looked like showing off, and it was, a little. But it also told Spark that human mastery didn't depend on the human standing on two legs.

"I'll be damned," Earp said softly from the corral fence, and Jesse smiled up at the sky. Yes, it was partly showing off.

When Spark breathed easier, Jesse stood up and went to his head. "Up," he said, and tugged gently at the halter. Spark got his feet under him and scrambled up. Then he stood quietly, head at shoulder level, as if he didn't want the lead horse in the herd to think he was feeling uppity. Jesse pulled a handful of weeds and rubbed Spark down with them. "You won't believe this," he assured the colt, "but I know just how you feel."

The hard work was done; now he could address Earp's complaint. He left Spark to rest while he fetched the harness from the lean-to. The headstall had blinders, of course. He took out his pocketknife and began to cut the stitching that fastened the leather squares to the cheek pieces.

"Hey!" Earp said.

Jesse kept cutting. "Don't use these."

"To hell with that. A horse'll spook if he sees things off to the side of him."

"Horses spook at what they can't see or can't understand. Let a horse have a good look at anything, and he'll see that it won't hurt him. A horse wearing blinders starts off nervous."

Jesse harnessed the colt, and tied up his left foot again. He let him feel the driving reins flapping against his back, sides, and legs. When Spark was quiet under that, Jesse freed his left foreleg and drove him around the corral, walking behind and talking to him all the while.

Jesse and Earp wheeled Earp's two-wheeled gig into the corral, and Jesse led Spark up to it. The colt was inclined to snort and balk. "Yes, you great ninny," Jesse told him kindly. "It's a terrible machine that eats horses. Have a good stare at it, and take your time."

When Spark decided it was safe to look away from the gig, Jesse walked him in an ever-wider circle that ended at the right front wheel. He led him slowly around the cart, letting him touch it with his nose whenever he liked. By the time they'd returned to the front of the gig, Spark seemed to think no more of it than he did the fence rail.

Jesse and Earp swung the gig shafts off to the left,

and Jesse led Spark in front of the cart, where he would stand when hitched. Then he tied up Spark's forefoot and rubbed his shoulder. "Last time, boyo, my word on it.

"Now," he told Earp, "I'm going to raise the shafts and set them down with him between them. You go to his head and hold the rein and talk to him. If he wants to look behind him, don't stop him. But if he gets fretful, tell me."

Jesse raised the shafts and swung them over Spark's back at a near-glacial rate. The colt's ears went back and stayed there only once. Earp stroked his muzzle and kept up a flow of endearments, and Jesse held the shafts at half cock until Spark forgot them.

When they were in place, he and Earp fastened them to the surcingle. Jesse gave them a jiggle once they were in place, and they rattled and brushed Spark's flanks. The colt's ears went back. He gave a half hop, but the pull of the strap on his foreleg reminded him that the tune wasn't his to call.

"You see?" Jesse said. "He knows this is when the Devil comes up on his heels. But he also knows he can't win a fight with us, and when he loses, no harm comes to him. He's starting to think we're so strong, we can protect him from the Devil himself. Now, lead him out slowly to the left."

"Not straight forward?" Earp asked.

"No. If he feels the weight of the gig and stops, you won't win a tug-of-war with him. But if you turn him left when his left foot's up, he has to go where you lead him or lose his balance."

"Huh," said Earp, sounding pleased.

When Spark hopped forward, the gig rattled behind him. He threw up his head and fought the strap that held his left foot, trying to strike out with it. He could only flail with his knee.

"There now, you damned fool," Earp said gently, stroking the colt's neck. Spark stood still, rolling his eyes a little. "Settle down. It won't do you any good to keep me from fatherin' children."

Jesse approved of his tone of voice, and the steadiness with which he led the colt out again, forward and to the left. This time when the gig rattled and squeaked behind his heels, Spark only laid his ears back. Jesse held the reins and worked his way back toward the gig. "You can let go his head," he told Earp.

And Spark was being driven. Not from the seat of the gig, and going on only three legs. But he was pulling the cart, and being commanded by the reins.

A few circles of the corral in either direction, and Spark gave up the fight. Jesse let down his forefoot and massaged the leg. "Lead him out of the corral and drive him once 'round the block," he said to Earp. "But only once; he's tired. Then bring him in and make a fuss over him."

While Earp did that, Jesse fetched the mare and the burro from the front porch railing and turned them loose in the corral. He pumped water into the trough and gave them each a handful of hay. Then he sat on the fence until Earp brought Spark back down Fremont at an easy trot. He helped Earp unhitch the colt and watched as he rubbed him down and fed him.

Then Earp joined Jesse on the outside of the fence. "And that's it? He's broke?"

"He might need another lesson, but I doubt it. He's a good horse. All he needed was to understand what you wanted, and that it wouldn't hurt him to do it."

"Not unlike some people I know," Earp said. It was a moment before Jesse remembered he'd said that to Earp, and realized that Earp was pulling his leg.

"Next time some drunk turns mean downtown, you could tie up his foreleg and see what happens."

Earp laughed. "There's more mean men than mean horses."

Jesse splashed the dirt off himself at the pump and, dripping, followed Earp to the kitchen door. As they reached it, Mrs. Earp flung it open. "I couldn't get a minute's work done for watching. Where'd you learn to make a horse lay down like that?"

Jeese took the towel she held out to him. "A man named John Rarey invented the system. He figured out some of how horses think. After that it was common sense and leverage."

Mrs. Earp *hmmph*'d. "It looked more like gypsy-work. I'd swear you were magicking that horse."

"No." It wasn't until it came out his mouth that Jesse realized how short and sharp he sounded. He took a deep breath. "Anyone can do it. Some tamers try to pass it off as a mystery to make more money, but it's just science." This skill was a rational, sensible thing. Wasn't it?

Mrs. Earp handed him his clothes. "I figure that was only ten dollars of horse-breakin'," she said. "The other ten I would've paid for a ticket to watch."

"Maybe the government could raise money that way. The cavalry uses Rarey's method."

"You were in the army?" Earp asked.

Jesse shook his head. "I don't think it'd suit me. I'd rather pick my own fights."

"We all would," said Earp. "But sometimes that's a luxury even civilians don't get."

Jesse studied his quiet face and felt a chill. Whatever Earp's inexplicable force was, for good or bad he'd quit fighting it.

⚛ 10 ⚛

Mildred slapped the letter down on Harry's desk. She wanted to hurl it, but even such thick, silky paper would have fluttered and dodged in the air, perhaps missing the desk and landing on the floor. Her righteous indignation was unsuited to bending over to retrieve it.

Harry unfolded it, making a rustle like new money. He raised his eyebrows at the letterhead; then his gaze passed down the rest. When he reached the bottom, he looked up. "Do they?"

"No, of course they don't! I have the deed. It's in a strongbox at the bank."

"It'd be in your husband's name."

It sounded more like thinking aloud than argument, but Mildred wanted *someone* to argue with. "My marriage license is in the box next to it. Or does this territory not allow widows to inherit real estate?"

Harry lowered the letter and frowned at her. "Don't rip up at me, Madam Grizzly. In fact, don't rip up at all. You've got documents to prove that the Gilded Age Mining Company doesn't own your lot, so why are you snarling and stamping?"

"Because—" Because, even knowing she had proof that the claim in the letter was a lie, it had frightened her. She was ashamed of the lurch of her heart, the catch of her breath when she'd read she was unlawfully in possession of property deeded to the Gilded Age Mining Company, and was required to quit said property immediately and surrender it to the Company.

And she was ashamed that for an instant she'd

wondered if it were true. If David, who'd never had much head for business, had left her a house and land that had never really belonged to him. That shame was enough grievance to justify a little snarling.

"Because it's outrageous," she said. "They can't have so much as a scrap of paper to support this claim. They've made it up out of whole cloth to see if I can be scared out of my own home."

Harry nodded. "So what's your problem?"

Mildred stared at him, her anger banging around inside her like a badger in a cage. But when it tried to escape out her mouth, it turned into something small and foolish-looking, and she couldn't find words to turn it back into a badger. She blew out a ferocious breath and dropped into the chair beside Harry's desk.

"That's better," Harry said. "Now, first off, you have your attorney answer that letter. They know they've got nothing, and a good knuckle-rapping lawyer's letter will warn 'em off."

"I don't have an attorney."

Harry snorted. "You've lived in Tombstone all this time and never had a legal ruckus with anyone? Damn, Mildred, even Saint Nellie Cashman has a lawyer."

"I can't imagine how you missed seeing my halo before now."

"Tell you what—I'll send this around to Allan English, with a note from me, and he'll take care of it."

Mildred had met Mr. English, with his spade beard, stage-actor's manner, and persistent odor of bourbon. "If he's sober."

"You best hope not. He's much better drunk. English'll write you a letter that'll singe their eyebrows off."

The notion of singeing the eyebrows of the owners of the Gilded Age Mining Company gave her a positive thrill. But she hadn't yet raised her second concern.

"Harry, I can't be the only lot owner to get one of these letters."

"I wouldn't think so, no."

"Well, what's to be done about it?"

Harry leaned slowly back in his chair and stared at her. She felt a prickle of alarm, and it grew when he smiled the small, sweet smile he wore when he'd got the last damning fact for an editorial. "You'd best visit your neighbors. Find out how many have gotten this letter. You'll want a few personal details, ideally about elderly widows and orphaned children—you know the sort of thing. After that, we'll talk about the best way for you to get a statement from the Gilded Age partners to include in the article."

"Me? Harry, have you run mad?"

"They're your neighbors, ain't they? They'll talk to you."

"But I'm not—"

"You're whatever you say you are, Millie. That's the point of coming west. I thought you knew that."

She thought, *I have to get out of this*, but nothing useful followed it.

"When you're done, bring it to Rule. He's city editor, after all." Harry pursed his lips. "Besides, I can't say I wouldn't recall all your corrections and take it out on your copy."

Mildred had to laugh, but she added, "There must be an easier way to get revenge than this."

"Hell, no. I don't have to lift a finger, and I get a breaking story covered."

She waited for a good rebuttal to come to her. *I'm only a typesetter.* That wouldn't do; Harry knew that, and it weighed with him not at all.

She was startled by the pressure of his hand on her shoulder, and she realized he'd stood up. "Don't fret, Millie. If it's no good, Rule will rewrite it. But he might not have to." As he started toward the pressroom, he shouted back, "Get on it, damn it! I don't want the *Epitaph* printing this first!"

"What about today's type?" A forlorn hope, but it had to be tried.

"Dugan wants the overtime, and I don't mind the typos half as much as you do. The news won't come to the office. Git!"

She was routed. She rose, straightened her shoulders, and retreated with as much dignity as haste would allow.

All her neighbors had received the letter. Everyone on the block had been told they were squatters, and some of them had believed it. White-haired Mr. Matucek, whose shack was barely more than a weather-shelter for the hole that was his mining claim, told her, "I break nothing law! Where I go, I not stay here?" Mrs. Corrigan, whose husband worked at the Gird mill in Contention, stood in her kitchen with three children hiding in her skirts and a fourth in her arms, and said, "All our savings went for this house. They'll put my kids out on the street!"

Others, wiser in business and law, were steaming mad and ready to drag Gilded Age into court if they could. And a few, not wise but even more angry, declared the partners in the Gilded Age Mining Company ought to be careful about sitting down to dinner with their backs to the window. Mildred documented all of it.

Each person's story and situation added itself to the last. A structure began to take shape in her head, the shape of the story of Gilded Age's attempted theft. And theft it was, just like a rustler's attempt to brand someone else's cow.

The article grew, in fact, just as one of her fictional stories did. Ideas, figures, phrases at first drifted unconnected in an alarming void, and Mildred wondered how they would ever become something linear and convincing. But the more information she gathered, the more bits stuck together. Facts demanded a certain order to be understood. Witness accounts built to an emotional peak. By the time she'd collected the statement from the Gilded Age lawyer that, in many words, said nothing at all, she was rushing along on a tide of elation.

The clerk in the office of the Justice of the Peace didn't look up at her entrance. "I need to speak with the justice, please," she said.

The clerk still didn't look up from the ledger in front of him. He had thin, fox-colored hair and a face like risen bread dough, and smelled strongly of macassar oil. "Make an appointment. Next week's the first you can get."

"I need to see him immediately."

"Sorry. Soonest is next week."

The elation emptied out of her.

She could go back to Harry with her job unfinished. He could send Richard Rule to get the last piece, to write the story, and he would see that she was a typesetter after all, as she'd known from the start. There was no shame in being right.

But the story was in her head, nearly finished and *hers*. Rule might reject it when it was done, but until then she had a responsibility—not to the *Nugget*, but to the story itself—to bring it safe home.

She dropped her handbag with a satisfying bang on the clerk's ledger, and set her palms on either side of it so that she leaned over him. He jerked back and finally met her eyes. His looked unnaturally large behind his spectacles.

Well-bred ladies did not behave like this. She had always been a well-bred lady, however much she flirted with eccentricity. Well-bred ladies descended no farther than to setting type.

But they didn't sell sensation stories to magazines, either.

"I'm loath to impede the business of the city of Tombstone," she said in her kindest voice. Inwardly she trembled: that sentence sounded like Harry at his most vitriolic. "But I'm afraid the justice would be deeply disappointed to learn you'd denied him a chance to re-but the story he'll read in tomorrow's *Nugget*."

"What story?" the clerk said, a little too sharply.

Mildred smiled and shook her head. "Now, how would we sell papers if we told everyone what was in them before they were printed?"

"You're . . . with the *Nugget*?"

You're not any more surprised than I am. "Yes, I'm with the *Nugget*. My heavens, did you think I'd come for tea and gossip? Be a good lad and announce me."

He stood up with a scrape of chair, as cowed as if she'd transformed into Mayor Clum before his eyes. Mildred wondered if it was the "lad" that had finished him off, as if he weren't Mildred's age or maybe more.

The clerk disappeared into the inner office, and popped back out a minute later. "Right this way, ma'am."

Mildred picked up her bag, smoothed her gloves to hide the shaking of her hands, and set out on her first interview of a city official.

Richard Rule was a darkly handsome man who could charm the shoes off a draft mule. Mildred had always liked him, though not half as much, she suspected, as he liked himself. But he wrote outstanding copy.

After his first stammering surprise at finding that the sheaf of papers she handed him was an article assigned by his boss, he set charm aside and went to work. Mildred watched as he drove his pencil through lines and phrases. "Too intellectual," he said of one, and "Redundant," of another. He cut one whole sentence at the end of a paragraph, and turned the page.

"But that's the conclusion the earlier statements lead to," she protested.

"That's right. And if you let the reader reach it by himself, he'll be convinced it's true." Rule plunged on, and Mildred watched, her heart sinking lower with each page.

But she didn't want to be a journalist, did she? She'd done a bad job, and proved she had no business outside the railing that fenced her type cases. She was a very good typesetter. Nothing was changed.

So why did she feel so melancholy?

Rule finished the last page and tucked it behind the rest. Not a page had escaped penciling.

"Good work," he said.

Mildred wasn't sure at first what she'd heard. Then she glanced up at Rule's face. He stared rather impatiently back.

"Good?" Mildred asked. It came out as a croak.

Rule's expression softened. He didn't smile, but he didn't seem like a man trying to communicate with someone who spoke no English, either. "Here, look it over." He passed the pages back to her. "If I've marked anything that you don't understand, ask."

She read them as he waited. He'd removed words as a gardener might prune the topiary. He'd cut phrases that separated facts from their meaning. He'd made workmanlike sentences graceful, and made halting paragraphs flow. She'd thought he was making her work his own. Instead he'd made it into what she'd meant it to be.

She handed the pages back. No, not pages—*copy*. "I see." What she wanted to say was, "I have been given a revelation," but she didn't think Richard Rule would be comfortable in the role of a literary burning bush.

"By the time this comes out tomorrow, there'll be some fur flying. Follow up, see if you can get a statement from one of the partners. I'd like some background on town lot claims, too. The records office is open for a few hours yet."

"You want me to write another?" *You sound as if you fell on your head*, Mildred scolded herself. But she had to be sure.

Rule frowned. "Don't you want to?"

"Yes. I do."

"All right then." He handed her pages—her copy— to Joe Dugan at the type cases. When Rule turned away, Joe looked across the aisle at her, grinned, and winked.

Tombstone's citizens had begun to move into the town before it existed, that was the problem. Goose Flats and the Tombstone Hills had belonged to the Apaches, until one day they were the property of a hundred prospectors and speculators chasing veins of silver and claiming land not by its surface virtues but by what might be underneath it.

Then the saloons and bordellos and general stores and boardinghouses appeared: tents put up on any level patch by people come to get rich on silver secondhand. Someone replaced his tent with adobe, and another built a wood-frame building. Next thing anyone knew, there were streets with names, and lot boundaries. And other than the old mining claims, there was no proof of ownership of those lots besides occupancy. The Apaches had never deeded them to anyone, after all.

The Gilded Age Mining Company was claiming large chunks of town on no better authority than that Tombstone could as well belong to the Gilded Age as to anyone. It was nonsense. But they had only to intimidate a few lot owners, or win a few court cases, and the partners could leave town as wealthy men. They would, of course, have to leave town.

Mildred left the records office with her mind on her opening sentence, and ran hard into a fellow pedestrian. The shock drove a squeak out of her, and a huff of wind out of her victim. A grip on her shoulders kept her from stumbling. "Oh, Lord, I'm sorry, Miss Benjamin," said the voice that went with the grip.

She looked into the face of Tom McLaury, and her own grew hot as a stovetop. "No, it was me—I wasn't looking—I'm so sorry—"

McLaury let go of her shoulders, but she felt the pressure of his fingers still. "Are you all right?"

"Yes. Thank you. Are you?"

He shook his head and looked grave. "I don't mean to brag, but it takes more than one young lady to do me lasting harm."

"How many *does* it take?" Mildred asked. She was annoyingly aware of the physicalness of him. Harry Woods could stand this close, and she never thought about it.

He blushed and laughed. "I guess I'm not sure. I haven't put it to the test."

"I expect it depends on the circumstances." He wasn't shocked or offended. That was nice. "And your goat?"

"Living a life of ease, Miss Benjamin, and mighty ungrateful for it. No prison built can hold him."

"If you decide he's for the stewpot after all, don't tell me. I'd feel responsible." Then she registered what he'd called her. "It's 'Mrs. Benjamin.' " McLaury's expression went a little stiff, before she could finish with, "I'm a widow."

"Oh." His face unfroze. "Oh. I'm sorry."

"It was a while ago." She realized that for the first time she didn't have the precise number of weeks at her mental fingertips. Maybe there wasn't room, with all that town lot information.

"I went along by the *Nugget* office, and they said I might find you here."

"You were looking for me?" Mildred would have to talk to someone about forwarding gentlemen callers. Probably Harry.

McLaury turned red again. "There's a play at the Opera House tonight. I know it's not much warning, but my brother and I are in town until tomorrow noon . . ." He took a breath and set his jaw, as if expecting to be punched. "Would you care to go with me?"

For the first time, Mildred noticed McLaury's clothes. Not the drover rig that the ranchers wore into town. He wore a smart dark town suit and a starched white shirt, a satin-stripe waistcoat and matching tie. His unruly brown hair had been slicked smooth, and the hat he turned in his hands might be new. She looked down, embarrassed, and saw that his shoes were shined.

She couldn't. Well, why not? Because she hadn't for so long, that was why. She remembered going to the theater, concerts, cotillions—but that was before David. She didn't know how to behave, how to talk to a man who wasn't her husband or her coworker.

Silly—she was talking to him now, wasn't she? And what made her think her debutante behavior would apply to widowhood, anyway? Here was a friend, asking her to a play. She didn't need to flirt with him.

But what if he flirted with her? Well, what if he did? If she didn't like it, she could discourage it, gently. If she recalled how. Oh, heavens, it was just a play!

She looked up into Tom McLaury's face, and found his blush had drained away. "Thank you," she said. "I'd like to go to the play with you."

He grinned the wide white grin that had disarmed her at their first meeting, in the street over the goat. "Shall I come for you at your place? Oh, except I don't know where that is."

She told him, as she thought, *Dear God, what have I done?* She supposed she'd be asking that until the evening was over. She watched McLaury walk down the street and swore to postpone all internal debate until he brought her home at evening's end.

She couldn't keep the vow, but at least she had it to remind herself of when she backslid. The Opera House was enough distraction that she didn't need the reminder very often.

The theaters of Philadelphia were larger, grander, and brighter, but Philadelphia was very far away. She and David had been perpetually short of money, and sometimes too far from a town to spend it on the theater if they had it. Now that she was a working woman, she had money but less time—and a lady didn't go to the theater unescorted. She'd never been in the Opera House.

In the foyer, the chandeliers and the lamps along the walls had cut-glass chimneys that scattered the light like a bright morning. The walls were hung with gold-printed paper, and gold-framed mirrors that doubled the lamps and the room and the company that filled it. Mildred struggled to keep her gloved hand light on

Tom McLaury's arm; the brilliance and heat and racket of conversation made her dizzy.

At least her evening gown—dark blue silk, a bit severe for the occasion—didn't have a bustle. However far Tombstone was from Philadelphia, it got all the eastern magazines and newspapers; the ladies present wore the fashionable column-like silhouette with overskirts elaborately ornamented and trained. They made the room vivid as a stained-glass window, their silk and satin in scarlet, emerald, aubergine, ashes-of-roses, sapphire, daffodil, apple-green. Some ladies wore splendid jewelry, and faceted stones winked from men's cravats. It was a reminder of how rich Tombstone could be. Mildred resisted the temptation to tug at her bodice and smooth her overskirt. That much she remembered of her debutante wisdom: dress well, then behave as if you never gave your clothes a thought.

Mildred saw the county sheriff, John Behan, near the wall, with a lovely little dark-haired woman on his arm. The woman laughed up at him, then dropped her eyes as if ashamed of her daring. But if she were uncomfortable with daring, she wouldn't have worn that gown.

Tom guided her toward the sheriff and his companion. Behan saw them and smiled. John Behan would disappoint the eastern readers of *Gallagher's Illustrated*, who had a very different picture of how an Arizona Territory lawman looked. He was not tall or lean or weather-beaten, though he was tall enough, and athletic. Instead of a cool, narrowed gaze squinting into some inconceivable distance, Behan's eyes were large and dreaming and rather sad. He lacked the canonical mane of hair burnt pale by the sun; the sheriff's high forehead was getting higher as his hair receded prematurely. He looked like a history professor who wrote poetry in secret. But as far as she could tell, he did the job in spite of his cosmetic shortcomings. She recalled John Dunbar's assessment: "As long as the county stays quiet, it's live and let live with Johnny." She couldn't fault Behan for that; it was hard work to keep Cochise County quiet.

"Good evening, Tom," Behan said when they were in earshot. The dark-haired woman turned and smiled at Tom, then gave Mildred an evaluating stare that no smile could soften. Mildred smiled graciously back.

"Hello, Johnny. Sheriff John Behan, this is Mrs. Mildred Benjamin."

Mildred heard a note of—was it pride?—in McLaury's voice. Flirting she could discourage; what was she to do about this? Not to mention that by using her first name instead of David's, Tom had suggested that she was a divorcée.

"I know the sheriff by sight and reputation, at least," Mildred said. "I work for Harry Woods at the *Nugget*." She held out her hand to Behan, and he clasped it. His stare was admiring.

"That's where I've seen you! The *Nugget*'s a fine newspaper."

Mildred kept her face very straight. "And we support the Democrats."

Behan laughed. "That doesn't hurt you with me, that's for sure. I don't think you've met Sadie Marcus, Mrs. Benjamin."

"Pleased to meet you," Miss Marcus said stiffly.

Mildred wondered if Sadie Marcus had caught the unconscious message in her escort's words: *I doubt you and she move in the same circles*. Miss Marcus's gown, low-cut and overtrimmed, had told her that. Still, her opinion of Behan sank a hair, and she smiled more warmly at Miss Marcus when she replied, "Delighted. Have you been long in Tombstone?"

Miss Marcus's eyes widened, as if she hadn't expected to be talked to. "Only a few months."

"That's nearly an old-timer in a three-year-old town."

"How long have you been here?"

"Almost a year. I'm old as dirt."

"Hey!" Tom protested. "Frank and I started ranching longer ago than that. What does that make me?"

Mildred shook her head and sighed. "A founding father, Mr. McLaury, and that's an antique by definition."

Tom looked tragic, and Sadie Marcus laughed, sweet and clear like a child.

"Good evening, Johnny," came a voice over Mildred's shoulder.

Mildred sometimes thought that the Earp brothers were the only people in town that everyone knew. Working on a newspaper gave one a skewed view; still, everyone seemed to have an opinion on the Earps, whether they'd met them or not. One opinion was usually considered sufficient to cover all four of them.

It was Wyatt who'd come up behind her and greeted Behan. He'd make the readers of *Gallagher's* happy: he was the very pattern of a western lawman. Cochise County had failed to reward his appearance with the sheriff's job, however, which just showed what happened when people didn't read enough fiction.

She felt Tom McLaury stiffen at her side, and remembered Lucy Austerberg's story about a quarrel between Earp and the McLaurys over missing government mules. She glanced at Tom's face—stern, but not fierce.

Mildred studied Earp's profile while he shook hands with Behan. What she'd overheard at Allie and

Virgil Earp's house couldn't be true. But why would Kate Holliday call Wyatt Earp a con man and a thief, and what were the "disguises" she'd referred to? And if there was no truth in it, why had Allie been crying?

Earp nodded to Tom. "Evening, McLaury." Yes, there was a grudge there.

Behan stepped in quickly. "Let me make you known to the ladies. Wyatt Earp, Mrs. Mildred Benjamin and Miss Sadie Marcus."

Earp took Mildred's hand. His narrowed blue eyes weren't gazing into inconceivable distance, but into her. She felt as if the blood were chilling in her veins. She blinked, and the spell was broken. Earp smiled and inclined his head over her fingers. "My pleasure, Mrs. Benjamin."

"Likewise, Mr. Earp." She glanced past him. "Is your wife with you this evening? I'd like to say hello."

Earp kept smiling, but it was warm as a glacier. "Mattie isn't comfortable in a crowd." He turned abruptly to Miss Marcus.

Miss Marcus hadn't liked the mention of a wife, either. Heavens, the woman had been clutching John Behan like a hundred-dollar gold piece. Then she'd given Tom as warm a look as a woman on another man's arm could. Now she was sparkling at Earp. If men were fish, Sadie Marcus seemed determined to catch more than she could salt.

Behan broke in smoothly with, "I appreciate the work you and your brothers did, trailing Jim Crane and Head and Leonard. That was a long, hard ride."

Earp's jaw worked. What made him look so speculative? Was it that the speech reminded Earp that John Behan was in charge? Or was there something about the pursuit of the stage robbers that Mildred hadn't heard?

"It was that. Shame we couldn't run 'em down for you."

Behan flushed, and his smile was forced. "We can't catch them all."

"That's what I hear."

The bell chimed for the audience to take their seats, cutting off the discussion and leaving Mildred divided between relief and disappointment. She laid her hand on Tom McLaury's offered arm. Something made her look over Behan's shoulder to the open double doors— and into the eyes of Jesse Fox.

She jumped at a shock—but no, there was nothing she could have gotten a shock from. There was no reading Fox's expression. Blast the man. Couldn't he have left town when he said he would? And why should she care if he left or stayed? She felt as if she'd been caught at something underhanded.

She was sitting down in the middle of a row of chairs, and couldn't remember getting there. Tom settled into the chair next to her. "Are you all right?" he asked.

"Oh, yes. Just thinking." She looked for Fox, but couldn't see him. Then the lights went down, the little orchestra produced an overture of sentimental strings, and the curtain parted.

The play was "The Ticket-of-Leave Man." She'd seen it years ago in Philadelphia. Her mother had thought it unsuitable for a young lady, dealing as it did with counterfeiters, drunks, jailbirds, actresses, and maidens who earned their living singing in tea gardens. But her father, surprisingly, had disagreed. "If playwrights wrote only about upright, moral people, there'd be nothing to write about. I believe the righteous triumph in the end in this story. She'll come to no harm."

And of course, she'd enjoyed herself immensely.

This company had modified the play for its audience. The hero's broad Lancashire accent was replaced by a Vermont Yankee dialect, which was just as difficult to follow but more familiar. (The dialect was gone by Act Two, when Bob returned from prison. The actor was probably disappointed, but the audience was relieved.) Currency was changed to dollars, and the whole was colored with local references and topical jokes.

The actress playing May was so small and frail that Mildred wondered if she'd get through the first scene, but when she performed May's song, it filled the room with no apparent effort. She sang "The Cuckoo" so sweetly, sadly, that when the tea garden patrons refused to tip her, hisses rose up from the audience.

The best members of the company were the comic male and female leads. The woman, especially; her Emily St. Evremond was drily funny, and even her vulgar moments were charming. When she announced, "I call this life—the music and the company, and the singing and the trapeze. I thought the man must break his neck. It was beautiful," the audience howled.

When Mildred had first seen the play, she'd longed to take May's part. The character seemed bland now. But one could do worse than go through life as Emily St. Evremond, adapting with courage and humor to every change of fortune.

The final scene in the churchyard was so luridly staged that Mildred half expected ghosts to be added to the climax. But no, Bob made his heroic stand—which would have been useless if Detective Hawkshaw and young Sam hadn't been there to back his play—and banker Gibson learned he'd misjudged his clerk, all without supernatural intervention. The applause was mighty, and when the comic male lead, at the curtain call, waved his basket and offered to sell the audience "nice boiled pig's feet, two for a penny!" he was cheered.

When the curtain came down and the lights up, Tom McLaury asked, "Did you enjoy it?"

"Oh, so much! The actors were splendid. And I liked the changes that made it seem local."

Tom looked dismayed. "You didn't say you'd already seen it."

"Years ago. It was more fun the second time, because I knew what to watch for. Don't you ever reread a book you liked?" Once the words were out of her mouth, she regretted them; there were plenty of people who didn't read for pleasure, let alone reread.

But Tom smiled and shook his head. "I used to, when I was a tyke. But how can you read a book you've already read when you know there are all those other ones out there?"

"An excellent argument, Mr. McLaury. I can only defend my position by saying that I use my old books as seasoning for the new ones—I sprinkle them lightly through my reading."

He grinned. "Seasoning, not saleratus?"

"No, unlike biscuits, books rise by themselves."

Tom laughed and helped her to her feet. It was pleasant to exchange nonsense with a nice-looking man. Too pleasant, perhaps: she couldn't see herself walking out evenings with Tom McLaury, or with anyone. She'd had a husband. Now she was creating a very nice life without one, and she meant to give it a fair trial.

"Wasn't it mighty odd," Tom added as they passed into the foyer, "when Emily said she wanted to see the banker's office, because she'd only ever seen an office onstage?"

"And what she was seeing was an office onstage? That made me laugh."

"Yes, but it made me think, too. Not that you can't tell what's real, because you can. But that you can't always tell the truth of a thing by looking, no matter how clear you can see it."

"I suppose that's one of the lessons of the play."

"That and, 'Don't get drunk with fellows you don't know.' "

As Mildred laughed, Sadie Marcus came up with Behan close behind. "Did you like the play, Mrs. Benjamin?" Miss Marcus asked.

"Very much. And you?"

"Oh, I always love the theater. I used to think I'd be a fine actress, if I had the chance. Johnny, wouldn't I be a treat in the boy parts, like that Sam in the play?"

Behan's eyes dropped as if against his will to Miss Marcus's striking *décolletage*; he seemed dazed when he replied, "That you would, Sadie." Mildred bit the inside of her lip to keep from laughing.

That was when Jesse Fox appeared, slipping as cleverly between the densely packed patrons in the foyer as his namesake would evade hunters. "Good evening, Mrs. Benjamin." He looked as if he, too, was trying not to laugh. Mildred rejected the notion that he might be laughing at her. "And Tom McLaury, isn't it? I've met your brother Frank."

"I remember—you were playing cards at the Oriental." Tom shook his hand cheerfully.

"Did you win?" Mildred asked.

"I wish people would stop asking me that," Fox sighed. "No."

Which didn't mean he wasn't a cardsharp. Then she recalled that in doing her a favor he'd involved himself in a much worse business. She felt her face go hot.

Fox's attention had moved to Behan and Miss Marcus as Tom introduced them. Fox asked what Miss Marcus thought of the play.

"Lovely. And true, the way all the men in the story would starve if it weren't for their wives working and being clever." She shot a teasing glance at the men. But Mildred thought there was a kernel of something harder in the teasing.

At that moment she found Wyatt Earp at her shoulder. Mildred remembered a parlor full of Earp wives sewing tents, and wondered if he'd heard what Miss Marcus had said about the play.

Mildred watched Miss Marcus gaze into Earp's eyes, then drop hers. It made her appear flustered, but Mildred imagined it would take more than a man's eyes to fluster Sadie Marcus.

On the other hand, if she felt what Mildred had on meeting Earp's eyes . . . Ridiculous. The man wasn't a mesmerist.

Behan introduced Fox, but instead of shaking his hand, Earp said, "We met. You were playing cards with John Ringo."

Was that the same game? If so, Mildred wished she could have been a fly on the wall, to know what made Earp sound so frosty.

"And I lately trained a horse for your brother," Fox said, as if he hadn't noticed the cold.

"I hope he got his money's worth."

McLaury and Behan went rigid on either side of her, and Mildred didn't blame them. If Earp wanted to pick a quarrel with Jesse Fox, that was his business, but to do it in the foyer of the Opera House called for more provocation than she could imagine.

Fox only smiled. "You'll have to ask him. A good horse, though."

"That bay of his?" Earp asked, interested, it seemed, in spite of himself.

Fox nodded.

Earp made a little noise in his throat, like suppressed laughter. "Well, I hope the buggy can be fixed."

"Your brother would know best about that, too."

Fox was clearly not to be drawn. Earp turned to Behan and asked about some piece of county tax business.

Tom stepped aside to join in the discussion, and Fox moved closer to Mildred. "I still have something to ask you, and again these aren't the best circumstances for it."

"You can't think I appreciate being reminded of the previous ones."

He dropped his gaze. "No. Sorry. But are you working tomorrow? Might I come by the newspaper office?"

"You can come, but you might not find me there."

"Then you're not working?"

"I'll be covering a story." How pretentious it sounded!

Fox looked up, his face alert and pleased. "You're a reporter now? Congratulations!"

"My goodness, no sly comments about lady journalists?"

"Do you get many of those? I'd rather not offend the press."

"Still angling for the social column?"

"No, I've decided I'd rather stay out of the news altogether."

"And you don't think you can manage without a friend at the paper."

"At least I don't mean to throw away the advantage."

Curse the man—he had a way of making her forget that she didn't want to talk to him. By being good to talk to, in fact. He seemed to hone her faculties just by being there; she felt she could grapple with any subject, like a fencer meeting his opponent at the peak of his training.

Of course, wariness and the hint of danger always did hone one's faculties.

Then she saw a man working his way through the

crowd from the front doors. His uncovered hair was short and black, and that was all she could tell about him. He kept his chin tucked, and ducked his head apologetically whenever he had to press past anyone. The men he passed frowned after him, and the ladies drew closer to their escorts. It wasn't until he arrived at Fox's left shoulder that the man looked up. He was Chinese.

Mildred hoped her gasp of surprise wasn't audible. What was a Chinaman doing in the foyer of the Opera House?

The man's eyes passed swiftly over her before they dropped to the floor. He said, "So solly. Missa Fox?"

Fox's eyes widened. He turned sharply and stared at the Chinaman.

"Missa Fox, is big message for you. Gotta go, chop-chop. Velly solly." And the Chinaman folded his hands over his stomach and bowed.

Jesse Fox still stared. Not angry, not alarmed, just staring. And biting his lip. The Chinaman rose from his bow, looked into Fox's face . . . and winked. Mildred was sure of it.

Fox turned to her. "Mrs. Benjamin, I'm very sorry"—that, for some reason, seemed to give him trouble; he bit his lip again before he went on—"but it seems I'm needed elsewhere. Perhaps I'll catch you at the newspaper office tomorrow."

All the questions she wanted to ask would have to wait. "Perhaps you will. Good night, Mr. Fox."

She watched him follow the Chinaman out of the Opera House. She'd been happy to think that he *wouldn't* be able to catch her at the office. But he'd roused her curiosity, and she found herself wondering how she could be sure to be there if he stopped by. *You have plenty to ask questions about*, she scolded herself, *without adding Jesse Fox to the list.*

Mildred found that the rest of her party had also watched Fox leave. "I just don't like them," Miss Marcus declared with an exaggerated shiver. "You hear such stories."

Behan smiled at her. "The Celestials? They're all right. Even their vices are quiet. In fact, if some of the county's yahoos would go on the dope instead of drinking, you wouldn't hear me complain."

"Quiet can cover a lot of troublemaking." Earp's eyes were still on the door.

Tom touched her elbow. In the lights of the foyer his high-boned face looked like some lovely statue's. His blue eyes crinkled at the corners as he smiled at her. There was no question—Tom McLaury was a very good-looking man. "May I take you home, Mrs. Benjamin?"

"Yes, thank you." She took his arm, and they stepped out into the night.

Mildred tugged her shawl closer around her throat and looked up at the sky. The West could make an astronomer out of anyone. The brilliant company of the stars was laid out overhead for her to see and marvel at, undimmed by streetlights.

"Beautiful, isn't it?" Tom murmured beside her.

She looked at him, startled. In spite of his arm under her fingers, she'd almost forgotten he was with her.

When she was younger, when David was courting her—well, to be fair, when she was sneaking out to see him—stars had existed in the context of him. Why admire a clear night sky, if there was no one beside her to declare it beautiful, and to agree with? Rapture wasn't a private emotion; beauty required consensus.

It was years since she'd felt that way. Even before David died, she'd discovered that where she saw planets and nebulae, David saw a poet's sequined dome.

He'd gazed across the plains and seen an ocean made of grass, while she'd seen prairie dog towns, pronghorn antelope tracks, and the earth-binding roots of bluestem and buffalo grass.

She'd loved David, and she'd loved the differences between them. But she had only begun to discover her adult self, who she was in the privacy of her own heart and mind when she wasn't standing with her hand on someone's arm.

They'd reached her front door. She looked up at Tom McLaury, so handsome, so earnest, so ready to smile and laugh. Was she done discovering—was it time to think of joining this new self to someone else?

Tom took off his hat and returned her gaze, and she saw the signs of some mental struggle in his face. Then, quick and shy as a boy stealing fruit, he touched his lips to hers.

It was a sweet shock, familiar and strange at once. It made it hard to think—but not impossible.

"Mr. McLaury, I don't—"

"No, no, wait," he begged. He looked alarmed; whether at his own daring or her response, she couldn't tell. "I shouldn't have done that. You don't hardly know me. But you looked—" He took one of Mildred's gloved hands in both of his. She wanted to warn him not to drop his hat, but that would suggest her mind wasn't on the business at hand. And it was, wasn't it?

"Mr. McLaury, I'm glad to be your friend. But I'm not sure I'm ready to be anything more."

He kept his eyes on her knuckles. "Would it be all right if we stayed friends while you think about it?"

Her afternoon's worth of mental arguments came back to her. They could be friends, couldn't they, without an implied promise to be more? And would it be fair to either of them if she made it impossible to get to know him better? But what if she didn't learn to love him? He seemed halfway to being in love with her.

"Nothing may come of it," Mildred said.

He looked up, a grin barely turning his lips. "Something always comes of friendship."

"Very philosophical, Mr. McLaury." She found herself smiling. "All right. We'll stay friends."

He squeezed her hand, and his grin bloomed. "In that case, will you go riding with me tomorrow?"

"I thought you and your brother were leaving town tomorrow?"

"I'm sure there's something needs doing before we go," he said gravely, and winked.

"I work tomorrow for the *Nugget*." She noticed she didn't mention her story this time.

"Could you manage afternoon, maybe?"

Fox had said he'd look for her at the *Nugget* office. Well, she hadn't promised to be there. "Afternoon it is."

He let go of her hand to put his hat on. "I'll come for you here." He looked so happy that Mildred doubted the wisdom of her decision.

"Good night, Mr. McLaury." She watched him head down the street into the darkness.

She went indoors and lit the parlor lamp. It lit up the same room, the same shabby comfort, it had shone on when she left. What did she expect? She'd gone to a play, and was going riding tomorrow. With a friend.

David had given her a volume of Tennyson in the early days of their romance. Her mother had asked where she'd gotten it. "From a friend," she'd answered. As she'd said it, she'd felt her heart recoil from that betrayal.

Now—she was going riding with a friend. No, no

turmoil in her breast. Her brain was in disarray, but her breast was fine. Was that because she didn't love Tom McLaury, or only because she was no longer young and foolish?

Tonight David seemed nearer in her memory than he had been for months. It was only the associations of dressing up, of being in a gentleman's company. But it was easy to remember his hollow-cheeked face, his large, dark eyes that always seemed to yearn for something, the sound of his uneven steps across the floor.

His gravity had appealed to her. He wasn't like the blythe young men who had never been crossed, who courted rich and pretty girls with every expectation of winning them. David—older, lamed by war and sobered by circumstance—was a romantic figure. And she'd needed romance.

Whatever she needed now, it wasn't that. But only for this moment, in this spot of lamplight, it was David she wished for.

She found she had to sit down and cry just a little bit.

⇜ 11 ⇝

Jesse contained himself until they were a block away. Then he said, "I can't decide if you should be on the stage or the gallows. Heaven knows you nearly killed me back there."

"The barbarian stage," Lung declared, "is a child's play with dolls compared to the great theaters of China. What imagined trouble were you dying of?"

"Apoplexy, from trying not to laugh."

"Velly solly," Lung said, singsong. He looked smug.

"Do you do that often?"

"When it is useful. They expect it, and what they expect is invisible to them."

" 'They' meaning 'us.' "

Lung raised his eyebrows, surprised. "Are you one of them?"

Jesse shrugged. "I can pass."

They crossed through the light of the lamps outside the O.K. Corral livery stable, and he noticed how Lung was dressed. His black padded jacket was silk, patterned with medallions visible only when the light fell on them. His loose trousers looked like silk, too, and he wore tooled leather slippers. At his throat and wrists a thin band of starched and blinding white showed from under the jacket. He even wore the silk button cap that Jesse had heard him make fun of, which he'd pulled out of his pocket as soon as they left the theater. Sober magnificence—and staggering conformity, for Lung. Except for the lack of a queue, he was just what a successful professional Chinese man ought to look like.

"Lung, where are we going?"

Lung looked over his shoulder. "I was beginning to think you would prefer to be surprised."

"Good God, not by you."

"Better you be prepared for this. Are you confident of your Chinese?"

Jesse stopped. "No," he replied in Chinese.

"You understand it, at least. Do the best you can. I have been summoned to meet with the—you might say 'mayor'—of the Chinese in Tombstone, and I wish to introduce you."

"And why is that?"

"Because if I am summoned for the purpose I suspect, I will need your aid."

"Well, I certainly feel all prepared now. You could at least tell me as much as you know."

"Oh, that would require lifetimes."

"Don't make me duck your wily heathen head in that water butt."

"Could you?" Lung said.

"If we have time, I'll try."

"Alas, we do not. How lucky for you!" Then Lung relented. "I know very little. I have heard rumors of a crime, but as is the way of rumors, they cannot all be true. I hope we will learn more soon."

Jesse digested that, and decided to suspend judgment.

"Your manners are good, at least. It would be appropriate to show respect as if to the governor—"

"I have limited respect for the governor."

"Behave as if the territory were governed by someone you respect. And whatever I say you are, you must be, for the next hour."

"A deaf-mute? A lunatic? A gypsy fiddler?"

Lung sighed. "This is serious."

Jesse could see from Lung's face that it was. "I'll behave."

"Thank you. Here we are."

They'd arrived at the edge of Hoptown, and at a sprawling single-story adobe house with a deep porch all around. At the windows, a few stray knife edges of light showed between heavy curtains. A Chinese man sat beside the front door in a straight-backed wooden chair. He rose as they reached the porch.

"I am expected," Lung said in Chinese.

"He is not," said the guard, looking at Jesse.

"His presence is required, even so. Perhaps I should go home, and return at some better hour."

To Jesse, Lung sounded perfectly polite, but the guard's jaw muscles sprang into relief. "You may pass."

Instead of opening the door or announcing them, the man sat down. Lung used the knocker. The door was opened by a Chinese maidservant in a plain dark blue silk coat, who bowed low to Lung.

Outside the house, they were in the Arizona Territory. Inside they were in China. This wasn't like Lung's house, a convenient hodgepodge of cultures. Here the furniture, the ornaments, even the scent of the air, were imported.

The maid pointed smiling at the hat in Jesse's hand, then to the top of a filigreed walnut side table. He laid the hat down between two yellow-glazed porcelain vases each large enough to hide a small child. The mirror above the table was framed in walnut carved with phoenixes.

The maid led them past a lacquer screen to a red-painted double door. She nodded at Lung and Jesse and pushed the doors open.

Jesse stared into a narrow room lit with so many lamps that the heat of them greeted him in the doorway. A glossy carpet lay before him, blood-colored and brimming with dragons. At its other end was a tall heavily carved rosewood chair, the only furniture in the room. In the chair sat a Chinese woman.

Jesse knew enough of Chinese standards to know that she was beautiful. Her wide face was pale and smooth-skinned under her powder, and her black hair, drawn into an elaborate knot, shone like still water. Her white hands were folded in her lap and ornamented with gold nail guards. Her coat was gold silk embroidered with butterflies, with a wide border of blue, and the heavy blue silk skirt under it pooled on the floor.

Awe stunned his brain as he followed Lung down the carpet and bowed to her. Then he realized the nail guards hid the true length of her nails, and the skirt kept her feet out of sight. She appeared to be a noble-woman, congenitally idle and helpless. But appearances might be deceiving.

She raised her exquisitely arched brows. In Chinese, she said to Lung, "Doctor, a dog has followed you in." Immediately she turned to Jesse, smiled, and said in English, "I not know you, honored sir. Pardon humble woman, please."

If he replied in Chinese, he would shame her: she would know her first sentence had been understood. If he answered in English, he would be lying by omission, assuring her of privacy where she had none. Either way, he'd be rude. Of course, she'd been rude first. He shot a glance at Lung. Lung stared blankly at the wall over the Chinese woman's head.

He bowed again, even lower; then straightened and said gravely, "Esteemed lady, how should you know me? I am a humble traveler lately arrived in this city. Necessity brings me to you uninvited, but not unwelcome, I hope." He'd spoken in Chinese.

As he watched her face turn crimson, he thanked whatever part of his memory had allowed him to get all three sentences out without a hitch. He hoped he wouldn't have to do it again.

Lung stepped forward quickly. "Madam, this is my colleague, Jesse Fox. His skill is the equal of mine, and his knowledge of the world outside ours is greater. His assistance will be of benefit to you in this matter."

Lung's speech had given her time to cool off. She looked calmly down her little nose at him. "You know, then, why I asked you to come?"

Lung inclined his head. The posture suggested that of course he knew, but that to say so would be showing off. Lung had always been good at that sort of thing.

Jesse thought he could feel the force of the woman's will in the room, like pressure in a column of water.

Her dark eyes were fierce in her still face. "Dr. Fox, I am known here as China Mary." She said the name in English. "I prefer that to the barbarian custom of calling a woman by the name of her husband."

"And your own name, madam?" he asked in English.

"I keep it for my private life, of which this is not part."

Jesse suspected that putting him in his place had also improved her temper. "Dr. Chow knows why we're here, but he hasn't had time to tell me. If you'd do me the kindness . . ."

He was careful not to look at Lung. It would be undignified to gloat.

"This afternoon one of our people was traveling with a message from the town of Charleston. As he followed the river, he saw what he thought was a bundle of clothing at the foot of a tree. When he approached, he saw it was a girl. A Chinese girl," China Mary added sharply. "She was dead—her throat had been cut."

And Lung thought he ought to be involved in this?

"The barbarians will not look further into such a crime. But we must know if there is danger yet to come."

"Where is the girl now?" Lung asked.

"At the—" Jesse didn't recognize the word she used. "Her friends wish her to be prepared for the funeral soon."

"We will go immediately." Lung bowed, and Jesse did the same.

When they turned to go, Jesse saw the two Chinese men in dark clothes who stood one on each side of the doorway. They were so silent, he'd never realized they were there. Now they opened the doors, and Jesse followed Lung into the hall. The maidservant smiled and bowed, led them to the front door and handed Jesse his hat, and they passed back out into the night, and the West. Lung pulled the silk cap off and stuffed it back in his pocket.

"Lung, you're the doctor," Jesse said as he caught up with him. "Do I really have to be there when you examine the body?"

"It will do you no harm."

"You'll be sorry if I throw up."

"No, I will be sorry if you faint." Lung stopped in the fitful light of a torch and gripped Jesse's shoulder. "Jesse, I need your help in this. Even untrained and unwilling, you have strengths I will not set aside."

"You think this is . . ."

Lung stepped back and folded his arms.

"That . . . the thing we talked about."

"You are trying to make me hit you."

"You do, and see how much help you get."

Lung sighed. "Yes, I think this is something . . . 'scientific.' I am nearly sure of it. Knowing that, will you assist me?"

"I've got no notion what to do or how to do it, but yes. But I meant it about the throwing up."

"I will see that you have a basin." By the torchlight Jesse saw Lung's face relax.

As they started off again, Jesse asked, "Why's China Mary so concerned, or are you usually the Hop-town coroner?"

"We are always wary. But there is talk against us in the town—because of your severed arm, I am sorry to say."

"What?"

Lung shrugged. "The firecrackers."

"Good God. Anyone can buy firecrackers."

"These matters are rarely reasonable. A dead girl

could be the first of many attacks. The community must be prepared."

The building they approached had been a miner's cabin, or possibly had been built to pass as one, with board-and-batten walls and a tin roof. At the front door, a black paper banner lifted gently in the night breeze; its gold lettering caught the light of the kerosene lamp beside the entrance.

Before they reached it, Lung turned right and led Jesse to a side door. He could hardly see it in the dark between the buildings. Lung knocked, and the door opened.

A small, well-dressed Chinese man let them into a hallway.

"The girl?" said Lung.

The little man replied very quickly and bowed a great deal. Jesse missed most of what he said, but his expression and even his bowing was solemn. The undertaker, Jesse realized.

The little man turned and called what might have been a name. A Chinese woman in a cheap western gown and wrap rose from a chair down the hall and hurried up to them. Her nose and her downcast eyes were red.

"Answer all of this wise doctor's questions," the undertaker ordered. The woman cast a frightened glance up at Lung. She was younger than Jesse had first thought.

"Do not be afraid," Lung said. "You are very brave to be here, and I am grateful. You were a friend of the dead girl's?"

"Cha Ye, yes. We were at the house of Mrs. Cray. Some of the houses will not have Chinese girls, but Mrs. Cray says that if a man likes it, it is her business to have it. If a Chinese man comes to Mrs. Cray's with money, he is welcome."

So the girls were prostitutes. And Mrs. Cray might be open-mindedness personified, but that hadn't kept Cha Ye safe.

"When did you last see Cha Ye?"

"Yesterday, after dinner. A man came to the parlor, and though we were all beautiful and smiled at him, he liked her best."

"A Chinese man?"

"Oh, no, a big-nose." She must have seen Jesse's eyebrows go up; she blushed and hid behind her hands. "A white."

Lung shot Jesse a grin and went on. "Had you seen him before? Do you know his name?"

The girl shook her head. "Mrs. Cray called him 'sir' and 'the gentleman.' She calls them by their names when she knows them."

"What was his appearance?"

The girl frowned. "Like a white."

Lung took a deep breath and let it out. "Was he old or young? Tall or short? Fat or thin?"

"Not so old. Tall, maybe, for a big-nose. Dirt-colored hair, and a little dirt-colored moustache." She curled her lip. "Not so good a moustache, so I think maybe he is not very manly. Ugly white eyes."

"Light-colored eyes."

She nodded.

"Did he show interest in any other girl?"

"Only in Cha Ye and me."

If a Chinese prostitute disappeared, only the Chinese would ask after her. A white whore's disappearance would be looked into.

"Did you see the man leave?"

"Yes. He was very loud after, downstairs, saying he had made Cha Ye happy, and she would need to rest. While he talked, he was laughing always. It made him sound stupid."

Lung looked at Jesse and shrugged. "What then?"

"He paid double, so Mrs. Cray was happy. He drank two whiskeys." She frowned. "I made him drink, but Mrs. Cray said the money was for Cha Ye, because he was her customer. Cha Ye would have shared with me." Her eyes filled with tears.

"When did you know that Cha Ye was not in the house?"

"Today, at midday. I went to wake her. She was not there."

"But her window was open," Jesse said, in Chinese.

The girl stared at him, her mouth open. "Yes, it was."

"Were things in the room broken, or upset, or out of order?"

The girl shook her head.

"Did you smell anything strange?"

When the girl shook her head she gave him a look she probably reserved for people who talked to themselves on the street.

"Thank you," Lung said. "You have helped your friend's ghost to rest."

"She will not haunt me?"

"You will not be troubled."

The girl bowed low, awkward with her western skirts. Then she scurried past and out the door.

"We can find her again if we have more questions," Lung said.

"Should I talk to the madam?"

"Do you think she knows more than the girl does?"

Jesse thought back over the story. "Less, probably."

"Then you will have to stay and face the unpleasantness." Lung opened the door and went in, and Jesse followed.

Smoke hung under the ceiling like a layer of cloud, and plumed upward from a thicket of joss sticks on a bench in the corner. Under the sweet burnt smell of the incense Jesse could still catch the slaughterhouse odor it covered. A fly blundered through the air before him, drugged by smoke.

The girl lay on a wooden table in the middle of the room. She wore a pink silk wrapper that closed up the front with ribbons. The silk was stained red-brown all down the front. Above it the girl's face was gray-white, and the wound under her chin was blue-black and white-lipped.

Her eyes were open. Lung closed them. Then he pressed the skin of her throat, so the wound opened slightly.

Jesse didn't need the basin, after all; he made it out the door in time. Afterward he stood leaning against the wall, breathing, thinking how good it was to be able to do that.

Lung looked up when he came back in the room, and asked a question with his eyebrows.

"All over," Jesse assured him.

"Bullet wounds don't trouble you."

"Of course they do. Just not as much as *that*." He jerked his head at the body on the table. "What do you know so far?"

"Either her murderer was right-handed, or left-handed and made the cut from behind."

"How can you tell?" If he could deal with it on the level of details, it would be easier.

"The difference in the depth of the wound from one side to the other."

He swallowed hard. Details weren't much help after all. "What else?"

"You were not gone long. Come and help."

Jesse stiffened his spine and approached the table. The girl's face and throat were bruised. The ribbon at the neck of her wrapper was still tied, but one end had torn away from the silk. The blood—an unimaginable quantity; how much was there in a human being?—was dry and stiff down the front of her, and kept the gown from completely following the contours of her body. There were smears of dirt on the front and hem, and a long three-cornered tear in the thin fabric. The girl's feet were caked with orange-brown dirt, and there were cuts on the soles.

"Look," Lung said, and pointed to the front of the skirt of the wrapper. It had little holes and tears in it, two groups of them on either side of the opening. Under the blood Jesse thought he could see grains of something as well.

Lung untied the lower ties of the gown with gentle fingers and drew it back to reveal the girl's knees. There was sand embedded in the skin.

Jesse looked at her feet again. Other than the cuts, there was no blood on them.

"Do you have a knife?" Lung asked.

Jesse handed over his pocketknife. Lung used it to cut away the ruined gown. "Bruises on her arms and her wrists. She was bound." Lung leaned over the girl's face, examined the corners of her mouth. "But not gagged, I think."

Jesse looked down at the girl, but what he was trying to see had happened perhaps twenty-four hours earlier. "Her customer's job was to drug her and open the window. He wouldn't have dressed her afterward—"

"Possibly she never undressed."

"Either he didn't get what he'd paid Mrs. Cray for, or he didn't insist on viewing the merchandise."

"Then he left," Lung said, "and someone else took the girl from her room. She woke at last, which required her to be bound. But by then she was not where anyone would hear her cries."

"Left-handed," Jesse said.

"Pardon?"

"She was killed on her knees. Her killer stood behind her."

"She might only have fallen to her knees as she was taken to the place where she was killed."

"There's no blood on her feet. She wasn't standing when—" He could almost see a man pulling the stumbling girl barefoot down the riverbank, forcing her to her knees, yanking the neck of her wrapper open, tearing the ribbon. She was screaming, pleading in broken English. He stood behind her, gripped her hair, forced her head back. His face was . . . What face? What did he look like? Jesse tried to step forward, to call out, so the man would look up. But he seemed to be stepping back instead; the man and the girl receded—

"Jesse?" Lung's voice came from nearby.

He was in the undertaker's back room, breathing hard, and the girl was dead on the table.

"It is already done," Lung said.

Jesse rubbed his eyes. "My God, it didn't feel like it."

"It was not what is called a crime of passion, was it?"

"You're asking me?"

"You saw it."

Jesse shook his head angrily. "I imagined it."

Lung lowered his head and glared at Jesse from under his eyebrows. "I will explain the nature of your abilities again, if there is the smallest chance it will make you wise."

"But I did imagine it." Honesty compelled him to add, "I started by imagining it."

"Could you see anything of the murderer?"

"No. Not much. I *thought* it was a man, but I might have assumed that."

Lung turned back to the girl. "She was the victim

because she was easily taken, and would not be missed by anyone of consequence. She died because someone required a death."

"Why?"

"That cannot be answered here. Fetch your horse and meet me at my home." Lung turned abruptly and went to the door. The latch resisted him, and he wrenched it open with more force than it needed. Then he strode off down the hall.

Jesse hadn't realized until it was gone how much leashed anger there had been in the room.

Underlying every philosophy was the inevitability of death. The moral and ethical questions, the search for right living, the weighing of the evidence of one's senses—it all came down to how fast, how far, and which way you could run before you hit the end of the rope.

Of course, it wasn't until he was diagnosed with consumption that Doc had understood that. A death sentence had a way of focusing one's thinking. Until then he'd studied other men's philosophies and believed himself to be partaking of great thoughts. Now Doc had less interest in greatness and more in the length of the rope.

Presiding over the Oriental's faro table, he was reminded of his own philosophy. He'd left Georgia choosing glory over length of days. Did glory consist of sitting all night in rooms stinking of cigars and stale beer, listening to bad music badly played and rough voices shouting nothing worth hearing, drinking one watery julep after another and taking fools' money?

Perhaps not. But all that would certainly work against length of days. He was half true to his ideals, at least.

Doc studied the faces of the men crowded up to the faro table. Desperate, eager, predatory, sullen, happy-drunk; whatever their attitude, whatever system they played or what fabulous run of luck they thought they were on, their immediate destinies were the same. They were here to lose their money to him.

More precisely, to lose to the dealer as the representative of the bank, that faceless concept on which losers could vent their spleen. The bank itself, of course, was a polite fiction. The bank was Wyatt Earp, who owned the gambling in the Oriental, and Doc was his surrogate.

"Place your bets, gentlemen," Doc ordered. Markers hit the felt like hailstones. He noted their placement with detached interest. George Parsons, that old woman, bet king, queen, and ace to win. He'd once tried to explain to Doc why that was the perfect bet, but Doc hadn't gotten much out of it except that Parsons was pretty much on the go but could still add. John Dunbar bet the deuce and the trey to lose. Dunbar always said he played for fun. Well, he had it to throw away, but that wasn't Doc's idea of a good time. The young miner, Pinkham, laid one chip down for the six and the nine, and stared intently at the painted cards on the board. Cleaned out, Doc was sure. He could go to the Devil or not as he pleased; it was none of Doc's business.

He was aware of Whitey Martin at the casekeeper, ready to tally the cards as they came out of the dealing box, and Frank Leslie on his left working lookout. Doc could keep track of the betting himself—if he'd stay sober. But that wasn't the way the game was played, thank God.

He dealt the soda out of the box and onto its spot on the table beside him. A murmur rose from the players at the sight of the seven of hearts under it. "Seven to

lose, and . . ." He dealt the seven onto the soda card.
Ten of clubs underneath. ". . . ten to win." Someone
had bet the ten to lose, he saw; there was a coppered
marker on the ten card painted on the table. And someone had bet lucky seven to win. Not so lucky, after all.
No winners on those cards.

The three of clubs came off the deck next, so Dunbar won some money and left his marker where it was.
A red five after it, and another payout, since someone
had bet odd to win.

He continued to deal the cards. Martin moved beads
on the casekeeper, and Leslie droned out the bets, win
or lose. He'd been here for four hours, and it seemed
like weeks. Unless he passed out drunk (not likely) or
someone got mad and shot him (possible), he'd be
here 'til dawn.

Kate had stood at his elbow for a while, earlier in
the night. He liked knowing she was there; he imagined he could feel her warmth on whichever side she
stood, could smell her jasmine scent over the saloon
reek. She'd been restless, though, and had wandered
away after an hour. He wondered where she'd found to
go, and resolved not to ask.

"Gentlemen, time to call the turn," he said, to remind the hard drinkers that he was about to show the
last two bettable cards in the deck. There was a flurry
of markers on the board.

Into them spun a gold dollar, like a goldfinch in a
flock of sparrows. It fell just shy of the high card spot.
Doc frowned and looked up to see where it had come
from.

"You might want to use a marker like the common
folk do," he said to John Ringo.

"Just wanted to get your attention," Ringo replied,
with a smile that involved only his mouth. "Money

usually works." He wore town clothes—coat, waist-coat, and silk tie—and his hair and moustache were fresh-trimmed.

Doc laughed. He wondered what Ringo would say if he knew Doc was glad to see him. Hatred drove away boredom. "Wait until I've finished with these gentlemen, and I am at your service." He turned back to the dealing box and, in quick succession, revealed the last cards. "King to lose, trey to win, and ace hock."

Groans around the table: no one had called it cor-rectly. Doc collected the bets, picked up Ringo's dol-lar, and dropped it in with the rest. Then he rose and smiled at his flock, and waved Frank Leslie into the dealer's chair.

"My time is usually worth more," Doc said to Ringo as they moved away from the table, "but I'll let you have it at the friends and kin rate."

Ringo's lips twitched. Doc thought that meant he might be genuinely amused. "I may be a better friend to you than you think."

"Quite likely; you couldn't be a worse one." Doc picked up one of the fresh decks from the bar and snapped the paper off. He might want something to do with his hands if the conversation went on long.

Ringo flicked a speck of lint off one of his grosgrain lapels. A damned nice coat, Doc observed, and new; and a pearl-and-garnet pin glowed in the folds of Ringo's tie.

"Why, how respectable you look, Mr. Ringo. People do say your . . . business is thriving."

"They'll say what they please, won't they?" Ringo looked around the room, narrow-eyed. "I don't see the Earp brothers in the house."

"Were you looking for a particular one?"

"It's safe to say I never have a use for any of the Earps."

"They would speak just as highly of you, I'm sure. They're all elsewhere at the moment."

"Good. They're what I want to talk to you about." Ringo pulled out a chair at a little table in the back meant for customers bent on two-handed games.

And so this was. "You understand there are things you can say about the Earps that I will not listen to politely."

Ringo nodded. "I don't come to pick a quarrel. Let's call this a truce, for as long as we're sitting here."

Doc took the other chair. "Truce it is. Send in your herald." He shuffled the cards without taking his eyes off Ringo.

Ringo flagged the bartender, and a minute later drinks arrived: another julep for Doc, and Old Overholt for Ringo.

Doc eyed the prearranged refreshments. "You were pretty sure I'd say yes."

Ringo shrugged. "Just because I don't like you don't mean I don't know you. I'd even say I can't afford not to."

"Then you know I am not susceptible to flattery." He was, though. He liked to be considered a worthy opponent.

Ringo drank off half the contents of his glass and set it down with a click. "I came to warn you."

Doc answered that by raising his eyebrows.

"Whatever else you and I are, we're honest men by our lights. If we're going to do a man down, we'll do it to his face in daylight."

"I suppose that's something to congratulate ourselves on."

"Not everyone in town can say the same."

Doc laughed and fanned the cards. "I am shocked.

Shocked, I say. This is mighty entertaining, but you might want to come to some point or other."

"I'm offering you a chance to throw in with me."

That stilled Doc's hands in sheer surprise. "Well. Why would I do a thing like that?"

"Because the . . . the people you travel with now are dirty. And worse."

"Worse than dirty."

Ringo looked down at his glass, and suddenly tossed the rest down his throat. "There're unnatural things being done in this town. You wouldn't believe half what I know."

Doc squared the cards and leaned back in his chair. "Oh, I am wonderfully gullible." He remembered Wyatt on all fours behind the Redfields' barn, the cold power he'd felt from him when he'd confronted him later. And his own troubled dreams. But how would Ringo know any of that?

"It's a poison, what they're doing. And you're part of it, however hard you try to keep your hands clean. They'll use you, and leave you to take the blame and burn in hell for it."

With an effort, Doc began to lay out cards. "And I would be better off if I joined you in stealing other men's cattle?"

Ringo flushed, and a muscle stood out in his jaw. "By God, you're bound up in worse than that. I'd treat you fair, at least, and not like a dog."

"And what would be the advantage to you? Other than the fact that Wyatt would have one friend the less."

"I'd have one friend more. A sharp one. The only people in town who ain't afraid of you are the Earps, and that's because they think they run you." Ringo leaned across the table. "Stand with me, and you'll be a partner and your own man."

Doc met Ringo's cold, straight gaze—wonderfully

like Wyatt's, in its way. "Mr. Ringo, I thank you for your concern for my reputation and my soul. But I have chosen my ground."

"Time comes you regret that, you remember my offer."

Doc looked down at the cards he'd dealt face up on the table. "I always wonder why people will gamble. They seem to think the cards are angels, sent down to Earth to do them a kindness."

Ringo rose from his chair. Judging by his expression, he thought Doc had drunk too much. Not enough, never enough.

"The truth is," Doc went on, "the cards hate us, no matter what we do, no matter what we give them. They hate us because they're trapped in there, and we're free, changing all manner of things, taking charge of the world. They can't do that. They can only hold our luck, and twist it around, and ruin us for spite. Because we have everything they want and can't ever get." Doc leaned back and smiled up at Ringo. "If you want to give good advice to someone, tell that to the poor souls around the faro table. They're more likely to be able to use it."

Ringo stood rigid for an instant. Then he turned and pushed out through the crowd to the door.

Doc studied the cards on the table before him. What had made Ringo come to him, now or ever? He ran his fingertip lightly over his spade flush and meditated on darkness, and swords, and one's life in someone else's keeping.

⚜ 12 ⚜

Even for Hoptown, it was too damned early. Jesse rode Sam down Second Street past ground-floor windows dark behind their wooden shutters, second-floor windows with only a rare candle burning. A hanging sign squeaked once on its hook and fell silent, as if rolling over in bed.

In the east the night sky seemed to be thinning at its edge, tarnished silver instead of ink. He could make out the shapes of things, the contrast of light railings against dark walls, walls against the light dust. But deep darkness knocked the corners off, lied about distances, turned passageways between buildings into shallow embrasures and embrasures into passageways.

Jesse felt vulnerable, itchy between the shoulder blades. It had been years since the world had looked like this to him. Had looked, in fact, the way it did to normal people. Had he minded, back then, not being able to see in the dark? Probably he had. He'd certainly minded when, after falling off a river ferry in Kansas and being fished out again, he had found his eyes painfully sensitive to light. A doctor in San Francisco hadn't seen anything wrong with him. Then Jesse had been afraid the effect was a hallucination; after all, his sister had gone mad.

Lung had told him it wasn't, of course. Jesse had ignored him: even very clever men could be fools now and then, he'd thought, not noticing that it applied to himself as well.

His eyes had returned to normal, but Jesse rather regretted the timing. Tombstone didn't feel like the sort of place one should be blind in at night.

He wanted eggs, bacon, biscuits, a cup of strong coffee, and at least three hours of sleep. Sam seemed dozy beneath him, head low, ears lax on either side of his black forelock. Grooming and saddling him at the livery had given Jesse a chance to come to terms with their errand, but one didn't, it seemed, take every chance one was given.

He turned the corner and saw a long-legged black riding mule tethered to Lung's porch post. There was a pack roll tied behind the saddle. How long were they going to be at this?

As he rode up, the mule swiveled its ears and turned to look at him. Jesse could make out its molasses-colored muzzle and the rings around its eyes. Sam gave a little chuckle of greeting, and the mule stamped.

Lung stepped out his front door, a roll of something under his arm. He looked up and down the street with what, even at a distance in the dark, seemed like brittle cheerfulness. "What a beautiful day!" he said, shockingly loud in the sleeping street.

So they were playacting. Jesse had no idea why, but he stepped into a role. "It can't be. It isn't day yet. Do you have any coffee?"

"The fresh air will wake you. If not, we shall beg some for you in Saint David." Lung tied the roll he carried onto the back of Jesse's saddle.

"Mormons don't drink coffee."

"Even in Saint David, I am sure there are unbelievers." Lung untied the mule and swung easily into the saddle.

Lung wore ordinary drover's clothes: an old brown sack coat, striped cotton shirt, woolen vest, pants, and boots. There was a dark felt hat hanging by a lanyard from the saddle horn.

It seemed wrong. It didn't look wrong; dressed this way, Lung looked more Indian than Chinese—almost like the Apache scouts who rode with the cavalry. But he *was* Chinese. As far as Jesse had been able to tell, that meant more to the Chinese than being German or Italian or Irish meant to other immigrants. Clothes, food, neighbors, customs, religion—if you were Chinese, everything was Chinese, and stayed that way.

Yet Lung had seemed unconcerned about the loss of his queue, which no respectable Chinese man would be. It was true that Lung wasn't perfectly respectable—he'd befriended Jesse, after all. Jesse pondered a way to broach the subject.

Lung crammed the hat on and grinned out from under the wide brim, as if he were going to a masquerade and was particularly proud of his costume. If there had been a moment when Jesse could say something, it was gone. He settled for, "Nice sombrero."

"Thank you. How well can you see it?"

"Is it *not* a nice sombrero?"

"Very. How are your eyes?"

Jesse wrestled with a surge of illogical resentment. "They're fine."

Lung reined the mule closer. "I told you that your sight would be cured when you no longer struggled against your nature. When did it happen?"

"Maybe a week ago."

"Ah," said Lung, a world of self-satisfaction in the syllable.

Jesse scowled at Lung, then relented. "I miss the night vision."

Lung cocked his head. "Summon it, then."

"What?"

"You will learn how." Lung turned the mule's nose to the Benson Road.

Jesse waited until they were well past the outlying houses to say, "We're going to the river?"

"We are."

"It's thataway." He jerked his head to the left.

Lung's artificial good cheer was gone. "The murderer may already have removed the signs of his presence from the place. If so, we will have ridden far for nothing."

"But in case he hasn't, we're trying to get there unnoticed."

"Exactly so." Lung's mule broke into a trot.

A few minutes later they left the road and headed west, toward the line of cone-shaped hills and the rolling country that circled Tombstone like a moat. They could have taken the Charleston road, blending in with traffic. But there was no reason not to be careful. As the sun rose behind his back, Jesse watched the fine detail of the land grow back up around him: creosote bush, sage, and tough high desert grasses; the shadow of a rock cast on a bare patch of ground; a lizard motionless on the rock. Prickly poppy waved its papery white cups, and globe mallow stretched clustered spires of orange against the green-brown landscape of spring. If it wasn't for their grim errand, he would have been enjoying himself.

They headed up the slope toward a little pass between the hills, dodging spiked buggy whips of ocotillo as they went. "How long will this take?" Jesse asked. "I'd had plans." Like, say, talking Mildred Benjamin into having dinner with him. He wanted very much to know what she was like with her guard lowered. So far they hadn't met under the best of conditions for that.

"Mmm," Lung replied.

"Couldn't we, I don't know, conjure up the girl's ghost and ask her who did it?"

Lung looked scornful. "Ghosts are a peasant superstition."

"At the undertaker's, you said—"

Lung gave a dismissive snort.

Jesse resolved not to offer any more suggestions.

They came out of the hills at last. Before them the ground dropped steadily to the San Pedro River, then stretched out flat, a sea of shivering pale grass, to the high, ragged Huachucas and the Mustang range. Jesse could see the line of intermittent green that marked the San Pedro and the bottom of the valley, the line of mesquite *bosque* and ground that would be marsh when the summer rains came. It was a sharp contrast to the subtle colors of the hills they'd just traveled. But it was a broken line. From the rise they stood on, Jesse could see the smoke and dust rising from the town of Charleston to the south, and from the stamping mills at Contention northward. North of that, he knew, where the eastern banks rose above the river, were more mills, and the endless roar of giant hammers crushing rock.

Dark satanic mills, he thought suddenly, and was startled. They were neither dark nor evil; they were just what happened to silver ore after it came out of the ground. They were part of the architecture of prosperity. Was it the business they were on that made him think dark thoughts? He couldn't shake the idea, though, that there was a shadow threading the hills that the clear, clean morning couldn't wipe away.

With a downhill slope ahead, Sam was prepared for more than a trot after a soft life in town. He was obeying Jesse's hands, but only with considerable head-tossing and bit-mouthing. The mule cut a path through the grass, and it sprang back to hiss against Sam's legs as they followed.

"Does that long-eared coat rack of yours canter?" Jesse asked.

"He knows better than to waste his strength. Mules are more intelligent than horses."

Jesse rode up next to Lung again. "Few things are more intelligent than Sam. Including most people I know."

"Sam was a Confucian scholar in a life long past."

Jesse stared at the spot between Sam's flicking ears directly over his brain. He felt suddenly odd about holding the reins. "Is that true?"

A grin split Lung's face. "What a shame you will not always believe everything you are told."

"You," Jesse declared, "are the biggest son of a bitch who ever drank tea."

"Speaking of tea . . ." Lung reined the mule into a thicket of mesquite and slid off. He untied a leather-covered bottle from his saddle and held it out to Jesse.

Jesse dismounted, opened the bottle, and sniffed. "You couldn't have handed me this back in town?" He took a good-sized swallow of strong lukewarm tea and passed it back to Lung.

"We were in haste." Lung drank, and sat on his heels in the freckling shade of the mesquite.

"You know where on the river she was found?"

Lung nodded. "I spoke to the man who found her."

Jesse looked down the slope of the valley, to the line of green that wandered to both horizons. "How did he just happen to find her?"

Lung pursed his lips and frowned at the sky.

"Never mind—it was something illegal that involved following the riverbank, and you're sworn to secrecy."

"That was very good."

"I've seen that expression before. When we get to the place, what are we looking for?"

Lung stretched his hands and studied them. "I would rather not say."

"Can you at least say why you brought me?"

"You may be useful."

Jesse sighed. "I'll do my best to brighten the corner where I am."

Lung corked the bottle with a smack of his palm. For a long moment he stared out at the mountains across the valley. Jesse couldn't read anything from his profile, but he was certain something was simmering under that hat. Something about the dead girl, perhaps?

But when Lung turned, Jesse had an instant's warning—it wasn't the girl. "I am treating you like a fool, and proposing to use you as if you were a chisel or a rake. Once you would have been offended."

"That was when I thought it was personal. Now I know you're just naturally ornery."

Lung shook his head. "No, listen to me. You have changed. Why do you allow others to direct the course of your life?"

"Just because I let you boss me around doesn't mean everyone gets the privilege."

"You have been 'bossed around' by circumstance since you arrived in Tombstone. You were not like this before."

Jesse tried to suppress his annoyance, but he heard it in his voice when he said, "Before what?"

"In San Francisco, you chose your own path. Not always wisely, I admit, but . . ."

"You're a fine one to complain," Jesse snapped. "I had a path picked out. I was on my way to Mexico. Now look at me."

Lung did, sideways and with a question in it.

"You did take credit for getting me here, if you recall."

"I do not seem to have got the person I thought I called."

"What's that supposed to mean?"

Lung frowned at the dirt between his boots. "The

old Jesse would not be waiting to be shown what to do."

"For God's sake, Lung, what choice do I have?"

"Do you not wish to know the nature of the thing that troubles your dreams? Or even the identity of the sorcerer who threatened you?"

And how did Lung know about his dreams? "No. I want to take care of whatever you got me here to deal with, so I can leave."

"They are the same matter. I thought you knew."

He was caught in the spiderweb of this town. He felt it when he'd arrived. He should have paid more attention. "Fine. Show me what it is, so I can do it."

Lung lifted his hands, then abruptly, angrily, let them drop. "You want me to show you what is already in front of you. How do I do that?"

"You could start by sounding less like a circus fortune-teller. If I'm so damned blind, I'm no use to you. I'll just be getting back to my own business."

"Breaking horses? That is not your business."

Like a blow, the memory: standing over the fallen horse in Earp's corral, and realizing that there were ropes around his own body, around his mind, a force that made him fight himself to a standstill. A force that could master him.

Another blow: his sister in her hospital bed, broken by this thing. Unlike the horse taming, it didn't care if it destroyed what it mastered. He felt sick with fury and despair.

"So I should take my destiny into my own hands, and do what you tell me?" Jesse stood and dusted off his trousers. "You can't have it both ways, Lung." He walked over to Sam, who raised his head from his grazing and pointed both ears at him.

"Where are you going?" Lung called behind him.

"I'm going to the river with you and doing whatever

damned thing needs doing. Then I'm going back to Tombstone, getting a night's sleep, and riding on in the morning." His life might not be his own, but he could at least wrench it away from this place. Not seeing Mrs. Benjamin. That caused him a pang. But he couldn't stay.

And then what? What could he do but wait for the power to ride him where it pleased? Lung expected him to pick his own direction, but how could he, knowing this thing might pick another, and make him take it? He felt like a plague carrier. He needed to go before he spread the infection.

By the time Jesse was mounted, Lung was there, tying the bottle back in place on his saddle. He swung up on the mule and urged it off at a canter. Jesse followed.

They rode in silence until they passed out of the shadows of the hills, and their own shadows were shortening before them. Jesse lost sight of the river as they dropped down to lower ground.

"I apologize," Lung said.

"What?"

"You are correct. I had no right to complain that you let others direct your life, when I was one of those others."

Jesse could remember fewer than a handful of times when he'd heard Lung apologize, and all of those had been demanded of him. He was still angry, but not, he realized, with his companion.

"Perhaps," Lung added after a pause, "it is because I envy you."

Surprise made Jesse tense in the saddle, and Sam tossed his head. "You what? Why?"

"You are expected to choose your own way. Your duty to family and community come second to your duty to yourself."

That wasn't entirely true. But Jesse only said, "As I recall, you've always done pretty much as you pleased."

Lung smiled crookedly at the mule's ears. "And it has always pleased me to be Chinese."

Jesse opened his mouth to ask what that meant. Something in Lung's expression made him say instead, "I expect I'm driving you crazy."

Lung shrugged. "I am used to that."

"Very funny."

They rode on in something evolving toward peace.

At present, the San Pedro River was a narrow, quiet body, flowing along the bottom of its bed in the orange earth. The trees cast a broad line of breathing shade on either side and rose above it in places like flowers in a vase. But Jesse could see the marks the river had made in previous floods: snags of branches and trunks flung up on the banks far from the water's edge, tumbled stones pushed to higher ground, now dry until the rainy season. The trees would have their feet in swift water then.

They followed the edge of the *bosque* north until they struck a wash, and followed it down the slope through thickening mesquite scrub. Lung stopped when it got too dense for the mule to pass, and slid down from the saddle. He looped the reins to a good-sized branch and unbuckled his cinch. Their mounts would have shade and grazing here—and they'd be out of sight from almost anywhere.

"I take it we'll be here a while," Jesse said as he dismounted.

Lung shrugged. "That will depend on what we find. But I would rather pamper this creature than try to ride him home when he has a bad opinion of me."

Jesse made Sam comfortable. "Where's the scene of the crime?"

"I believe we are just above it."

A big cottonwood leaned its boughs out over the mesquite here. Between the scrub, hidden from all angles but one, Jesse saw a winding narrow course of dry grass. It ducked under one of the tree limbs and disappeared into gray-green gloom toward the river. Probably a smugglers' trail. Jesse waved at it. "After you."

Lung quirked an eyebrow at him and started down toward the river.

Jesse went slowly, picking his way down the bank, studying the trees and the ground ahead for blood. There would have been enough to be hard to miss.

Ahead of him, Lung stopped. He must have found it—

Ice closed over Jesse's head. He couldn't breathe. Then the feeling passed, and he was on his hands and knees in the grass. Lung crouched over him. Lung's lips moved, but nothing came out. No, it was that Jesse couldn't hear him. He shook his head hard, and realized that Lung was saying Jesse's name.

"Don't tell me," Jesse said when he got his breath back. "We're there."

"What was it?"

"Do you remember when the bridge plank let go and you fell in the Russian River?"

"Ah." Lung helped him to his feet. "Do you need to be thawed?"

"Just fine now." It wasn't, of course. Not as long as something like that could happen to him without warning. But it would be worse if he didn't know what was happening to him, and was surrounded by people who didn't believe it was happening at all—if this had come to him as it had to Lily.

There was no sign anyone had been here since the girl was found. Dark dried blood stained the ground and the grass and the roots of the tree she'd been killed under. Jesse felt as if tiny things were crawling over the skin of his arms and back. He had no idea if it was simple revulsion or something more.

He searched for marks, fallen buttons or scraps of cloth, whatever might hint at the murderer's identity. Lung, meanwhile, was behaving oddly.

He stood behind the tree and craned his neck around it, peering through the scrub first upriver, then down, then back across the valley. Then he strode off down the riverbank, stopped, and squinted back at the tree. He took what looked like a small carpenter's pro-tractor from a pocket of his jacket, held it before him, and fiddled with it. Then he sprang up the bank and through the trees. Jesse could hear him just beyond the cottonwood and mesquite, moving back and forth.

When he came back to the riverbank his face was grim.

"What is it?" Jesse asked.

Lung sat heavily on a fallen tree trunk and frowned at Jesse. Or rather, as if Jesse were something else en-tirely, something Lung didn't like the looks of. Finally he said, "It is difficult to explain. In China, it is under-stood that the fortunes of a family may be made or de-stroyed by where they choose to build their house, or where their ancestors are buried."

"They can't do much about that last, can they?"

"Oh, yes. Everyone knows the location of his fam-ily's graves. The wealthy hire sorcerers to travel the country in disguise, to find the most auspicious sites for graves. Poorly located relatives may be moved to better burial places to improve one's luck. And of course, one's own grave must be carefully chosen. But the details are not important here."

Jesse itched to ask Lung if he had his burial spot picked out. But he was afraid teasing would derail Lung's explanation. "You did say it would be hard to make me understand."

Lung gave a little embarrassed grin. "It is a lifetime's study, and not, I am afraid, mine. But it is the study of the power in the earth itself, and its effect on human lives. The flow of that power can be read in the relationships of rivers to mountains, the shapes of bodies of water, the direction of light and wind, the presence of one element next to another. A sorcerer who studies these things can use the earthly power as his own."

"Wait, wait—are you working up to saying that the person who killed that girl has studied this stuff? Because I don't think many barbarians—I mean, whites—"

"He may have. But it is more likely that he is guided not by study but by instinct. The land itself has taught him, because he can feel the movement of power in it. He need not measure and observe the elements, as I did moments ago. He need only feel, and act."

"In my experience, education beats instinct every time."

"I hope not, because I cannot possibly educate you well enough to defeat this person."

"Oh."

"I have met others of this kind. They follow the gold and silver strikes, because they can feel the metals speaking to them. Often they do not know what they feel or how to use it. They say they have a 'hunch.' However they explain it to themselves, they will follow the voice of the ore and find it."

"Then all these fellows get rich?"

Lung shook his head. "If, as you did, they deny their gift, they will move from hunch to hunch, from one strike to the next. They believe they seek wealth, but when they get it, they find it is hollow, and they spend or wager it all and set out to search again. What they truly crave is control of the power they feel. But they do not understand what they are, and are helpless to seize what they crave."

Jesse looked over the valley to the line of hills, then back at the bloodstained grass at his feet. "The one who did this. He understands."

"If I have not mistaken the distances and compass points, he is attempting to place a very large area under his command, with Tombstone at its center."

"You're saying this"—Jesse pointed at the blood—"is a claim stake."

A pause; then Lung nodded.

"How do we pull it up?"

"I beg your pardon?"

"If a man marks a claim that isn't his, he'll come back to find his stakes have been pulled. If he made an honest mistake, it's a warning to check his boundaries. If he's not honest—then it's a different kind of warning."

"You are certain, then, that it is not his to claim?"

The idea stopped Jesse's thoughts like a wall.

"Tombstone is full of those who have claimed riches by their strength and skill," Lung continued. "Why should this man not be another? What law forbids it?"

"The one against murdering for gain."

"Then if this man is brought before a judge, there will be justice for him in the court, and punishment if he is guilty?"

Jesse looked down again at the blood on the grass. The killer might get a year in prison, or six months, or nothing. It depended on how the judge felt about whores, Chinese girls, and the killer himself. Meanwhile, whoever he was, he would control this power that Lung talked about. The dead girl would continue to work for her murderer.

"I believe in the rule of law," Jesse said at last. His voice was harsh in his own ears. "The law will deal with the murder. But the other . . . Lung, does getting control of this . . . thing usually call for killing someone?"

"It is not unknown, but it is not the common method." Lung was watching him warily.

"If he'd done it some other way, I'd let his claim stand. But not . . . like this."

"If you undo his work, you are correct—it will warn him."

"I don't even know if it *can* be undone. I was hoping you could do it."

Lung shook his head. "My skills lie elsewhere."

"Can you *tell* me how to do it?"

Again, Lung shook his head.

Back the way they had come, barely visible through the brush, the pointed hills bordered the valley like lace on a tablecloth. Beyond them, out of sight, lay the plateau where Tombstone was growing, sprawling, building, and at its rim lay the Tombstone Hills, studded with mine shafts. Those were the hills he'd dreamed of, sleeping on the cot in Lung's house when he'd first arrived. He'd dreamed he *was* the hills, full of silver—

"Never mind," he said. "I think I know how."

There was a wild, reckless energy in him woven of manic confidence and anger. He sat on a rock and pulled off his boots and socks, then shed his coat and vest. He found himself humming a lively tune in a minor key, and realized it was the heroine's song from the play. *Oh, the cuckoo, she's a pretty bird, she warbles as she flies.*

He sat down cross-legged in a space of bare dry

earth, arm's length from the spilled blood, laid his hands on his knees, and stared at the ground before him. *Talk to me*, he thought.

He felt a fool, even with no one but Lung to see him. Foolish, and angry, and impatient. Only patience availed in taming horses. But he *was* the horse this time. The anger would wear him out. He had to surrender, not fight.

He tried to think the way one does before sleep, the mind skimming its contents, brushing past images and ideas but never grabbing hold of them. Pleasant, undemanding thoughts—last night's play, *not* Mrs. Benjamin, other plays and other theaters he'd seen, the dark red stage curtain in a New York theater that reminded him of a parlor rug in his parents' house, a big chair in that parlor, and China Mary sitting in it—no, that was another chair, or was it?—and her gold filigree nail guards, and the carpet rolled back in her long narrow room to reveal a hole that went down below the foundations of the house, with a carved oak banister and polished stairs—how did the carpet lie flat over that banister, and why didn't people fall into the stairwell when they walked across the carpet?—and he walked down the stairs into cool, stone-scented darkness.

He saw the rough face of volcanic rock at the foot of the stairs, but kept walking. The sparkling black flecks in the stone were the spaces where he would fit himself, expanded and fragmented and still whole. For an instant it resisted him. He claimed the stone, made it his own flesh and wrapped himself in it, and that was the end of resistance.

There was a solidness about it that felt comfortable, right. He was stronger here where he could be stone against stone, all hard, skinless strength. Not skinless, no—his skin was dry in the sun above, but here in his bones was a netting of moisture, water moving drop by drop down to join the aquifer below him and to feed the river itself. Lines and nodes of water, of silver, of copper—

—and something else, that moved in a creeping, unbroken vein. A long loop of it lay like a noose over him, binding, freezing, sealed and stagnant. Near him, very near, he could feel a tangling in the loop, cold against his bones. He didn't think it was supposed to be cold.

The cold gave him a focus for his senses. He thought he would be lost in richness otherwise, the textures of stone and mud and water and sand, the stillness of old limestone, the memory of turbulence imprisoned in igneous rock.

There it was: two strands knotted, throttling each other. One reeked of iron and smoke; the other was poison, carrion, bitter dark. They didn't belong here, twisting through his bones. The knot was wedged in the stone like water frozen in a pipe, crystalline and razor-edged. The edges and the temperature seemed to warn him away, to say, *This is not yours to meddle with.*

This frail, corrupt thing wedged into the stone of him, not his to meddle with? If he'd had a mouth, he'd have laughed.

He possessed the earth around it, and shrugged. It felt like shrugging, anyway: a flexing of stone, a contraction around that brittle shape. It shattered.

The power it had dammed and directed was no longer stagnant. What had been cold was hot enough to melt stone. What had been sluggish roared and plunged. It swept over him, more fluid than water.

Like negative images on a photographer's plate, he saw the storefronts of Allen Street swamped by a running, leaping darkness; he saw dark men with white eyes carrying coffins, a parade of coffins. Pain scorched his frail human hands and arms, drove a long spike into his soft human belly. The flood filled his mind, his nerves, the places where he kept his memory, his name, his self. It was endless. It was drowning him.

He couldn't get free. He was made of inflexible stone, and the force that attacked him was part of him. Once he'd been softer, smaller. He'd had arms and legs, and could run. He'd crawled on the skin of the earth, where he'd been safe from this uncontrollable tide. There, if water closed over his head, he would swim upward, toward light, growing light, until his face broke the surface and the sun would dazzle him blind through his closed eyelids, and his lungs would fill with sweet air—

He coughed, and opened his eyes. Then he had to blink to try to clear them of what felt like a sandstorm's worth of grit. He wanted to rub them, but he seemed to have lost his arms somewhere.

Above him, Lung swore in Chinese.

Jesse was lying on his back on the dirt. He'd been sitting when he started, hadn't he? He tried to sit up, and found his hands and arms attached just where they'd always been, but inclined to tremble embarrassingly when asked to work.

Lung helped prop him up. "Keep your eyes closed," Lung said. "There is dirt in them still."

There was dirt in his eyes? A piece of cloth swept his face. A moment later it came back with water on it, and covered the same ground. He wanted to push it away—was he a baby, that he couldn't wipe his own face? But it was all he could do to keep from falling over.

"Better," Lung said. "You may open your eyes."

The view, when he did, was of himself from the chest down. Clumps of orange-brown dirt lay in every fold of his shirt and trousers. "I look as if I've been buried alive." It came out as a whisper, and scraped his throat.

Lung's silence made him look up. Lung was pale, and wore an expression Jesse had never seen on him before. "And so you should," he said at last.

Jesse looked down again. The soil around him was loose, as if it had been dug. In anger and fear, he asked, "What did you do?"

"Nothing. I watched. You fell backward, and I was concerned. Then you began to sink into the earth, and I was afraid."

He still was. Jesse could see it. "Go on."

"You sank into the earth, and it closed over you. I was too frightened to move, until you were already out of sight. Then I dug into the dirt after you. I dug down until I reached stone. You were not there." Lung swept his hands over his face, and Jesse saw that they were dirty and bleeding and broken-nailed. "I thought you had died."

"How long?" Jesse asked.

"Longer than you could have held your breath."

The earth had its own way of breathing. Stone didn't need lungs. "Did anything happen while I . . ."

"A tremor. Then the soil began to move, as if a corpse were digging itself out of its grave. You rose up through it, lying flat and still. Then the earth closed beneath you."

His strength was coming back. That was nice. He felt as if he ought to say something. The only thing that occurred to him was, "I want a bath."

Lung laughed a little, but it sounded more like hysteria than amusement. "It seems that instinct may be as effective as education, after all."

"No. No, the damned thing nearly killed me." Jesse got himself up onto his knees, and only swayed a little. A bit more effort and he was on his feet. Yes, he was nearly back to normal. If there was any normal, any-more.

He unbuttoned his shirt, wrestled it off over his head, and shook dirt out of it. It would probably never be the same, but he thought he could get it presentable enough to wear back to town.

Lung stood. "You will need to eat." He turned and headed upstream to where they'd left Sam and the mule.

Jesse pulled off his trousers and drawers and shook them, too. He tossed them over a branch, stepped down the bank, and waded into the San Pedro up to his knees.

The water was cool under the trees, and though the river was shrunken, it was relatively clear. In flood, it would be brown with silt chewed out of its bed and flung downstream—

He stiffened; the image was too much like what he'd felt under the earth. Another wave of fear: He had been under the earth. He had been buried alive. He had buried *himself* alive.

He plunged his head into the water and scrubbed hard at his face, dug his fingers into his scalp until it hurt. Only time would wash away the memory of drowning in power, but he'd damned well try to give time some help.

He lay in the streambed and let the water flow around him. The dropping sun blinked and flashed through the breeze-turned leaves. Slowly the fear subsided; not gone, but shrunk to a size he didn't have to struggle against for each breath. Maybe the Baptists were right. Maybe water was grace, and its touch could wash the Devil away.

But it had felt good. He'd felt strong and *right* as part of the bedrock, as if he'd come to a place that had been made just for him.

Not unlike a grave.

Lung thought Jesse could stand up to the force that had destroyed Lily. Jesse would have to tell him he was wrong. No one could. The man who'd murdered the Chinese girl may have felt and used that power, but it had turned his mind already. Jesse wouldn't follow him there, not even to avenge the girl. Not even to help Lung.

He fetched his shirt and scrubbed it as best he could against the river rocks. Then he put his trousers back on, and his boots, and carried the rest of his clothes upstream, in the direction Lung had gone.

Lung sat in a pleasant, open space between three shrubby mesquite trees, above the wash they'd followed to the river. He'd tethered the mule and Sam nearby. He had a tiny fire burning in a nest of rocks, and a tin kettle propped over it. He was staring at something far away, or nothing, more likely.

Jesse took the animals down to the river to drink. When he came back, he spread his shirt over a bush to dry in the sun, and sat across the fire from Lung. That seemed to draw Lung back from wherever he'd gone.

"The water will boil in a moment. Meanwhile, here."

Lung had unrolled a slicker and laid out a sort of Chinese picnic on it. There was sticky rice in a large, primeval-looking leaf; strips of dried, spiced chicken; and preserved vegetables in a stoneware crock.

"Now *that's* magic," Jesse said, but Lung didn't smile.

Instead, he looked away through the mesquite and said, "I thought you were dead. Dead, and I had killed you. You are right to leave. Do it soon, before I have your death on my conscience and your ghost at my heels."

"There's no such thing as ghosts."

Lung turned his gaze on Jesse. *There are ghosts and ghosts*, it replied. "You asked if a death was required, to bind the earth."

"What? Oh."

"If I had said yes, would you have done it?"

"Cold-blooded murder? Of course not!"

Lung's face was tight with pain. "And would you now?"

Cicadas buzzed in the trees around them. A dragonfly rose, shining and improbable, from the river. Suddenly he understood what Lung was asking; understanding swept away his anger. He shut away the memory of living, powerful and whole, in stone. "No, Lung."

The teakettle rumbled gently, and Lung took it off the fire.

"Pass the chicken," Jesse said.

They were both wolf-hungry, but the greatest virtue of the food was that it required attention and requests and comments. It prevented awkwardness. Jesse was pinching up the last rice grains with his chopsticks when Lung asked, "How early will you leave?"

Jesse poured more tea into his tin cup. "No. I won't leave you sitting in this."

"If I must, I will drug you and put you on a train in Tucson."

"Look, Lung—" Jesse glared at the surface of his tea, but no useful words formed there. "I—what I did today, down there—I can't do that again."

"Do you think I wish—"

"Let me finish before you get your hackles up. I can't do that again, but I must be good for something. Whoever killed that girl moved this . . . stuff around as if he were making a sand castle. And he's crazy, which maybe goes without saying. If I leave, what do you plan to do about him?"

"Hide under the bed."

"What?"

"Jesse, the Chinese have survived in this country as the mouse survives in the presence of the fox. If there is nothing I can do but wait this man out, I will wait him out."

"Why don't we both leave? Come on, we'll go to Mexico. You can doctor the president and all the rich *gringos*, and I'll train their horses."

Lung poked the fire. It didn't need poking that Jesse could see, but Lung took his time about it. At last he said, "I am needed here."

"By whom, for what?" But Jesse suspected he already knew.

"If China Mary is the mayor of Hoptown, I am its doctor, its"—Lung smiled crookedly—"medicine man."

"They'll get another one."

"In San Francisco there were many who did what I do. Here, there is only me. In San Francisco I could do as I pleased. I could be a child. Here I must be a man. They need me."

"They" being the Chinese. It was the answer to the question Jesse had asked himself that morning. Lung might live without his queue, dress in western clothes, and eat off a western kitchen table. But at the center of him, where hard choices were made, he was Chinese. He would choose the community over himself.

Lung prodded the fire. "Ask anyone in Hoptown. They work, and save, and send money home to China. They mean to return there, as rich men, or as bones."

"What about you?"

The silence seemed long to Jesse, before Lung said, "I will never return to China."

The words sounded like a door closing. Jesse didn't know if he could open it again, or if he should.

"We had fun in San Francisco," Jesse said.

That made Lung smile again, a real one this time. "We did."

"I can't leave you to grow up all by yourself."

"You could not grow up if you lived to be one hundred."

"Can so."

"Hah."

"Bet you a hundred dollars."

"Where would you get one hundred dollars?"

"That's my problem. Fish or cut bait."

Lung raised an eyebrow. "And who decides if you have grown up?"

"You do."

"Just give me the hundred dollars, then."

Jesse laughed. "All right, we'll take this up again later. Lung, is there a reason why someone can't just find this bastard and throw down on him?"

Lung crooked his eyebrows.

"Call him out." When the eyebrows didn't change, Jesse sighed and said, "Draw a gun and try to be the first one to pull the trigger."

"Ah. By 'someone,' do you mean you? A pity you are not in the habit of shooting people."

"I try not to be," Jesse said, thinking of Arthur Ortega. "And I'd rather the law dealt with the fellow. But if it comes to it—*Can* he . . . be killed?"

Lung swirled the tea in his cup. "It depends."

"Now that's the wrong answer if ever there was one."

"A sorcerer may bind others to his service. Those bound become . . . I do not know the word. They become images of him. The sorcerer draws strength from them, and blows directed at him strike them."

"But he'd have to be trained to do that—to bind people. Wouldn't he?"

Lung snorted. "Loyalty, friendship—are you trained

to feel them? He need not be taught. He may be doing it without knowing."

"Or he may not be doing it at all."

"But if he is, he would be difficult to kill. Certainly he would have to be taken alone, far from his allies."

"Well, let's hope it doesn't come to that."

"It may not. He will know his work here has been undone, and will seek the one responsible. If he finds you before you identify him, he can shoot you in the back and spare you the anguish of dealing with him."

Jesse had the vulnerable feeling between his shoulder blades again.

"Jesse. Leave town."

"No."

Lung banged his cup down in the dirt. "First you go wherever you are pushed, and now this! Is this your stupid way of proving me wrong?"

"Shh." In his bones and flesh, a beating rhythm.

The sound of horses cantering toward the river. His revolver was in his saddle holster, fifteen feet away. Whoever it was might ride past, might not see them. Unless he stood up and went for his pistol. The fire— would they have seen smoke? Hell, go for the pistol. It could be Apaches.

He was halfway to his saddle when Sam neighed. He crossed the last feet of ground, the back of his head buzzing with that target feeling, snatched the pistol, and turned.

The two riders must not have noticed anything until he stood up; they were just now reining their horses in. A gray roan and a sorrel. The sorrel's rider was a woman. In fact, it was Mrs. Benjamin.

He should have bolted for his shirt instead of his pistol.

He avoided meeting Mrs. Benjamin's gaze and turned to the other rider. It was Tom McLaury, and even as Jesse watched his expression changed from surprise to amusement.

"Good afternoon," Jesse said in as ordinary a voice as he could manage, and turned away to holster the pistol. If this damned nonsense of Lung's worked the way it ought, Jesse would be able to sink into the ground right now.

"Nearer evening, really," McLaury said, as if desperate for something innocuous to say. It was true: the sun burned low through the trees on the other side of the river.

Lung popped up like a jack-in-the-box from beside the fire, startling the horses and riders about equally. Jesse used the moment to fetch his shirt. He buttoned it as Lung bowed to the new arrivals, ridiculously low. A mesquite branch scratched at his cropped hair, and he swatted it like a fly, looking offended. If he'd still had his queue, he'd likely have found a way to get it tangled in the thorns.

"Greetings, honorable sir, honorable missy. I make Missa Fox tea. You wantee tea?"

Jesse sighed. "Lung, please don't."

Lung straightened up. If Jesse hadn't been struggling with so many other emotions he'd have laughed out loud to see the grinning idiot expression fall from Lung's face, replaced by a raised eyebrow and a quirk at the corner of his mouth.

Jesse turned to Mrs. Benjamin. She was looking from Jesse to Lung with blank politeness, as if she'd found herself at a stranger's party. "My friend, Chow Lung. Lung, this is Mrs. David Benjamin, and Mr. Tom McLaury."

"Delighted," Lung said, with a perfect, modest bow and a straight face.

Mrs. Benjamin inclined her head, making the veil of her neat little riding hat bob. "Mr. Chow."

How did she know about Chinese family names?
Dear God, she was the perfect woman, and he had no
chance of making an impression good enough to off-
set all the previous ones.

"There *is* tea," Lung said. "Would you care to join
us?"

McLaury frowned at Lung, then at Jesse. But Mrs.
Benjamin smiled and replied, "Thank you, but I'm
afraid we need to start back. Perhaps another time."
And she turned the smile on Jesse. Her lips pressed together as if she were trying not to laugh.

She could laugh at him; he didn't mind. Better that
than scorn. He'd like to make her laugh. "Have a good
ride," he said. She nodded and wheeled her horse. It
wasn't until they were out of sight that he realized he
hadn't looked at McLaury since Mrs. Benjamin had
smiled.

"What do you know about that woman?" Lung asked.

Jesse turned to find Lung watching after their visitors, his eyes narrowed. "She's a widow, works for the
Nugget, Jewish, lives in a little house just off Fremont." *And clever, and brave, and I like the way her
face moves*. "Why?"

"She is . . ." Lung shrugged. "I cannot say."

"Not the fortune-teller business again."

"It is only a feeling."

"Well, stop feeling. That's what I'm trying to do."

"And you have had such success in the past." Lung
looked up at the sky, smiling sweetly.

"I'm going to finish putting my damned clothes on."

Jesse wasn't sure, but he thought he heard Lung
murmur, "Too late," and snicker.

The sorrel mare was tired, and willing to trot peace-
fully toward the line of conical hills between the river

and Tombstone. From this side, Mildred reflected,
they looked like a range of little volcanoes. For all she
knew, they *were* volcanoes.

Was there anything in the world that was precisely
what it looked? Hills, perhaps, but Mildred doubted it.

Tom's roan came up alongside the mare. "Do you
know anything about those hills?" she asked Tom.

"No."

There was a line marked between his brows. He was
dwelling on something unpleasant, and Mildred was
almost certain it was Jesse Fox.

But it was a few moments before he said, "He had
no business introducing you to a Chinaman."

"I don't know how he could have *not* introduced
me." She had to struggle again to keep from laughing.
The feelings that had crossed Fox's unguarded face!
Horror, dismay at the sight of her, resignation as he'd
told his friend to leave off playing the Oriental clown.
Now *that* had produced a dramatic transformation. But
not, perhaps, as dramatic as the change in Fox when
she'd smiled at him.

Fox had felt like a fool, so much so he hadn't bothered to hide it. But he wasn't a fool. Mildred remembered her first impression, when she'd found herself
facing a shirtless man, his hair wild and dark and wet,
looking at her over the barrel of a pistol.

Just for an instant, she'd thought she knew what the
Angel of Death looked like.

Tom said, "He could have kept his mouth shut. It
wasn't right."

She drew rein and looked into his face. It was still
handsome, even when sullen. Handsome, and uncom-
plicated, and safe.

A sudden contrary seizure made her say, "It would
have been rude not to introduce someone standing in
plain sight. I'm surprised at you, Mr. McLaury." She

touched the sorrel mare with her spur and cantered ahead. When Tom caught up with her, the subject and the chill between them were both dropped.

But the fact was that Tom was right. No one she knew would have introduced a Chinese man to a white woman as if they were social equals.

The sorrel mare jigged sideways under her. Tom grabbed for her bridle, but Mildred had the mare in hand before he could reach it. A coyote might have startled the horse, or a ringtail—

A creak of leather, a jingle of metal as a horse shook its head. There was a mounted man in the shadows beside the road.

Tom had a pistol in the pocket of his coat. Mildred reined the mare back, trying to make it seem as if the horse were only sidling with nerves, clearing the way between Tom and the horseman.

The figure rode forward, right hand raised and empty. He was light-haired, round-faced, and smiling.

"Why, hello, Tom. Ain't it fine to meet with friends on the road of an evening?" The man chuckled as he spoke. Well, if he was the sort to be amused at other people's reasonable caution, it was good to know it right off.

Tom nodded, unsmiling and stiff. "Jim. Didn't think to see you here."

"Oh, likely you haven't. Business bring you this way? Or pleasure?" The stranger smirked at Mildred.

Tom's horse flung up its head.

The stranger laughed at that. "I'd best be going. Give your brother my regards, hear, Tom?" He tugged his hat brim at Mildred and turned his horse down the road, away from town. Dust rose behind him, pearly in the twilight, and in moments he was out of sight.

"Speaking of introductions," said Mildred, "I assume that was someone I don't want to know."

"That was Jim Crane."

It was an instant before Mildred realized why she knew that name. "He's wanted for the Benson stage holdup!"

Tom nodded, tight-mouthed.

"He must be crazy. Why isn't he in Mexico?"

"I don't expect he's welcome there, either. If that makes odds with him."

"We'll find the sheriff when we get to town."

Tom's horse sped up, and Mildred had a good view of his shoulders, stiff in silhouette. She nudged the mare until they rode in tandem again, and looked at Tom.

His gaze stayed between his horse's ears as he said, "I run cattle for a living."

For a moment, Mildred didn't understand. "Oh. And he's a rustler."

"If I talk to Behan, word will get back. The best that'll happen is that they'll clean us out. The *best*."

His jaw muscles stood out in ridges. She wanted to say *I'm sorry*, but that was wrong—it would sound like pity. But wasn't pity the right response to the sight of a man in a trap? "If he takes this sort of risk often, he'll be caught soon, anyway."

His face softened, and he looked at her, an apology in his eyes and his voice. "He will, right enough."

Lamps shone in windows and beside doors, and dark was chasing down the western sky, by the time they rode up to her house. Tom swung himself off his horse and tied hers to the porch rail. As he did, Mildred slid down from her sidesaddle, too quickly for grace.

He turned from the railing, surprised. Something wary in his face said he suspected what she meant to do.

Mildred squared her shoulders and held her hand out to him. "Thank you for a lovely afternoon."

"May I call—may I see you when I come back into town?"

She'd done few things harder than meeting his eyes. "I—I'm sorry, Mr. McLaury."

"Not even friends, then?"

He sounded so hopeful. How dreadful to hurt another person like this! Had she really done it before, at balls and parties and picnics, to young men who'd begged her to be kind? But she had been kind, though they would have denied it.

"Not the way we used the word last night."

He looked down at the toes of his boots. "No, I guess I wasn't playing a straight game then." He looked up swiftly, and his eyes shone in his grave face. "I was playing to win, though."

"I'm sorry. I'd make an awfully bad rancher's wife, and I can't see you as a—as a newspaperwoman's husband. I shouldn't have let you hope."

He lifted his chin. "Is this about me not going to Behan? D'you think I'm a coward?"

"No! But more talk like that, and I'll think you're a damned fool."

She sounded like Harry, she realized. But it cracked a grin into Tom's stern face.

"Time won't change your mind?"

"No, Tom. I can be your friend, but . . ."

Tom's eyes were on his fingers as they turned his hat around and around. "But not more." He took a breath. "Well, I can't say I'm not sorry. But one of the things I like in you is that you know your mind." He shrugged, and smiled. Mildred thought it cost him some effort. "I'll wish you a good night, then."

He untied the mare from the rail, mounted his own

horse, and led the mare away toward the livery stable.

Mildred watched him go. Was she closing a door, or opening one? She tried hard not to think about the way the light had come into Jesse Fox's face when she smiled.

Jesse woke to thunder. But the rains weren't due for months. And if it was thunder, it was right overhead and he was outdoors. He certainly wasn't outdoors. This was his bed at Brown's Hotel.

When the thunder came again, it was someone pounding on the door of his room. "All right, all right," he shouted.

He sat up and remembered that he'd fallen down on the bed in his clothes, so at least he was decent. As he stumbled to the door, he noticed that the sun was setting. He'd slept the clock 'round. He wondered how long he'd have slept if this pounding wasn't going on.

He opened the door just wide enough to look out. At first he didn't recognize the boy in the hall. Then he remembered.

"Chu, right?"

The Chinese boy, Lung's servant, was wide-eyed and pale. Beyond him he saw the inhabitants of the other rooms up and down the hall peering out, scowling.

"Mr. Fox. Come now, please!"

Suddenly he was awake. "What is it?"

"Please, you come!" The boy turned and bolted down the hall, down the stairs, gone.

Jesse grabbed his coat and hat and followed him.

By the time he got to the street, the boy was nowhere in sight. But there was plenty to make up for his absence. Tombstone was wide awake.

Hafford's Saloon was crowded, and men lounged on the sidewalk outside, smoking and talking. Music rolled out the doors of the Grand Hotel across the street. Down the street at the Eagle Brewery, a drunk complained loudly, unintelligibly. Brightly dressed women leaned over a balcony railing, smiling and calling to men on the sidewalk. A handsome Negress in orange ruffles shouted to him, "Over here, good-lookin'!" A coach rattled around the corner, its four horses piebald with foam.

He couldn't run; it was too crowded. He forced a path through knots of people and heard angry voices behind him. He bolted across a street under the nose of a horse, and the buggy driver swore as he dragged on the reins.

Then the faces glaring at him were mostly Chinese, the swearing in Chinese in a handful of dialects. He saw Lung's sign with its gilded edges, the knot missing from the bottom. Chu stood in one corner of the porch. Jesse's boots sounded like carpenters at work as he leaped up the wooden step.

The door was ajar. There was splintered wood, raw and white, on the latch side. His heartbeat roared in his ears as he pushed the door wide.

Lung lay on the floor, on his back. His arms were flung out, as if he'd tried to catch himself as he fell. His eyes were open below the bullet hole in his forehead.

Jesse felt the floor under his knees.

"Mr. Fox?" he heard Chu say behind him. He could hear the tears in his voice. "Mr. Fox, what you want me do? Mr. Fox?"

They need me. If he finds you, he can shoot you in the back. So solly. Loyalty, friendship. Jesse couldn't blink. His muscles were so tight they'd begun to quake.

If you undo his work, it will warn him. You want me to show you what is already in front of you. Your ghost at my heels. The clamor in his head bore little resemblance to thinking. He'd start to think again soon. He dreaded it.

Someone grabbed his shoulder and shook it. "Mr. Fox!"

The sensation that went through him was more fluid than water. The boy hissed and yanked his hand away.

I should have asked him where he wanted to be buried.

⤜ 13 ⤛

Mildred breathed in the scents of the cedar boughs and lilies in her arms. Where had the Methodist church ladies found lilies? Lilies liked their feet in the shade and their heads in the sun, and there was precious little shade to be had anywhere south of Prescott at the end of May. She thought of Decoration Days in Philadelphia, bright green and smelling of crushed grass and lilacs and the peonies that grew on her grandfather's grave. Decoration Day in Arizona was more like living on a blacksmith's anvil, with a red-hot hammer poised overhead.

Well, wherever they'd come from, there were lilies, and Mildred was pleased. David had been fond of them. The Baptist and Catholic ladies must be gnashing their teeth, though, and planning their next year's revenge. If it was a slow news day, she'd give Harry and Richard a nudge about mentioning it in the tit-bits.

Oh, but it was hot, and at seven in the morning, too!

She couldn't carry a parasol with all this greenery, and wasn't about to ask Lucy Austerberg, who had no graves to visit here, to give her a ride in their surrey. And the cemetery hadn't a stick of shade. She was glad she'd lost a little weight since last summer; a bit of space between her skin and her clothes was a welcome thing.

Two dry-stone pillars flanked the cemetery entrance. She saw a few people decking graves, and two little boys chasing each other between the markers. She grinned, remembering how much she'd wanted to do that when she was small, and a cemetery seemed like a grand green meadow.

This one wasn't green, except for the decorations. But it had the most beautiful view in town. The cemetery lay at the north end of Goose Flats like the prow of the ship of Tombstone, sailing toward the Dragoon Mountains. The ground dropped sharply away beyond it, down to the big wash and the valley beyond, gray-green and tan-green with summer. The morning sun made the Dragoons a misty purple island, almost featureless. The afternoon sun would pick out the details in rosy light and blue shadow, and show the shape of a reclining lamb in the upthrust faces of rock.

If the departed were tethered to their grave sites and aware of their surroundings, she could think of worse places to spend eternity.

She walked between the rows of dead to David's grave. It was a good-sized village, Tombstone's Boot Hill, its population swelled by the nature of frontier life. Killed by Apaches, dead in a wagon accident, taken by the influenza, shot by a lawman or a bad man. Even a few suicides, as if it might be better to beat hardship at its own game. The town was too new to have lost many people to old age. No, by far the most common cause of death in Boot Hill was bad luck.

David's wooden tablet was sun-bleached, but still in fine shape. She laid out the cedar in a herringbone pattern like a blanket over the grave, and wove the lilies into the boughs. If a breeze came up, the whole thing would stay put.

Mildred sat on her heels at the foot of the plot. Her first Decoration Day with a husband's grave to adorn. Shouldn't the occasion freshen her grief, give her cause for a good cry? She ought to have things to say to him, at least.

She did; but he was dead and beyond hearing them. Instead of grief, she found a thread of irritation in her thoughts, surprisingly dear for its familiarity. She was annoyed at David in death as she'd been in life. Feckless man, given to mad projects he couldn't complete, committing their money and strength to plans that, if they needed to be carried out at all, would have been better done by someone who had even a pinch of experience in the subject. Their marriage had turned out to be one of those uncompleted projects.

She smiled and shook her head. She'd loved him so much, for his idealism, his wild flights, his ardent soul, his vivid conversation, his passion for her. And he'd exasperated her with his occasional snobbery, his naiveté, his inflexibility. He became her dear friend during their life together. If there'd been any provision in her youth for a young lady to be dear friends with a man she wasn't married to, she and David would likely have settled for friendship. Even so, she wondered if they would have married if her parents hadn't forbidden it.

But she was spoiled now for the company of the more down-to-earth man she probably ought to have. Where was one to find a mate who offered fireworks of the mind and heart *and* knew how to fix the pump?

She blew a little kiss to David's grave marker and

stood up. There was an hour yet before she needed to be at the *Nugget* office, and there was no telling what waited for her there. It had been a quiet month. There'd been a shooting in Galeyville, involving Curly Bill Brocius as, unexpectedly, the victim. But Brocius was recovering, and his friends had chosen not to lynch the man who shot him. Sheriff Behan had deputized men to stand guard at the Mountain Bay mine after a dispute sprang up about its ownership, but that settled peacefully. Though she'd had little to write about besides the progress on the city water supply, Richard Rule continued to give her assignments.

She hadn't mentioned to Harry what she'd heard at Virgil Earp's house. Kate Holliday wasn't the most reliable source, and eavesdropping wasn't enough to base a story on, not without some corroboration. Officially, there was no mystery about who had attacked the Benson stage in March: William Leonard, Harry Head, and Jim Crane, with Luther King and Arthur Ortega to hold the horses. But the rumors continued to fly that Doc Holliday had been involved, that the Earps had emptied the Wells Fargo strongbox before it was loaded and had engineered the holdup as a cover-up, that James Earp's real purpose in taking his wife on a visit to California was to take the stolen money away.

And who was fueling that fire, anyway? The holdup had failed; if the strongbox had arrived empty, it would have been discovered. Mildred had said as much to Harry. He'd replied that the emptying-the-strongbox story was nonsense, but that Holliday was still the likely fourth shooter in the robbery attempt. Had Mrs. Holliday been covering for her man when she suggested the fourth robber was Morgan Earp? If so, what good did it do her to make the suggestion to an audience as hostile as the Earp women?

The only certain facts were that Wyatt Earp was a hard man to like, and that a lot of people in town had found reason not to make the effort. Mildred found it very easy indeed to like the Earp women, and watched, troubled, as the bad feeling over Wyatt spread to his brothers and their wives.

She hadn't told anyone about meeting Jim Crane, either. It troubled her; but Tom McLaury's name would come out if she did. And people would ask, rightly, why hadn't she spoken sooner? Tom McLaury wasn't a coward, but she wasn't so sure about herself.

It had been a quiet month—but the sort of quiet that left the whole town holding its breath. A hundred head of rustled cattle or an Apache raid might have relieved the pressure.

She gazed north for another view of the Dragoons to take back to town. A man stood at the far end of the cemetery, a straight dark brushstroke against the cloud-like mountains. He was hatless, and seemed familiar. When he turned his profile to her, she realized it was Jesse Fox.

Mildred walked toward him, trusting the crunch of her steps and the swish of her skirts to warn him. The graves around him were Chinese ones. Perhaps he'd come to admire the view.

"Good morning, Mr. Fox," she said, when she was close enough not to need to call.

Fox turned. He wasn't startled, but for a moment Mildred thought he didn't recognize her. His face was cool and empty. Something gave her heart a curious pinch; the sensation made her feel guilty and foolish, and her face grew hot.

Then Fox blinked, or rather squeezed his eyes shut as if they pained him, and opened them again. "Mrs. Benjamin. Good morning. Your husband's grave?"

"Yes. David's buried over there." She turned and pointed.

"You seem too young to have been married to a soldier." He shook his head sharply and pinched the bridge of his nose. "I'm sorry, that's no business of mine."

"David was older than me. And a passionate abolitionist, so he felt he ought to leave school and enlist. He was with Sherman in Georgia."

"Dear God."

"He said something very similar. But he was wounded and discharged, and I met him when I was eighteen."

Fox was silent. Mildred saw the distance in his eyes, and wondered if she'd said too much. "What brings you to Boot Hill at this hour?" she asked, to smooth over the awkward place.

One corner of his mouth twitched, a half smile. "Decoration Day." He nodded toward the slope at his feet.

There was a new grave there, with Chinese characters on its marker. Pinned to the marker was a strip of paper with rows of calligraphy in black ink.

"A friend of yours?" Mildred asked, confused. Such a fresh grave, such stillness in the way Fox held himself.

Fox nodded. "You met him."

Mildred stared at the grave, and at Fox. "Your friend from the river? But—Oh, no. I'm so sorry."

His lips parted; then he frowned and shut them and eyed the ground at his feet. After a moment he turned back to her. He looked younger and a little lost. "I feel very stupid—is 'thank you' the right thing to say?"

"For the first few months, one may say any blasted thing at all and be excused. That was my experience, anyway." What was she angry about? Did she resent being dragged into someone else's grief, when she was nearly done with hers? Or was she angry that the world continued to offer things to grieve over?

"Then thank you."

"Was there . . . was it an accident?"

"No. You couldn't call it that."

His voice was unsteady, almost as if he wanted to laugh. She felt another pinch at her heart.

"I'm sorry, I didn't mean to pry."

"He was shot." Fox said it carefully, as if reciting. "Someone broke into his home and shot him."

"Good God." *A robbery?* she wanted to ask, but she was afraid it would be salt in the wound. With illness, the story was over once the cause was named. The story of a violent death went on and on, question after cruel question.

What had she not minded talking about, after David was buried? After Eli died? There had been safe subjects. There had even been some she'd welcomed. "How long did you know him? Mr. . . . Chow, was it?"

Fox nodded. "Five years, on and off. I met him in Virginia City. Then later, in San Francisco . . . Our favorite recreation was getting into trouble and seeing if we could get ourselves out." He smiled a little. "We didn't think of it that way at the time, of course."

"How did you meet?" Unspoken in the question, Mildred realized, was the one that went, *How did a white man come to be friends with an Oriental?*

"Now that *was* an accident," Fox said to the Dragoons. "Mine, in fact. I'd likely have lost my arm if Lung hadn't decided I was worth the trouble of saving."

"He was a doctor?"

"Among other things. In Virginia City he was pretending to be a miner."

"Pretending?"

"He wasn't really convincing anyone. Himself

included." Fox shook his head, smiling. "The Chinese came here to get rich, just like everyone else. But I think Lung already knew there were many kinds of rich, even if he hadn't admitted it to himself. It's hard to feel wealthy when you're spending all your time sitting on a mountain defending your claim from Indians, and white men who don't think a Chinaman should have a claim at all."

"So he gave up prospecting."

"It's a damn fool way to make a living."

"I know. My husband tried it."

Fox flushed. "Sorry. I didn't—"

"I was agreeing with you. Having seen the results firsthand." Mildred studied the grave, and nodded at the strip of paper. "What's that?"

"A sutra for the dead." He must have read her expression. "A prayer."

"Is that . . . Confucian?"

"Buddhist. You seem to know a little about the Chinese."

A question without asking a question. Mildred couldn't decide if that was delicacy on his part, or presumption—if he was sure she would answer because he wanted to know.

"My parents had a Chinese cook. Oh, gracious, that sounds all wrong, doesn't it?" Mildred found Fox watching her, his head a little tilted, his lips a little pinched. "Don't laugh."

"I swear, I wouldn't dream of it."

"You're dreaming of nothing else at the moment. I was the sort of child who preferred the kitchen to the nursery, and Mr. Weh didn't mind."

"That's where you learned that in Chinese, the patronymic comes before the given name?"

"And how to shell peas."

There, he laughed. It rang out pleasantly across the

open ground of Boot Hill. "What did your parents think?"

"I have no idea. I certainly wasn't going to tell them where I went when my nanny couldn't find me. Mr. Weh even taught me a few Chinese words, though I never tried them out on anyone but him."

"What were they?"

"Oh, little-girl things. 'Please,' 'thank you,' 'hello,' 'good-bye.'"

"Try them on me."

"No. I'd rather pretend I don't remember them than have you make fun of my pronunciation."

"Have it your way. But your pride is safe with me." He gazed out over the valley again. "Lung taught me a bit of Chinese, enough to scrape by in the Chinatowns. He was a good teacher—patient and mean at the same time."

"What, did he abuse you when you got things wrong?"

Fox grinned. "Colorfully. The first things I learned well in Chinese were insults."

"But the Chinese are always so polite!"

"Not to their friends."

"I suppose Americans do the same thing, or we wouldn't have the phrase 'company manners.'"

He smiled at her. "You know, you don't have to distract me. I haven't had anyone to talk to about him. It helps."

Mildred remembered that, too. "Good. Can you tell me—is someone investigating?"

He looked down at the grave, and Mildred saw his face go still. "Oh, yes."

She hadn't the nerve to ask any more questions. "I should get back to town. Good-bye, Mr. Fox, and good luck." She gathered up her skirts and started back the way she'd come.

"Mrs. Benjamin!" he called, and she looked over her shoulder at him. "Will you have dinner with me?"

She almost said yes, in a moment's impulse she didn't understand. Was it pity? Curiosity? But she'd discouraged Tom, with good reasons. They applied to Jesse Fox, too.

"Thank you, Mr. Fox, but no." Suddenly she remembered something he'd said in the foyer of the opera house after the play. "Is that what you were waiting for the right circumstances to ask?"

"Yes."

Mildred looked around Boot Hill. "And these are the right circumstances?"

"I've learned lately that you can't wait for what might never happen."

That lesson, too, she remembered. What things unsaid and undone did Jesse Fox regret? She turned to go.

"What if I ask again later?" he said.

If she told him her answer would be the same, he would probably believe her. "It's a free country."

She walked on to the entrance. Clearly the heat had gotten to her brain.

Jesse climbed the stairs of Brown's Hotel and turned toward his room. A figure crouched against the wall by his door.

Lung's murder should have warned him. He should have been wary. How many people died thinking that?

But it was Chu, Lung's servant. He sat huddled on the floor, wedged between Jesse's door frame and an enormous carpetbag. As Jesse approached, he shot to his feet. The boy's eyes were red, his face stiffly impassive.

Jesse hadn't seen him since the funeral, when one

of Lung's neighbors had promised to look after him. His queue was bristly with hair that had worked free of its plait, and his cotton jacket was wrinkled. Not excessively looked-after.

"Good morning," Jesse said. Chu pressed his lips together and bobbed his head. "Did you come through the lobby?"

Chu raised his chin. "Back stair. No let Chinese front way."

"Very resourceful. What can I do for you?"

"We talk?"

"All right."

Chu frowned. ". . . Man to man." He looked up and down the hall, and back to Jesse.

"In . . . the room?" Jesse asked.

Chu nodded shortly. Jesse unlocked the door and waved him in.

The boy walked to the middle of the room, dropped his carpetbag, and scowled at Jesse. "I no wash goddamn dish, I no sweep goddamn floor, I no do goddamn laundry. I take care Sam, you pay me."

Jesse felt behind himself for a chair and sat down. "You no . . . I beg your pardon?"

Chu clenched his fists and looked desperate. "I no wash goddamn—"

"Wait, never mind. You won't wash dishes, sweep floors, or do laundry. But didn't you do those things for Chow Lung?"

"Chow Lung, me, okay! No all day wash, all day sweep!"

Light dawned, more or less. "You mean, a job." Chu nodded, relieved. "You're not old enough for one."

Chu stared as if Jesse had sprouted wings.

He hadn't seen many Chinese children. The ones he had seen . . . had all been at work. If they were old enough to walk, talk, and carry, they worked. Chu had

worked for Chow Lung, keeping house, maybe helping with medicines or accounts or running messages.
In return he got room and board and training.

One wasn't guaranteed food and a place to sleep
just because one happened to be a child. No wonder
Chu had looked at him that way.

"The people who took you in—didn't they have
work? Or help you find some?"

Chu snorted. It reminded Jesse powerfully of Lung.

It reminded him of Lung's resources as well. He
stood up. "Come along. We're going to talk to someone."

By the time they reached China Mary's, Chu was
sweating and lugging the carpetbag with both hands.
He refused Jesse's offers to carry it, just as he'd refused to leave it at the hotel.

There was no bodyguard on the porch this time, but
Jesse would bet he wasn't far away. He knocked, and
looked at Chu, whose chin was jutting again.

A different young woman, just as pleasant as the
first, opened the door. "Mr. Fox to see China Mary,
please," he said.

Her face drooped, as if she were genuinely disappointed for him. "Mister not expected—so sorry. Lady
not seeing visitors now."

Chu dropped the carpetbag; the porch quaked. "Dr.
Fox," he said, with awful intensity. "Friend Chow Lung.
Important wise person. You shit under shoe Dr. Fox."

The maid's mouth opened and stayed that way.
Jesse's face stung with blushing. The maid darted
down the hall, knocked on the double doors, and
passed through them. Jesse was afraid to look at Chu.

Moments later she returned. "Please, come now."
Jesse and Chu followed her.

China Mary sat in the same sort of state Jesse had seen on the evening of the play. They'd barely entered the room when she called "Stop!" in Chinese.

Jesse bowed low. "Madam, I've come—"

"Is this a matter concerning the child?"

"Yes, ma'am." Jesse stole a glance at Chu. Chu was scowling at the dragon rug.

"Then it is of no interest to me."

"Madam, Dr. Chow suggested that the Chinese look to you for help."

"And they brought the boy to me. I would have placed him in honest work, safe among his people, to rise and be respected as he deserved. He refused all I offered. Is he perhaps a nephew of the emperor? Does work insult his hands?"

Jesse raised his eyebrows at Chu. "Dishes, floors, and laundry?" he murmured. Chu flushed and bit his lip.

"He's very young. Surely for the sake of Dr. Chow's memory, you could give him another chance."

"Is that his wish?"

Chu's gaze stayed on the rug, his teeth in his lip. But at last, stiffly, he shook his head.

"It is as you see," said China Mary. "Good day, Doctor."

They tramped halfway to Brown's in silence. Finally Jesse said, "I'll carry the carpetbag."

Chu shook his head.

"Oh, for God's sake. You've decided to drop yourself into my care; you'd damned well better trust me. Give me the carpetbag."

Eyes downcast, Chu handed it over. Well, from the evidence, the boy was strong enough to take care of a horse. The bag was heavier than Sam's saddle.

At Crabtree's Livery Stable, Jesse arranged for Chu to have a room in the loft for his own. He'd gotten enough baffled outrage directed at him for one day; he wasn't going to invite it from Brown's by asking them to house a Chinese boy.

The room was a little larger than a good-sized armoire. Chu examined it, grinning. He took the carpetbag from Jesse and set it in the corner. "Okay," he said. "Work now. Sam need thing, I tell you. Pay me good, dollar week."

Well, at least someone was comfortable with the arrangement.

It was insane. What was he to do when he left Tombstone? Get a donkey and let the boy follow behind, Sancho Panza to his Don Quixote? "Chu, let me buy you a ticket—hell, let me buy two of 'em and hire someone to look after you on the way—and send you back to your family. You must have family in China."

Chu had to raise his nose quite a lot before he could look down it at Jesse. "Hah! I goddamn American!" He banged down the loft ladder. A moment later Jesse heard him below, whistling inexpertly.

Mildred stood for a moment on Freemont, shading her eyes and admiring Schieffelin Hall. It was finished on the outside, a mighty barn of adobe bricks fronted with a fine big porch. Piles of buckets and sacks and lumber on that porch and the men carrying tools in and out showed that the inside work was still under way.

"Millie!" a woman's voice called, and Mildred stopped. Allie Earp was hurrying down Freemont toward her, waving. Behind her came another woman— or a girl, really. She was taller than Allie, but almost everyone over the age of twelve was.

"Millie, it's out," Allie said between breaths as she came up. She handed Mildred a folded newspaper.

Gallagher's Illustrated Weekly. The engraving under the banner stretched from one margin to the other, and showed a raging flood of longhorn cattle under a full moon, with two riders at their head. Their horses were wild-eyed, foam flying from their open mouths. One rider, a man in fringed buckskin and a noble moustache, reached for the reeling rider of the other horse, a lady in a riding habit. She was hatless, and her light hair, in improbable quantities, streamed behind her like the storm clouds that boiled around the printed moon.

A New Tale of Thrilling Frontier Adventure, Never Before Available in Any Form! STAMPEDE AT MIDNIGHT! And below the title, in lovely large, bold type, *By M. E. Benjamin.*

Mildred unfolded the paper and stared at the columns of type. They had indents and capital letters, quotation marks and italics: all the authority of print. Had Dickens looked at his first typeset story this way? Had he, too, felt as if it was no longer entirely his, like a child married and moved away? She felt a mad desire to read the thing from beginning to end, right away, even though she knew every word in it.

"Lucia isn't blond," she said, entirely at random.

"Oh, it's just the moonlight," Allie scolded happily. "Besides, it shows better in the picture this way. *Now* can I tell Mattie and Lou?"

"What if they don't like it?" Suddenly it seemed possible that no one would like it. The editor had, but editors were human and fallible.

"Tell you what—I'll let 'em read it, and ask 'em what they think. When they say it's about the finest story they ever read, I'll tell 'em who wrote it."

"Oh, Allie," Mildred said, and realized she hadn't much to say beyond that. But Allie grinned at her, as if she understood the feeling behind the lack of words.

The young woman still stood just behind Allie, watching the two of them with her head a little to one side and her eyes wide. Allie laughed. "Oh, Lord, you'd think I didn't have manners at all! This is Hattie Earp, Jim and Bessie's girl. Hattie, I expect you've worked out that this is Mrs. Benjamin."

Hattie took Mildred's offered hand. Her blue eyes met Mildred's and then dropped, and her face turned pink. "Pleased to meet you," she murmured.

My, but the child was pretty. She had wheat-colored hair that sprang out of its pins and curled around her temples. Her face was still soft and rounded, with a snubbed nose and a sweet, small mouth. She had a straight back and shoulders, and curves that were womanly without being opulent. Her rust-red calico dress was plain, but that only added to her air of maiden modesty.

"Delighted," Mildred said.

"I never met an authoress before," Hattie breathed.

"Allie, you didn't tell her, did you?"

"It just popped out when I saw the story." Allie nodded at the paper in Mildred's hands. "Hattie's staying with Virge and me while Jim and Bessie are off in California, so how could I keep it secret?"

Mildred smiled at Hattie, who looked a little nervous. "I don't know that you can say you've met an authoress even now. Maybe you ought to wait and see if they take another story from me."

"They will," Allie said with a brisk nod.

Mildred heard the tramp of a man's boots behind her and stepped away from the street to let him pass. When he came abreast of them, she saw it was Tom McLaury.

"Good morning, Mr. McLaury."

He smiled at her and her companions—she had to admit, she'd never seen a man smile sweeter than Tom

McLaury—and touched his hat brim. "Mighty hot. I was hoping for a little more spring."

"Do you know these ladies? This is Mrs. Virgil Earp, and this is Miss Hattie Earp."

He swept off his hat and shook Allie's hand. When he turned to Hattie, the girl seemed to have forgotten the existence of her hands, and was staring at Tom, her lips parted. "Miss Earp," he said, and the smile faded as he looked at her.

Oh, dear, Mildred thought.

She could ask Tom for his escort to the *Nugget* office, thereby giving him unwarranted encouragement but keeping him out of trouble. Or she could suggest that he escort the Earp ladies, which would allow Hattie to encourage him. But what good could come of encouraging one of the McLaury brothers to buzz around Wyatt Earp's niece? She'd best distract him.

But the moment for action was lost. Hattie smiled shyly, and Tom took her belatedly offered hand. Hattie asked, in a voice that sounded as if she'd been running, "Are you a rancher, Mr. McLaury?"

"My brother and I raise cattle. May I carry that for you, Miss Earp?" Tom nodded at the string bag on Hattie's arm.

Mildred exchanged glances with Allie. Allie made a little sour face. "We're not going so far that we can't carry our odds and ends," Allie told him briskly. "Nice to meet you, Mr. McLaury. Hattie, we'd best hurry if we want to finish before Lou comes. Millie, I'll talk to you later." She waggled the copy of *Gallagher's*.

"Please do," Mildred called after her as Allie hurried Hattie down the street. Hattie, Mildred was impressed to see, didn't look back over her shoulder.

"Do you know the Earps much?" Tom asked.

"I know most of the Earp women pretty well. I just met Miss Earp."

"She seems like a nice girl."

"Tom," Mildred said, "Wyatt Earp is her uncle."

"Uncles don't have much say-so in who a girl meets."

"You know better. Earp has two older brothers, but he's still the head of the clan. He won't stand for it."

Tom raised his chin and said coolly, "I haven't given him anything to stand for. I've got no quarrel with the Earp family."

Mildred sighed. "I hope not."

Doc considered his cards with satisfaction. He had a pair of kings, and a few other things that could prove useful, depending how the draw went. And he had a good sense, now, of the four men he was playing poker with. He didn't know them, couldn't remember their names. But he knew their play. That was enough.

He preferred to play in the card room downstairs in the Grand Hotel during his nights off. It seemed as if everyone who came to the Oriental of an evening felt obliged to prove he was Doc's friend by buying him a drink and inquiring into his business. The Grand's barroom was cramped and dark, but people let you alone. It wasn't the sort of place one passed through just to see who was there; the smart lobby with its aura of respectability made the real loungers think twice before they sauntered through it to get to the saloon.

He laid down his bet and discarded the three of clubs. The dealer slid him another card. He didn't reach for it until all the men at the table had got theirs. Then he tucked it in his hand. A reward for his patience and good nature: a third king. Now all he had to do was make the other players bet their wages away.

A hand fell on his shoulder. A surge of anger shot

through him, so strong that he was surprised when he realized habit had kept it off his face.

"I am otherwise engaged, Wyatt."

"How'd you know it was me?"

"Because anyone else would know that if he laid a hand on me, I'd cut it off."

"I want a word with you."

"You'll have to wait until I'm done."

A moment of silence behind him. Then Wyatt said, "Finish the hand."

That was Wyatt in a nutshell; he'd do as you asked, if he could make it sound like his idea. Doc played the hand out, but the fun had gone out of it. Even when the red-haired man across the table slapped his chips down on the felt as if he were squashing a spider, so Doc knew he was bluffing, it was an empty triumph.

He won the hand, and made a display of pulling out his watch and consulting it. Light caught the engraved initials on the inside of the case, as if to remind him who was waiting. He snorted and snapped it closed.

"Gentlemen," he said as he rose, with a general nod to the table.

No one protested; there was no "Leaving already?" or "You can't go while you're winning!" They seemed to expect when Wyatt said "hop," he'd hop. He dusted off his coat front, turned to Wyatt, and said in a voice that would carry to all the cardplayers, "All right, Wyatt, let's go pull your fat out of the fire." Petty, but he felt better.

Doc cashed out, and Wyatt led the way through the lobby and out to Allen Street. There were plenty of people on the street; between them, Doc and Wyatt must have nodded to a dozen or more acquaintances. Wyatt turned east and Doc followed, and eventually the evening strollers thinned. As they crossed Seventh a big Sonoran jackrabbit shot out from under a building, nearly under their feet, and dashed across the street.

"I know what it means when a black cat crosses your path, but what does a bunny signify?" Doc asked.

"It means it's too damned hot and dry, and he's looking for water."

"There is no poetry in your soul, Wyatt."

"That's because I don't have one. Listen, I've been talking to Ike Clanton."

"No wonder you were desperate for my conversation."

"Someone saw Jim Crane in town."

Doc said, "People have also seen the Virgin Mary and the ghost of Abraham Lincoln." What he thought wasn't words; more a cold place in his vitals, and the conflicting urges to save Morgan and to beat him senseless.

Wyatt ignored him. "Clanton claims to know where Head, Crane, and Leonard are holed up."

Doc stopped walking. "That's a mighty big stick he has."

"He's got no notion of it. I told him I wanted to bring 'em in to win votes in the election for sheriff. Said I'd divide the Wells Fargo reward money with him."

"And he suggested you go straight to hell."

Wyatt's teeth showed under his moustache, white in the gloom. "You know me better than that."

"You're telling me that Ike Clanton split on his dear friends just to keep you happy?"

"Clanton can see which side of the bread the butter's on. Though he did ask me not to say where I found out." Wyatt lifted his head as if to study the deep blue of the sky above the rooftops. "If Ike does as I told him, it should roll a few rocks out of the road."

"And if he doesn't?"

Wyatt shrugged. "No harm done to us. But Ike's got no cause to doubt me. He'll play."

Doc considered the implications. The Clantons raised beef down on the San Pedro near Charleston, and raised hell everywhere else. Old Man Clanton had almost certainly built his herd on other men's cattle, like many a more successful and respected rancher. But unlike his predecessors he was still skimming stock, and giving corral room to fellows who did the same. His oldest boy, Finn, was no better or worse than most. But Ike ran his mouth and didn't back it with anything. And Billy followed the likes of John Ringo around like a pup, too much of a fool to be a sensible coward in the mold of his brother Ike.

Taken together, they were an unchancy family. "If you're seen to have the Clantons parading behind you, you can whistle for those votes for sheriff."

"Now didn't I just say Ike swore me to secrecy?" Wyatt was smiling widely now. "And when I get Virgil set proper, he'll be able to put me where I need to be."

That was Wyatt talking to himself; Doc had no idea what he meant. It fanned a small, resentful flame in him. "If you really want to win that election, you ought to cut the disreputable members of your acquaintance. Meaning me."

"Isn't that the point of finding Crane and his boys? So folks will know you ain't a road agent, too?"

He was still smiling, leaning against a sapling tree that had somehow survived the wholesale clearance of the lot it stood on. Overhead the stars blinked through the smoke and dust from the workings. Doc felt them singing to him, muted through the haze; he knew what they said, but it did him no good. "Dear heaven, Wyatt, I am not Ike Clanton, nor any other idiot of your acquaintance. I am aware that you can either clear me or protect Morgan, and I know which you'll choose."

Wyatt shook his head. "You stood by me when there wasn't much in it for you, when you didn't have to. I know that."

"And now I have to."

Wyatt shook his head. "My friends wear no chains. I say I'll keep you out of Yuma or a noose, but saying isn't doing, even for me. So go if you want to, Doc."

He meant it. Didn't he? He was saying that Doc could pack up and head out, back to Las Vegas or Fort Griffin or out to California if it pleased him. He could pull until the silk thread that connected them snapped, and he was free. He felt Wyatt's eyes on him.

And he felt the strength slipping out of his limbs. His heart labored and accomplished little, and his lungs ached. He doubted he could walk as far as his room at Fly's, let alone to a livery stable to mount a horse and ride away.

He should have been dead years ago. He'd always said so. When he was ready to surrender to the inevitable, he could walk away, but until then, he would stand by Wyatt. Because by some devilish device, he was taking part of Wyatt's bottomless strength for his own. Wyatt was what kept him alive.

Wyatt broke the long silence. "I can't do without you, Doc." There was an apology in the words, an earnest sorrow.

"I know. You won't have to."

He was strong again, and the stars were decently muzzled. If he had the sense to stay a little more sober, he wouldn't have these fits and fancies.

"What will you do about Crane and Head and Leonard?"

Wyatt turned his face south, toward the hills. "I'll take care of it."

* * *

Doc put the whole business out of his head for upwards of a week. Kate was restless and irritable, and wanted Doc to take her north to cooler air. "It's bad for me," he told her, without specifying the sort of badness. He set himself to amuse her in Tombstone instead, and hoped that, intermittently, he was successful.

He was on his way to the barber, thinking that the heat and his own sweat was softening his beard better than hot towels could, when he saw Virgil Earp coming down Fremont.

"How did that horse breaker do for you?" Doc asked.

"Seems like a decent fellow. And it was a treat to watch him work."

In the middle of that, Doc saw the badge on Virgil's breast pocket. "Good God. What have you gone and done?"

Virgil tucked his chin to look down at his own chest. "Didn't you hear? Sippy's gone out of town. I'm city marshal in his place."

"Well. I expect congratulations are in order." That was a foothold for Wyatt; if Virgil got a chance to make his mark as marshal, it would give luster to the name of Earp in the county elections. "How long do you have Marshal Sippy's seat?"

"Good question. He said he'd be away two weeks, but there are folks who swear he's cleared out for good. Seems he owes a little money here and there."

"O ye of little faith. Shall I make the town hot for you, so you can show what you're made of?"

"Plenty hot as it is." Virgil nodded and raised his hand to a man across the street, and turned back to Doc. "Oh, did you hear about Billy Leonard and Harry Head?"

Doc felt his insides drop a little, though he couldn't have said why. "Not as yet."

"Killed, over by Hachita. The Haslett boys thought Leonard and Head had come into New Mexico to murder them and take their land. So they shot 'em."

"Who the hell told them such a thing?" Doc asked, before he thought better of asking.

But Virgil only shrugged. "Wyatt sent Morgan to scout after Leonard, Head, and Crane, but he got there after the Hasletts. Leonard lived long enough to clear you, by the way."

That and the direct intervention of Jesus Christ would prove him innocent in the eyes of Tombstone. Morgan was a well-meaning idiot. "What about Jim Crane?"

"Away when the Hasletts came. If I were those boys, I'd be trying to grow eyes in the back of my head."

The Haslett brothers would certainly have to fear Crane's vengeance. Whether they had anyone else to fear depended on whether the rest of the world shared Virgil's ignorance on the subject of who put the notion in their heads to kill Crane's pals. "If this keeps up, the call for coffin wood will have us all living in tents."

"They can kill each other as they please. My house is built."

Doc watched him cross the street. *Not quite*, he thought. *It's building, but the Earp family is not weathertight yet.* And a lot could happen to a structure even after it was finished. He'd entrusted his future to Wyatt, as Wyatt's brothers had. He hoped to God that whatever Wyatt chose to build would shelter them all.

⇟ 14 ⇞

Mildred looked out the window of the Nugget office as another gust of wind rattled the glass. For a moment, dust hid the buildings across the street, as if a curtain had been yanked across her view.

"It's not as bad as last week," Harry said behind her, sounding resigned.

"The knowledge that I'm biting down on infinitesimally less grit every time I chew is *such* a comfort."

"Then there's the pleasure of wiping mud out of the corners of your eyes."

"And knowing that, no matter how much you sweat, there will always be enough dust to stick to you and blot it up."

"Ugh. You've gone too far for me. Besides, I thought ladies don't sweat."

"You thought no such thing. My God, Harry, it's like living in a furnace with a bellows going, and we're only two-thirds through June. None of us will survive to see the rains."

Harry mopped his face with his handkerchief. He no longer bothered to put it back in his pocket. "If you'll quit yammering, I can edit your copy."

The sound was like a cannon, and the way the ground shook, and the windows rattled—"Are they blasting at the mines?" Mildred asked, even as she thought, *That was downtown.*

Harry shook his head, his face blank with listening.

She threw open the door. Over the sound of the wind she heard, growing from mutter to thunder like the sound of an approaching train, voices shouting, and screaming.

"Get your things," Harry said.

She could smell smoke on the wind.

Brown's Hotel lurched. For a disorienting instant, Jesse thought Allen Street was under attack. Then he heard the shouting, and the crackle of fire.

He grabbed his gunbelt and his coat. The corridor was jammed with guests. One man clutched his arm. "What was that?"

"Out," Jesse said, and then again, much louder, "everyone out. Down the stairs and out the side door. Whatever's in your rooms can stay there. Move!"

For a wonder, they did, scurrying down the stairs and pouring out into the lobby like cattle into a stockyard pen. But the hotel staff had the herd moving, out the doors, and the new arrivals had a current of other guests to join.

It occurred to Jesse, finally, to doubt what he knew and how he knew it. But by then he could feel unseen things being broken down, transformed by heat and oxygen. The web of the world was being ripped apart and remade.

He heard, "Mr. Fox!" as he came out on Fourth Street. Chu ran across the street and stopped, puffing. "Mr. Fox, what you want me do?" Chu was wide-eyed, but not, Jesse thought, with fear.

"Saddle Sam and be ready to get him someplace safe if the fire comes that way."

Chu made a rude noise past his front teeth. "Already saddle. Feed in damn saddlebag, too. That all?"

Lung's efforts to impress Chu with Jesse's importance hadn't been entirely successful. Jesse handed him his coat. "Take care of this. And don't leave Sam alone no matter what."

Chu pelted off toward the livery stable.

Allen Street was bedlam. Men filled buckets and ran with them, east toward Fifth Street. Others staggered out of businesses with armloads of ledger books, boxes, piles of whatever needed saving. A Negro man in miner's denim ran toward him, carrying a crowbar. Jesse grabbed his shoulder to slow him down.

"Where'd you get that?"

"Vizina Works. But the hardware's closer."

Jesse let him go and ran for the hardware store.

Doc lay on the floor and thought, Damned if I drink *here again.* After I gut the man who did that. Then it dawned on him that he didn't know what "that" was.

He looked out across the floor of the Arcade Saloon, across shards of glass and mirror and splintered wood and shattered ornamental millwork, and understood that whatever had knocked him down hadn't been anything personal. He was on his feet and moving before he realized he'd seen the front wall of the saloon burning, flames floor to ceiling like wallpaper.

One of the bartenders stood wobbling in the middle of the floor, staring down at his apron, which was on fire. Doc yanked it off him. The man's moustache and eyebrows and the hair above his forehead were singed half away, but otherwise he seemed all right. Doc pushed him toward the back and hoped he wouldn't fall down before he got to the door.

The few other customers were already cramming out the back entrance. If this had happened only hours before, the place would have been jammed for the free lunch. Now there weren't half a dozen people in the room.

The other bartender staggered to his feet behind the bar. Blood poured down his face from a cut in his hair.

Doc grabbed him by his vest and pulled him into the room.

"The receipts," the man gasped.

"To hell with 'em." Doc stuffed the bartender out behind the others and looked back the way he'd come.

He couldn't see the front of the room for the smoke. It roiled toward him along the ceiling like storm clouds, like an animal stalking him. There were flames in the smoke—the cloth-covered ceiling had caught. The fire passed from growling to roaring.

He crouched and squinted—was there anyone left, anyone lying on the floor, maybe unconscious? Flames ran along the seams of the floor planks, smoldered and burst in the carpet edges. Between the daylight and the fire, there should be plenty of light, but the room was in eclipse. Something crashed to the street outside.

His collar came up sharp against his windpipe and half choked him. He fell over backward—no, was dragged. Then the sunlight blinded him, and the air, though hot, was almost clean. He coughed and coughed, and thought an apology to what was left of his lungs.

"Christ, did you want to see how long it would take you to catch?" someone snapped above him.

Against the dazzle of light, the silhouette of a head and shoulders. As his eyes adjusted, he recognized Jesse Fox. "Couldn't—" He coughed and tried again. "Looking for others."

"Was there anyone?"

Doc shook his head.

Fox turned to a frightened man in a sack suit. "Help him out of here. Get north of Fremont and stay there." He hoisted Doc onto his feet and passed him to the man in the suit. "You may now leave the barbecue to the rest of us."

Startled, Doc looked into Fox's face and found him grinning. "Don't burn anything," Doc croaked.

Fox laughed.

Doc tried to keep as much of his weight on his own feet as he could, but he was afraid he still made a good bit of work for the man in the suit. *A lunger with a chest full of smoke*, he thought. *My, I do know how to pick my fights*. And he laughed, even though it hurt.

"Fly's Boarding House," he ordered the man whose shoulders were under his arm. He needed to make sure of Kate.

The balcony outside the Arcade Saloon had fallen in a fountain of spark and flame. Now the porch of the building next door had begun to burn. Allen Street was lined with verandas and second-floor balconies that shaded the sidewalks. They would spread the fire down the street the way forests carried wildfires through the treetops, handing it across the faces of brick and adobe buildings to ignite the wood frame ones beyond.

Jesse thrust the handle of his borrowed axe into his gunbelt and climbed a post of the balcony next to the burning porch. The turned wood gave him hand- and footholds.

He dragged himself over the railing and ran back to the burning structure. Below him, men were hacking away at its support posts. He chopped at the beams that held the porch to the building. Jesse felt the floor shudder and sway beneath him, and leaped for the next-door balcony. The porch groaned, gave way, crashed into the street.

Too late. A spark had found the dry wood shingles of the roof. Jesse swung the axe blade into the fancy painted posts of the railing. After that balcony, there was another. It caught, too.

Soon he lived in a bubble of blazing heat and deafening noise. He knew there were things outside the bubble—shouting, sweating men throwing buckets of water at wooden façades, people running to save belongings, horses screaming in fear. He thought, *Is this what Shiloh was like, and Gettysburg?* This was battle. On the other side of the charge, instead of men, there was fire, that advanced on all fronts in all directions, breaking their lines everywhere.

He swung the axe until his shoulders and arms burned with weariness. Then, because he had to keep on, they ceased to burn. At some point they would stop doing what he asked.

The fire had jumped ahead of him. He knew without looking; he could feel it as he'd felt the metal ore and the water in the rock. It was netted along Allen Street like the workings of a drunken spider, devouring air and wood and turning them to ash. Straw into gold, in reverse.

Suddenly his bubble had another soul in it. A man climbed over the railing with an iron bar, nodded to him, and began to pry away at the the supports on the other side of the balcony they stood on. It was hard to say what he looked like, other than that he had thin hair in disarray, and that his long face around his moustache was black with soot and striped with sweat. Jesse swung harder at the post on his side.

Fire ran in rivulets over their heads in the roof beams. Jesse heard the crack of heated wood exploding. He screamed, "Jump!" to the other man, but there was no time. The beam dropped toward Jesse.

Then it caught, changed course. It struck the other man in the face, splintered end first, and he fell back over the swaying railing.

Daylight gaped between the front wall and the balcony. It was coming down.

Jesse jumped to the balcony rail and felt it wrench loose under his feet as he leaped again, into the blazing air above Allen Street.

The dirt slammed into the soles of his feet, his shoulders and back. He knew he'd rolled once he stopped, but not until then. Someone grabbed his arms and yanked him out of the road.

He wanted to shout that the balcony was about to fall. He couldn't get breath in his lungs to do it. The fire fighters fled as the balcony leaned outward, wood screaming, and toppled in a curtain of sparks. He looked for the man who'd been hit by the timber. Two men carried him off at a half run.

Jesse stood up and promptly fell down again. "You're all in," said the man who'd dragged him out of danger. "Garza!" he bellowed. "Get him out!"

A big man, his eyes black and red in his smoke-black face, appeared and flung Jesse over his shoulder like a child. Jesse wanted to protest; but it was that, or lie in the street in everyone's way. He calculated that Garza carried him at least two blocks before letting him slide off and propping him against a wagon bed.

Then Garza was gone, and a dark-haired lady was helping him sit up against the wagon wheel in the wagon's long shadow. She held out a dipper of water. He was so dry he could hardly pull his tongue away from his teeth. He didn't know whether he was glad of the water that dribbled over his chin and onto his chest, or sorry that it hadn't made it down his throat with the rest.

After that he leaned his head against the wagon wheel and just sat. He was gradually aware of other men around him, in various states of exhaustion or injury, and women hurrying between them, carrying water or bandages. The air was full of smoke, tinted by the setting sun behind him until the street looked like a view of Hell.

"Mr. Fox?" one of the women said, somewhere above him.

He tilted his head up and squinted. "Mrs. Benjamin." It came out in a whisper.

She squatted next to him. "Have you started to hurt anywhere yet?"

"Will I?"

"I had a fellow mad at me for cutting his hair, a minute ago. I did it to get at the scalp wound he didn't know he had."

"Ingrate."

"I forgave him. After I told him what I thought of him." She picked up Jesse's right hand, and he saw the knuckles were torn and bleeding. He couldn't remember when that had happened. From a burlap sack beside her she produced a bottle, opened it, and held it over his hand.

He saw the label. "That's the *good* whiskey."

"Yes, and there's more of it in town than there is of tincture of iodine."

"Half the saloons just burned."

"And the liquor still wins over the iodine." She poured it over his knuckles, and over the back of his left hand, too, where the skin was torn away. Then she made a pad of a scrap of bandage, soaked it with whiskey, and dabbed his face.

The alcohol bit into the raw places, and he concentrated on the pain as he looked at her bent head, her curling brown hair escaping from its ruthless knot, her face in profile calm under the dirt. If he thought about the pain in his knuckles and the cuts and burns on his face, he could ignore her strong fingers holding his hands still and steady. In Renaissance paintings, angels had the same look of calm strength, of remote mercy for humanity. He wanted, absurdly, to cry like a child. Instead he leaned his head back against the wagon wheel and closed his eyes.

"You're not going to faint, are you?" she asked.

Jesse shook his head. He felt her wrapping his knuckles in something. When she was done she let his hands fall back in his lap, and he opened his eyes.

"There was a fellow hit in the face by a falling timber. I was with him . . ."

She frowned, then seemed to understand it was a question. "George Parsons. If he lives—" She stopped with a little shudder. "I understand Doc Goodfellow likes a challenge."

"How far's the fire spread?"

"Nearly half of downtown." She shook her head and smiled crookedly. "Want to hear a nice ironic bit?"

"That depends."

"John Clum, in his mayor's hat, is out of town on a mission to buy us a fire engine."

Jesse was afraid to start laughing, for fear it wouldn't end well. "That's going to be a hell of a homecoming."

"Won't it be?" Still with that cracked smile, she looked east and a little north. "That pillar of smoke on the left would be my house, among other things."

It was like a slap, though he was pretty sure she hadn't meant it to be. "I'm sorry." *I'm sorry I didn't save your house, and let the rest of this damned town burn.*

Why in heaven's name did I tell him about the house? Mildred scolded herself. "I'm still better off than a lot of people. Unless the *Nugget* office burned." Fox closed his eyes again, and Mildred thought his face lost color under the dirt. "Mr. Fox, are you sure you're not going to faint?"

"I'm sure. Anyone know how it started?"

Mildred took a deep breath. "The story I heard was that the owner of the Arcade Saloon was checking the level in a barrel of whiskey, couldn't see well enough through the bung hole, and so held a match to it. I honestly don't know whether to laugh or cry."

"I see the dilemma." He coughed. It sounded painful. "Do you think, under the circumstances, you could call me Jesse?"

His hair stuck to his forehead. She wanted to push it back to look for cuts or bruises, but something kept her from touching him. "You give a lot of weight to circumstance."

"It's shorter than 'Mr. Fox.' "

Hearing it in his mouth reminded her of a nursery story she'd loved, because it terrified her, and because the heroine was brave. There was an old song, too, on the same story. "Be glad of 'Mr. Fox.' I could be calling you Reynardine."

His eyes opened, startled and unfocused. Then he grinned, not at her but like a schoolboy who'd remembered the answer just in time to forestall the ruler. His teeth shone in his dirty face. " 'Oh, no, my dear, I am no rake brought up in Venus' train.' "

"And the next line of the song? Something about being on the run from the sheriff's men?"

He shook his head. Then he frowned. "Well, I'm not welcome in Sacramento and environs. A disagreement about right of way for the Central Pacific."

"Which side were you on?"

"Not the Central Pacific's, or I'd be welcome in Sacramento."

Somehow that seemed in character. Other men quarreled with their fellows, one or a few at a time. Jesse Fox tilted at entire railroads. She said, "No one would want to go to Sacramento, anyway."

A Chinese boy pushed past her suddenly and stood over Fox, scowling. "You look shit," the boy declared.

"Chu! Ladies present."

The boy transferred the scowl to Mildred.

"Is Sam all right?"

"He not okay, I no leave." The boy spat into the street and looked pleased with himself.

Fox winced and let his head fall back against the wagon wheel. "I apologize for Chu. He's sleeping at the livery stable. I think he's learning these things from the teamsters. Chu, you can go back to Sam."

"Sam okay. I take care you."

Mildred smiled and stood up. "Then I can leave you with a clear conscience, Mr. Fox." She started to brush dust off her skirt. No point; there was mud, soot, and a little blood on it as well. "There's food down the street, under the tent, whenever you want it."

"I get chuck, bring here," Chu assured her, his chin up.

Fox looked down at his hands, and ran a finger over his bandaged knuckles. "Thank you, Mrs. Benjamin."

It did sound odd, the careful formality in the midst of chaos. But it was the mortar of society. "You're welcome, Mr. Fox. Master Chu, a pleasure to make your acquaintance."

Two stiff drinks and the knowledge that Kate was safe had set Doc nearly back on his feet. She'd insisted on going out by herself once he was accounted for. He worried about her until she came back to Fly's, a bit before sunset.

"Miss Nightingale," he greeted her.

"Make fun if you want. But there's streets full of hurt men out there. Least I could do was fetch and carry for 'em." She yanked out her hat pin as she stood before the bureau mirror.

The scene was almost a parody of Kate at the mirror. A hundred times he'd seen her stand before it to create a flawless self: hair, clothes, a little rouge for her cheeks and lips. Now her face and gown were dirty, strands of hair stuck to her sweat-damp neck, and her perfume was smoke. Doc wondered if she saw those things in the mirror, and missed seeing her strong bones, her eyes full of light, the energy that made her every motion arresting.

"That was admiration, not making fun." There'd been an element of teasing, too, because he liked the way she fired up when he teased her.

"You could have pitched in."

"I had leave to absent myself." In fact, Fox had made a command of it. It had weighed with him, the Devil only knew why.

Kate dropped to her knees by his chair. "I'm sorry, Doc. What a damned shrew I am! I wouldn't have wanted you out there."

"Why? Did you flirt with all the wounded?"

"Don't be a fool." She laid her head on his knee, a thoroughly uncharacteristic gesture. He stroked the loose hair off her neck. "I'm just tired. And hungry."

"My God, woman, you eat like a draft mule."

She pinched his thigh. "Only when I work like one. Come on, Doc, let's see if there's anything in town to eat that hasn't been burnt up."

She pulled herself to her feet. She *was* tired; ordinarily she'd make something like that look effortless. Doc levered himself out of the armchair and checked his own appearance in the mirror. Yes, all clean and respectable again.

"Doc?" Kate said from the window. Her voice was

a little too casual. "Did you dream anything last night?"

He turned around. She stood with her chin up, her shoulders squared, but her hands wrung each other as if they belonged to another body. For an instant he was angry, but the sight of her courage and fear holding each other in check softened him.

"No," he lied. "Let's find you some dinner."

Allie stood back and surveyed their work. "Well," she said, doubt heavy in her voice, "it's up. Though the Lord knows what'll happen if the wind blows."

Mildred looked at the tent they'd erected where her house used to be. They'd used the shovels Allie had brought and cleared rubble to make room for it, and pounded the pegs in with rocks where they could (Allie had forgotten the hammer). Where they couldn't, they'd piled more rocks to hold the canvas and the guy ropes down. The result clung to its poles looking as if it hadn't a right angle sewn in it anywhere. Mildred tried to stifle a giggle, but it escaped.

Allie looked at her doubtfully. That made Mildred snort with trying not to laugh.

"What?" Allie said.

Mildred waved at the tent and whooped with laughter. "I swear not to tell anyone who sewed it!"

"Well, if it was put up proper, and not by two crazy women with no tools almost in the dark—" Then Allie, too, started laughing. "If Virge comes by and sees this, he'll tease me to the end of my days!"

"I'd be sorry for your reputation, but I hope he does come by."

Allie sobered instantly. "Damn the lot claim, Millie. You come bed down in our house tonight and deal with this after a good night's sleep."

"And waste this handsome tent?" Mildred had meant to make Allie laugh again, but it didn't work. "If I stay on the lot, I won't have anything to deal with. I've got a structure up, and I'm in residence. Anyone who wants to make a grab at a town lot will look for easier pickings."

Allie sighed. "Sometimes I don't know why anybody'd want a piece of this place."

"I felt like that when I saw what was left of the house." And Mildred had been doing her best, ever since, to avoid making a mental catalog of what she'd lost, what might have been saved if she'd lived in a place with a fire company, and plenty of water for them. "If you can offer me a bed, Hattie must be home with her parents."

"Lord, I love that girl, but if you hung a big sign that said 'Trouble,' she'd run right up ag'in' it and break her nose."

Mildred put the shovels back in Allie's gig. "Tom McLaury still?"

"I warned her."

"And I warned him. It made me feel like his mother. I wish people would remember that *Romeo and Juliet* doesn't end well."

Allie gave her a searching look. "You sweet on him?"

"No." Allie seemed unconvinced, so Mildred went on, "I might have been, a little, but it wore off. Tom's a nice boy. But that's just it—I'm the younger, I think, but I *still* feel like his mother."

"You seen more of life, and lost somebody. Sweet Jesus, I don't know what I'd do if I lost Virge. Run crazy, I think."

"Don't lose him, then. You'd make an awful madwoman."

Allie frowned at the gathering dark. Then she rummaged under the seat of the gig and brought something out. "You take this."

A big kitchen knife flashed in Allie's hand. "I won't need it," Mildred said.

"Then you won't use it."

Mildred took it from her.

Allie sighed. "I guess if you holler, someone'll hear you."

"I bet I won't have to."

"Feel sure enough to put four bits on it?"

"You'd better have the egg money to back that up tomorrow morning," Mildred said sternly.

Allie grinned. "You want the egg money, or the eggs? I'll make you breakfast."

"The eggs, oh, please." Mildred bent over and hugged Allie hard, and was surprised when Allie hugged back. "Thank you so much. I don't know what I would have done."

"Fiddle. You take care, now." Allie climbed up to the seat of the gig and clucked to the horse, reining it around debris in the street. Mildred waved after her, and listened until the squeak of the wheels faded away.

She clutched her arms around herself and looked out over the ravaged block. The walls of three adobe buildings still stood, but they were shells, the roofs and windows gone. Everything else was desolation—black, broken timbers, twisted pipe and railings, bent strips of stamped tin. The smell of smoke closed out all other smells. Here and there coals glowed red under the rubble, but there was little left to feed them.

She saw other lights around her, across the block. Someone else's tent, glowing with a lamp inside. A campfire that blinked in and out of sight when someone passed between her and the light. The flickering of a candle lamp at another neighbor's lot. Allie was right; she could shout, and someone would hear.

Mildred looked again at the little drunken tent. She and David had spent nights in less certain shelter.

She even had the luxury of an army cot that Allie had unearthed, and a blanket. The cot filled the tent almost from edge to edge.

She refused to be afraid. She was in the middle of the city of Tombstone, with neighbors and peace officers around. She was hardly less safe than she would be in a wooden house with a bolt on the door.

Mildred crawled into the tent, turned so her head was to the flap, and lay staring up into darkness, the knife at her side.

She dozed a few times, her mind drifting just to the border of dreaming. But when she did, her own disjointed thoughts were enough to wake her. So when she heard several pairs of feet crunching in the rubble outside, she was off the end of the cot and outside in a flash. She kept the knife hidden in a fold of her skirt.

There were three men with a lantern. It was half shuttered so that it shone on her, not them. She couldn't see their faces.

"You're squattin', missy," one said.

"I own this lot." Good, her voice didn't shake.

"Let's see the paper, then."

No point in answering that; they knew she wouldn't have it with her. "Who do you work for?"

That stopped them for a second. Hadn't they ever been talked back to? Mildred glanced past the men. The lights she'd seen elsewhere on the block were out.

Finally one of them, not the first man who'd spoke, said, "None of your damn business. You run off or we'll make you run."

The man with the lantern moved toward the side of the tent, and the light fell on a shard of kindling in his hand.

Rage crested in her. "Just what we need, fire. Get the hell off my lot!"

Before she could dodge, one of them had the collar

of her dress twisted in his fist. She raised the knife and brought it down as hard as she could. It struck something, caught there. The man grunted and grabbed her wrist. She smelled drink on him as he growled, "I don't think you can make us."

Behind her, Jesse Fox said, "But I can."

The man let go and stepped back. "Stay out of this. We got law on our side."

Fox laughed—not the free laugh that had rung out over Boot Hill, but a soft, private sound. He stood beside her now. "Sure you do. I can see your badges from here."

The night was warm—Mildred was certain of it—but she was shivering uncontrollably. She had never been so cold.

The man with the lantern swung it up, so the light fell on Fox. He didn't squint. "There's three of us," said the man with the lantern. "I only count one of you."

"And my five little friends," Fox said, and raised his right hand. There was a revolver in it.

The three men moved back a pace. The one with the lantern shuttered it. There was no moon, but the smoke made a kind of ceiling that reflected the lights of town. The men were silhouetted against it.

Out of the darkness beside her came an oiled clicking as the pistol's cylinder rotated.

"We're going," said the first man.

Fox said nothing. Mildred couldn't, past her clenched teeth. She saw the shapes of the three men slide away across the ruined block.

Mildred's knees wobbled. She sat down where she was, with no care for rocks or anything else.

"Mrs. Benjamin! Are you all right?"

"Oh, for God's sake, go ahead and call me Mildred."

She heard him uncock his pistol, and felt him crouch beside her. A match caught and flared, and she blinked.

She saw him on the other side of the flame. He still wore the filthy shirt he'd fought the fire in, but most of the soot was off his face and hair. Under and above the stubble of his beard his skin was freckled with little burns and cuts. The hand that held the match was wrapped in her bandage, dingy now.

"You're not hurt?" he asked.

"I'm offended. There were *two* of us, plus your little friends." Her voice shook so, she didn't expect him to understand a word.

He smiled and blew out the match. "If they could count, they'd find other work." His voice came from a few feet away. "Do you have a lantern?"

Mildred shook her head, then remembered that he probably couldn't see it. "No."

"Just as well, maybe. No sense lighting the way for unwelcome guests." Her blanket settled over her shoulders; he drew it snug around her arms and throat, and she felt bandage brush her chin. "Always stab upward."

"I beg your pardon?"

"With the knife. Stab upward from below. Overhand only works for stage villains."

She had hit something, but it might only have been a sleeve button. Her stomach gave a lurch. And was he laughing at her? He'd better not.

"I'm not complaining, mind you," she said as sharply as she could with her teeth chattering, "but what are you doing here?"

Silence from beside her. She couldn't see him even silhouetted; crouched, they were both below the artificial horizon of ruined and half-ruined buildings. But something about that silence suggested irritation.

"I was in the neighborhood and thought I'd stop by," he answered. No doubt, now, about the irritation.

"Don't bite me. It was a fair question."

"No, it wasn't. Go to bed. I'll be out here if you need anything."

"You will?"

"Go," he said with such force that she went.

She knew she'd fallen asleep, because she woke up. Alarmed, she looked out to see what had roused her.

Fox sat in front of the tent near a little campfire; the night had turned cool after all. Heaven only knew where he'd found anything to burn. He sat cross-legged, his pistol on his knee.

The footsteps that had wakened her belonged to Virgil Earp. His coat front was tucked back to show the revolver in his waistband, and the firelight flashed on his badge. He shone a lantern over her tent and over Fox. Fox nodded to him. After a moment, Earp nodded back and walked on.

She laid her head down on the cot and went back to sleep.

⇥ 15 ⇤

There was a crash from the other side of the canvas wall, as if an entire lumber yard had been thrown over the edge of Heaven to land in Allen Street. Doc groaned and laid his head on his folded arms on the table.

"That's it," he muttered. "I am pulling up stakes and moving to a town that's already finished."

Morgan laughed, which resonated vilely in Doc's skull. "You'd stand it better if you didn't have the hangover all the time."

"I drink to stand it. The hangover is inevitable."

Morgan shook his head. "Raw egg and two thimbles of ground chile pepper in a glass of beer. Drink it right down, soon's you get out of bed. Then you'll be all right."

Doc shuddered. "As compared to what, being stone dead?"

Morgan creased his newspaper. It sounded like a rifle volley. "You at least eat some oysters?"

"Oysters ought not be eaten more than a mile from the sea." Though there had been grand fried oysters in Philadelphia. He and his college friends had eaten platters of them on Friday nights and washed them down with beer, playing at being working men instead of the young gentlemen with money they were the rest of the week. They'd been good fellows, for Yankees. Thank God he didn't have to see any of them again.

Or had they all ended up drinking at ten o'clock in the morning, sitting on a nail keg at a wobbling table knocked together out of scraps, in a tent that called itself a saloon by virtue of six bottles of liquor, a barrel of beer, and the sign over the door?

"Damn!" Morgan reared back and frowned at his newspaper.

"What now?" Disaster, death, or financial ruin?

"They've canceled the fireworks for Fourth of July!"

Doc laughed, though it made his head throb. "Oh, Morgan, you are a treat."

"What?" Morgan transferred his affronted expression from the paper to Doc.

"They just finished burning the place down, and you crave to do it again?"

"It won't be the Fourth without fireworks."

"It will, though, all over the world."

"You know what I mean." Morgan set the paper aside and leaned his elbows on the table. "Doc, I know I'm better off not asking—"

"Then don't ask."

"Now when did you know me to do what was good for me?" Morgan asked, grinning.

"When you set up housekeeping with Lou."

Morgan was startled. "Is that so?"

"I like Lou. She has a spine. Which cannot be said of that poor little brown bird of Wyatt's."

"Mattie?" Morgan snorted. "You live with Lou for a while, you'll like Mattie better."

"I doubt it. And don't speak ill of your woman to others. It's ungentlemanly."

"Oh, hell, Doc, you're almost family."

Heaven forfend, Doc thought.

"What do you think of the new one?" Morgan asked with a wink.

By which he meant Wyatt's new one. Sadie Marcus, that force of nature. "I think she's still hanging on Johnny Behan's arm."

"That won't last long. You wait 'til Wyatt crooks his finger."

"No, thank you. Miss Sadie is one of the few things on which Wyatt and I don't see eye to eye."

"Jealous?" Morgan leered across the table.

"I think Wyatt believes no woman can make a fool of him. There's no bigger fool than that."

Morgan was silent a moment, thoughtful. Doc was pleased. He liked to think he was, ridiculous as it sounded, a good influence on Morgan. Morgan and he were nearly of an age—in fact, Morgan was a hair older—but Doc suspected that proximity to Wyatt had kept Morgan from growing up, as a tall plant might shade a smaller one and keep it spindly.

Suddenly Morgan laughed. "Hell, you almost made me forget my question. Look here, you're a Reb and a college man, and we're Union men who went through the schoolhouse and that's all. Why'd you partner up with the Earps?"

It was a revealing speech, Doc thought. "We," for Morgan, meant what it did to Wyatt: his brothers. Whatever associations they had, whatever groups they each could claim membership in, the Earp brothers were a fraternal order beyond the dreams of Masons. And like Wyatt, Morgan saw a block, one man with many bodies, where Doc saw four men. It was funny that the town seemed to accept Morgan's and Wyatt's version over the evidence of their own senses.

"I have not partnered up with the Earps," Doc said. Morgan's eyes narrowed. Before he could speak, Doc continued. "I have no use for your brother Jim. We are speaking plainly, so I'll tell you that I think he is a damned storekeeper, and one who would put his thumb on the scales besides. And you may have noticed that Virgil and I are not bosom beaux."

"Virgil's a good man."

"Perhaps that's why. I am Wyatt's friend, for reasons that have nothing to do with North or South, or whether he reads Latin. As for you . . ." Doc leaned against the tent pole behind him and hooked his thumbs in his vest pockets. "Hell, have you ever seen me kick a dog?"

"Damn it, Doc, I oughta give you one in the nose!" Morgan laughed.

"You try and see what you get for it."

"Wyatt'll protect me."

"Wyatt will wipe your eye for you. Now, I answered your question. Will you answer one for me?"

Morgan's brows drew together. "Why wouldn't I?"

"Oh, possibly because you have more sense than I give you credit for. I'll take that as a 'yes.'" Doc leaned over the table, though he doubted he could be heard a foot away, given the constant racket of wrecking and rebuilding. "Why did you do it?"

Morgan was puzzling back over their conversation; Doc could see it in his face. "Do what?"

"Go out that night with Crane and his damned familiars."

A muscle sprang up in Morgan's jaw; for a moment his eyes were nearly cold as Wyatt's. Then he turned his head aside. "Oh, Jesus Christ, Doc. I don't know. You've done as bad or worse—why'd *you* do it?"

"Don't believe all you hear. I never turned road agent and killed two men who didn't raise a hand against me."

"I didn't! I fired over the horses, but I didn't shoot Philpot or the other fellow, I swear."

"In the dark? With your share of a bottle inside you? Plenty of big talk to prove?"

Morgan was gray and sweating, and not just from the heat in the tent, Doc was sure. "I don't . . . it ain't clear, all of it. I don't think so."

"So, led astray by false companions? That must have gone down a treat with Wyatt."

Morgan looked down at the splintery wood of the table.

"Well, you're right in one respect: I've some sympathy for ordinary human weakness, having experienced it at close range. Next time you commence to weaken, come to me first, all right?"

Morgan nodded.

Doc finished his drink and stood up. "Come on, let's see what's building that requires a commotion like unto the battle of Jericho."

"It won't be the Fourth without fireworks," Mildred said, scanning the text in the *Epitaph* again.

"Will you hold that thing down below the rail?" scolded Harry. "What'll folks think if they walk by the *Nugget* office and see our lady reporter reading the *Epitaph*?"

"They'll think we're keeping an eye on the competition." Mildred sat beside Harry's desk. Even so, she could barely hear him for the commotion of getting the weekly edition out. She had a story in it she was particularly proud of, about the Sycamore Springs Water Company, and was hoping she could dawdle in the office until the pressmen pulled a proof of that page. It was lowering to think that Harry probably knew exactly what she was doing.

Mildred added, "I suppose we'll have to be content with the delights of a fire company parade and a grand oration from Mr. Fitch." She looked across at Harry, who sat with his feet on his desk. "Harry, do we call it an oration because we know if we say 'speech,' everyone will avoid it like smallpox?"

"There's a ball, too," Harry reminded her.

"Yes, there's a ball. Which is another reason to regret the lack of fireworks." Harry gave her a stare like a baffled hound, so she said, "One need not go partnered to a fireworks display."

"No one says you have to go partnered to the dance."

"It looks odd. Do you think, if it rains every day between now and then, they'll change their minds about the fireworks?"

"Millie, if you stick at looking odd, I've got some mighty bad news for you. D'you want me to take you?"

"That'd be nice. Who'll take your wife?"

"Can't I walk into a ballroom with a handsome lady on each arm?"

"Only if one is your sister."

"Huh. Sounds like hoity-toity eastern manners to me."

Mildred gave up on suppressing a grin. "Harry, I'm trying to sulk, and you're making it very difficult."

From the open door, someone laughed; she turned and saw Jesse Fox. He took off his hat and stepped in.

Mildred sprang from the chair, her face hot. She felt as if she'd been caught at something. "Mr. Fox. You've met Harry Woods." Then she remembered—they'd met over Luther King's severed arm. She felt a sudden envy of people who never stayed long in one place: there would be so much less to keep track of.

Fox and Harry shook hands. Then Fox turned to her, and to her astonishment, flushed. It made her feel better.

She hadn't seen him since the night of the fire. Were they friends now? Were they something she had no name for, a thing forged of danger and fear, and if so, what public behavior did it call for? It was up to her to set the tone, but she had no idea what it should be.

Meanwhile Harry's gaze went from her to Fox, good-natured and intrusive. Newspapermen were a pack of gossipy old biddies at heart. She glared at him, and he beamed.

"This is a business call," Fox said, waving his hat vaguely toward the type cases. "Earl and Banning's Ice Cream Saloon opened for business this morning, and I thought the paper might want to cover the commencement of such a significant venture."

Mildred pressed her lips together. When she thought her voice would be steady, she said, "You rehearsed that."

"I thought you wouldn't let me finish if I didn't say it all at once."

Harry took his feet off his desk. "The man's right, Mildred. If we ignore it and the *Epitaph* covers it, we'll look nohow."

"It's not quite in the same league as the county elections."

"News is news. Don't forget your notebook."

She had no choice; she pinned her hat on and swept out the door Fox held for her.

Outside, Fox offered his arm and she laid her hand lightly on it. It felt warm through her glove, but that might be a product of her embarrassment.

"I'm going to skin Harry when I get back to the office," she said, "and it'll be all your fault."

"You notice that I didn't ask you to have dinner with me. I decided it was bad luck."

"Remarkable restraint on your part."

"Thank you. Are you rebuilding your house yet?"

She blushed again. "I feel silly saying this . . ."

"Are you selling?"

"John Fitzhenry made me a ridiculously good offer. They're moving the store to Sixth and Fremont, and my little lot is now an 'ideal location for mercantile ventures.' So says Mr. Fitzhenry."

"Good. Why do you feel silly?"

Mildred looked at the toes of her boots as they appeared and disappeared at her skirt hem. "We . . . went to so much trouble that night."

"If we hadn't, you might not have the lot to sell. Will you stay in Tombstone?"

Something in his tone—a kind of weight—made her look into his face. All she saw was polite interest. "I'm the *Nugget*'s celebrated lady reporter. How can I leave, after tasting fame?"

He laughed, as she'd meant him to. But he added, "You mean that, a little."

"What if I do?"

"You want to be famous?"

"I think fame would be dreadful. No, I enjoy writing for the paper. I took pride in being a good typesetter, and in being able to support myself. But this—" Mildred shrugged. "I do it for its own sake."

"Will you buy another lot?"

"There's a house I like at the corner of Third and Fremont. Not so much in the middle of things. The owner hasn't positively decided to sell, though."

"Here we are," said Fox. They stood before a yellow and white storefront with two plate-glass windows showing red velvet half curtains on brass rods. The gilded lettering on the glass declared, *Fresh Candy*, *Ice Cream*, *Coffee*, and *Lunches*. She could smell the new paint, the burnt sugar and roasting coffee.

In a moment she would be sitting across a table from Jesse Fox, trying to make conversation face-to-face. The thought made her freeze like a rabbit.

"Is your heart set on ice cream?" she asked.

He stopped at the door. "The ice cream was mostly bait."

"What were you fishing for?"

"Idle talk with present company."

Mildred looked down the street. "In that case, could we stroll a bit? It's a lovely day. . . ." Easier to walk and talk, surely, chinking the awkward pauses with mentions of weather or scenery.

Fox put out his elbow again. "It is, isn't it?"

And of course, she promptly couldn't think of a thing to say.

He saved her by taking up where he'd left off. "Are you comfortable in the meantime? Without your own place, I mean."

Mildred nodded. "Miss Gilchrist was so pleased about renting a room to a writer that she subscribed to the *Nugget*." And to *Gallagher's*, but Mildred wasn't going to mention that. "There's something to be said for moving house when one hasn't anything to move."

"Good Lord. That's a little too much making the best of things for me."

"I regret the photographs and letters, mostly. At that first view of the wreckage, I felt as if I'd lost my whole life."

"You couldn't salvage anything?"

"I had the dress I stood up in. And my savings in the bank, thank goodness."

"I see you spent it on adornment."

"Nonsense. Someone had ordered this and hadn't paid, so I got it cheap." She'd never bought a dress with her own money before. She wouldn't have bought this one if she hadn't been forced to it, but she felt astonishing pride in the striped silk twill with tiers of pleated ruffles, the square neck filled in with a lace chemisette. She shrugged again. "I won't say it wasn't a nuisance."

"So much for your stoic façade. Are you telling me you didn't lose books?" Fox asked as they waited for a wagon to pass.

"Twenty-three. Hardly a library." Recalling them made her heart sink. The manuscript of "The Spectre of Spaniard's Mine" was safe; she'd lent it to Allie to read days before. But Keats and Dickens and their companions were gone.

"I'm sorry for your loss," Fox said. "I've been traveling horseback for years, and even I have two books."

Mildred imagined him riding alone through the Sierras, hunched against the weather, with his books in his saddlebags. "Which two?"

"Emerson's *Nature*—"

"Really?"

"What's wrong with Emerson?"

"He's very . . . serious."

"Oh, so am I."

"What's the other?"

He smiled down at the sidewalk. "*Twelfth Night*."

"Aha! Shakespeare, and a comedy! Your favorite?"

"No, *Hamlet*'s my favorite." He shot her a quick, embarrassed look. "I told you I was serious. But the sort of day that can be brightened by *Hamlet* doesn't give you time to read."

"Tragedy lifts you out of yourself. Someone else's, anyway."

"Yes, but Maria making fun of Sir Andrew makes me laugh."

"I read it aloud to my younger sisters. They said it was very pretty, but that no one would really have taken Viola for a boy."

"They did if Shakespeare said they did," Fox declared.

"I hope you aren't that trusting with every author." Mildred contemplated anyone getting their notions of human nature from "Stampede at Midnight" and quaked with guilt.

"I assume they're trustworthy until proven otherwise."

"How," Mildred asked, feeling like a spy, "do they prove they're not?"

Fox looked up at the sky, or possibly the roof peak of Dr. Goodfellow's house. Mildred was startled; not only had she not needed weather or scenery, she'd entirely missed when they'd turned onto Toughnut Street. "Notable recent examples," Fox declared, "include horses that gallop through the night without pause, heroines who regularly faint when startled, and heroes who simultaneously and accurately fire a rifle in one hand and a revolver in the other."

She resolved that in "The Spectre of Spaniard's Mine," Regina wouldn't faint at all, whatever her provocation. "I'm afraid I have an adversarial relationship with authors. I open a book thinking, '*Try* to impress me.'"

Fox chuckled. "But you do like fiction."

Mildred clasped her hands hard on the chain of her purse, which enabled her to say, "Oh, yes," in an almost-level voice.

A breeze tried to lift Fox's hat, and he grabbed the brim.

"Walking's dusty work. What would you say to ice cream?" said Mildred.

If she'd meant to record the opening of Earl and Banning's, she should have paid it more mind. She knew they ordered ice cream and coffee, but neither held its own against the distraction of talking with Jesse Fox. He didn't flirt, not really, or salt his observations with compliments. It wasn't that he spoke to her as he might to a man; Harry did that, and it was refreshing, but it wasn't this. David had treated her like an intelligent being, but not an equal; the gap in their ages and experience made that seem just.

She couldn't explain it, quite; but she could enjoy it.

While Fox drank his coffee, Mildred noticed new skin on his knuckles, and no scabs. He healed fast, it seemed. He saw her gaze, and his eyebrows lifted. She felt as if she'd been caught prying, and to soften it asked, "Who was the Chinese boy who came to find you the day of the fire?"

"Chu? He was Chow Lung's servant."

"He seems to have taken possession of you."

Fox sighed. "That almost sums it up. Though, strictly speaking, he's Sam's servant, not mine. My horse," he added, when Mildred tilted her head and frowned.

"He seems young to be working."

"Apparently not," Fox said, in a discouraging tone. "I have no idea how old he is. Ten? Twelve? He says he doesn't know."

"When did you decide to hire a servant?"

"Never, but you see how that turned out."

Mildred laughed. "So not a houseboy, but a stable-boy."

"And since I don't have either a house or a stable, that's pretty ridiculous. Do you know anyone who might hire him and be decent to him?"

Perhaps this was the real reason he'd come to the *Nugget* office. "Why can't he stay where he is?"

His gaze dropped to the cup in his hands, and his face had iron in it. "It's not a good idea."

She could ask him what he was thinking, and he might tell her. She chose not to ask.

He sipped his coffee and looked across the cup at her, and became ordinary again. "I think the coffee's good. Don't you?"

"They'll get a daisy of a mention in the *Nugget*, unless someone robs a stagecoach tonight and there's no room. Have you noticed that news is entirely relative?"

The bell over the shop door rang. Fox raised his head and frowned, though his back was to the street. Mildred looked toward the door.

It was Wyatt Earp, with Sadie Marcus on his arm. At least, she'd been on his arm, and would be again as soon as Earp followed her through the door he held. Miss Marcus's eyes were downcast, and a little smile curled the corners of her mouth. Her dress was apple-green, embroidered with flowers and birds in the Oriental style. It was just the sort of dress Earp's wife ought to own and didn't.

Mildred thought of shy, pretty Mattie Earp, who always struggled to please everyone, and felt her hackles rise. Did Sadie Marcus know about a wife at home? Of course she did—Mildred had mentioned her at the theater. And if Sadie had forgotten, Earp wasn't reminding her.

Mildred tried to keep her thoughts off her face. Maybe John Behan had asked Earp to entertain Miss Marcus while he attended to business. Maybe they were going to meet Behan now. And maybe Mildred would grow a third arm.

Earp's chilly eyes stopped at their table, and Mildred caught a fleeting sharp scent, like a struck match. Then Earp smiled and crossed the room, Miss Marcus in tow. "Mr. Fox, isn't it? And Mrs. Benjamin. How d'you do."

Fox rose, smiling, too. "Miss Marcus." Mildred wasn't surprised when the woman tucked her chin and looked up at Fox through her eyelashes as he clasped her hand. "And Mr. Earp."

Earp took Jesse's hand in both of his, as one might greet a good friend. "Pleased, Mr. Fox, very pleased."

Fox looked puzzled. And well he might; Mildred recalled the way Earp had greeted him at the theater. "And here I'd thought I hadn't made a good impression."

Earp shook his head. "I beg your pardon for that. I'm colder than I mean to be, sometimes."

He hadn't been cold; he'd been rude and quarrelsome. Jesse blinked, as if the sun had struck into his eyes.

"Have supper with me this evening," Earp continued, "and we'll call it square. Mrs. Benjamin, I'd be delighted if you'd consent to come." Earp held out a hand to her.

It's not right, she thought, then wondered what she meant. But she laughed and gestured toward their empty dishes. "I'm afraid I'm too sticky to shake hands. What a shocking thing, when a grown woman can't eat ice cream and stay tidy."

Almost too quick to see, Earp's face stiffened. But she had seen it. The smile that followed, wide and delighted, didn't change that. "As long as you enjoy yourself."

Miss Marcus frowned at him, and at her. Mildred was afraid to look at Jesse Fox.

Fox said, "Awfully kind of you, Mr. Earp, but I'm afraid I'm engaged tonight. Maybe another time."

Mildred felt the tension go out of her. "I'm sorry, Mr. Earp; I'm busy tonight, as well."

"How have you been, Mrs. Benjamin?" Miss Marcus asked. A flash of irritation on Earp's face; for him, the conversation was over. "I heard you'd lost your house."

"Yes, but Mr. Earp's wife and sisters-in-law rallied to my cause. I don't know what I would have done without their help."

"That's good to hear," Earp said, biting the words off. Well, if his conscience troubled him, he knew what to do about it.

"I should get back to work," Mildred announced. "So nice to see you again, Miss Marcus, Mr. Earp." She stood and began to pull on her gloves, and Earp led Miss Marcus to a table. Fox offered Mildred his arm. His face above it was thoughtful.

"Well," she said when they reached the street. "That was bracing."

Fox eyed her curiously. "What was going on between you and Earp?"

"Nothing at all."

"It was just something he ate that disagreed with him?"

"Did you see *me* disagree with him?"

"Yes, I did." With a little shake of his head, he added, "Something like it, anyway."

"Did you also see him making up to you?"

"No." Fox wrinkled his nose and looked vaguely

up, as if working to remember. "I did see Miss Marcus making up to me."

"Not like that! It sounds suspicious-minded of me, but I wanted to ask him what he was selling."

"Hmm. I must have been in Cochise County long enough to vote."

"Maybe that's all it was. It will all come out eventually. Tombstone's like that. But didn't you think it was odd?"

"Mrs. Benjamin—"

"I thought I told you once to call me Mildred."

"You did, but that was . . ."

"In more trying times? I expect they'll come again, and it will save effort if I don't have to repeat myself when they do."

"Mildred, then." He looked ridiculously pleased. "Mildred, will you go to the Fourth of July ball with me?"

"You're changing the subject."

"No," he said, wary, "I'm asking you to the ball."

She realized belatedly that he had, indeed, asked her to the ball. "Did you overhear me talking to Harry?"

Fox stopped in the middle of the sidewalk. "How in heaven's name did you ever end up married? Pretend we're still talking about Shakespeare. Just answer."

"Shakespeare doesn't require a motive." It wasn't quite what she meant, but she was too flustered to do better.

Fox took a long breath and let it out. "All right. I'm a single gentleman. I'm still new in town. I know very few single ladies. I'm fond of dancing, and haven't had a chance to do it in a while. If you'd be so kind as to accept my escort to the Fourth of July ball, I'd be grateful. There. Motive." He crossed his

arms over his chest and waited. Mildred was reminded of a cigar-store Indian, except that they never
looked out of temper.

And that made her laugh. "I don't think I've ever
been asked to a dance by a man wearing quite that expression."

"I'm surprised it doesn't happen regularly."

"Are you certain you want to spend an evening in
such irksome company?"

"Yes."

"Then I accept. Thank you very much, Mr. Fox."
Before she turned toward the door of the *Nugget* office, she saw his face go blank with surprise.

"Jesse," he called after her.

She gave him a nod and a smile of what she hoped
looked like queenly condescension. It wasn't until she
was in the office and halfway to Harry's desk that she
understood what she'd done. She pressed her fingers
to her lips.

"Oh, blazes."

"What?" said Harry.

The fuller implications of what she'd done occurred
to her suddenly, and she said, "Oh, hell!"

"*What?*"

"The Fourth is two days away."

"Yes, it is," said Harry.

Mildred dropped into a chair, weak with the magni-
tude of the problem she'd created. "I haven't got a
gown."

"Mildred," Harry said. She was suddenly aware that
he was not smiling. He ought to be gloating at her, at
the way he'd gotten her out of the office in the company of a personable young man. Instead he sat very
still, his hands on the arms of his chair, his face stiff.

"What is it?" she asked.

Harry looked down at his knees, then back up. "The president's been shot."

Doc leaned back on his elbows and looked up into the willow leaves that fluttered overhead. "You were right. This is worth the trip." They were at the foot of the Dragoon Mountains, in the mouth of a canyon that was probably too small to have a name, on the lip of a spring, likewise. The sound of the water trickling from stone to stone was like harp strings brushed with a feather.

Kate sat beside the picnic blanket, smiling at him, her flowered cotton dress pooled around her. If the prairies and the high desert had spawned mermaids, they would look like that. "Did you get enough to eat?"

"I may need another piece of cake in a while."

"There's only the one piece left," she said, her eyes narrowing.

"I am not going to have to wrassle you for it, am I?"

One of her dimples showed, and he felt delight quicken his heartbeat. Her hand crept toward the basket.

"Oh, no you don't," he growled, and grabbed for her. Kate shrieked and laughed, and ended up as she'd probably planned, pinned under him on the blanket.

"All right," she said. "You can have your cake."

"Thank you, ma'am. I shall." Slowly he lowered his lips to her throat, and heard her breath hiss in through her teeth. She arched beneath him.

He pretended to be lazy about it, and took his time, though she groaned and clutched at him and tried to hurry him up. His reward was the look of her afterward, flushed and sleepy and sated. She looked like he felt, in fact. But there were too many people in the world who disliked him for him to be comfortable dozing outdoors in broad daylight.

He put most of his clothes back on and took the last piece of cake out of the basket. Kate watched him under her eyelids, pouting. "A man has to keep up his strength," he told her. She continued to pout. He grinned and held the cake out, and she took a bite. He watched her lick the crumbs off her lips. "You missed one," he said, and leaned over to touch his tongue to the corner of her mouth.

They finished the cake like that, alternating bites and kisses. "A girl needs her strength, too," Kate said when it was done.

"If you were any stronger, I would be frightened."

Kate quirked her mouth at him and proceeded to dress.

"Oh, don't do that," Doc said.

"You wouldn't want me to get a sunburn, would you?"

"No, I would not." He watched her dress, enjoying her self-possession.

They'd been happy together since the fire. Doc didn't want to inquire into the reasons. But he thought he could get used to being happy, being comfortable, even.

Kate settled down next to him, her hip against his. "Doc, this town's getting to be pretty flat."

"That can't be, darlin'. Don't you read Mayor Clum's editorials? Why, Tombstone is the Paris of the West."

Kate made a rude noise. "I'm damned glad John Clum is having a good time. But I'll bet even Paris gets slow after a while."

"Where would you rather be?"

He heard her keeping her voice light, her words casual. "Leadville sounds lively."

"I had heard that."

She turned abruptly to him. "Doc, why don't we go? We could make an excursion of it. We wouldn't have to stay away forever. Come on, we'll have a good time."

He looked into her eyes. Her voice was bright and cheery, but her eyes were begging. Kate never begged for anything. "I imagine you would be the queen of Leadville."

"Hell with that. As long as I'm with you, I don't care."

"You'd like to go."

She nodded, and he saw hope creep into her face. He could make her happy. The enormity of it, that he had this glorious woman's happiness in his two hands, humbled him.

"All right. Leadville it is."

"Oh, Doc!" Kate threw her arms around him and buried her face in his neck.

"My God, you would think I'd given you diamonds." The smell of her hair engulfed him.

"Maybe you have. Who knows what we'll find in Leadville?"

"I doubt it will be a diamond mine."

She laughed. "When do we go?"

"Not until after the Fourth." Wyatt would just have to do without him for a while. He'd done it before.

"Why not?"

He tipped her head up and kissed her fiercely. "Because I have bought two tickets to the Fourth of July ball, and I plan to dance with you."

She took his face between her palms and studied it. "All right, then. But after the Fourth—"

"After the Fourth," he agreed.

≈ **16** ≈

Allie Earp answered her door, pushing a strand of hair off her forehead with the back of her wrist. Even that careful gesture left a smudge of flour behind. "Millie! Lord, what a nice surprise. Come on in."

Mildred suddenly felt ashamed of herself. Allie had enough to do without taking care of Mildred, and certainly without anything as frivolous as this. But oh, how she wanted to concentrate on frivolity for an hour or two! The news from Washington was bad, but inconclusive; Harry had taken to hovering around the telegraph office, waiting for reports on President Garfield's condition.

She clutched her muslin-sheet-wrapped burden closer, and heard the taffeta inside whisper. "No, you're working. I'll come back some other time."

"Gracious, no, I'm playin'. Virge is partial to sweet things, so I'm surprisin' him with an angel cake."

"I should let you get back to it."

"It's in the oven. Now come on, we're letting flies in." Allie peered at the bundle in Mildred's arms.

Mildred looked down at it herself. Sunlight caught the crystals even through the muslin, and they winked at her.

So she stepped into the little parlor. "I've got myself in a fix, Allie. I've been invited to the July Fourth ball."

Allie's eyes got big. "Who by?"

"I don't think you know him. His name is Jesse Fox."

Allie squeaked and clapped her hands together. "Sure I do! The horse tamer!"

"Horse tamer?" *I don't even know what he does for a living,* Mildred realized.

"He broke that bay of ours to drive in an afternoon. Lord, Millie, it was like the man with the lions at the circus. You'd think he'd put a spell on that horse."

"Gracious." Mildred sat down. "I wish I'd seen it."

Allie frowned with remembering. "He was nice and polite. Handsome, too. Careless of his clothes, but men mostly are."

Mildred could personally recall several instances of Jesse Fox being less than faultlessly dressed. She grinned, and hoped it would pass for a response to Allie's words. "Speaking of clothes—that's my fix. I had a perfectly decent evening gown, until the house burned down. Lucy Austerberg gave me this one," Mildred said, hoisting the bundled dress, "but it needs to be altered to fit, and you've seen what I'm like with a needle."

"Mighty good of her," Allie said stiffly.

"I know she's a terrible gossip. But she'll empty her pantry for someone in trouble."

Allie sighed. "Lord knows she just says what everybody else does. And it's not so hard, knowing we've true friends out there." She smiled shyly at Mildred.

Mildred recalled Wyatt Earp with Sadie Marcus in the ice cream saloon. He stirred up talk, and the Earp women had to listen to it. "I went to all the dressmakers in town, but they're busy straight through until the ball, no time even for alterations. So I thought of you—but it's awfully short notice, and you're . . ." Mildred waved a hand around the parlor, trying to include house, chores, and husband in the gesture.

"Depends on how fussy it is to fit. Let's see this dress."

Mildred unwrapped the sheet. Allie's mouth formed an "O," but no sound came out. Finally she said, "I better go wash my hands."

While Allie washed, Mildred looked down at the

mass of changeable taffeta in her lap. It was brown and black by turns, shifting from one to the other as the folds of fabric moved. The color made her think of black coffee.

Allie bustled back in and scooped the pieces of the gown out of Mildred's lap and laid them over the furniture. The cap-sleeved bodice opened down the front with tiny faceted jet buttons, on an overlaid panel of black reembroidered lace. The lace was sewn with crystals and edged with black satin cord. The overskirt had a pointed apron of the same black lace, glittering with crystals and edged with silk floss fringe; black silk cord and tassels appeared and disappeared in the folds at the back. The hem of the skirt was trimmed with knife pleats and satin cord. The three pieces, spread out in Allie's parlor, looked exotic as an orchid. It was the sort of dress Mildred had dreamed of owning, when she was a debutante looking forward to wearing the sophisticated gowns of a married lady.

"My goodness," Allie said, smiling softly at the parts of the dress. Then she gave her head a shake, as if waking herself up. "You scoot across the street and fetch Lou and Mattie. Tell 'em to bring their silk pins."

For the next half hour Mildred stood in the Earp parlor in various stages of undress while the Earp ladies tucked, pinned, and marked around her.

Finally Allie and Lou carried in the cheval mirror from the bedroom and set it in front of Mildred.

She was entirely held together with pins, and afraid to move for fear of being pricked to death. But the woman in the mirror didn't look stiff or self-conscious. Beside the dark fabric her skin was creamy, and her hair showed sparks of red in the brown.

"You look like a queen of Spain," Lou said proudly.

"If I get any compliments, I'm going to point across

the room to you three and say, 'Those are my fairy god-mothers.'"

"Oh, we won't be at the dance," Allie replied, her voice flat and firm. Mildred glanced at the other two Earp women. Mattie was rolling up a tape measure with more than necessary care. Lou stood with her arms folded.

"Wyatt doesn't like for me to go out much," Mattie said quietly, to her lap. "He says Tombstone's a rough town, and men wouldn't show me proper respect." Then she raised her head and met Mildred's eyes. Hers were full of pain and pride.

Mildred looked from Mattie to Allie, who quirked her mouth in a mirthless smile. "The Earps are power-ful concerned about respect for their women," she said. Beside her, Lou's face was stony.

Mattie had only repeated the polite fiction that kept the Earp women isolated from their neighbors. A fic-tion, because isolation didn't protect their reputations. The less the town knew of them, the more it would imagine and spread reasons why three supposedly re-spectable married ladies didn't join in the social life of Tombstone.

Mildred's presence among them, from her first visit, had destroyed that fiction. Allie, Mattie, and Lou had only to look at Mildred, both respectable and free, to know it was a lie. But of course, they'd always known. Mildred just made the truth harder to ignore.

Some of her knowledge must have showed on her face, because Allie gripped her arm and smiled. "Lord, can you imagine a big pine tree like Virgil tryin' to waltz with a little acorn like me? No, hon, you dance with your horse tamer and tell us all about it afterward."

"I will, if you want me to." Mildred laid her hand over Allie's and squeezed.

"But just one glass of champagne," Lou warned.

"And if they have tea sandwiches, don't eat any with onions," Mattie added. "In case he kisses you." The Earp women giggled like girls.

"He only asked me because he doesn't know many ladies in town," Mildred said desperately.

Her companions looked at her as if she'd just assured them her mother had found her in an eggshell. "You bet he did," Allie replied. "Now, let's get you out of that so we can sew it up. You come by tomorrow morning, and we'll have it ready."

"Addie Bourland charges ten dollars for altering a gown."

"Well, good for her," Lou said brightly, sliding the skirt down over Mildred's petticoat. "Ouch! Allie, did you put this pin in wrong-way up?"

Which disposed of the question of payment, since Mildred didn't have the courage to raise it again. But she resolved to do ten dollars' worth of favors for the three Mrs. Earp.

*The parade, which should have been silly and provin*cial, caused her to have to pretend she'd gotten dust in her eye. The new company of firemen, with their bright wagon and its shining hose and brass fittings, marched through the streets of Tombstone, accompanied by the almost-as-new town band and representatives of every fraternal order and church group in town. All along the route, the citizens of Tombstone cheered the fire company like war heroes. Which they would be, Mildred reflected—they just hadn't gone into battle yet. Less than two weeks ago the town had experienced firsthand what these men would face. It loved them for stepping forward to carry the burden. Mildred found herself more moved than she ever had been by the larger, finer parades of Philadelphia.

Even Tom Fitch's oration was a splendid event. The subject (the vision of the Founding Fathers) was familiar, but he spoke in an excellent, heartfelt style. And through the day's activities ran a thread of hope. In Washington, the president still fought for his life, and the people around her spoke of him with cautious optimism.

She hadn't seen Jesse Fox at either the parade or the speech, but there was no surprise in that; the population of Tombstone was plenty of haystack to hide a needle in. Her stomach fluttered a little when she thought of evening, of the dance, of being in company. There was nothing to be nervous about. She would be nicely dressed, she knew the steps, her manners were sufficiently good that she wasn't likely to do something disgraceful by accident, and if she sat out a few dances, it would be only a chance to rest her feet. Still, she found she had to reassure herself more than once.

A cooler wind gusted suddenly down the street, flapping ribbons and lace on parasols, lifting swags of tricolored bunting like sails, and tossing several straw hats off heads and over the crowd. Mildred looked up to see clouds piling high over the Dragoons. The rainy season had arrived.

As she made herself an early dinner in Miss Gilchrist's kitchen, she heard thunder mutter in the distance. The air through the open window was sharp and promising.

She imagined picking her way through muddy streets in several pounds of taffeta skirt and petticoat and her dancing slippers, and her heart sank for an instant. But she took another breath of wind with rain in it and changed her mind. The first storm of the summer was a happy madness, a reckless joy, that infected anyone it fell on. Even the skies had chosen to celebrate the Fourth. She would dance wet and muddy, if it came to that.

She put her hair up in a twist at the back, and held it with a pair of ebony combs she'd got at Austerberg's. Then the slippers with their little heels—she'd been lucky to find a pair to fit ready-made—her gown, long gloves, and a black lace fan to hang on her wrist. Her pearl necklet had been lost in the fire, but it would have been too plain, anyway. She fastened a black velvet ribbon around her throat, and pinned the rhinestone brooch Lucy had lent her to it.

There, she was ready. And terrified. Suddenly she was certain that Fox wouldn't come, that something had happened. *Stop it*, she scolded. *You've used up all the bad luck in your lifetime. From now on, you're safe*.

She heard a horse's hooves and the rattle of wheels, and heard them stop outside the house. She peeked out the curtains to see Jesse Fox step down from a covered buggy. His bucskin horse was between the shafts, and the boy, Chu, stood at the horse's head.

She opened the door before he could knock. "It's going to rain," he said, in answer to her look past him at the buggy.

"That's true," Mildred admitted, and let him into the parlor.

He was neatly clad in formal black and white. He held out a gloved hand that for an instant appeared to be on fire. But it was a silk tiger lily blossom in his palm.

"There are no fresh flowers in Cochise County in early July. I admit, I didn't search the whole of it, but I have it on good authority."

"That's also true. Wait 'til the middle of the rains, though, and you'll be shocked at what blooms."

"Shocked?"

"Impressed, at least. I was downright stunned when I first saw it happen." She took a pin from Miss Gilchrist's store on the hall table and pinned the silk lily high on her right shoulder. The fierce red-orange made her skin look like porcelain.

In the mirror she caught Fox's eyes. He was smiling a little, in a strange, private way that was almost sad. Images flooded her mind: a fire in a fireplace, leaves rustling overhead in summer, sunlight on snow. She felt, not perfect happiness, but the memory of it. Why would Jesse Fox remind her of past joys, when he hadn't provided her with any present ones? Not yet, anyway.

She turned briskly from the mirror. "Look all right?"

"Perfect." He held out his hand, and she laid hers on it.

It was raining, light, pattering drops, by the time Jesse drew Sam up in front of Schieffelin Hall. He pulled an umbrella from under the seat, climbed out, and handed Mrs. Benjamin—Mildred—out of the buggy under its shelter. He walked her inside and to the door of the ladies' retiring room, then came back. Chu had hopped down from the back and onto the bench, and had the reins in his hand.

"Thank you, Chu. Bring the rig back around midnight, all right?"

"Huh. Be raining like horse piss then."

"I expect. There's a slicker folded up in back if you need it. And thunder and lightning don't trouble Sam."

Chu looked toward the hall, where the new windows sparkled with gaslight, and the ladies and gentlemen inside passed before them, bright-colored and black. Jesse would have sworn his expression was wistful. "Huh," he said, and clucked to Sam. The buggy rolled away.

Mildred had disposed of her wrap and was waiting for him outside the retiring room. The foyer was full of women who had gone to every length possible to look their best, but not one of them made his heart feel tight and his lungs empty the way Mildred Benjamin did. Funny that such an unpleasant sensation should be so welcome. She seemed to stand in a better-lit room than the rest of the company. He wondered why everyone there hadn't turned to stare at her by now.

As he came up she grinned like a schoolboy, which contrasted wildly with her gown and hair. Jesse was glad she couldn't see it; she'd probably try not to do it again.

"This has all the signs of being a bang-up party. Wait 'til you get a squint at the ballroom."

"Mrs. Benjamin, such vulgar expressions!"

"You sound like my mother."

"Yoiks. I'll stop, then. Did you give her much reason to sound like that?"

"Now and then. I decided that a bit of tasteful disregard for convention would set me apart from the other debs."

"Dear heaven," Jesse said. "You're a society girl?"

She lifted her lovely head and drooped her eyelids, like an actress playing Queen Elizabeth. "My papa is a very *warm* man."

Laughter burst out of him. He hoped she wouldn't make him laugh like that on the dance floor. "Let's get you a dance card. I need to put my name down before the fortune-hunters get to you."

He exchanged his ticket for dance cards, and opened them immediately.

"Here, you, one of those is mine," Mildred protested.

He'd remembered to bring a pencil, which impressed even him. It had been a while since he'd been to an event that involved dance cards. He wrote his name down for the grand march and quadrille, the Lancers, a waltz contredanse, a mazourka, and the last waltz. Then he handed one card to Mildred with a little bow.

She looked at it and shook her head. "You can't have five. If you dance more than four dances with the same lady, people will talk."

Jesse knew that, but he didn't plan to let it weigh with him. "Remember, I know so few ladies in town. And it's such a long program of dances. Won't you feel cold-hearted when you see me standing against the wall, watching all those happier gentlemen whose partners aren't so cruel?"

She blushed. "I think I'm being hoisted on my own petard. All right, but if the Methodist ladies cut me on the street tomorrow, I'll sue you for loss of character. Come see the ballroom."

He held out his arm, and she laid her hand on it. Looking at her profile, he wondered if anything short of loss of character would convince her to think of him as more than a friend. No, that was ridiculous— Mildred Benjamin was not the sort of woman whose reputation demanded a husband to prop it up.

Then he realized the madness of the thought. He was no fit suitor, and a barely acceptable friend, for anyone. His friendship had been no protection for Lung, and Lung had been better able to defend himself than Mildred was. He tried to imagine telling Mildred Benjamin, "I can light candles with my thoughts and bury myself alive. My friend Chow Lung was a Chinese sorcerer. And somewhere in Tombstone, there's another sorcerer who'll probably kill me if he finds me."

He almost wished he were a cattle rustler. It would be just as dangerous, but easier to explain.

The band was tuning up. He led Mildred into the

stream of good citizens of Tombstone, and they flowed through the big doors into the ballroom.

In the east there were grand theaters with three balconies that held a thousand people, ornamented with gold leaf and velvet and crystal. There were ballrooms two full stories high, with allegorical murals on the ceilings, a dozen French doors hung with silk, and more gas lighting than the entire Arizona Territory could boast. But since he'd passed St. Louis, Jesse had found that elegance was a thing hung on context. Here in the heart of Apache country, Schieffelin Hall was a marvel.

Some of the effect, he supposed, was the company. But the many bright brass chandeliers shone down on elaborate ornamental paintwork, a wide, deep stage curtained with purple velvet and gold fringe and tassels, and a floor that shone like glass. The walls were swagged with red, white, and blue bunting, held up by the claws of gold-painted plaster eagles.

Two large framed prints hung above the proscenium arch of the stage. One was a portrait of George Washington, a reproduction of the Stuart painting. The other was of President Garfield, a tinted engraving from his inauguration photograph. Beside the print of Washington it looked faded and ghostly. Jesse hoped it wasn't an omen.

But were there omens in the natural laws of his strange new country? How was he supposed to sort out superstition from fact, when what ought to be superstition had become the heart of a sort of bastard engineering?

The prints were flanked by a pair of American flags threaded with wire along their edges and shaped so they seemed caught in the midst of billowing in the wind. Young trees in pots, their branches studded with artificial flowers among the real leaves, stood on either side of the stage and at intervals along the walls. They interrupted the many gilt chairs placed along the room's edges for the dancers' relief.

"What did I tell you?" Mildred said happily. "Bang-up. There's really no other expression that will do."

"Passable."

"If you're going to tease, I wash my hands of you."

"No, no, I'll be very good." Jesse looked into Mildred's open, smiling face and knew that in spite of danger, loss, and every other dark fact of life, he would rather be here, now, than anywhere else in the world or time.

The band on the stage consisted of piano, string bass, snare drum, clarinet and fife, and two violins. The floor director called out from the stage, "Ladies and gentlemen! Take places, please, for the grand march!"

Jesse led Mildred to a place in the line of what were about to become dancers. "You *have* done this before?" Mildred asked suddenly.

He looked across their hands and saw that it was a serious question. "A little bit," he assured her, and the fiddles began to scrape out the opening bars of the march.

The line of marching couples snaked through the hall, admiring one another's clothes, noting the presence or absence of friends, and who was on whose arm. Mildred nodded and smiled at a daunting number of people. He tried not to feel jealous of any of them. Mildred had been here for over a year, a long time in the life of the camp; she had work and a position in the social fabric, and so she had friends. Jesse was a drifter on his way to Mexico.

Worse, she was a woman in a man's profession, so she could hardly be starved for sensible male company. In a dime novel, he could rescue her from a runaway coach, and that would settle both their futures. Life set the bar considerably higher.

By the time the floor director called sets for the quadrille, Jesse despaired of ever seeing a particle of happiness again. He turned to look longingly at Mildred on his right, and found her grinning at him.

"Jesse, if you let your thoughts wander, you're going to forget the figures."

That pleasant, uncommon sound: his name in her voice. And he was happy again, just like that. Ballrooms were for tonight's pleasure, not tomorrow's worries. He could agonize like an undergraduate over breakfast.

"I never forget the figures," he assured her. The fiddles struck up again, and he bowed to his partner.

*They arrived late, but since Kate arrived late every-*where, Doc hadn't expected anything else. He had no great fancy for the opening promenade, anyway.

They hurried under the overhang and Doc folded the umbrella. Kate peered through the windows at the latecomers in the foyer, and beyond them the dancers in the ballroom swirling through the figures of a quadrille. In the light from the window she was flushed, and her eyes were bright. She smiled at Doc dizzyingly. "Oh, Doc, this beats anything for fun."

"Even if I take all your waltzes?"

"Now, you have plenty of chances to get your arm around me."

"Never enough." Best not to say that he had little enough opportunity to thwart the chances of other men. But he loved to waltz, and Kate was graceful and bird-light on a dance floor.

The end of a cigar glowed red in the shadows near the door. Doc stepped between it and Kate. But it was Morgan's voice that said, "Hello, Doc. That Johnson boy growed up yet?"

"If it were any business of yours, I would tell you," Doc said cheerfully.

Morgan moved into the light and tipped his hat to Kate. "Evening, Mrs. H. Save me a polka?"

"Oh, no," Kate replied, laughing. "My shoes are brand-new."

"I promise I won't tread on 'em."

"Then I guess if you wrote your name down for a polka, I wouldn't hide when it came 'round."

Morgan turned to Doc. "Jim Crane's at Gray's ranch. Frank Leslie went out to bring him in."

Even tonight, the Earps' concerns would intrude. Kate was right: they needed time away from Tombstone. "Really?" Doc raised his eyebrows, to make sure even Morgan couldn't mistake his tone. "Well, then, that's all taken care of, isn't it?"

"Hell, yes. Either Frank'll shoot him, or he'll shoot Frank and run for Mexico. Either way we'll be done with him."

Only Kate's presence kept Doc from saying, *If you hadn't thrown in with him, none of us would give a damn about Jim Crane*. Instead he replied, "Of course Frank Leslie will draw on Jim Crane. If Crane is dead drunk and unarmed. Or were you thinking of a back-shooting?"

Morgan's eyes narrowed; he looked for a moment so like Wyatt that Doc had to review the conversation to make sure he wasn't talking to the wrong brother. "Frank's no coward."

"Did I say so? I only do him the favor of thinking he's not stupid."

Morgan sighed. "Damn. I guess we'll be riding out with a posse after all."

"Not I," Doc declared. He felt Kate beside him, a warm presence in the wet night air. "Kate and I are going to Leadville for a while."

"No, really? Hell, wish I could go with you. But you know how it is—Wyatt's got all of us runnin' after something."

"Don't let him wear you to a stub."

Morgan laughed. "There's too much of me for that." Doc took Kate's arm, and Morgan added, "Mrs. Holliday, you remember that polka."

"You remember it yourself," she retorted.

As Doc opened the door for her, she squeezed his arm and smiled up at him. "You're welcome," he murmured as they passed into the light and heat of the ball.

*Mildred had forgotten an important fact about Tomb-*stone. However sophisticated it had become, it was a mining camp still. There were more men than women in it.

Her dance card was full; she'd had to decline the honor of dancing with half a dozen gentlemen. She danced the schottische with Frederick Austerberg, who begged for a repeat of the pleasure at the ball the Turnverein Society planned for August. She enjoyed a breathless, light-footed polka with Richard Rule, who was smiling for the first time since the news about Garfield had arrived. Sheriff Behan partnered her in a mazourka, good-natured when she couldn't at first remember the steps; after the dance, until her next partner claimed her, he talked sensibly about town politics. She danced with a young officer from Camp Huachuca, who told her about his sisters back in Minnesota. She thanked God that her shoes fit her well, because she didn't sit down for five minutes together.

Jesse Fox's name was on her card for the Lancers, the last dance before the intermission. She'd seen him in the sets in the course of the evening, and had even

been on his left in one of the quadrilles. His partner
for that dance was a very young lady whose name Mildred couldn't remember, a fey-looking brown-eyed
creature. During the schottische he'd caught her eye;
he was standing against the wall near the stage, and
when she looked, he donned a mournful expression.
She'd grinned at him.

"So, Mrs. Benjamin," said John Dunbar, beaming
and blotting his face with his handkerchief. He'd just
galloped her through a polka redowa. "Who shall I deliver you to?"

Mildred checked her dance card to be sure. Yes,
she'd been looking forward to this. "Mr. Wyatt Earp
has put his name down for the waltz."

"And here comes the lucky fellow."

Wyatt Earp slipped sideways between the milling
couples at the edge of the floor. He looked surprisingly grim; but as he approached, he smiled at Mildred.

"Hi, Wyatt, good thing you didn't waste any time, or
I'd have been tempted to keep the lady," Dunbar said
to him. "She's like dancing with a feather."

"Good to hear. I'm no great hand at dancing, but I'll
try to do you justice, Mrs. Benjamin."

Interesting, she thought. A man who's not much for
dancing comes to a ball anyway, and not to escort his
wife. Why, then? "Oh, I'm sure we'll get along, Mr.
Earp. Thank you, Mr. Dunbar."

Dunbar bowed to her. "Pleasure's mine, Mrs. Benjamin."

When she turned back to Earp, he said, "If I get in a
scrape, you'll pull me out, won't you?"

Mildred folded her fan. "But, Mr. Earp, on the
dance floor the lady must be guided by the gentleman.
Besides, you wouldn't want to be rescued by a female,
would you?"

To her surprise, Earp only smiled wider. "Oh, a little nudge with your elbow or a nod the way I'm supposed to go—that wouldn't be against the rules. Would it?"

"You may count on me," she said gravely. He nodded and, when the floor manager called for the couples to assemble for the Aurora waltz, led her onto the floor.

Earp was in luck, then, and so was she; the Aurora was the simplest waltz she knew. One didn't need to pay careful attention to the figures, and could converse with one's partner. Earp proved to be a precise, rather stiff dancer, but he knew what the calls meant, and didn't lag behind the measure in executing them.

When they reached the top of the set and came together to waltz, it was Earp who began the conversation.

"How do you like your work, Mrs. Benjamin?"

"Very much."

"I'd think it would put you in the way of a rough crowd."

"Oh, reporters are the most protected of creatures. Even the roughest fellow knows that if he gives us trouble, he'll suffer for it in print." She smiled brilliantly at him.

He quirked his eyebrows, and his mouth under his moustache. Mildred thought he knew she'd meant that as a barb. But he was amused, or chose to be amused. As they circled decorously back to the top of the set, Earp asked, "How did you meet Mr. Jesse Fox?"

"He came in to buy a paper. Is he one of the rough crowd?"

"He's not much known, and doesn't always keep good company. I'd worry to see a sister of mine take up with him."

He looked sincerely concerned for her. Mildred found herself warming toward him; he was kind, and had more of a sense of humor than she'd expected. Then she remembered Mattie Earp, and Sadie Marcus, and Allie's ironic comment. "But then," she replied, "you're very protective of your womenfolk."

At that point they cast off, turning away from each other at the top of the set and passing to the bottom. When they reached it, whatever reaction he might have shown was gone. They had little chance to talk until they were head couple again, and waltzing.

"I suppose Virgil's missus has been giving you an earful," he said as they went up the set.

"It does seem hard that your wife has so little social life."

Another man might have recommended, as delicately as possible, that she mind her own business. Earp smiled sadly instead. "You'd have to know Mattie. I'll bet she seems shy to you. But on her own, she does things she regrets mightily later. I have to protect her from herself."

"Really?"

"I think she's . . . well, maybe not quite right. It's good of you to offer her a little decent female company."

Which, in two short sentences, dealt with both his wife and his sisters-in-law. By the time Mildred arrived at the top of the set she had an entirely new opinion of Wyatt Earp.

They cast off again, and when they arrived at the bottom of the set it was Mildred who had her social face fastened on once more. The dance called for couples to all swing as the last figure in the sequence, and when they did, Earp said, "You won't say anything about that to anyone, will you?"

They were parted by the dance, and the top couple whirled up and back and up the set between them. When Mildred came together with Earp again, she said to him, as sweetly as she knew how, "Of course not, Mr. Earp. What sort of name would I deserve, if I blackened a helpless woman's character behind her back?"

His face turned red and rigid. They finished the dance in silence, and Earp's arm, when he led her off the floor, was like stone under her hand. He left her without a bow, and without giving her over to her next partner.

She'd made an enemy. But a man who could say such things about the woman under his protection to a near-stranger was no one she wanted for a friend. She found she'd clenched her hands into fists. She snapped her fan open and used it vigorously, and tried to re-assemble her ballroom composure.

"Whom would you like killed?" Jesse Fox asked at her elbow.

Apparently she hadn't entirely succeeded. "No one. Don't encourage me. Gracious, is it our dance already?"

His face fell like a pantomime clown's. "And here I've been counting the minutes."

She had to laugh, which made her feel better immediately. "You're certain that wasn't steps you were counting?"

"*One*-two-three, *one*-two-three," he muttered. "I'm fine for the waltz, but if I have to count to four, there'll be trouble. You know, if you're worn to a shadow and would rather sit out, I'll keep you company."

"Gracious, no, I love the Lancers. There'll be sitting enough during the intermission."

"I'll make sure you restore your strength with cake then." He led her into a set.

Mildred realized when they got there that they were top couple in the square. "You're sure—"

"Rest content. We'll be fine."

She didn't know the lady of the couple across the set, but the gentleman was Frank McLaury, Tom's brother. It made sense that they would come into town for the Fourth of July festivities. She took a deep breath and sent out an unaimed prayer that neither Frank McLaury nor Jesse Fox were overestimating their abilities. The top and bottom couples would lead off the figure, and the Lancers was an unforgiving quadrille.

Then the fiddles leaped onto the melody in fine, wild harmony, and the snare drum and string bass seemed to lift her feet from the floor when they joined in. Disaster might lurk ahead. But she was suddenly, uncontainably happy.

Jesse Fox swept them into the figure without hesitation or misstep. When the top and bottom couples crossed over and back, with Jesse and Mildred passing between Frank and his partner on the way down and outside them on the way back, none of them collided, and she relaxed.

Jesse leaned his head a fraction toward her. "Told you," he murmured. He had a grin unsuited to a ballroom and a light in his eye as wild as the fiddles. He looked like she felt.

When the figure called for the gentlemen to turn the opposite lady, she said, "Good evening, Mr. McLaury. Is your brother here, too?"

He flushed. "No, ma'am."

She knew Frank McLaury was proud and inclined to take offense, but this, she thought, was simple embarrassment. At the next cross, she added, "I don't mean to pry. But is he well?"

McLaury seemed to be thinking about that—and about her as well, perhaps. When the dance brought them back together, he answered, "Tom's well. He's got the bit between his teeth on something, that's all."

Mildred felt a stab of alarm. "Not—?" She swallowed the name as the dance moved them on. One did not bandy another woman's name about on a dance floor, especially one so young. At the next opportunity, she ventured, "A certain very young lady?"

Frank shrugged. "Tom's a grown man. He knows his own mind." But Mildred knew from McLaury's face that he was worried.

And Tom wasn't here. Had he taken advantage of the distraction the celebrations provided to visit Hattie Earp? If so, they were having a wet time of it. She didn't think Tom would risk Hattie's reputation by sitting with her indoors unchaperoned. Perhaps the rain would discourage them. Perhaps they'd give up their rendezvous, and Tom would go back to his hotel room, and nothing would come of it.

Jesse bowed to her as the musicians finished and the sets broke up.

"Thank you," she said, "that was splendid."

"Now, why is it that you doubted my dancing skills?"

She felt a blush creep over her face. "It's just that— Not everyone has a chance to learn the dances well, you know."

"You did."

"Of course I did. Along with all the less entertaining things young ladies are taught before they go into society."

He smiled warmly at her, and she had the impression he was relenting. "Columbia University has high standards for gentlemanly accomplishments."

"You went to Columbia?"

"For two years." He shrugged. "Until a family crisis."

Mildred longed to ask, but she settled for, "What did you study?"

"Ironically, geology and engineering. I was planning

a career in mining. And here I am, at one of the biggest
silver strikes in history, training horses."

"And aren't you lucky you learned to dance before
you came?"

He laughed. "Uncommon lucky."

She went into the tea room on Jesse's arm, and he
pulled out a chair for her at one of the tables. "What
can I fetch you?"

"I believe you promised me cake. Champagne never
goes amiss. And anything else that looks good, because I'm sorry to say I'm starving."

He laughed. "If anyone gives me the eye for filling a
plate, I'll tell 'em it's for me." And he slipped into the
crowd at the buffet tables.

Frederick and Lucy Austerberg came in from the
ballroom. "Mrs. Benjamin, may I seat my lovely partner beside you?" Frederick asked, and Lucy giggled.

"Of course."

He was sliding Lucy's chair under her when Sheriff
Behan approached. He had Sadie Marcus on his arm,
but Sadie seemed determined not to notice Behan beyond what was absolutely necessary. Mildred was surprised; good manners generally prevented a quarrel of
that size in a ballroom, and she'd always thought John
Behan's manners especially good.

"Have you got two seats for a weary pair of terpsi-
choreans?" Behan asked, a little too hearty.

Mildred took pity on him. "Certainly. Welcome to
the Footsore Club."

Behan seated Sadie next to what would be Frederick's chair, bowed to the ladies, and joined Frederick
on the way to the buffet. Sadie seemed absorbed in
disapproving of one of the wall sconces. Lucy, at the
other extreme, was staring at Sadie as if Behan had
just seated a wild animal at the table. She was probably taking in the amount of bosom visible above the

quantities of bullion fringe and spangles on Sadie's bodice.

If she was going to feel pity, Mildred reflected, it ought to be dispensed generally. She smiled at Sadie and said, "Lovely ball, don't you think?"

Sadie's gaze dropped from the wall sconce to Mildred, her eyes wide with surprise. "Yes—yes, it *is* nice."

"I expect it to get even nicer. My favorite dance is in the second half. Do you know Portland Fancy?"

"Oh, yes, we danced that at home." To Mildred's amazement, an entirely new Sadie Marcus appeared before her. This one was much younger, and seemed to have forgotten anger, coquetry, and calculation all in a lump. "I don't know why it is, but it's so exciting to pass through the line like that and dance with another set each time."

"Where is home?" Mildred almost preferred the calculating Sadie. With her guard down, the girl made Mildred feel like someone's elderly auntie.

"San Francisco. We had lots of fun, even though we weren't allowed to go to public balls like this. Of course"—and the veneer went back up—"that was many years ago."

Jesse returned, carrying two plates and two glasses of champagne with no apparent difficulty. He looked around the table, put on an affronted face, and said to Mildred, "But you told me you were a pariah!"

"I'm restored to grace, having acquitted myself decently in the Lancers. Jesse Fox, this is Mrs. Frederick Austerberg, the original owner of my gown. And you know Miss Marcus."

They all declared themselves pleased. Mildred was relieved when Lucy struck up a conversation with Sadie about routes to Arizona Territory from San Francisco.

"I'm sorry," Jesse murmured as he set her plate down. "Was I outrageous?"

"Yes, but anyone *I* introduce you to is probably accustomed."

"I've noticed that about you. You have a bizarre and singular sense of humor."

"I'm taking that for a compliment," Mildred sighed, and studied her plate. "Oh, macaroons! Jesse, you're a trump."

"The smoked oysters and salad are there to make it seem as if you don't live on sweets."

She compared the contents of his plate. He had just as many macaroons as she did. He must have seen her look; he added, "I only got them in case you needed extra. To your health." He lifted his glass.

She'd called him by name again, as easily as she did with Harry. No, not quite as easily, since with Harry she didn't think about it after she'd done it. Nor would she ever feel this nervous flutter at the thought if she did.

By the time Behan returned, Sadie seemed to have decided to forgive him for whatever he had or hadn't done. Frederick Austerberg was always good fun, being fond of any kind of socializing. Jesse set himself to charm Lucy, and wasn't outrageous at all. It was a thoroughly pleasant meal.

It was interrupted now and then by thunder, and once a flash of lightning through the windows that made the gas lamps seem dim. There was considerable hubbub in the room, but Mildred thought she could hear the rush of rain outside.

When she finished, Jesse asked, "Would you like to take a turn around the foyer? I think that's as close to the fresh air as we're likely to want to get."

"Yes, please. We can look out the windows."

"Do you like storms?" he asked as he escorted her out.

"To watch. Riding through one is nothing I want to do again."

"Where were you when you did that?"

"Kansas. It left me with a low opinion of the whole state."

Jesse shook his head. "I nearly froze to death in Colorado, but you don't see me holding a grudge."

"Obviously, you're a better person than I am."

The view from the foyer windows was excellent. They could see the street running with water, the roofs shining, and beyond the roofs, the lightning knifing down to strike behind the Tombstone Hills. The dark sky seemed to tear like paper, and each bolt looked like harsh white light revealed through the rip. Thunder rattled the window they stood at. They ooohed and ahhhed at the display, and Mildred laughed.

"We have fireworks after all," she said.

Three forks of lightning lit the street for an instant like daylight. In the flash Mildred saw two men on the porch of Schieffelin Hall. They were hatless, but in the frozen moment of light, she couldn't tell who they were or what they were doing.

She heard hurrying footsteps behind her and turned. Kate Holliday had just come through the ballroom doors; she was crossing the foyer at a near-run, the skirt of her gown caught up in both hands. "Where is he?" she demanded.

Jesse stepped forward. "Can I help you?"

Kate stopped. "I'm sorry. Have you seen Dr. Holliday?" Her breath came quick and hard, and her gaze flew around the room, as if her husband might appear there at any moment. What would frighten a woman as tough as Kate Holliday?

Doc shivered in the cold, damp air on the porch. Only a few feet from him, the rain fell off the roof edge in a sheet, and frothed away tumbling and brown toward

the nearest wash. Lightning blazed like a great match
striking, and thunder cracked hard on its heels.

"This is a damned fine place for a chat," he said to
Wyatt. "I hope there's a reason why we couldn't have
it indoors."

"Privacy," Wyatt replied. "Morgan says you're leaving town."

The chill he felt was not from the wind. "I am. Kate
and I are going to Colorado."

"For how long?"

Doc shrugged. "I expect we'll be back eventually.
And the telegraph works, you know."

Wyatt was silent. Doc knew he should let the silence
stand, or bid Wyatt good evening and go back inside to
Kate. But something about Wyatt's posture, or the
charged air of the storm, or his own cold skin, made
him say, "I am not one of your brothers. I don't have to
account to you for my movements."

He heard Wyatt take a long breath. "Of course not,"
Wyatt said softly, so softly that Doc had to strain to
hear him over the sound of the water. "But I can't
spare you just now, Doc."

"The devil you can't. You've got your whole family,
the mayor, and three dozen or so upright citizens ready
to come when you whistle. What do you need me for?"

Wyatt turned his head, and Doc saw blue fire in his
eyes from the lightning flash. "You're essential. I
thought you knew that."

"You've been drinking," Doc snapped, and started
for the door.

"Don't do that," Wyatt said.

Doc stopped. He had every intention of going
through that door, going back to the ballroom, finding
Kate and waltzing with her. Instead he stopped.

He heard the doorknob in front of him rattle as
someone inside took hold of it. At the same time he

heard Wyatt step toward him, felt Wyatt's hand on his shoulder. He heard Wyatt's breath hiss in through his teeth.

Sweat soaked Doc's clothes. His lungs were a burning, compacted mass in his chest, good for nothing. The world tilted and began to spin.

He fell forward and caught at the door frame, but there was no strength in his hands or arms. He slid to the walkway, and felt the rainwater and tracked mud on the boards beneath his cheek.

"Doc!" Kate screamed above him. He smelled jasmine. He hoped it was her perfume, and not a fever dream.

Just as Kate Holliday reached for the doorknob, Jesse tasted something metallic, caught a scent like the air around an electrical generator. *Lightning.* "No," he said, and reached to stop her.

Whatever it was went off, but it wasn't lightning.

It hit him in the chest. He staggered and fell, and found himself sitting on the floor of the foyer looking out the door, past Mrs. Holliday's skirt. He heard her shriek, saw her drop to her knees to clutch at the man lying in the doorway.

The man behind the fallen man, the one who stood outside with the rain lashing behind him, had done the thing. Not a shot, not a blow. Not a thing given, but rather something drawn off and gathered in. The force that had struck Jesse was the excess, whatever passed over the spillway because it wasn't needed to fill the reservoir of power.

It was Wyatt Earp outside the door. He caught and held Jesse's eyes. Then the second blow came.

Pain shot through his temples. His stomach flopped as if he'd been turned upside down. And he saw, for an instant, two things: Earp standing in the doorway, his eyes cold, one hand raised; and Earp crouching over Holliday, supporting his shoulders, his face twisted with concern. He saw them both at once, as if someone had put the wrong picture in one half of a stereopticon slide. In his memory, too, there were two versions of the last few seconds, and one of them had nothing uncanny in it.

Then he saw Mildred Benjamin. She was clutching the edge of the parlor table under the window. She was pale, and her eyes were wide and fixed on Earp. At the sight of her Jesse's vision cleared, and his memory as well. The false versions were still there, but transparent as steam.

It had only been seconds since Mrs. Holliday opened the door. Jesse crouched and got his arms under Holliday's shoulders and knees—his hands passing through the illusion of Earp's arm—and hoisted. It didn't take as much strength as he'd expected; Holliday was tall, but Jesse could feel his bones even through the layers of cloth.

"On the settee," Mildred ordered, breathless. Kate Holliday held Doc's hand as Jesse carried him across the foyer and draped him over the settee. He heard Earp's boots on the floor behind him.

Mildred felt Holliday's pulse and his forehead. "Give me one of your feathers," she ordered Mrs. Holliday. When the other woman looked blank, Mildred reached out and plucked one of the peacock feather eyes out of Mrs. Holliday's coiffure. "Do you have a match?" she asked Jesse.

He shook his head. She made an irritable noise, pulled a handkerchief out of her tiny purse, and used it to lift the chimney of one of the wall sconces. She held the feather's tip in the flame until it smoldered.

She waved the smoking feather under Holliday's

nose. He jerked his head back, coughing, and his eyes opened. They focused on something over Jesse's shoulder, widened, and closed tight again.

Jesse knew what Holliday had seen: Wyatt Earp.

Kate Holliday whirled from her place by the settee and turned on Earp. "He told you we were leaving!" Her fingers were curved and stiff like claws.

"Good God, Kate, he can't travel like this!" Earp protested. He looked past Mrs. Holliday to Mildred, frowning. "How is he?"

"I don't know. Get a doctor." Mildred had never sounded so cold. "Goodfellow's here—fetch him."

Under other circumstances, Jesse could have laughed at the way he, Mrs. Holliday, and Earp looked at each other. Jesse wasn't about to leave Mildred with Earp, with only Kate Holliday for protection. Kate wouldn't leave Holliday, not being sure how much protection Mildred and Jesse would be. And Earp could go, but none of them trusted him to be quick.

"Go," Jesse said to Mrs. Holliday. "I'll look out for your husband." She drew a sobbing breath and bolted for the tea room.

Holliday began to stir before the doctor arrived. "Lie still," Mildred ordered him.

Holliday gave a little puff of a laugh and fumbled in his coat pocket. He could slide the flask out, but couldn't lift it. Jesse reached past Mildred and held it while he drank. Mildred glared at Jesse.

Holliday lay with his eyes closed, frowning, but breathing more easily. All the while Jesse was aware of Earp standing silent behind him.

Goodfellow arrived as the sound of the musicians tuning filtered out of the ballroom. Kate Holliday followed close behind him. Mildred stepped back as the doctor took Holliday's wrist. "He was unconscious for half a minute or so," Mildred told him.

"Thank you, Mrs. Benjamin." Goodfellow bent over Holliday, and Mildred came away from the settee.

Jesse saw her look from him to Earp and back. She walked up to Jesse and said, "I would like a glass of wine." Her voice was firm but low, and Jesse knew it wouldn't have carried to Earp.

Jesse held out his arm, and she twined hers in it. She leaned on him more than she had at the start of the evening.

The tea room was nearly empty, but there were still waiters tending the buffet, and two boys clearing away the used china and whisking off the tablecloths. Jesse led Mildred to a chair at a bare table and fetched two glasses of claret. When he handed one to her, she drank a third of it straight off.

"If they'd had brandy, I'd have brought that instead," Jesse told her. Out in the ballroom the band struck up a tune.

"Thank you. Oh, the devil, is that the first dance? I had a partner . . ." She fumbled for her dance card, dropped it. Jesse picked it up and gave it back to her. "It's Harry. That's all right, I can apologize tomorrow, and explain—"

At that, she crossed her arms on the table and dropped her head on them.

"Mrs.—Mildred. Are you all right?"

"I think," she said, muffled, "I might faint."

And not a feather in sight. "Put your head between your knees," Jesse ordered.

"Can't. Corset."

He could insist she lie down. Or he could be poised to catch her if she fell, which, he realized, he was. When she slowly straightened up, Jesse handed her her wine and felt helpless.

She took a sip. "I don't want to be a model for one of your unrealistic heroines."

It took him a moment to remember their conversation about authors. "You've been very realistic so far."

"I don't think I *can* explain to Harry," she said thinly.

"Doc Holliday had the bad grace to pass out, you helped care for him until the doctor came, and as a result, you missed your dance."

"It sounds so simple and normal, doesn't it?" Mildred took another swallow of wine.

"Maybe it is in Tombstone," Jesse said, hoping she'd laugh.

Instead she looked down at her wineglass. "I think . . . I don't know what to think." She pressed a hand to her forehead. "I'm sorry. What a fuss I'm making!"

Her smile was bright and desperate and false. He couldn't think what it reminded him of . . . Yes, he could. His mother had smiled that way when she said that Lily was only suffering from nervous prostration and would be fine with rest. Lily herself had smiled that way when she'd said, "I'm just a little fevered, Jess. It's nothing."

Jesse leaned forward and laid his hand over Mildred's on the table. "What did you see?"

She drew her hand away. "Nothing."

"I think you saw two things that can't both be true. You may convince yourself to believe one, and the other will fade out of your memory. Or you may decide you have a brain fever. Except that, now that we're having this conversation, you probably won't be able to do either."

Mildred stared at him, fear in her face. She shook her head.

It required almost more nerve than he had, but he went on. "What happened out front was real. Knowing that, knowing there are people who can . . . can make you see things that aren't there, or keep you from seeing things that are. . . . It's like confidence games and horse-coping. Knowing gives you some protection against them."

She sat silent, staring down into her wine, and his courage failed him. Now wasn't the moment to tell her everything. Let her get used to it a little at a time.

At last she drank off the rest of her wine and said, "I'd like to go home."

"Of course. I'll send someone to tell Chu."

Mildred went off to the ladies' retiring room while he found someone to run to the livery stable. She didn't come out until the buggy was at the door. Then she appeared, her wrap tight around her shoulders and her face pale and closed. He handed her in and took the reins from Chu.

The rain had slowed to a sputtering drizzle, but the streets were still like creek beds. He steered Sam to the highest parts, which kept him busy enough to excuse the silence between them. He wanted to say something, but everything he thought of sounded jolly and false in his head.

At Mildred's lodging house, he put up the umbrella and handed her to her front door. His voice came out rusty when he said, "May I call tomorrow to see how you are?"

She paused with her hand on the latch. At last she said, "That won't be necessary, Mr. Fox. I'll be fine." She opened the door. "Thank you for your escort."

She went inside. The key turned in the lock with a sound like a bark of bitter laughter.

Mr. Fox.

What had he done? If he'd leaped to a false conclusion, if she *hadn't* seen something like what he'd seen in the foyer, then she thought he was trying to hoax her. Or she thought he was insane. Which would he rather be: cruel, or mad?

He climbed back into the buggy and clicked his tongue at Sam.

"I drive," Chu suggested as they splashed down the street.

"No, thank you."

"I drive good!"

"'Well.' If you want to say you're skilled at it, you say, 'I drive well.' And if I didn't already know that, you wouldn't have been driving Sam in the first place."

"'I drive well.' Now I drive?"

Jesse shook his head. "I need something to do."

"Huh," said Chu.

⇀ 17 ⇀

Doc woke to the irregular ticking of rain on the window glass. The light through the draperies looked like six in the morning, which was a hell of a time to be awake. He fumbled at the nightstand for his pocket watch and couldn't find it. He always put it on the nightstand.

"Doc?" Kate leaped up from the easy chair and leaned over him. "You all right?"

"Playing nurse after the fire has gone to your head. What time is it?"

The watch he'd bought her was pinned to her bodice. She consulted it. "Nearly noon. You want coffee, or whiskey?"

"I take it back. You must have gone to a pretty fair nursing school. Both."

He struggled to sit up. Why was he so weak?

Kate had a spirit lamp burning on the bureau, and a little pot of coffee over it. She poured some into a flowered china cup, then held the whiskey bottle over the cup and raised her eyebrows. Doc nodded.

"Where's my watch?" he asked as she poured.

"Right here. I took it off you last night with everything else." Kate brought him the cup, and laid the watch on the nightstand beside him.

Kate had undressed him? He must have gotten uncommonly drunk. He prided himself on being able to get home and into bed no matter what.

He thumbed the watch open. *JHH from WBSE.* He shivered and closed the cover, and realized he'd forgotten to check the time. He put the watch back on the nightstand.

Kate sat on the bed and watched him while he sipped the coffee, which made him nervous. But she kept silent until he had enough inside him to feel as if life was worth living.

"We've got to leave, Doc," she said.

"Don't start in on me when I've just woken up."

"I talk to you when I can get you to listen. You can't stay here. Didn't last night tell you anything?"

Last night. Last night was July Fourth, and the ball. At the intermission, he and Wyatt had talked on the porch, and Wyatt had convinced him not to go to Colorado, and then he'd had an attack, probably from the moist air—

That wasn't how it happened. He wasn't sure of the truth, but he knew that wasn't it. All he remembered for sure was being afraid of Wyatt, in a way that he was afraid of no other man living or dead.

"I can't travel like this," he snapped. As he said it, it echoed something from last night.

"The hell you can't. If we light out now, you won't *be* like this. Doc, I don't stand in your way. Most times you choose Hell over Heaven, and I back your play whatever it is."

"Good. Don't stop now."

"This is no choice of yours! This is Wyatt's doing!"

"Neither he nor you can tell me how to live my life." But he shivered as he said it. It wasn't true, was it?

Kate leaned forward and grabbed his wrists. A little coffee slopped over the edge of the cup and onto the bedsheet. "You know better, God damn it! And you're going to admit it. Wyatt Earp is a black magician."

Doc threw the cup. It missed Kate's head by several inches and smashed against the wall. Coffee stained the wallpaper. "If you talk any more gypsy claptrap, I will pack you off to Colorado by yourself."

"He's doing some kind of hoodoo on you. He has been for years. He turns it on everyone who comes near. My God, if I can see it, why can't you?"

He could. He'd been watching Wyatt do strange things for years, averting censure and bullets, getting knowledge he couldn't have through natural means.

"Doc, my daddy was a medical man. I'm not an ignorant hick like Virgil's woman, reading cards and tea leaves. But I know what I've seen."

He'd seen Wyatt walk through gunfire in Dodge City and never get a scratch. He'd seen him find Luther King at Redfield's ranch, using something that was neither sight nor hearing. He'd ridden with Wyatt afterward on what was supposed to be a search for Leonard, Head, and Crane. It had followed four hundred miles of river and mountain range all the way to

Tucson, the Mexican border, and back, an irregular figure eight that enclosed every watershed and road of service to Tombstone.

"He can do things. Unnatural things. I don't know anything to call it but witchcraft."

Again and again he had seen the truth, and refused to admit what he'd seen. Magic was for ignorant men and gamblers. Magic didn't rule an educated man. Magic couldn't make a man do what he didn't want to do, or make him stand by a friend who was prepared to betray him. Of all people, John Ringo had warned him about Wyatt, and he'd pretended even to himself that he had no idea what Ringo was talking about.

"But we can get clear of it. I know we can, if we just leave now."

Now Doc remembered last night clearly. And he knew that remembering and clarity didn't make one bit of difference. He was in Wyatt's power.

He studied the coffee spot on the sheet. "You go along, then. I'll meet you somewhere."

"No! My God, Doc—" Kate jumped up and paced halfway across the room. Then she stopped, and turned, and the pain in her face was terrible. "Are you saying we're through?"

There was a hurt in his chest that shamed the paltry hurt of the tuberculosis at the sight of her, wicked and devious and secretive, too honest not to meet the question head-on. "I will never be through with you," he whispered.

She stood straight-shouldered before him, her hands clenched in her skirts. "I won't let Wyatt have you. Not without a fight. I'm warning you, Doc."

She walked out of the room and slammed the door.

So—he had, unknowing, indentured himself to Wyatt. He couldn't recall doing it. In fact, he had suspected it was the other way around.

In college he'd had curious experiences: a lamp burning in his room when he was sure he'd snuffed it; a sudden comprehension of a stranger's intentions; dreams that seemed to come true. When his consumption was diagnosed, he decided the curious experiences were the product of fever.

He'd met Wyatt in Texas. He'd had an aura of self-reliance and a relentless focus that Doc liked. Wyatt urged him to come to Dodge City. "I expect they can use a dentist," he'd said. "I'm damned sure they need another faro dealer."

The proposal stuck in Doc's head and grew. In light of his present knowledge he was fairly sure it had been a baited hook, touched with a bit of hoodoo to see if Doc could be led. At the time it had seemed like the most normal thing in the world that he should be obsessed with the promise of Dodge City. Still, he didn't think Wyatt had laid claim to him in Texas.

As soon as he and Kate arrived in Dodge he felt stronger. Remission, it was called, when the disease huddled under its rock and waited, and that, too, seemed natural. Dodge was a roaring town, and Doc liked to be at the center of the noise. So did Wyatt. Did it happen in Dodge? While Doc thought he was making the only close friend of his adult life, was that friend clasping invisible fetters on him?

When Wyatt got wind of Tombstone, he whistled up his brothers and started packing. It had been then that Doc began to feel less than well, to think the cowtown dust was doing him a mischief. He'd convinced Kate of it, anyway, and she'd fancied the sound of the booming new camp.

But by the time they reached Arizona Territory, Kate and Wyatt were eyeing each other like cocks before a fight. In Globe, Doc hit a streak at the tables he hated to walk away from, and Kate suggested they stay in town and let the Earps go on.

He was certainly bound by the time they reached Globe. When Wyatt heard Doc and Kate were staying, his face went dark as a rain cloud. But his voice was easy when he said, "You'll see—Tombstone's the biggest thing you ever had a finger in. I'll make you rich, Doc. You come down when you've had enough."

Doc, God help him, had thought Wyatt was referring to Kate.

Globe was a disaster. The cards turned sour, and his strength began to fail. One afternoon as he lay in bed sweating and aching, his breath burning in his lungs, Kate burst into tears. It was the first time he'd seen her cry. "Hell with this," he told her. "Let's go to Tombstone."

As soon as he'd arrived, as soon as he shook Wyatt's hand, he knew he was better. The oddest notion sprang into his head and wouldn't be banished: that by some uncanny means he was borrowing Wyatt's strength. He'd felt guilty, but it didn't seem to do Wyatt any harm. So he'd called it fancy, laughed it off, and forgotten the whole business as much as he could.

Now he wondered if Kate had suspected the true state of affairs all along, and if that was what her tears had been for.

Doc pillowed his forehead on his raised knees and tried not to think about anything.

"Well," Harry said, even before the door of the Nugget office closed behind him, *"I was right about Holliday."*

Mildred jumped, inwardly if not visibly. She'd been thinking about Holliday, at least as he related to Wyatt Earp and Jesse Fox, almost to the exclusion of anything else. Did Harry know what had happened on July Fourth? Did he have any better understanding of it than she did?

"You were right?" she said, floundering.

Richard Rule looked up from her copy. "About the Benson stage holdup?"

Harry sat on the edge of his desk and looked smug. "Kate Elder, Mrs. Holliday by courtesy, just swore out an affidavit that Doc Holliday was one of the men who attempted the robbery."

Rule's "Huh!" and Mildred's outraged "What?" overlapped perfectly.

Harry shook his head at Mildred. "I know, you never believed it. But you have to believe it now."

"Harry, you're the one who told me to trust my instincts. And right now they're saying that mule won't pull." The image of Kate Holliday hovering fearful over her husband on the settee, and turning on Earp . . . What was it she'd said to him?

"What motive would she have for swearing to it, if it weren't true?" Rule asked.

"Why would she swear to it if it *is* true? Something's not right here."

Harry shrugged, irritated. "I'm writing it the way the sheriff tells it. If you've got a better source than Behan, you go ahead and use it." Rule got out of Harry's chair and Harry took it over, swinging around to face the typewriter.

Let it go, she ordered herself. The alternative was to face the difference between what she'd seen and what she believed. Unless this had nothing to do with the Fourth of July. Or Mrs. Holliday had a more sensible reason for what had happened that night than Jesse Fox had.

Mildred picked up her purse. "I'll see if I do," she said to Harry, and left the office.

She'd been angry at Fox since the ball. Anger had replaced confusion and panic while she was still in the tea room: at first just enough to get her up and moving, but more as she gathered her wits.

Fox had found out, somehow, about M. E. Benjamin's stories of ghosts and prophecies and wicked uncles. He was pretending to believe in them, in order to make a fool of Mildred, to laugh at her later. Weren't the ranks of the Theosophists swollen with hysterical lady authors? Did Fox think she scurried along at the skirt hems of mediums and crystal-gazers?

That was the thought that had kept her from sleeping the night of the ball. But in the time since, she'd had to admit that she'd clutched at anger to drive away fear.

She turned left at Fremont. The sinking sun glared in under the lid of the low clouds. She lifted her skirts to cross the muddy street and frowned at two miners who'd been waiting for a sight of her ankles. They flushed and pretended to be interested in something over her head. The mud made angry sucking sounds each time she pulled her boot heels free of it.

Holliday was boarding at Fly's. It wasn't likely his wife was still there, unless he'd been taken into custody. Still, when she saw the slender, energetic figure of Mrs. Fly sweeping the stoop, she stopped.

Mrs. Fly straightened and wiped her hair back. "Good afternoon, Mrs. Benjamin! Isn't this dratted mud the last straw? And neither the dogs nor the boarders'll wipe their feet." But she sounded cheerful anyway. "Won't you come in?"

"I'm sorry, I can't stay. I just wanted to know if Mrs. Holliday is still here."

Mrs. Fly rolled her eyes. "I'd hate to think what we'd do if she were. When they're quarreling, the Devil himself wouldn't stay in the next room."

"Dr. and Mrs. Holliday are quarreling?" Mildred asked innocently.

"You didn't hear? She got drunk and sicced Behan on her man. Holliday was in jail for all of fifteen minutes before Wyatt Earp and his gambling friends bailed him out."

"I don't suppose they could stay in the same house after that. Do you know where she went?"

Mrs. Fly cocked her head like a sparrow. "Heavens, Mrs. Benjamin, why would you want to find Mrs. Holliday?"

Some instinct told Mildred not to associate this with the *Nugget*. "I found a piece of jewelry she lost at the ball."

That satisfied Mrs. Fly, at least temporarily. "She packed her things off to the Cosmopolitan Hotel. You can leave a note for her there, anyway."

"I'll do that."

"And, Mrs. Benjamin, have you given thought to joining the Literary Society?"

"It sounds a treat," Mildred said. "But I don't seem to have a spare moment lately. Maybe when I'm moved into a new place."

"The little house on the corner?"

"If he'll come down on the price."

Mrs. Fly beamed. "Mr. Fly's been softening him up. We're set on having you for a neighbor."

"Tell your husband I appreciate the flanking maneuver. Good evening, Mrs. Fly."

As she headed back toward Allen Street, Mildred thought of the Earp women reading to each other as they sewed. She'd lay money nobody meant to invite them to join the Literary Society. For a few strides, she was angry with Mrs. Fly. But the fault didn't lie there, not really.

The Cosmopolitan Hotel and its whole block had

stood just west of the fire; it lifted its elegant façade over the north side of Allen Street untouched. The balcony over the sidewalk was edged with potted orange trees, which were thriving in the summer rains.

She stopped at the iron scraper by the entrance and got as much mud off her boots as she could. People passed in and out as she did. Half the downtown burned flat, she reflected, and Tombstone barely slowed to take a breath. The stages brought passengers every day, and most of them stayed.

She went through the hotel lobby, looking for Kate Holliday. There were three men in various upholstered chairs reading newspapers, and a lady at a writing desk making use of the hotel's pen and paper. Guests came down the stairs, headed for the Maison Doré restaurant. Mrs. Holliday wasn't among them.

"Do you know if Mrs. Holliday is in?" she asked the desk clerk.

He was a young man with thinning dark hair, and his mouth was pinched as if disapproval were his natural state. "She ain't in her room," the clerk said without checking the key box behind him. Instead his eyes went to the saloon. "You want to leave a message for her?"

"No, thank you." Ladies did not go unaccompanied into barrooms, ever. Not even in pursuit of the truth. Mildred straightened her spine, filled her lungs, and headed for the elaborate spindle-work doors of the saloon.

The room was thick with the odor of cigars long smoked or snuffed, beer long drunk or spilled. It was a smell she knew from passing open doors on Allen Street. But here it was uncontested and joined to the rainy-season smell of damp wool and mildew. New smoke lay in strata like layers in rock, from just above the heads of the patrons all the way to the high ceiling.

The air seemed a better barrier than the saloon doors were.

Kate Holliday stood at the bar like a man, in near solitary splendor; the men themselves were farther down the rail, watching her warily out of the corners of their eyes like spooky cattle. Was that because she was Doc Holliday's woman, and they had a healthy sense of self-preservation? Or was it fear of the unknown: an elegantly dressed woman in their preserve, ignoring them as a lioness might a flock of crows?

Association with the lioness might shield her from potential insult. Mildred crossed the room to Mrs. Holliday's side. "Good evening, Mrs. Holliday."

The woman turned a cold face on her, with no recognition in it. Then her eyes widened. "It's—Mrs. Benjamin, isn't it? Good God." There was a glass on the bar in front of her, almost empty. Mildred smelled gin and lemons and sugar on Mrs. Holliday's breath.

"Might I talk to you for a few minutes?"

Mrs. Holliday stared at her thoughtfully. She didn't look or sound drunk, but Mildred thought she was. At last she let out a puff of breath that might have been a laugh. "I don't suppose you want to do it here." She turned her hand to indicate the bar, a graceful gesture.

"If it's the best we've got," Mildred replied, though her heart sank an inch.

Mrs. Holliday smiled and shook her head. "It ain't fit. We'll go to my room." She sailed out through the lobby doors, dignified as a senator, and Mildred followed. When the doors swung closed behind her, she could hear a buzz of conversation spring up on the other side of them.

Kate Holliday's handsomely furnished room was untidy and impersonal, and looked like a place in which its inhabitant didn't plan to stay long. Mrs. Holliday dropped onto the mahogany bed, folded her arms on the carved footboard, and rested her chin on them, looking at Mildred. "Well, what is it? Oh"—and she raised her head to nod toward the bureau—"d'you want a drink?"

There was a half-full bottle of bourbon on the bureau, and a glass beside it. No need to go to the saloon to drink; Mrs. Holliday had been making a statement. "No, thank you," Mildred replied.

"Sorry I don't have tea," Mrs. Holliday said, with the hint of a sneer.

"Mrs. Holliday—" Mildred closed her lips on the rest of the sentence. "No, I'm not going to rise to that bait. Nor any other, I hope. Mrs. Holliday, did your husband really help stop the Benson stage in March?"

Mrs. Holliday returned her chin to its place on her crossed wrists. "You're here because I said so, aren't you?"

"That's not an answer."

"Who says I have to give you one?"

"No one." Mildred twitched a petticoat off the padded seat of an ornate chair, hung it over the chair's back by its drawstring, and sat down. "Maybe you don't want to talk about that."

Mrs. Holliday just stared at her, a little crooked smile on her lips. In the silence Mildred heard thunder mutter, miles away.

"Would you talk to me about what happened at the ball the night of the Fourth?"

The smile hardened like candy. "There was a lot of dancing."

"There's a lot being done right here and now, too. Mrs. Holliday, something happened between your husband and Wyatt Earp. What was it?"

Mrs. Holliday closed her eyes. "Call me Kate," she said. She seemed ten years older than she had a moment before. "Have you asked your gentleman friend? I wager he knows a little."

She felt a little cold jab at her insides. "He was with me. He wouldn't know any more than I do."

"If you think that, there's no point in my talking to you."

Mildred realized that her hands, which she'd folded in her lap, were clenched on each other, nails digging in. "You said something to Earp, something like, 'He told you we were going.'"

Kate nodded. "And Wyatt can't have that, not now. He's going to squeeze Doc like an orange until he's empty. Without Doc, he can't bring anything off."

"Squeeze him how? What do you mean, empty?"

"You wouldn't understand."

"But if you're concerned for Dr. Holliday, why did you swear to Sheriff Behan that he was a party to murder?"

"They'll put him in jail. They'll stick him in Yuma prison. And I defy even Wyatt God-damned Earp to get at him there."

Mildred sat limp in her chair as the statement sank in. "You accused him of a felony to keep him *safe*?"

"I won't let 'em hang him. But my God, hanging might be better. Quick and clean."

Kate was unquestionably drunk. But she was telling the truth. She'd blamed Doc Holliday for the stage holdup to get him arrested and imprisoned, so he'd be out of reach of Wyatt Earp.

"What do you want to keep him safe from?" Mildred asked.

Kate stared at her from under drooping eyelids. Mildred thought of the lioness, watching circus visitors through the bars, dreaming of how it would be if the bars were gone.

"Is Earp engaged in illegal activities?" Mildred added desperately. "Is he involving your husband in them?" There was no halo over Doc Holliday's head;

but it was possible for a man to draw the line somewhere, then find himself dragged across it.

Kate dropped her forehead onto her arms and made
a sound. For a horrid instant Mildred thought it might
be a sob—what was she to do if Kate turned maudlin-
drunk? But the sound continued, and Mildred realized
she was laughing. "Damn," she said, raising her head.
"It's just the way you said that, as if nobody would
have guessed. Hell, yes, to both questions. But I don't
give a Chinaman's curse about that."

"What, then?"

"If he'd chosen this, I could stand it, do you see? I
always say he can go to Hell by his own road. If this
was his choice, I'd bear it, though it makes me sick."

"If he'd chosen *what*? What is he being forced to
do?"

Kate's eyes held Mildred's, fixed and intense. No
drooping lids now, no drunken wandering. "Have a
drink," she breathed, "and I'll tell you."

"I don't like bourbon."

"That's all I've got. Have a drink, or we're done
talking."

It might be pure devilment—Kate might be playing
with her; there might be nothing more to be told. But
Mildred felt something moving around them, a deep
secret thing just beyond sound or sight. She rose and
poured a little bourbon into the glass. She started to
carry it back to the chair. But Kate was watching her
as if she wanted to see through to her bones. Mildred
stopped, took a deep breath, and swallowed the bourbon in a gulp. It tasted like sugar mixed with
kerosene. By an effort of will, she neither gasped nor
coughed.

Kate nodded at the glass. Mildred poured more
bourbon and handed it to her. Kate emptied the glass
and sighed. Then she sat with it cupped in her hands,

her hands in her lap, her head bent. Had the glass been a posy of flowers or a photograph, she might have been sitting for a sentimental painting.

Mildred sat down, straight-backed and businesslike. She opened her mouth to ask her question again. Then she closed it. The conversation was no longer hers to direct. She was the audience now; Kate would tell the story, or not.

The curtains were open. It was full dark outside, or close enough that the only thing to be seen in the window was the reflection of the room, lit by the lamp beside the bed. Where her own face was shadowed, it disappeared on the window glass, as if she were a puzzle with pieces missing. This time the thunder was close enough to make the glass shudder in its frame.

"There's people in this world," Kate began slowly, "that have a power about them. Most of 'em only have a little, and don't know they've got that much. But when a preacher makes you cry and shout and clap when you don't believe a word he said, that's one of 'em. When a salesman makes you buy something you don't fancy and can't use, that's another.

"Then there's those that have a lot of that power, but don't know it, and can't use it for anything. Some of those kind take hurt from it. It makes 'em sick, or crazy, or makes 'em try to hurt themselves.

"But there's a few that have it, and know it, and use it. They're the ones in the fairy tales turning men into beasts, or making water run uphill."

"Those things are impossible." Mildred's voice sounded thin in her ears.

Kate looked up from the empty glass. "Sure they are. But what do they mean?"

Mildred frowned at her.

"You saying you never knew a person to be

changed? A friend made into an enemy, a good man
into a monster?"

"That's nothing . . . strange."

"Not always," Kate said, and looked down again,
smiling. "Most people will brush right up against the
powerful ones, and never know it. They might be
brother and sister, or husband and wife, even. But
those powerful ones, you watch, they try to never be
alone in the world. They keep their friends or family
around them. That's their strength."

It could be metaphor, Mildred thought. All leaders
were made strong by their followers. The Earps believed in strength in numbers. "That's just the way a
community works."

"Are the Earp brothers a community? My God. I
don't suppose you heard about Bessie's little girl."

Did she mean Hattie? Mildred shook her head.

"Jim Earp found out she'd climbed out her bedroom
window to go for a buggy ride with some fellow, the
night of Fourth of July. He'd've been within his rights
to switch her when she got home. Instead he calls in
his brothers. You could hear the strap and her screech-
ing from down the block, and Wyatt—Wyatt!—
shouting at her. And her Bessie's daughter from before
she met Jim, and not even Wyatt's blood kin! There's
your *community*."

Mildred felt sick. However much the Earp clan
might object to the McLaurys, it couldn't justify that.
"I still don't understand why you're afraid for your
husband."

"He's one of those who has the power and can't use
it. But Wyatt Earp can. That's what happened on the
porch of Schieffelin Hall that night."

Perhaps it was the bourbon, but Mildred was angry
at the nonsense, the waste of time, the seduction of the
tale. "If these powerful people seem perfectly normal,

why do you know this? How could you possibly know that any of this was happening?"

Kate frowned, her face full of the dull puzzlement of drink. "Most people don't see the truth. But people like us see some of it."

"Like us. Who . . ."

"You and me," Kate said. "I wouldn't have talked to you if you didn't know some of it already."

People like us see. Wyatt Earp, crouched solicitously over his friend—or Earp framed in the doorway, netted with something that gleamed black and silver like hematite, but *alive*, moving and flickering and finally disappearing as if melting into his clothes. If reality lay with the first choice, why had she seen that other, that impossible thing?

"You're drunk," Mildred whispered.

"Hell, yes. I couldn't say all that without a few strong ones in me." Kate showed her teeth in a smile. "When I'm sober, I don't even like to think about it. Gives me the shakes."

Mildred stood up. "If this is what your affidavit against your husband is based on, I'd go to Behan tomorrow and withdraw it."

Kate threw back her head and laughed. "My God, you want to make me out a liar, don't you? You don't want to see it. Then you'd better stay away from that gentleman friend of yours."

"What do you mean?"

"Fox. He's got it. And I'd say he knows it. Worse, I'd say Wyatt knows it. You better be careful." And Kate laughed until she fell backward on the bed, snorting and whooping, and the empty glass rolled out of her hand and dropped to the rug.

Mildred let herself out of the room and went down the hall toward the stairs. At the head of them there was a window, its drapes drawn back in swags. For a

moment the lamps backlit her, so that, in the reflection
of the hall, she was an empty darkness. Then she
passed under the chandelier, and the light seemed to
re-create her like a summoned ghost.

She would give Harry an edited version of Kate's
motives. She'd tell him that Kate lied to get Doc away
from the Earps' plans and influence. But she knew
what he'd say. The *Nugget* couldn't give credence to a
drunk woman's angry slander . . . unless it told the
story the editor already believed. And why Kate had
done it didn't matter, anyway; she'd done it, and the
court would convict Holliday or it wouldn't. Harry
would be more interested in that, as evidence that the
Earps had the judge in their pockets.

She was almost jealous of him. For Harry the case
at hand was about crookedness, influence, politics,
jockeying for office. It could be described in a language he spoke. But if Kate was right, what language
had words for what was happening in Tombstone, and
who spoke it?

Besides, apparently, Jesse Fox and Wyatt Earp?

She remembered Earp's overtures to Jesse in the ice
cream parlor. She'd been certain something was
wrong. But not this. Let it not be this.

Outside, she hurried to Fifth and turned toward Safford Street and Miss Gilchrist's. She was barely to
Fremont when the sky opened up like a burst dam.

Of course she'd forgotten her umbrella in the
Nugget office. She ran for an overhang and the lamp
that hung under it, swinging in the wind. It was Crabtree's Livery Stable, she realized. Jesse Fox kept his
horse here.

There was no reason why he should be at the stable.
And the rain was coming off the overhanging roof hard
enough to splash her waist-high. Lightning slashed
sideways across the sky and dragged a deafening crack

of thunder close behind. That settled it. She opened the door and went in.

Her entrance stopped a conversation in midsentence; the night manager and a companion sat smoking with their feet on the unlit stove. From the fragment she'd heard, they'd either been comparing the merits of two racehorses, or two unusually colorfully named prostitutes.

Both men sprang up from their chairs and offered them to her. She could hear the rain hammering the roof. She could bolt for Miss Gilchrist's and probably ruin most of what she had on, including her boots; or she could make it impossible for these men to get comfortable again.

A third possibility occurred to her. "No, thank you, gentlemen. I'm going to visit a horse of my acquaintance until the rain lets up." She had a glimpse of their astonished faces before she headed for the back door.

The yard had deeper roof overhangs than the front of the building. Carriages and wagons sheltered in a big covered space on the right, beside the harness and feed rooms. On the left, lamplight showed a row of stalls, and closer to the office, boxes large enough for a horse to turn and lie down in. She'd put money on Fox's horse being in one of those.

The first one was empty. She heard noises from the next: a rustle of straw, chewing, and a sound like wet and difficult breathing.

She peered through the bars in the upper half of the box stall door, expecting to see a sick horse. Instead, a small, dark-clad figure leaned against a horse, face hidden in the black mane. The horse was Jesse Fox's, and the figure was Chu. And Chu was crying.

She must have made a noise. Chu whipped around and saw her. His eyes were red and swollen, and he gave a mighty sniff in lieu of blowing his nose. "What you want?" he snapped, hoarse with crying.

The scene shifted before her eyes. Nothing really changed, but the elements and their relation to each other settled into a new arrangement, one whose strangeness made her catch her breath.

"You're a girl," she said.

Chu's mouth opened, eyes wide in horror. "No, no, lady! No girl! You mighty stupid!"

"I'm not, though. Did Mr. Chow know you weren't a boy?" Mildred saw Chu flinch at the dead man's name, and knew why she was crying. "Yes, of course he did. You couldn't have kept up the disguise without help. Was it his idea?"

Chu's horror had grown into horrified fascination; she was watching Mildred as one might watch an earthquake in progress. Finally the girl nodded warily.

Jesse had thought Chu might be twelve at most. It was hard to tell in boy's clothes and a queue, but Mildred found herself revising the estimate downward slightly. "Were you related to Mr. Chow?"

At that, Chu turned back to the horse and hid her face. "Go away," she said, muffled.

"I'm sorry, but I can't," Mildred said in as matter-of-fact a tone as she could manage. She opened the stall door and stepped in, mindful of where she put her feet. "You can't expect me to walk away from a mystery like this." Chu still didn't look at her, so she put as much regret in her voice as she could and added, "Besides, I forgot my umbrella at the newspaper office."

Ah, there was the profile, and a glaring, sideways look. "Big stupid."

"So I've told myself. Once the rains start, one ought to *sleep* with one's umbrella. And I've lived here for over a year, so I ought to know better. Have you been in Arizona Territory long? Is this your first summer?"

"You fulla damn question."

It's a good way to stall for time. What was she going to do about this? Whatever "this" was. Did Fox know his stableboy was a girl? What did it mean if he did? "It would be rude to talk about myself all the time," she answered.

Chu scowled at her. "I got work. You goddamn talk someplace else." The girl yanked a brush out of her jacket pocket and began to make ferocious sweeps of the horse's already glossy side. The horse turned from the hay rack to look, as if in surprise.

Mildred had had experience lately with interviewing hostile persons. "Tell you what—I'll talk about you, instead. Since you won't tell me about yourself, I'll have to guess. I think you were born in this country—California, most likely. You came to Tombstone with Mr. Chow, but you didn't know Mr. Fox in San Francisco, so either you weren't with Mr. Chow then, or he kept you hidden." Mildred flinched inwardly, but she forced herself to finish what she'd started. "Since you won't say anything about it, I assume your relationship to Mr. Chow was one that people would disapprove of. Were you his mistress?"

Chu turned away from the horse. Instead of the angry face she'd expected, the girl looked baffled. "Huh? Were what?"

Oh, dear. She'd forgotten the language barrier. And it had been hard enough to say the first time. "Were you Mr. Chow's . . . lover?"

It might have been the word, or the pause before it, or Mildred's tone. Chu flushed dark as a thundercloud and threw the brush. Mildred dodged, but it hit her in the shoulder anyway. Fox's horse shied and fetched up against the far wall of the stall with his ears back.

"You dirty big-nose bitch, think like that! I no fuck nobody! Chow Lung good man, great man, take care me, you no speak his name, you dirty mouth!" Chu was screaming by the end of the speech, but screaming came too close to crying, and tipped over the edge. She collapsed into the straw, weeping so hard she barely had room to breathe.

Mildred dropped to her knees and put her arms tight around the girl. "I'm sorry. I didn't really think there was anything improper between you and Mr. Chow. I just wanted to make you mad so you would talk to me."

The horse seemed to find the sight of the two of them crouched in the straw disturbing; he stayed on the opposite side of the box and watched them. The girl, in contrast, suddenly relaxed in Mildred's arms and cried freely into her shoulder.

"You haven't had anyone to talk to about him," Mildred guessed.

Chu shook her head without lifting it from Mildred's shoulder.

"You could have talked to Mr. Fox. I think he misses Mr. Chow, too."

"No. Maybe I say something, he tell I no damn boy. I no talk to him so much."

"It might be that he's already guessed," Mildred suggested hopefully. Then at least Mildred wouldn't have to tell him.

Chu lifted her head from Mildred's shoulder, her swollen features eloquent of scorn and disbelief. "Hah," she said.

"No, you're right. Of course he hasn't."

Chu shook her head sadly. "Everybody stupid, too. Why not you?"

"I don't know. Hasn't anyone ever guessed before?"

"I shut up plenty. Stick to horses. Nobody know, only Chow Lung."

"Oh, dear." Chow Lung had been Chu's only friend,

the only person she could speak freely with, and he was gone. If she had to live under the same conditions, Mildred thought she might do something desperate. "Is Chu your real name?"

Chu gave an odd little shrug. "I keep."

And here, Mildred thought, *we are. Now what?* "Would you like to come home with me tonight? I worry about you here alone." Though Miss Gilchrist's response to the arrival of a Chinese child at her door would be anything but cheerful and welcoming.

Chu frowned, thinking. "No, safe here," she said at last. "Look funny, go your house. I goddamn stable-boy." She smiled at Mildred, a watery but genuine expression, and clambered to her feet.

Mildred rose, too, and refused to look down at her skirt for stains. "I have to tell Mr. Fox the truth."

"No, no! He kick me out!"

He might. It would be justifiable. It might be the only proper thing to do. "You can't go on pretending to be a boy and not tell him. It's . . . it's like lying."

Chu frowned. "So?"

Oh, dear. "One ought not to lie if one can help it. Especially not to people one wants as friends. Mr. Fox was good friends with Mr. Chow, and I think would be your friend, if you let him." She was aware she was promising a great deal in Jesse Fox's name.

Suddenly she remembered—Kate Holliday had as good as accused Fox of dealing in some kind of witch-craft. He had certainly been comfortable enough with the notion of the supernatural to know what she'd experienced in the foyer of Schieffelin Hall, and to suggest an explanation that was anything but scientific. It was nonsense; it was impossible. But true or not, how did it affect Chu's situation?

"What do you know of Mr. Fox?" Mildred asked carefully.

Chu shrugged. "He kind. I know from Sam." She jerked her head toward the horse, which had relaxed when she and Mildred had failed to do anything threatening. "Chow Lung say he smart. I not see so much."

Mildred bit her lip to keep from laughing. "Did Mr. Chow say anything about what Mr. Fox does?"

"I hear him plenty damn mad at Mr. Fox. Big damn waste, he say."

Mildred thought that over. "Because he's training horses instead of being a mining engineer?"

"Be what?"

"A mining engineer. Someone who tells people where to dig mines, and how to do it."

"Ohhhh." Chu nodded slowly. "And find water, and place for house and grave for good luck. Yes, Chow Lung, too. He try to teach Mr. Fox."

Mildred felt the same expression on her face as Chu had worn a moment ago. "I'm sorry. What was Mr. Chow trying to teach Mr. Fox?"

"What you say. Right? How to use magic in ground." Chu stamped her foot twice on the stall floor and grinned.

"No, not magic—" Mildred stopped herself.

Chu was saying that Chow Lung had been a magician—a *magician*—and was upset because Jesse Fox ought to be one, and wasn't.

And Kate insisted that Wyatt Earp was one, and Jesse was another. Mildred had seen Wyatt Earp engaged in magic. He'd attempted to change her perception of it, also through magic. Jesse had acknowledged it, corroborated the impossible evidence of her senses. They couldn't all be in cahoots, Chu, Kate Holliday, Wyatt Earp, and Jesse Fox. And they weren't all deluded, unless Mildred was deluded as well. There seemed to be only one conclusion to be drawn, the one she least wanted to be true.

"Miss?" Chu said, and tugged lightly on her sleeve. "Miss? You okay?"

"Yes," Mildred said, her voice cracking. "You understand, it's very hard to believe . . . to believe in magic."

Chu frowned. "No. Easy. Everybody Chinese know. Big noses crazy, is all."

She could declare, as others did, that the Chinese were foolish and superstitious. She could chalk Kate's account up to drink. She could assume that what she'd seen of Wyatt Earp on the porch the night of the ball was a product of the dark, the lightning, wrought-up nerves, and champagne. And she could decide that Jesse Fox had tried to play an unpleasant joke, to get her to say she believed in nonsense so he could make fun of her for it.

But it took four explanations, each one independent of the others, to answer all the questions. Only one theory covered everything, and that was Chu's, and Kate's, and Jesse's.

Knowledge, Jesse had said, was some protection. She owed him an apology.

She swam to the surface of her murky thoughts to find Chu looking at her a little sideways. "You're probably right," Mildred told her. "Big noses are crazy. But if you only ever have other crazy people to talk to, how would you know?"

"Huh," said Chu. "Please, you no tell Mr. Fox?"

Mildred sighed. "I won't tell him right this minute. You and a few other people have given me a lot to think about, and I want to go home and do that. Promise me you won't try something foolish, like running away, in the meanwhile?"

Chu's brow furrowed, but she said, "Okay. Promise." She stuck her hand out at Mildred.

Mildred stared at it, confused.

"Drover do all time like this," Chu said impatiently. "They say, 'Okay, I do,' shake on it." Mildred put out her hand. Chu shook it vigorously and beamed. "Lots time they spit."

"You needn't, really," Mildred hastened to say.

Chu drooped a little. "I spit good. No, I spit *well*."

"I'll take your word for it." She looked out into the yard. The eaves no longer streamed water; they'd settled to an irregular drip. "I have to go home. Chu, if you have trouble, or need help of any kind, you can come to me. Come to the white house with blue porch posts on Safford, at the end of the next block, and ask for Mrs. Benjamin."

Chu shook her head. "No say that."

"No?"

"No remember. *Pin-Ja-Min*?" Chu repeated, mincing the syllables, and made a rude, dismissive noise.

Oh, dear, Mildred thought. Continuing acquaintance with Chu would probably have her doing it regularly. "Millie, then," she offered. "Ask for Millie."

"Mei-li," Chu said carefully, and nodded. "Okay."

Mildred felt she ought to do something more, but short of tucking the wretched child into bed, she couldn't think of a thing. "Good night, then," she said, and headed for the door, Safford Street, and the likelihood of a sleepless night.

It was a terrible burden to be a man of principle. If Wyatt Earp had killed Lung, Jesse could bring him to justice, and maybe the voice of his conscience, which suggested that Lung had died because Jesse was too slow to believe what Lung had told him, would shut the hell up. But he had to prove Earp's guilt first, and his standards of proof were high.

Sam seemed resigned to plodding through the rain. It dripped steadily from Jesse's hat brim and darkened Sam's golden hide. The sound of his hoofbeats changed every few steps: stone, wet earth, slurried mud, the splash of water. The storm seemed to have snagged on the ragged tops of the Swisshelm Mountains behind him; lightning lashed the peaks as if the clouds were beating their fists against them, trying to break free. It ought to be possible to ride out of reach of the rain eventually. The other side of Yuma, maybe.

So, Earp was one of Lung's "knowledgeable men." He might have killed Luther King and left Jesse the silver token warning. Jesse tried to recall Earp's reaction on seeing the thing lying on the poker table. Recognition? Then he'd studied the players—of course. The token was supposed to tell its maker who had magicked King out of town, but the poker game had spoiled that.

Earp could have killed the Chinese girl by the San Pedro and made that knot in the binding-strings of the earth. He could have felt it when his work was undone—but how could he have known who'd done it? And why murder Lung instead of Jesse, if he wanted revenge?

Ahead the land sloped up to Goose Flats, with the block-shapes of Tombstone's buildings all over the top like a pile of parcels on a table. He'd be back in town in under half an hour, if the road hadn't washed out.

In town there was food made by someone else, and hot water, and a dry place to sleep. He'd had those things intermittently in the last week, as he'd ridden up the San Pedro from Charleston to Contention City, then as far east as the Chiricahuas and Galeyville. Between the towns he'd stopped at ranches and prospectors' camps. Always, he'd brought the conversation around to the night Lung died, each time figuring out new ways to get people to answer the questions he couldn't directly ask. He didn't want to be known as the man who was prying into Wyatt Earp's affairs.

A teamster in Millville said he'd been in Tombstone that night and seen Earp at the faro table in the Eagle Brewery. A bookkeeper for the Gird Mill said Earp had been in Charleston that evening, searching out a man he had a summons for. A hand at Chandler's ranch said he'd seen a man who looked like Earp, on what was for sure Earp's racehorse, riding hell-for-leather toward Tombstone that afternoon. But a Mexican camped in the Chiricahua foothills said he'd been with a pack train smuggling silver out of Sonora, and come across Earp in the San Simon Valley that night.

Jesse had asked around Hoptown. Some residents swore they'd heard a shot. Others swore there was none. One man had seen a tall barbarian with a blond moustache and light eyes in the neighborhood, laughing at a man with a dancing dog. His friend rattled a dice box irritably and insisted the barbarian had been ugly and red and not so tall. An old man said he'd seen such a barbarian on a large black horse. A stout woman with gray in her hair said she'd seen such a one, but his horse was brown, and perhaps his hair had not been any lighter than Jesse's. He'd improved his conversational Chinese, but not much else.

Anyone who said he'd seen Wyatt Earp might have actually seen one of his brothers. Unless they stood side by side, they could be hard to distinguish. And of course, there was that trick Earp had done in the foyer of Schieffelin Hall. What were the limits on his ability to make people see what he wanted them to see, where he wanted them to see it?

Jesse would have cursed the undependability of eyewitnesses if he weren't more than a little undependable himself at present. The wearier he got, the harder it was to stay in the real, concrete world he rode through. Time became an icy slope that he found himself halfway down with no warning. Sometimes he was sure Lung was behind him on his black mule, and they were headed toward the San Pedro. Sometimes he was headed for Mexico, and Tombstone was only a name he'd heard. And sometimes he knew where and when he was, and it didn't help. "You said there were no such things as ghosts," he complained to Lung in one instance, and Lung looked offended at being associated with a peasant superstition. He didn't speak. Jesse almost wished he had.

After two nights of sleeping on the ground and bolting awake, sweating, from a dream of lying under the earth, Jesse had gone to unusual lengths to sleep in a bed, any bed, or at least on a floor under a roof. It hadn't always been possible.

On top of everything else, there was the Mildred Benjamin question. He thought of it that way because he had no idea what he ought to do about it. He hadn't seen her since the night of July Fourth, though he'd stopped in at the *Nugget* office and passed her house when he could. Should he seek her out? But if he did, what could he say? He couldn't very well apologize for telling the truth. Should he avoid her? What excuse did he have for that? Besides, he didn't want to.

As the days he spent away from Tombstone piled up, she ought to have dwindled in his thoughts. Instead, the most unlikely things reminded him of her. At Kendall Station, a man's bandaged hand brought to mind the gauze she'd wrapped around Jesse's knuckles. A dentist's signboard in Charleston made him think, not of Holliday, but of the way Mildred Benjamin had stepped forward to make order out of chaos that night at Schieffelin Hall. Every newspaper was a memento of her. Even the sight of the Dragoons brought back to him that morning on Boot Hill, when he'd shared a little of his grief over Chow Lung. She trailed him, rode with him, rose ahead of him whatever direction he traveled.

He heard hoofbeats behind him on the road, and reined Sam to one side. He could make out four riders through the rain. There was a rifle in his saddle scabbard, and his revolver was at his hip beneath his slicker. If the riders intended him harm, he'd be dead from a rifle bullet already. Unless they wanted to get close enough to be sure of him?

The first figure was quite close before Jesse could identify him: John Ringo. With him were two men he didn't recognize, and Curly Bill Brocius bringing up the rear.

"Afternoon, Mr. Fox," Ringo said. When he nodded at Jesse, rain ran off his hat brim in a little stream. He pulled his horse up, and the men behind him stopped, too.

"I guess 'good afternoon' would be stretching it," Jesse said.

"Good if you're a damned fish. Can't even keep a cigarette lit," Ringo grumbled. "Soaker like this is more like winter than summer. Good for the grazing, though."

It occurred to Jesse that grazing meant as much to the man who stole cattle as to the man who raised them. Ringo grinned as if he guessed Jesse's train of thought.

Brocius rode up on a nervous gray roan. "Is that Fox? Well met." He stuck out his hand, but the gray shied sideways, and Brocius barely stayed in the saddle. "Stand still, you whore," he said, but not as if he expected the mare to pay attention.

Jesse eyed the partly healed wound in Brocius's cheek. It reduced the size of his grin by half, and he looked worn and pale. "Looks like you had a run-in with something."

Brocius shrugged. "Something named Wallace. Damned fool shot out a tooth. I'll be all right, though."

Ringo frowned in a general way at the weather. "How's the road into town?"

"I'm about to find out."

"Whatever it's like, I'm crossin'," growled one of Ringo's men. "I ain't campin' here 'til the goddamn water goes down."

Ringo nodded at the man. "Mr. Fox, I don't believe you've met Pete Spencer. You can probably tell he's got a woman in town." Spencer frowned and spat into the road. "This other fellow here is Frank Stilwell. He's a sheriff's deputy, now and then." Ringo beamed as he said it, and Stilwell, a round-faced young man, laughed as if it were an old joke.

"We goin' into town or not?" Spencer said.

"I guess we'll see. If you don't mind a little company, Mr. Fox?"

"Not at all."

Walnut Gulch, when they reached it, looked as if it meant to grow up to be the Colorado. It was creamy brown and churning, and Jesse saw branches and a

good-sized rock tumble past in the flood. The roadbed
was probably still under there, somewhere, but finding
out for certain would be an adventure.

Jesse looked up to where the road emerged from the
water. "If we sight on the center of the road between
the wagon tracks, that'll be the highest line through.
Barring anyplace where it's washed away."

Ringo nodded. "Single file, then."

"Mind the debris coming down with the water."

Ringo raised his voice to carry to the others. "Follow straight as string, boys. And don't press your
horses. There'll be plenty of holes for 'em to step in."
He touched his heels to his big bay and urged him into
the water.

Jesse reined Sam in behind him. The bay didn't go
as quietly as Sam did, but Ringo seemed to drive him
forward by sheer force of personality. Wherever the
horse would rather have headed, forward was where
he stepped.

The water was nearly up to Sam's belly. Once he put
a hoof in a washed-out place and went in up to the cinch
buckles, snorting and tossing his head. Jesse brought
him back into line, and they went on, slower.

Then the water was down to Sam's knees, then his
fetlocks, and finally they stood on the other side next
to Ringo.

Spencer and Stilwell were nearly across, but Brocius's gray was having none of it, even with the other
horses to follow. She reared and balked at the water's
edge. Finally Brocius smacked her over the tail with
his quirt, and the mare leaped into the flood. The
splash startled Stilwell's horse, which bolted the last
yard to dry land.

It frightened the gray even more. Brocius grabbed
for the saddle horn as the mare shied sideways,

crow-hopped—and with a scream that put ice in Jesse's veins, toppled sideways. Brocius went headfirst into the flood behind her. The water grabbed them both.

"Rope!" Jesse yelled. He yanked off his slicker and his gunbelt and threw them up the bank. Someone must have handed him a rope, because he found himself taking a hitch with it around the saddle horn. He knotted the other end around his waist and looped up the middle in his right hand. "Stand!" he ordered Sam, and jumped from the saddle into the water.

It dragged at him like angry hands, and flung him as far as the free length of rope would allow. It battered him with sand, stones, debris, and its own hurtling weight. He could feel it trying to wash him away—not just his body, but his identity, his past, his will, the very possibility of him.

Magic had overwhelmed him in the earth, that day with Lung. This was the same power transmuted, in water that had no proper place or destination. There was anger in the flood, looking for an object.

He concentrated on the feel of the loops of rope in his hand. The rope was real. As long as he had it, he was connected to air and life. He kicked, paddled with his free arm, and pushed his face up to the surface. A little more effort got his head out of the water. Then he looked for Brocius.

The gray mare was gone, swept down the gulch. She had likely broken a leg in the fall. But Brocius . . . There, by a torn-up sycamore stump, was what might be a wet head, and a hand. Jesse let go of the extra length of rope and let the water hurl him down the gulch.

He stopped with a jerk two yards short. It was Brocius; he peered groggily through wet hair and tree roots. Jesse looked back toward the road. The other three men were sliding off their horses. How long had it been since he jumped? Sam stood like the statue of a horse, stiff-legged. A good cow pony knew how to keep the rope taut.

Jesse whistled three notes, as loud as he could, and choked on a mouthful of muddy water. Sam's ears flicked. He stepped forward, and forward again. And Jesse, at the end of the rope, was swept nearer to Brocius, foot by foot.

When he came abreast of the uprooted tree Jesse bellowed, "Stand." Sam planted his feet.

Brocius was half-conscious, blood running down in front of one ear. Jesse fought the current to get behind him.

The fallen stump blocked some of the force of the flood. He ducked below the water and butted Brocius in the stomach with his shoulder, shaking the man's grip loose. Jesse pushed to the surface with Brocius draped half over his shoulder, and both hands hard on the rope.

When Jesse moved back into the rushing water, his weight and Brocius's on the line pulled Sam forward a step. Sam snorted and threw up his head, but he stood.

They had to get out of the gulch; one good-sized boulder rolling downstream could smash them both flat. But Brocius was a big man, and the force of the water was like pressing into a wall. Jesse looked down the length of the rope, wringing out water where it pulled taut over the bank. He had enough strength left to hang on, but no more. Soon he wouldn't have that. The water was grinding it away.

But he and Brocius were moving toward the bank. Jesse raised his head and saw Ringo, Stilwell, and Spencer on the rope, hauling them in. Soon his knees fetched up against the rock and mud under the water.

As soon as they were both clear, Jesse sat down hard in the mud. His legs felt like vines.

"So much for treeing the town," Brocius croaked, wearing his half grin.

"You weren't in shape to tree a mouse when we left Galeyville," Ringo grumbled. "I shouldn't have brought you."

"You can leave him at one of the houses on the edge of town and bring the doctor back to him," Jesse suggested.

Ringo looked at him as if he'd forgotten Jesse could talk. "Hell, you come with him and I'll bring the doc back for both of you."

Jesse shook his head. "I'm just wet and tired. And not much more of either than I was a mile back." It wasn't true, but it sounded good. He shoved himself to his feet and only staggered once. "I'm going to see if I can find his horse."

Spencer and Stilwell got Brocius onto Stilwell's mount, and Stilwell up behind. Jesse untied the rope from his waist and coiled it, and Ringo took it from him. Then Jesse buckled on his gunbelt. The slicker would be an exercise in futility; better to let the clean rain rinse the muddy water off him. He stroked Sam's neck and swung up into the saddle.

"That's a mighty good horse," Ringo observed. "You ever think of selling him?"

Jesse tried to think of a way to answer that would be forceful but not rude.

Ringo laughed. "I didn't figure you had."

Ringo turned his horse up the road toward town. Jesse was about to rein Sam around to head down the gulch when Brocius called weakly from Stilwell's saddle, "Fox. I believe I owe you."

Jesse looked at his pale, drawn face with the livid wound in the cheek. Once it had been Jesse, lying flat and almost too weak to speak, who'd said to Lung, "I think you just saved my life."

Jesse shook his head at Brocius and wheeled Sam around. Words wouldn't pass the tightness in his throat.

He found the gray mare several miles down the gulch, at the foot of a deep cut the water had made over several seasons. She was on her feet—or three of them, anyway. Her near hind leg was broken, and she carried her head low with pain.

Jesse took Brocius's gear off the mare. "I'm sorry," he told her. "This is all I can do for you." He took the rifle out of its scabbard, levered a cartridge into the chamber, and pulled the trigger.

As he bundled Brocius's saddle and belongings in a blanket and tied it behind his own saddle, he wondered if that was true. No, he couldn't do anything for a broken-legged horse except put it out of its misery. But Sam wouldn't have spooked and fallen like that, because he and his rider had been trained to understand each other. He looked back at the body of the gray and thought of thousands of half-broke cow ponies across the West and the drovers who rode them, and all of them in danger of ending up like the gray: a feast for the turkey vultures. Jesse could only train one horse and one rider at a time.

Sam snorted and put his ears back when Jesse added his weight to the load on Sam's back. "Oh, hush," Jesse told him. "You've done more work than this." He stroked Sam's rain-wet neck and watched his ears swivel to catch the sounds of the words. "Let's go home and see how many weeks it takes us to dry out."

They followed the gulch back to the road, and the road to town. They'd just crossed the first of the numbered streets when John Ringo's big bay trotted out from behind a barn and swung in beside Sam. "So," said Ringo, as if in the middle of a conversation, "you play poker to lose and swim pretty well. Any other surprises under that hat?"

"Since they wouldn't be surprises to me, how would I know?"

"No offense meant."

"None taken." He couldn't explain to Ringo that he didn't want company. He could afford to be civil for the few minutes it would take to deliver Sam to the livery stable and Brocius's gear to wherever it belonged.

"That was quick thinking back there. You do that a lot?"

"Accidents are pretty common in the goldfields."

"Now, that's true. I also know that's true whether you ever saw 'em or not. So you see, I'm not too sure if you told me anything I don't already know."

Jesse schooled his face into what he hoped was a good-natured expression and said, "That's what makes you well-informed fellows so hard to talk to."

Ringo cackled—a wicked old man's laugh, out of place in his mouth. "Damned good thing you didn't go to Mexico after all. I liked what you did back there, and how you did it."

"Thank you," Jesse said, since Ringo seemed to expect him to say something.

"If you're looking for work, I could use a man who thinks fast and acts on it. You and I could be a big help to each other, Mr. Fox."

"And what is your line of work, Mr. Ringo?" Jesse asked, because he wanted to know what Ringo would answer.

Ringo smiled. "Moving livestock."

Jesse wanted to ask, "Anyone's in particular?" But one didn't accuse a man to his face of being a rustler, even if it was widely known to be true. "Those four men killed near Fronteras a few months ago were doing much the same. The newspapers are full of letters calling for the heads of . . . livestock movers. It seems like a risky business to be in."

"I wouldn't have thought you'd stick at a little risk."

"Oh, I'm a terrible coward. Thanks for the offer, but I believe I'll stay as I am."

"Well, you think about it." Ringo touched his hat brim and spurred his horse down the puddled street.

Jesse pulled Sam up and sagged in the saddle. He had half an education as a mining engineer, a trade as a horse tamer, and a calling as a . . . a conjure man. Now here was John Ringo saying he had the makings of a cattle thief. "Tombstone, the land of opportunity," he said aloud. Sam's ears swiveled. "Never mind," he added. "Whatever happens, you'll get fed."

⇛ 19 ⇚

Mildred's shabby black umbrella had become a butt for jokes in the Nugget office. "Carrying an old umbrella is proof that my mind is on higher things," she assured Joe Dugan.

Joe pointed his composing stick at the window. "Higher than that rain cloud? If you've got nothing better than that bumbershoot between you and it, you'll have its innards on your mind and everything else."

She laughed. But on her way to the post office, a gust of wind nearly swatted the umbrella out of her hands, and she heard a snap as a rib broke.

She saw the *Gallagher's* name on an envelope in her bundle of mail, and tore it open to find the acceptance and payment for "The Spectre of Spaniard's Mine." Her thoughts weren't so firmly fixed on higher things that she couldn't take a hint. She went straight to Austerberg's Dry Goods.

Frederick Austerberg laid out half a dozen ladies' umbrellas on the counter at the rear of the store.

She ought to take the gunmetal-gray one. It was sensible. She was sensible, wasn't she? The one next to it was red as a cardinal, with a black silk ruffle around the edge and a pierced-work ebony handle. Opened, it was shaped like an Oriental minaret or a dome from a Russian palace.

"That one," she said, tapping the red umbrella with one finger. Her voice was a little unsteady, as befitted a sensible woman buying a red umbrella.

A long roll of thunder, like a battery of cannon, sounded outside. "You will get to try it pretty quick, eh?" Mr. Austerberg craned his neck to peer around a pile of folded dungarees at the front window. "Look at that, black as the Wicked Gentleman." He shook his head. "Such rain already. Look at these shelves!"

Mildred supposed that by Mr. Austerberg's standards, the store was dangerously understocked, but she didn't see any empty spaces.

"The freight wagon came not past St. David last week. The road is not safe. Those canned goods, no more I have in the storeroom. When they are gone, poof!" Mr. Austerberg tended to forget his English syntax when greatly moved.

"Well, we can eat mock apple pie as long as the soda crackers hold out. Harry's threatening to print the *Nugget* in smaller type to keep from running out of paper."

Mr. Austerberg harrumphed through his nose. "If we have more law and order, maybe there be not so much news to print."

"Heavens, we have enough peace officers in Tombstone to start a new town. U. S. deputy marshals, county sheriff, city constable, deputies for all of 'em—"

"And do we have law? No. That Sheriff Behan will not arrest his friends, though from every honest rancher they steal. Poor Bauer, the butcher—seventy head of beef from his corral he has lost to these cow-boys! I thank the good God I am not a butcher."

From his language, Mr. Austerberg had been reading the *Epitaph*. "Cochise County is seven thousand square miles of bad travel. The angel Gabriel himself might have trouble serving a warrant."

"And when they walk down the street of town, these cow-boys? Why do they not fear justice?"

"Because justice requires proof, not hearsay." Mildred kept her tone light, though it was an effort. "If one of Mr. Bauer's seventy cows will come forward and identify the men who took it, they can be arrested. Until then, I'm not prepared to hang my neighbors simply because someone is pretty sure they stole some stock from somewhere."

"Everyone knows these men are thieves!"

"Then everyone should swear out an affidavit. After that the accused men can be arrested, tried, and their guilt or innocence determined on the merits of the case, and if they're found guilty, an appropriate sentence handed down. You say we have no law, Mr. Austerberg, but that's what law is. Anything else is lawlessness, even if the people getting killed are the ones you think deserve it." She had to stop for breath. So much, it seemed, for keeping her tone light.

Mr. Austerberg shook his head sadly. "That is ideal, yes. But here the ones who know do not come forward, and the police their duty do not do. The citizens must act."

"Doing what?"

"We will form a Vigilance Committee."

Civilized words for an uncivil thing. Mildred

shivered. "Vigilantes are just more lawbreakers stirred into the mix. Citizens should insist the police and the courts do their jobs, not take those jobs over."

"You do not understand. Men must protect their homes and families."

If there was one thing Mildred hated, it was being told by someone she was out-arguing that she didn't understand. "All of us want to protect our homes and families. I don't think the way to do it is to increase the chance of them being caught in the crossfire."

"You will see," Mr. Austerberg said. "When these thieves know that honest men against them stand, they will leave. There will be no danger."

Mildred thought the rustlers' resolve was firmer than Mr. Austerberg gave them credit for. But she didn't want to lose a friend. "I hope you're right. Now, how is your stock of pen nibs?"

Mr. Austerberg went to fetch his stepstool as the bell over the door clanged. Mildred looked up.

Jesse Fox stood in the door, brushing raindrops off his hat.

After her encounter with Chu, she'd looked for him, and was ashamed of how glad she was that a respectable widowed woman didn't write notes to single gentlemen. But he'd disappeared. She'd finally asked Chu, who said, "He not come back long time, he say." That suggested he would eventually come back. When he did, she would know what to do about him.

Here, at last, he was, with no indication of where he'd been or what he'd done. His attention was focused downward; he seemed unaware that there might be anyone else in the room. The light from the door framed him like the center of a painting.

He looked up and saw her. She wanted to school her face to some appropriate expression, but couldn't think of one. He, on the other hand, looked as if he'd been caught at something.

His shoulders rose and fell. Then he walked straight to the back of the store, and her.

"Mrs. Benjamin—"

She forced her mouth open, her voice to work. "I'm sorry I didn't believe you."

He blinked. "What—"

"What you said after the Fourth of July ball." She was aware that Mr. Austerberg might be within hearing.

"Oh. I came over to apologize. For making you uncomfortable."

Surprise made her laugh, a stiff, humorless sound. "Uncomfortable. It was that." She looked past him, which left her staring at the pile of dungarees. "Children want to be told everything is all right. And if it's not, they prefer to be lied to."

"But it's not good to do," he said rather sadly.

"No, and I'm not a child. Which . . . which leads me to the next thing I have to say." She folded her hands tightly over the clasp of her purse just to feel the solidness of it. "Thank you for treating me like an adult. And for sharing what must be"—she lowered her voice—"a considerable secret."

He frowned as if she were faintly printed type that needed puzzling out. "Do you know more than I told you?"

"Yes," she said, with care.

"How did that happen?"

"I spoke with Mrs. Holliday. And Chu."

"Interviewing the witnesses. I should have known." They stood silent. Should she not have told him? Finally he said, "Does it frighten you?"

"Of course it does," she snapped. "Any reasonable person would find the very possibility terrifying."

"But you're still . . ." He raised his empty hands, as if he hoped she could fill them with the end of his sentence.

"A reasonable person, once convinced that . . . such things are possible, would need to understand them."

"Would he?"

"Darwin saw evidence of the principles of natural selection. He didn't turn away from it."

"This is a little more alarming."

"Darwin insisted the world wasn't created full-grown in seven days. So far you haven't been so alarming as to deny the validity of Scripture."

That surprised a smile out of him, but it was fleeting. " 'Thou shalt not suffer a witch to live.' "

"There, wasn't it a Christian heresy, once, to say they didn't exist? Besides, I think the Hebrew word is feminine, so you needn't worry." She pressed her hands to her face; her gloves were at least cooler than her flushed cheeks. "Heavens, I sound like a madwoman."

"Talking makes you feel better."

"I can't think and natter at the same time. And thinking about this makes my insides feel uncertain."

"No credit," Frederick Austerberg declared, up at the front counter. "Cash only. We do not give credit."

Mildred looked around a shelf to the front of the store. Mr. Austerberg was bristling at a tall, slender man with dark reddish brown hair in an oilcloth slicker and riding boots. The man's back was to Mildred.

"Funny," the man said. "I'd've sworn my friend Mr. Gray had an account with you."

Jesse lifted his head, as if listening.

"What he has is no matter. You will have to pay cash." Mr. Austerberg lifted his chin. "We do not need custom from such as you."

The man tilted his head, perhaps at the things on the

counter. "All right, then," he replied, sounding amused. "I'll just put these back."

Mildred looked away before the man could see her staring. But Jesse nodded at him, so Mildred felt justified in looking again. The man nodded and smiled at Jesse. He had piercing, light eyes, a longish, squared-off face, and an armload of merchandise. He looked familiar, but she thought he was someone she'd seen, not someone she'd been introduced to.

He began to set things back in their places on the other side of the store. Jesse frowned, his eyes focused on empty air, as if contemplating some inner trouble.

Curiosity got the better of her. She drifted a few steps down the counter to a display of hand mirrors and picked one up. Now she could see over her shoulder and around the end of the shelf. The man returned two pairs of socks, and laid a cotton blanket on a stack of others.

Then he held his hand out, palm upward, cupped and empty above the blankets. He stared into it. Mildred felt a prickling on the skin of her arms, like static electricity.

A light wavered on the man's face. A flame leaped and grew in the palm of his hand.

She was afraid he'd notice her if she moved, afraid he'd spot her trick with the mirror if she didn't. She watched as he raised his cupped hand and poured fire, like liquid from a ladle, over the blankets and the canvas tarps and the bulging paper sacks on the floor below them.

Then he walked out of the store.

"Fire," she choked, then sucked in air and shouted, "fire!"

Jesse was already there. "Bring water!" he yelled to Mr. Austerberg. The fire was spreading with unnatural speed. It behaved more like water or oil, soaking in, seeping, trickling in rivulets. A stack of wool shirts caught as if they'd been doused with kerosene. That wasn't right; wool ought to smolder.

She swallowed hysterical laughter. No, it wasn't right.

Jesse grabbed things off the shelves, threw them on the floor, and stamped on them. A thicket of brooms hung from a rafter; Mildred yanked one down and beat at the fire. The flames spattered across the wooden floor like hot grease. Mr. Austerberg ran up and threw a bucket of water into the heart of the blaze. It hissed and died—and sprang back up again. He ran for more water.

Jesse looked at her across the crawling flames. "Get out of here." She saw fear in his face.

He stretched his hands out over the flames. Her view of him rippled in the heat, but she could tell he was rigid with effort. Her skin was prickling again.

Nothing changed—no. The flames stopped spreading. Slowly they crept toward Jesse, leaving scorched trails behind.

Mildred gripped the broom handle until her fingers ached. She began to sweep in quick, short strokes, toward the center, as if the flames were muddy water. Together they could contain the fire; she hoped Jesse knew how to put it out.

The blaze became a thin, shoulder-high column of fire. The sound of the flames rose in pitch to a screech. They lapped at Jesse's hands. His eyes were closed tight, his teeth clenched, like a man under the lash.

And the fire was gone. A rack of ruined merchandise and six feet of black, smoking floor were all that remained. Mr. Austerberg materialized with another bucket of water, and Mildred wondered, *How long did that take?*

Jesse swayed and folded slowly, until he was on his

knees. Mildred crouched beside him as Mr. Austerberg soaked the blackened shelves.

"Are you all right?" Stupid question; of course he wasn't. He was rocking over his hands, which lay in his lap like dead things. They were scorched red and black.

"It had to go somewhere," he whispered. "I think I dodged some of it."

There wasn't time to try to understand that. "You have to go to the hospital. Are you burnt anywhere else?"

"Arms."

"Mr. Austerberg! Do you have a wagon?"

"No," Jesse said in a stronger voice. "I think . . . not the hospital."

Mildred was about to tell him he was in no fit state to judge. But he might be right. *Trust your instincts.* "Fine. What, then?"

"Brown's."

"We'll still need the wagon."

He shook his head. "I can walk. Less fuss."

"The hell you can." Mildred saw Mr. Austerberg flinch at her language.

"I can."

Less fuss? Yes, and it would suggest to anyone who saw or heard about it afterward that he was not as hurt as he was. But the truth would come out eventually, wouldn't it?

She decided. "Mr. Austerberg, do you have a delivery boy?"

Mr. Austerberg nodded.

Mildred fumbled in her purse, found her little notebook and a pencil. "Have him take this note to Crabtree's Livery Stable and deliver it to a Chinese boy named Chu. He's Mr. Fox's servant."

She began to scrawl, then thought of her reader. She

flipped to a new page and printed, "Mr. Fox is hurt. Meet us at his room. Millie." She started to tear out the page, then stopped. "Mr. Fox, can Chu read? English?"

Jesse nodded. Mildred ripped out the page and handed it to Mr. Austerberg.

She helped Jesse to his feet. She expected him to lean on her. Instead he stood very erect, and his face was distant, as if he were thinking hard about something.

It was a strange, dreamlike trip to Brown's. Even the rain seemed unreal, a performance staged in the street to be viewed from the covered sidewalk. Mildred walked slowly beside Jesse, ready to grab him if he stumbled or swayed. When they came to an intersection, she put up her new umbrella and tilted it to shelter him as well. But she was afraid to speak. Whatever he was doing inside his head, she knew she mustn't interrupt.

Chu met them, not at Jesse's room, but on the landing of the stairs. She seemed to grasp matters in one swift look; when they reached her, she wrapped her arm around Jesse's waist on one side, while Mildred got her shoulder under Jesse's on the other. She felt him surrender some of his weight.

Together they helped him into the room and sat him on the bed. He was breathing hard. Chu dashed to an old nail keg that sat by the door, incongruous in the elegance of the room.

"Thank you, Mrs. Benjamin," Jesse murmured. "You'd best go now."

Chu was pulling a curious set of objects out of the nail keg. Four tiny brass thimble-shaped things, a handful of incense sticks, half-a-dozen paper packets, a squat milk glass jar. She jammed the incense into the brass thimbles and set one on the floor at each corner of the room. Then she produced a tin box of matches from a pocket and lit the incense. She spoke Chinese as she did it, the words tumbling over each other. The room began to smell like a Hoptown shrine.

Mildred, out of an impulse she didn't understand, yanked the drapes across the windows. Then she fetched a towel from the washstand and stuffed it under the door. "You'll have the management down on you in a flash, otherwise," she told Chu.

Chu said nothing. But her face, turned up to Mildred, was frightened and hopeful at once. Mildred nodded to her and went back to Jesse.

He sat perfectly still on the edge of the bed.

"I have to get your coat off and see what the damage is."

"No. Go home."

He didn't seem able to reinforce the words with that tone that caused one to obey him without thinking. "Shut up, please," she told him. She unbuttoned his coat and slid it cautiously off his shoulders and down his arms. He didn't wince or make a noise. Mildred was afraid he might have gone beyond feeling anything.

His coat sleeves weren't burned. Neither was the white cotton of his shirt, even the cuffs. But she could see the burned skin disappearing beneath the cuff edges. What had that fire been, that it burned things that ought not to have caught, and what had Jesse done with it, that it harmed nothing but him?

She slid his suspenders carefully off his shoulders and down over his arms. The alternative was to unbutton them, and she simply wasn't going to fumble with the waistband of his trousers. She unbuttoned his shirt. There were no signs of burns on his chest. "I'm sorry, but I'm about to destroy your shirt," she said, trying to sound matter-of-fact. She got her scissors from her purse and snipped the sleeves of his shirt off at the shoulder seams, then cut them away from his arms.

The damage reached to above the elbow on both arms. His skin was charred black in places like an overdone roast, and smelled like one as well. Mildred swallowed her lunch when it threatened to come back up and was grateful for Chu's incense.

"Not to bone," Chu said, her voice shaking. "Not burnt away. Only skin." She twisted off the lid of the white glass jar and began to spread the contents over Jesse's hands and arms. It was an ointment that smelled sharply of an herb Mildred couldn't identify. The blackened places on Jesse's skin formed length-wise streaks on his arms that met and branched, fol-lowing the lines of his veins.

Jesse didn't react to Chu's touch on his arms. Had he fainted sitting up? Then Mildred realized he was shivering, though the room was warm. Shock, of course. Shock held back pain. She found a blanket in the bottom drawer of a chest across the room and wrapped it around as much of him as she could and still leave his arms free.

He was conscious, at least as she understood the word. But he seemed not to be aware of them, the room, anything. Mildred turned to Chu. "What's hap-pening?"

"He heal himself from inside. Chow Lung do, one time." Again Chu lifted frightened eyes to Mildred. "Maybe."

In other words, Jesse might be doing magic, or he might simply be too deep in shock to respond. "How can I help?"

"Need hot water for tea."

"Put the towel back under the door after I leave."

Mildred went down the back stairs to the kitchen and convinced the staff to give her a very large pot of hot water, and no, she was quite capable of carrying it up to her room, thank you, it was the most foolish thing, but she had a horror of room service, a sort of superstition, she supposed, and thank you so much, she would certainly let them know if she needed anything else. As she lugged the kettle up the back stairs she reflected that eccentricity, once embarked upon, lay always like a pit at one's feet.

Chu pinched bits of powder out of the paper packets, dropped them in a cup, and poured hot water over them. Another herb smell rose up, this one decidedly unpleasant.

"I don't know if we can get him to drink," Mildred warned.

"He maybe come back."

Come back—that was it exactly. It was as if he'd left his body to fend for itself, and gone somewhere else. Mildred found the idea irritating. "Give me the cup."

She sat down on the bed beside him and held the cup under his nose. "Jesse. I know you're in there. Come out and drink this, or I'll pour it on you."

He blinked and drew his head back from the steam. "Eeugh."

"Chu says you have to drink it." Chu hadn't, exactly, but Mildred felt it was a safe assumption.

Jesse looked past the cup to Chu and frowned. "Mustn't sleep."

Chu shook her head. "Not poppy. Only much *yang*."

A flutter of breath came out Jesse's mouth that might have been a laugh. "If you say so."

Mildred held the cup to his lips and he sipped. "Eeugh," he repeated.

"Drink."

"Too hot."

"Then drink slowly. It might help the shivering."

It did seem to help, and when the cup was empty, Jesse seemed stronger and more aware.

"Let me fetch a doctor," Mildred said.

Jesse shook his head. "He'd give me morphine."

"If you don't want it now, you will soon."

His smile was tight. "Now. But I think . . ." He shook his head again. "Don't dare lose the thread. Not yet."

"Do you mind the incense?"

"No. It . . . gives me something to come back to."

Oh, that explains everything, Mildred thought. How could he use so many plain English words and make no sense? "I need to get you propped up before you fall off the bed."

"Don't let me sleep."

Mildred suspected that pain would take care of that. But she pulled off his boots and dragged him, with much help from Chu and a little from him, to lean against the headboard. Chu lifted his arms while she piled pillows across his lap and spread a towel over them. Chu lowered his arms gently onto the towel. Jesse was breathing hard again when they'd finished.

"What else should we do?" Mildred asked Chu.

"I no goddamn doctor," she said apologetically. "Chow Lung teach, I watch, only not so long."

"We'll do the best we can. Could you fetch some soup? Something he can drink?"

Chu nodded briskly. Mildred searched her purse and gave her a dollar. Chu jabbed a finger toward the smoke rising in one corner. "Joss burn all time, hear? Keep safe inside, nobody see." She whisked out the door.

Mildred wanted to ask Jesse what that meant, but he had disappeared behind his eyes again. She tucked the towel back into the gap under the door.

Nobody would take that child for a girl, not in that hodgepodge of Western and Chinese clothes, with that vocabulary. But Mildred had spotted the truth; why hadn't Jesse? She ought to tell him, now, while Chu was gone. Chu would be furious. And given Jesse's condition, there was an even chance he wouldn't remember.

She drew a chair close to the bed and sat. Jesse's chest moved up and down in a quick, not-quite-regular rhythm. His arms lay still, red and black and clotted with Chu's ointment, like artificial things fastened to his shoulders. His face was grayish pale. His eyes had closed, and his lips were parted.

Suddenly he made a noise, a cut-off whimper like a dog dreaming. His eyes opened wide. "I said don't let me sleep."

That stung. "Why not? Sleep is good for healing."

"I'll lose the pieces."

"None of this makes sense to me, you know. Pieces of what?"

He was silent for so long that she thought he'd decided to ignore her. Then between breaths, he said, "Sometimes I can feel how things fit together. As if they're my body. I turned that around—to see my body as something else. . . . So I can find what's wrong and—and fix it."

Once when she was small she'd had a toothache, and Eli had told her about the holy men in India who could walk through fire and lie on beds of nails and not feel a thing. She pretended she was a great yogi who could ignore the ache. It had partly worked, but the dentist still had to pull the tooth. Could Jesse really heal himself, or was he just controlling the pain?

There was a faint cough from the bed that might have been laughter. "Wish you'd seen your face. What were you thinking?"

"I'll tell you if it's any of your business." She was still out of temper. What was wrong with her? "Do you know the man who started the fire?"

"Not well."

"Who is he?"

"John Ringo."

"The rustler?" Given Mr. Austerberg's feelings on the matter, it was no wonder he'd been rude. "How do you know him?"

Jesse's face shone with sweat. "Complicated relationship. Played cards with him once." Then his eyes squeezed tight shut. "Oh, God."

"What?"

"He's another one."

Mildred stared at him, baffled. Oh, of course: another one like Jesse. "No, really? I would never have guessed."

"I think—I think he killed Luther King."

Any impulse toward sarcasm was instantly driven out of her. "How do you know?"

"There was a . . . token in King's hand. It stung me when I touched it. Lung said another like me would feel it, too. Ringo didn't. Thought that meant he wasn't one. But it wouldn't have hurt the man who made it. Ringo could have killed King, or had him killed, and left the token for me to find."

Mildred sorted that out in her head. "But why would Ringo kill him? If King might have tattled on the Earps—"

"No love lost, I know."

"Might he . . . might he have murdered your friend?"

He sighed. "Wonder where he was that night. Don't think anyone in Hoptown saw him." He opened his eyes. "When you found us by the river. It was the night after."

The night after Tom McLaury had been angry at Jesse. Until riding back, they'd met—"Did anyone see a white man, a stranger?"

"Plenty," he grumbled.

"A light-haired man with a round red face, who laughed too much."

Jesse's eyes were suddenly sharp on hers. "Who?"

"Jim Crane, the stage robber. Tom and I met him on the road back to town. Then Crane rode toward the river."

He drew breath through his teeth and shook his head.

"What is it?"

"Something I'd forgotten. Thank you."

He was an unpromising color, and the muscles stood out in his jaw. "I'm sorry," she said quickly. "I shouldn't distract you."

"It hurts, is all. But I think it's working."

Mildred's eyes flew to his ravaged arms. The backs of his hands were red and pink, instead of black and red. The black seemed to have flaked and fallen away onto the towel. Where it had been was exposed new skin, shiny and vulnerable-looking.

"It's working," she assured him. Her voice shook.

The doorknob rattled, and her heart leaped into her throat. But it was Chu, with a basket in one hand. "Dollar get plenty food, Hoptown," she announced smugly. "I get for everybody." She gave Mildred a wicked look. "You no like, I eat for you."

"Don't sass Mrs. Benjamin," Jesse murmured.

Chu winked at her and lifted a covered lacquer bowl from the basket. "Soup."

Mildred lifted the cover and coughed. "Good heavens. You're certain it's not linament?"

Chu glared. "Good soup! Hot, salt, sour, all *yang*! I find special!"

"I'm sorry. I'm sure you know best." She gave Jesse a hopeful look. He nodded. She sat down beside him to hold the bowl to his lips, as she'd held the cup.

The edge of the mattress gave a little under her, and she reached out a hand for balance. It landed on Jesse's shoulder.

There was a chill in the room after all, though Jesse's skin was warm where she'd cut his sleeve off. He drew in a swift breath, like a gasp. She snatched her hand away.

"I'm sorry, did I hurt you?"

Jesse shook his head. A set of curious expressions flew across his face: confusion, wonder, fear. Then they were gone. Or rather, he had shuttered them away.

"You'd better go," he said. "Chu can look after me."

She was mildly offended. He was right, of course. Still, what had happened? Did he not like to be touched? She'd laid the same hand on his same shoulder when they danced. Admittedly, there'd been three layers of cloth between them. Was he shy? Ridiculous. She must have hurt him—but he needn't send her packing for it.

She could tell him his stableboy was a girl; that would be a sort of revenge. But it would leave Chu to deal with the aftermath, which didn't seem fair.

She stood up and handed the bowl to Chu. "If you need anything . . ."

"I come, okay," Chu assured her.

"If he gets worse, go for a doctor, whatever he says."

"If I'm that much worse," Jesse growled, "I won't be able to say anything."

She bent to pick up her umbrella from the floor by the bed. As she did, she shot another glance at Jesse's arms. The charring and blisters were almost gone.

She went to the door. "Good-bye, then, and good luck."

His face looked hollowed and bleak. "Good-bye, Mildred."

As she walked down the hall to the back stairs, she thought, *I'm staying out of hotel rooms in future. They're bad for my peace of mind.*

⇝ 20 ⇜

Jesse stood at the open door of the Nugget office, watching Mildred Benjamin.

She frowned at the sheet of newsprint in her hands. Light shone through it, showing printing on the other side, though the side toward him was blank. A printer's proof? He knew nothing about newspapers, not the way she did.

He hadn't seen her since she'd left his hotel room. Ladies didn't visit single men in their lodgings, even to inquire about their health. But she'd seemed pretty thick with Chu; she might have gotten a report from that quarter. He'd no business asking Chu if she had. Besides, Chu had taken to watching him in a grave, evaluating way that made it hard to ask him anything.

Mildred's red-brown hair was pulled fiercely back from her face at the temples, but a few strands had got away and curled around her ears. Little silver drops caught the light at her earlobes. Her lips were crimped together—probably at whatever made her frown—which produced a shallow dimple beside her mouth. Her figure was straight-backed and slender in a gray-green twill dress. He remembered her in her ball gown on Fourth of July, her rounded arms and pale bosom. Slender, but not meager.

She looked up, and he felt his face flush. He hoped the light wasn't on him. But of course, her eyes went to his gloved hands first.

"They're fine," he said, and cleared his throat. "I need some information."

She searched his face. "That's what we do here," she said at last, holding up the sheet in her hand. "I warn you, Harry will be back any moment, and I'm guessing you don't want what you're asking about to make the next edition."

"Not really."

She frowned again. "Wait here." She disappeared into the back room for a minute, then returned. "Ask away."

"Where can I find a good description of Jim Crane?"

Mildred turned to a chest of long, flat drawers, read the label on one, and opened it. She took out a sheet of paper and handed it to him. "We keep copies of all the job printing."

It was the wanted poster for the Benson stage robbers. He found the second name. "C-R-A-I-N?"

She smiled for the first time since he'd arrived. "It's not my fault Bob Paul can't spell."

American; about 27 years old; about 5 feet, 11 inches high; weight, 175 or 180 lbs.; light complexion; light, sandy hair; light eyes; has worn light mustache; full, round face, and florid, healthy appearance; talks and laughs at same time; talks slow and hesitating; illiterate; cattle driver or cow-boy. Jesse nodded and handed the sheet back to Mildred.

"Here's what I know," he said briskly. "Crane sounds like the man who kidnapped a Chinese girl, and may have murdered her down by the river. One of the girls she worked with described him pretty well."

"When I met you at the river—"

"Lung and I were looking into it. It was . . . She was killed as part of a, a sort of binding."

"The sort of thing you do."

He felt a flash of anger. "Since I don't practice blood sacrifice, no."

"I'm sorry. I only meant—" She thumped down on a wooden stool and flourished her hands, as if they were full of words and it would help to throw them. "Couldn't you be something ordinary, like a scholar of ancient Etruscan or a camel breeder? It would be so much easier to *talk* about!"

The tension that had stood like a sheet of glass between them dissolved, and he laughed. "I've been trying to find words for months. You're the writer; I was counting on you."

"I suppose I'm the wrong sort of writer," she said, then blushed and looked away.

"I'm sorry, did I say—"

"No, no. What else do you know?"

"You said you saw Crane heading toward the San Pedro after you left Lung and me there. He may have come to see who was lurking around the river after . . ." How much should he explain? And how to do it? He looked desperately at Mildred, but this time she didn't have enough of the sentence to leap over the hard part for him. "Well, Lung and I . . . dismantled something. Or blew it up, really. Not a physical thing, a—"

Mildred giggled. "You should see your face."

"Teach me to expect sympathy from you."

"Was that the thing you had to do without your shirt? Oh, now you really *should* see your face."

Jesse covered it with one hand. "That wasn't fair."

"You're right. Ungentlemanly of me. So you . . . demolished something. Do you think that got Crane's attention?"

"His, or someone he was working for. Lung said rich strikes like Tombstone's attract people who can ... feel what's in the earth. They don't always know what they're doing. But if Wyatt Earp is one, and John Ringo another, Crane could be one, too. Or he could be fetching and carrying for one."

Her smile fell away. "Do you think Jim Crane killed your friend?"

"Someone who looked like Crane was seen in Hoptown the night Lung was murdered."

A monumental clatter sounded from the back room, and a man's voice: "God damn it to hell, someone tell that bastard Heintz to put the new bars on the folder or store 'em somewhere safe!"

Unlike Jesse, Mildred hadn't flinched at the noise. "Harry?" she called without looking 'round. "Are you all right?"

"Fine!" Harry Woods shouted. Then he muttered, "God damn it."

"I need to step out for a few minutes, Harry." Mildred snatched up the hat and purse lying on a table and jerked her head toward the front door. Jesse left by it and waited out of sight of the windows.

Mildred joined him moments later. "Sorry. I think we'll be private enough if we keep walking."

Jesse nodded back toward the office. "You don't trust him?"

"I trust him to be unnecessarily interested in my personal life. Best possible motives, of course."

He studied her out of the corner of his eye. Her cheeks were pink, and she seemed deeply involved in pulling on her gloves. "Did the whatever-they-weres survive?"

"If they were fragile, I wouldn't have used them."

"Oh," said Jesse. No other response seemed worthy.

"Where were we? So you blame Crane?"

"I suspect him. If I can get to him before someone else does, I may be able to find out if he did it, and if he did it on his own."

Mildred walked in silence for a moment, her eyes on the view of the Dragoons at the end of the street. "Do you know why one can't take the law into one's own hands?"

"Why?" he said warily. She didn't sound as if she was changing the subject.

"Because the law is too big to fit in one pair of hands. So if you feel you've got a comfortable grip on whatever you're holding, you can be pretty sure it's not the law." She looked into his face. "If you find Crane, what will you do?"

"Bring him in. He'll hang for the two killings in the stage holdup."

"And possibly for killing the Haslett brothers and another man in Hachita." Jesse missed his footing on the sidewalk. She nodded. "You must have been out of town. It was revenge, they say, and that might even be true; the Hasletts killed Head and Leonard."

The avalanche of death turned Jesse's stomach. "I guess I'd better find him soon."

"If he were easy to find, it would have been done." Mildred stopped at the frontage of a vacant lot. It had been cleared after the fire, but a pile of new-sawn pine was its only occupant. "There was another man who took part in that holdup."

"Your paper said Holliday—"

"Not Dr. Holliday." She gazed up and down the street, as if admiring the scenery, of which there was precious little. "I overheard Kate Holliday say that Morgan Earp was there."

He drew breath to ask if she thought it was true. But she wouldn't have told him if she didn't. "The Earps

won't want Crane tried. How far would they go to pre-
vent it?"

Mildred shook her head. "You said that Crane is
bound to hang. But what if he agrees to name the last
robber?" She met his eyes again. "Do you want him
tried, or dead? Because you should remember they
may not be the same thing."

If Crane bargained for his life—No, surely he
couldn't. He was accused of five murders; six, counting Lung's. But how good was the case against Crane
in those deaths? "Until I find out if he pulled the trigger, I don't want him one or the other."

She was troubled, and he couldn't blame her. Did he
want Lung's murderer dead? It was right to want it.
Lung himself had said there was a balance. Did he want
it so much that he'd do the job himself, if he had to?

Lung had asked him if he would kill in cold blood if
that was what it took to right a wrong. He'd said no.
That was the person he was. Wasn't it?

"Who would know where Crane's gone to ground?"

Mildred closed her eyes and rubbed the space between her eyebrows. "Even if you asked all his bosom
friends, why would they tell you?"

"That's for me to worry about."

"John Gray, possibly—Crane was sighted at Gray's
ranch at the beginning of last month. Rumor put him
with the rustlers on the border a few weeks ago, which
might mean John Ringo and William Brocius. I
wouldn't count on that, though. The moment anyone
steals anything from anybody in Cochise County, the
credit goes to those two and the latest bogeyman. I'm
waiting for the story that joins Ringo, Brocius, and
Geronimo." She spoke fast, and her voice was hard, a
shell over her emotions. "They all have land over the
New Mexico line, in the Bootheel around Cloverdale.
Gray, Ringo, the Clantons, Crane before he went on

the run. It's good land. Good for cattle." She pressed one hand to her mouth, as if she were afraid of the words that might follow.

"My compliments on your news-gathering. That's where I'll look."

"He could be anywhere. You can't just—"

Jesse took her chin between his thumb and forefinger. Even through his gloves, he could feel . . . what was it? Strength, fear, anger, resignation, all tumbled like stones in swift water. He thought she'd pull away, but she didn't. "I think I can. I mean to try, at least." He smiled, and wished she would smile back. "It may work to my advantage that Earp and Ringo and . . . whoever else is out there can't be sure I know what I'm doing."

She glared and pushed his hand away. "Do you?"

"Depends on what I'm doing."

Mildred sighed. "Just remember that the Earps have an interest in this. Be prepared to duck if they act on it."

"Are you worried about me?"

"Shouldn't I be?" She looked swiftly away; then she turned back and laid her hand on his wrist. "Yes." She pressed her lips together, and her hand slipped off his arm. "The *Nugget* has plenty of material as it is. Don't give us any more to write about."

At Crabtree's Livery, Jesse stuffed supplies into his saddlebags, aware that Chu was watching. It wasn't until he tucked a box of cartridges in the top of each bag that Chu spoke.

"You pack plenty stupid. Too heavy, put on top."

Jesse decided not to say that things on the top could be got at quickly. Chu talked to Mildred, after all. "When I get back, we'll work on your verbs."

"I know plenty goddamn English!"

Jesse grinned. "Maybe even too much."

Chu checked the fit of Sam's bridle, though the buckles were fastened on the usual holes. "You go long?"

"It depends on how long it takes to find what I'm after."

Chu sat down cross-legged on the floor in front of him, which gave the boy an unobstructed view of Jesse's face. Why did everyone feel they had to catch his every expression?

"Sumbitch kill Chow Lung," Chu said calmly.

"Pardon?"

"Who you go find."

Jesse fastened the bags, aware that stalling for time was cowardly. "What makes you think so?"

Chu shrugged. "I go with. Watch you back."

There was no heat in Chu's face, no anger or outrage, only an implacable steadiness. Jesse swallowed through a tight throat. A child shouldn't know how to look like that. "You're better off here."

"Chow Lung live, he go with you. You come get, I bet."

"If Chow Lung were alive, I wouldn't be going." His voice was harsh, which he hadn't intended. It was true; he would have ridden straight to Lung. They would have set out with a half-formed and improbable plan that they would change in midstream without needing to consult over it. They would likely have gotten on the bad side of everyone involved and had to leave town.

But Lung was dead, and this was nothing like the trouble they used to get into.

Jesse crouched next to Chu. "Lung probably taught you a lot. But he didn't teach you enough for this. It's dangerous."

Chu snorted. "How much *you* know?"

"Nothing like you and Mrs. Benjamin to build a fellow up," Jesse grumbled. He stood and picked up the saddlebags. "This isn't going to be about . . . knowledge. Not that kind."

"Stupid. About magic always. You see pretty soon."

"I'll tell you if it is." He strapped the bags behind the saddle cantle and tied his bedroll and slicker across them. "If I don't come back, go to Mrs. Benjamin. She'll help you." He felt reasonably comfortable committing Mildred to that. He stroked Sam's neck and swung into the saddle.

Chu took hold of Sam's reins. "Not do stupid thing."

"I thought I couldn't help that." He smiled, though his throat was tight again.

"Not do *big* stupid thing."

"Ah. Well, I'll try."

Chu stepped aside, and Jesse rode out into the sun.

Animas was a scramble of wood and adobe buildings, a country village that served the surrounding ranches. Hachita, ten miles away, had ambitions; from the looks of it, Animas had no plans to be more than it was right now.

Jesse drew rein at a squat building with "HOTEL" painted on the front. He sat in the saddle, bracing himself with both hands on the swell, and trying to look as if he was studying the street. But staying where he was wouldn't make him any less weary. Besides, it was time to get his weight off Sam's back and legs. The horse had worked hard enough.

He stumbled when his feet touched the ground, and half fell against Sam. Sam threw up his head and sidled away. Jesse landed on his hands and knees in the dirt of the street.

Water, sounding like his own blood in his ears—lots of it not far from the surface. Tombstone's bones were silver, but water was the flesh and bone of this place, feeding the grass and filling the creeks that ran in clefts between the hills. He tasted silver here, too, but fleeting and faint across his tongue.

Jesse gasped and shook his head, and the knowledge let go of him. He staggered to his feet.

He wasn't weak anymore. His first frightened thought was that he'd stolen from Sam when he stumbled against him. Then he remembered his fingers in the dirt. He'd pulled strength as well as knowledge out of the earth. Not as much strength as a good dinner and a full night's sleep, but enough to keep him upright.

Jesse stabled Sam and took possession of a small room with stained and faded wallpaper and a suspiciously trough-shaped bed. Unpromising as it was, it called him strongly. No, dinner first.

He found it across the street by the smell of onions and bacon fat coming from a whitewashed adobe. The inside was low-ceilinged and dark as a casket, but it offered dinners as well as home-brewed beer, a dozen varieties of alcohol, and a locally made peach liqueur the bartender described as "like a pretty whore with brass knuckles." Jesse got the beer and a plate of mixed fry with biscuits and sat down at the nearest of three tables.

He was halfway through the food and done with the beer when a familiar-looking man came in. His curly hair and pointed beard showed dusty red when he passed through the light of a lamp. He crossed the room to the counter like a regular. "Tom Collins whiskey," he ordered. "Make it rye, none of that hog feed corn shit you got."

As the bartender squeezed a lemon, the man turned

to scan the room. His eyes met Jesse's, and he frowned. "Don't I know you?"

"I've met you somewhere," Jesse acknowledged.

The man smirked. "Likely so. There's plenty around here who count me in when they need a steady hand."

Something about the words brought it back. "You were in the Oriental Saloon when the Ortega boy was brought in shot."

The red-haired man peered at him, and his face cleared. "You're the fellow with the horse! Sure, I remember you." His eyebrows lowered again. "Not your name, though."

"Jesse Fox."

"Ike Clanton. You're a ways from Tombstone."

Clanton was one of the men on Mildred's list of Bootheel ranchers. Jesse lifted his empty glass. "And it's a dry trip. May I buy you that whiskey, as long as I'm getting another?"

Clanton's eyes opened wider, and he smiled. "Can't turn that down."

From the look of him, Jesse thought that was truer than Clanton meant it. He got himself another beer.

Clanton tipped half the drink down his throat and said, "That boy died, I hear."

Jesse sighed. "Not what I'd intended."

"Law make a fuss?"

Jesse stole a glance at Clanton as he lifted his glass. Should he say yes? But it was easy to disprove. "Not a bit. Seems wrong, that a man should die and nobody care about it."

Clanton shook his head. "Territory's a hard place. You got to be hard to get by." He drained his whiskey.

Jesse flagged the bartender for another before he said, "You have to be hard just to get across it. I swear I've ridden every foot of ground between the Tombstone Hills and here in the last few days."

"What for?"

"Looking for someone."

"Who?"

Jesse gave Clanton an arrested look. "I suppose if you're pretty well connected around here, you might know the man. He used to have land north of here. Jim Crane?"

Clanton coughed, and covered it with a swallow of his fresh drink. "Crane's place was south of here, by Cloverdale. Hell, I guess it's still his, but it's the last place you'll find him, account of his being a wanted man." Clanton grinned. "Guess you want him, too. What for?"

"Just a couple of pressing questions."

"You hidin' a badge? If you are, I'd keep hidin' it. Unless you got a dozen deputies outside."

Jesse laughed. "I'm no lawman. I've got a story he can straighten out for me, is all."

Clanton tossed the rest of the second drink down. Even in the gloom, his cheeks and nose showed red. "Jim ain't very obliging."

"And he doesn't sound like a man I'd want to disoblige. I'd do what I could to make it worth his while, though."

Clanton opened his mouth as if to ask what with, but shut it again. No one riding alone on the border would answer a question like that.

"Need another?" Jesse asked, nodding at Clanton's glass.

Clanton shook his head regretfully. "Nah, I'm high enough to see in the window. How long you 'round for?"

"I leave at first light. What is it, thirty miles to Cloverdale? I'll ask again there."

"Well, if I hear anything about Jim before then, I'll pass it on."

"Mighty good of you. Nice to meet you again, Mr. Clanton."

In the ice cream parlor in Tombstone, Jesse had shaken Wyatt Earp's hand. Mildred had given Earp some ridiculous tale about mess, and hadn't. They'd seen the rest of the encounter differently. Jesse put out his hand, and Clanton took it.

He hadn't expected the strength of Clanton's handshake, or the calluses. How did this work? Not taking, not this time. How to gather honesty and good intentions and deliver them out through his skin—

Clanton smiled. "Well met anytime, Mr. Fox."

It might have worked; he couldn't tell. He put his hat on and headed for his room and its unpromising bed.

The sky was still gray when Jesse led Sam out of a stall the next morning. He almost wished he hadn't slept so soundly; whatever position he'd ended up in had left him sore in every muscle. He felt Sam's legs to see if he suffered anything similar, but there was no heat or swelling there.

As he snugged up the front cinch, he saw movement at the stable yard gate. He looked past Sam's nose to see Ike Clanton coming toward him.

"Guess I damn near missed you." Clanton's heartiness rang a little hollow. "Still mean to find Jim?"

"I do. Thought of anything that might help?"

Clanton shook his head. "Ask in Cloverdale—I can't do better than that. You could do me a favor, though."

"I'll try."

Clanton took a leather pouch out of his coat pocket. "I been keepin' this for Jim. Seems like you got as much chance to come on him as any, and more than most. Would you pass it along?"

The pouch was moose or elk hide, thick and scarred.

The contents shifted and clinked, heavy in Jesse's palm. He raised his eyebrows at Clanton.

Clanton flushed. "It's to get him out of the country."

"You trust me with it?"

"Ain't you trustworthy?"

Jesse hefted the pouch. "Oh, yes."

"If you don't find him, I guess you better fetch it back to me. I'll be in Tombstone for a couple-few days. But likely you'll find him." Clanton tugged his hat brim and hurried away.

Jesse stared at the sack of money in his hand and sighed. *This is what happens when you meddle with people's minds.*

John Gray was away from his house. His ranch foreman shook his heavy head and grinned when Jesse asked about Crane. "Ain't you heard?" the foreman asked. "The fellow's a wanted criminal." Whatever was involved in the "trust me" hex, it didn't seem to work every time. Jesse smiled and thanked him and turned Sam's nose south and west toward Cloverdale.

He'd sleep rough again; there wasn't enough of the long twilight left to reach town in. The sky above him was a luminous deep purple, with little clouds like rabbit scut dyed orange dotting the western horizon.

Until Clanton gave him the bag of money, Jesse had managed not to think about what he really wanted. He could find Crane, and decide then. Crane might not even be Lung's murderer, and he wouldn't have to decide at all. The chickens could stay uncounted.

But the weight of the leather bag in his pocket clarified things. He wanted Jim Crane dead. He wanted him to know he was about to die, as Lung must have known. He didn't want Crane to get away, and he didn't want to carry the money that could help him do it. Assuming Jesse could find him by riding blind through the benighted wilderness at the tip of Arizona Territory.

Except he wasn't blind.

Jesse squinted at the rough track that led away from Gray's ranch. Something like a scarf of mist lay above the ground. It disappeared one moment, then reappeared the next, like a hawk turning in a clear sky.

He urged Sam forward. The horse's knees touched the wisp of light and it vanished. But there was more ahead, curling down the track and out of sight.

It could be mist—but the evening wind didn't stir it.

I miss the night vision, he'd said to Lung. And Lung had told him to summon it, as if it could be called like a dog.

At the memory, anger and grief flashed in him like a struck match; he snuffed them as well as he could. Lung would have enjoyed seeing Jesse forced to accept everything he'd told him.

"Here, boy," he whispered. It didn't work, of course.

He concentrated on the trail of light ahead, willed it to grow stronger, surer. The effort made him squeeze his eyes shut—

When he opened them, the world was an image printed on silver. Underexposed, but brighter, sharper than a full-moon night. The track ahead showed wheel ruts, stones, puddles, and clear footing. A ringtail shot across the path—a flash from its eyes, a flick of its tail—and disappeared into the brush.

But the wisp of light was still frail and faint. He laughed softly. What would Lung have had to say about that? He nudged Sam forward, following the streak of light that might, or might not, be Jim Crane's trail.

*   *   *

Judging by the stars, it was next to morning. Was
Crane going into Mexico? For all Jesse could tell, he
might be across the border. The dry ravines and scrub
oaks didn't distinguish between nations.

Light flickered ahead, reflected up the face of a
bluff. A campfire.

Jesse dismounted, led Sam into a hollow in the
rocks, and tied him. He took the boxes of cartridges
from his saddlebags and put one in each coat pocket.

The rifle would look damned unfriendly if he
walked into the camp with it. But he didn't want his
last thought in life to be, "Well, that was stupid." He
slid the rifle out of its scabbard and tucked it under his
arm.

Closer in, he heard men's voices and the rustle of
the fire. He also heard the small sounds of a herd of
cattle: a snort, the scrape of a hoof, an irritable bleat.
Crane might be at that fire; and he might be in the
company of men moving cattle that weren't theirs,
who wouldn't care for a stranger arriving armed in the
darkness.

A twisted cedar, its branches lost in shadow, stood
where the light changed from the polished-pewter
darkness he'd conjured to the yellow of the firelight.
Jesse propped the rifle against the cedar's trunk and
laid a box of cartridges by the stock. Then he walked
into the camp, his hands away from his sides.

Two men sat at the fire. A third rummaged in the
back of a buckboard. Four dark shapes at the firelight's margins might have been sleeping men in their
blankets. As Jesse stepped into the light the men by the
fire rose, hands on the pistols in their belts. Jesse
shaded his eyes. The thread of light that had led him
was gone.

"Who're you?" the shorter of the men called. "And
what do you want?"

The glare of the little campfire made his eyes water. Now that he had the night vision, how did he turn it off? "My name is Jesse Fox. I'm looking for Jim Crane."

Something hard and cold pressed the skin below his left ear. "What d'you want him for?" asked a leisurely voice at his shoulder.

Jesse weighed possible answers, searching for one that would get the gun barrel out of his jaw hinge. "Ike Clanton asked me to give him something."

"Where'd you meet my boy?" That was the man by the buckboard. Jesse could see him at the corner of his eye, his long white beard and dense eyebrows catching the light.

"I beg your pardon?"

"Ike's my son."

"Animas. In a saloon."

The old man snorted. "Likely he was in Animas."

The man at the fire said, "Crane, don't be a damned fool."

The gun barrel stayed where it was as Crane reached around Jesse, pulled the revolver out of his holster, and tossed it to one side. "I'm just protectin' myself. Now you keep your hands right there," he said in a kind of slow chuckle. " 'Cause if you got a hideout on you, I will shoot you if you go for it." He gripped Jesse's lapel and pulled him around.

Jesse looked at Crane's round, smiling face and pale eyes, at the pistol in his left hand, and felt a shudder pass through him. This was what Lung had seen, the last thing.

He had seen a man whose terror ran so deep that no uncertain light, no cocky posing or gunman talk, could hide it from the sight of a knowledgeable man. Lung would have known that nothing he could do would outweigh whatever caused that fear, whoever ordered Lung's death.

"Who was it?" Jesse asked him.

Outside the circle of light a cow scrambled to its feet and shook, then another. "Oh, Christ Jesus, not now," muttered the short man by the fire. "Crane, put that gun down."

The taller one beside him said, "Want me to check 'em, Will?"

"Wait, maybe they'll settle. Crane, you pull that trigger and I'll have a hundred cows on the run. And I swear to God I'll send you to your Maker before I head after 'em."

Crane tapped his temple in a mock salute. "Whatever you say, Mr. Lang, sir. Me and my guest'll go attend to business elsewheres." He stepped back and jerked his head. Jesse walked past the buckboard out of the camp, with Crane behind.

It was a relief to be out of the fire-glare. Here he could see better than Crane, and that might prove useful. More useful still would be to know how to turn this witch-sight on and off when he needed it, but learning to do it with a gun at his back was beyond him.

"Stop. Turn around." Crane lowered his voice. "Who was who?"

"What?"

"You asked back there, who was it?"

Jesse studied his face again. "Who are you so afraid of?"

Crane laughed. "I ain't afraid of no one. And you ain't gonna be the first."

"All right. Who told you to kill the Chinese doctor in his home, and kidnap and kill the Chinese whore?"

Starlight winked on the pistol as Crane's hand jerked. "What the hell—"

"The doctor was a friend of mine."

Jesse watched Crane's face work, and finally settle into a parody of his cocksure grin. "Never knew a fella was friends with a Chinee."

"You can tell me. It won't get back to him."

Crane laughed again—at least, it was probably supposed to be a laugh. "How'll you stop it? Shit, I could whisper it to you on a church altar. God hisself couldn't keep it mum. You got no notion."

Jesse wanted to tell him otherwise. But there was a good chance Crane would shoot him if he did.

"What did Ike send for me? Or was that just talk?"

"It's in my right coat pocket. Can I take it out?"

"No. Turn the hell around."

Jesse did, and Crane reached around him from behind and pulled out the bag. Jesse heard Crane step away, but nothing else. He kept his hands up and turned slowly back.

Crane clutched the bag, feeling the shape of the contents and shaking his head. "Shit," he said.

"Clanton said it was to get you out of the country."

"Heh." He kept shaking his head, but slowly, as if it hurt him. "Heh. God damn." Finally he raised his eyes to Jesse's. "It's too late. It's too goddamn late. Couldn't run far enough anyway."

"Who was it?"

"Why? One's bad as t'other. Earp done his best to kill us all, ever since the holdup. His baby brother 'bout pissed himself when the shootin' started, and I thought maybe the Earps was all mouth and no sand. Out here, you can't kill your man, might as well stay home and stick to your sewin'." Crane gave another snort of laughter. "But Wyatt don't have no such trouble. He got Bill and Harry, though Jesus knows how—"

"That was the Hasletts."

"And Pontius Pilate didn't hammer no nails, neither."

"Why'd you keep working for him?"

Crane frowned and tucked his chin. "I never worked for Earp. You think I walked bang up to him and said, 'What can I do for you, Mr. Wyatt?' He'd'a said, 'Why, Jim, I'd take it kindly if you'd just lay right down and die.'"

"Then who ordered the murders?" But he knew.

"I went to John Ringo to save my skin from Earp. And he agreed, oh, yes. All I got to do is any goddamn thing he tells me. Killin' the Chinee gal damn near made me puke my guts up."

Crane was kneading the leather bag, over and over, as if he'd forgotten what it was. The pistol no longer pointed quite at Jesse.

Another voice, muted, rose from the camp behind them. Jesse thought he caught the word "bear." He heard more men stirring, the clink of a bridle. The cattle stirred, too, and grumbled nervously. "Take it and go," Jesse said. "Get to South America."

"No. I made my mind up. I'm goin' back to Tombstone."

"You'll hang."

"I know. But before I do"—Crane showed his teeth, a badger-grin of anger—"I'll talk on both of 'em." Crane lifted the bag. "You want this?"

Jesse shook his head.

"It can stay here then." Crane flung it down.

The contents spilled across the dirt: the shining coach wheels of new-minted Mexican silver. On one, like a shadow on the moon, lay a single gold dollar.

Jesse's heart slammed in his ribs. "Get out of here," he said to Crane. The gold coin winked and winked, like a sly, cruel face. How could he not have felt it until now? He'd carried it—

And as he had, it had called. Whatever it was meant to call was on its way, and had been, probably, since morning, when Clanton had given him the bag. It was still calling now.

"What—"

"Go!" Jesse shoved him toward the camp, ignoring the pistol. "Get your horse and go. Hurry!"

As Crane stepped into the circle of firelight, a shot cracked from above, and another. The old man, Ike Clanton's father, grunted and fell forward in the dirt. The bluff lit up with gunfire. The roar of it echoed off the rocks. Bullets stitched the earth, the buckboard, the shapes of the bedrolls.

Crane turned back toward him, his eyes wide and blind. His chest was torn open. He dropped at Jesse's feet.

Jesse's pistol lay wherever Crane had tossed it. Crane's had fallen from his hand somewhere near the fire. Jesse dived for the edge of the camp, rolled, came up running. He had to get to the rifle.

He came down hard in a jumble of rocks. The pain in his side didn't feel like a cramp—no, it felt wet. A shining dark trickle crept like an insect past his face across the dirt.

Funny. It started with this. This time I won't happen on Lung. Unless, of course, he did.

I never did make it to Mexico.

Doc hated riding the stage in the rain. With the canvas curtains down on all the windows, it was like being shut in a wardrobe with three strangers.

He'd caught enough of the casual chat to know that the short, red-faced man with the heavy moustache was an engineer at the Gird Mill; that the thin, sallow, sour-looking man who ought to have been a preacher claimed to be a first-class mixologist seeking employment; and that the quadroonish fellow in need of a haircut was a Hooker Ranch drover. They'd been in the coach since Tucson, and once they'd exhausted the president's health and the washed-out rail line, they hadn't much common ground to sustain the conversation.

That was fine with Doc. There'd be damned little opportunity for peaceful reflection once the stage arrived in Tombstone. Not that his present reflections were peaceful, though resignation to an unpleasant reality could bring a degree of peace with it.

Suddenly he hated the idea of arriving back in Tombstone without a little warning. He unbuckled the curtain at his elbow and rolled it up.

Gray light broke the gloom in the coach, and sage-scented moist air fought the fug of damp wool and sweat. He felt the frowns of his fellow passengers. But the howling thunderstorm that had held them up in Benson had turned into a slow, dreary rain, more like February than August. It seemed to be blowing from the south and west, which kept it out of his window. So long as the other three men weren't getting wet, they wouldn't complain. Or maybe it was Doc's face that kept them quiet.

He was on the wrong side of the coach to see the Tombstone Hills, but he had landmarks enough to know how far they were from town. All for the best. It was one sort of evil to come on trouble unaware, and another to watch it loom, like a condemned man watching his gallows building.

Beside and before the coach lay the Dragoon Mountains, blue through the drizzle. He remembered his picnic in the foothills with Kate. A man ought not to have a taste of that kind of happiness; it would make him believe he was entitled to more of it.

He took a certain bitter satisfaction in breathing the wet air. It wouldn't kill him. Wyatt wouldn't let it.

By the time the stage bumped and splattered to a stop on Allen Street, Doc felt he'd mustered sufficient fortitude and resignation. But the sight of Wyatt under the sidewalk overhang, clearly waiting for the stage, made him shiver. He pretended to stretch while his fellow passengers climbed down, and took his time getting out the door and onto the sidewalk.

"Thought you might need help with your bags," Wyatt said by way of greeting.

"Oh, no, I traveled light. For reasons of health, I couldn't afford to make a long stay." Doc smiled as sweetly as he knew how. "I'd think you'd be too busy to meet the stage. Hasn't Virgil put you on the police force yet?"

A knot of muscle stood out in Wyatt's jaw. "He will when he needs to."

Doc had known he hadn't. He smiled again, and Wyatt flushed.

The driver tossed down Doc's leather portmanteau. Wyatt caught it before Doc could. "How was Tucson?"

"Oh, grand, grand. A fine place for a man's tether to end."

That shut Wyatt up for the length of a few store-fronts. Finally he said, "Kate left town."

"I thought that was the purpose of charging her with threats against life."

"She was threatening your life, wasn't she? Stage robbery and double murder is a hanging offense."

"If that didn't bother me, I fail to see how it was any concern of yours."

Wyatt stopped in the middle of the sidewalk. "God damn it, Doc. I'm your friend. If I see someone doing you dirt, what the hell am I supposed to do?"

"Punish them for usurping your prerogative?"

Whatever Wyatt had expected Doc to say, it had not, apparently, been that. He stood glaring at Doc. Doc's sudden mean-spirited thought was that Wyatt was trying to remember what "usurping" and "prerogative" meant.

"If you can say that about me," Wyatt replied, "you're not the man I thought you were."

"If we're to have this discussion, we should have it with a little more privacy."

Wyatt involved his head and one shoulder in an irri-table shrug. "Nobody's noticing."

It was true. Doc suppressed a shudder. He was wrapped in Wyatt's manipulations again, without warn-ing or consent. "I take it that does not strike you as high-handed?"

"I'm doing no one harm, and you and me some good."

"And all that's left is for me to thank you for your consideration."

"Doc—" Wyatt took a long breath and continued in a milder tone, "I'm looking out for your interests."

"A subject I have no say in, it seems. Now take the hoodoo off us and come along to someplace quiet. Or give me my bag and go your way—it's all one to me."

He met Wyatt's eyes, watched his cold and angry

face. Then the stiffness went out of it. "I owe you an apology, don't I?"

"Yes, you do." Doc felt his own anger seeping away. Wyatt was always like this: high-handed, single-minded, convinced what he did was right and the way he did it was the only possible way. It was one of the things Doc liked about him, most of the time. But expecting consideration from Wyatt was like expecting tact from the occupants of a beehive. And like the bees, Wyatt was only obeying his nature—however unnatural it might seem.

Wyatt smiled, one of his rare real ones. "Let's go to the Can-Can. If I'm going to have to eat crow, I'd rather it was cooked decent."

John Dunbar and another man, walking toward them from Hafford's Corner, nodded to Wyatt, then to Doc. They had become noticeable again.

It was pleasant to come from the rain into the Can-Can Restaurant, that steamed with wet coats and cooking, and smelled of peppers and roasting coffee and bread. The little Chinaman who managed the place hurried up smiling.

"Got good table for you, Mr. Earp, up front where you like."

Wyatt grinned and shook his head. "No thanks, Qwong, you old heathen. The doctor and I want a little peace and quiet. You find us one out of the way."

The Chinaman led them to a table toward the back, out of the path from the kitchen, and waved a waiter over. Wyatt ordered breakfast; Doc ordered coffee.

Wyatt frowned at him over the menu. "When'd you last eat?"

"I believe it was when I was last hungry. Funny how that works."

Wyatt turned back to the waiter. "The same again for Dr. Holliday."

The waiter stole a nervous glance at Doc, nodded, and hurried away.

"I'm buying," Wyatt assured Doc.

"Damned ungrateful of me, but I'm still not hungry. Did it occur to you that the rest of the world would like to arrange things for itself on occasion?"

"Is that what this is about?"

Doc laughed; he couldn't help himself. "Blessed saints and angels, Wyatt, this is about such a passel of things I don't believe I could pick one if you put a gun to my head. Yes, it is about free will. Also conjuration, blackmail, and threats against life. That should do to start."

Wyatt sat with his hands flat on the table, his eyes on them as if a good explanation might appear printed on his knuckles. "I never meant to do anything but right by you, Doc."

"Ah, but was that just the best way to do right by you?"

Wyatt looked up, cold-eyed. Doc found it had very little effect on him for once.

"You're using me, aren't you?" Doc continued. "I will be damned if I know how, but you're using me, and your brothers, and if this were the Middle Ages, even Judge Spicer would call it the Black Arts and burn you at the God-damned stake."

"Used to be, if you approved of the ends, you weren't too nice about the means."

"Just when were the ends presented for my approval in this case?"

The waiter brought Doc's coffee, wary as a horse led up to a bonfire. Doc wondered if he and Wyatt looked like a quarrel; he'd swear they didn't sound like one. They could both say the most dreadful things in a voice that would barely cross the table.

Wyatt waited until Doc swallowed some coffee.

Then he replied, "I told you once. I'm making us all rich." The waiter hurried back with two platters of beefsteak and eggs, which hit the table with an impressive clunk. Wyatt tucked his napkin into his shirtfront and picked up his knife and fork. "I'm also," he added, his attention on his meat, "keeping you alive."

To hear Wyatt say it like that, offhand and unconcerned, struck at Doc's heart and stilled his breath. The odor of the beef, sickly sweet, reached him anyway. "How?" he asked. There was a break in his voice that shamed him.

Wyatt raised his eyebrows. "Conjuration," he drawled.

"What do I owe my life to? Do you sacrifice pigeons and boil black cats alive?"

"Would that trouble you?"

"Does keeping me alive require you to kill something else?"

Wyatt frowned, baffled. "If a man threw down on you, you'd jerk your pistol, wouldn't you? You'd kill to stay alive."

"God damn you, Wyatt—" Doc clenched his teeth on what was better left unsaid. "You don't see a difference, do you? A man chooses to play his life against mine. I choose to take him up on it. We take our chances, man to man. In your game, where did I have a choice?"

Wyatt stared down at his plate. "It *is* my game. I couldn't gamble on you choosing to back me. I'm sorry, Doc, but you're my ace. I couldn't risk letting go of you."

By God, he actually was sorry. Doc saw it in his averted eyes, heard it in his voice. "Then let go now."

"Not now. Don't ask it of me, Doc."

"Why not?"

"Because I'm in a fight I can't win without you."

"With whom, and what about?"

"You don't believe me, do you?" Wyatt said with a bitter grin. He put his fork down. "All right, listen. I'm not the only one in town who boils black cats. Do you understand? Those others are prepared to make a fight. And if I don't defend what's mine, they'll take it. They'll put us in the ground if they can."

"You don't think your brothers and I can do our own defending?"

Wyatt leaned over his plate. "What'll you do? Christ, Doc, you won't even know when it comes at you. As long as you stand with me, I can protect us all. I'm gaining on 'em now."

Doc wondered how he could tell. What were the markers in this game? Did one pile up the bodies of one's enemies like chips at the card table? Or was advantage something harder to measure, something intangible to anyone but the players? Doc thought back over the conversation and realized that he wasn't even sure he and Wyatt were talking about the same thing. Witchcraft and black cats. They couldn't really be talking about that.

Wyatt watched him, regret in his face. "I've gone about it wrong, I know. But I swear to God I never meant you harm. You've helped me in some mighty tight spots. Will you do it again?"

There was an aching tightness in Doc's throat. His only real friend turned out to be next door to the Devil himself, and was asking forgiveness for something they both knew he'd do again as soon as it seemed good. None of which changed the fact that Wyatt was indeed his friend. Dear God, did one laugh or cry at times like this?

"I know some of what you can do," Doc said, "having been on the receiving end. What else is there?"

Wyatt took a mouthful of eggs and swallowed them before he replied. "It ain't like a steam engine, that you can say will pull so much weight up such-and-such grade."

"Fine. What is it like?"

Wyatt shrugged. "I can do what I need to, when I need to do it. I call it, I guess I'd say, and it comes."

"Not unlike Elijah and the wrath of God." If that was how Wyatt thought of himself, Doc wanted to know.

But Wyatt frowned and didn't answer. Perhaps he'd weighed himself according to that biblical scale, and been troubled by the results.

Doc drank his coffee in silence, and let Wyatt eat in peace. When Wyatt slowed down, Doc said, "When did it start?"

Wyatt wiped his moustache with his napkin. "Somewhere between boy and man. I could feel where my family was, like I had a string tied tight between me and them. Nearly drove me crazy. I tried to run off, thinking that would break the string."

Doc asked the appropriate question with his eyebrows.

"That's how I found out my pa was the same way. He knew right where I was." Wyatt shook his head. "I wonder, though, if he still is. Seemed like the better at it I got, the less he had."

"But that's not all you can do."

Wyatt looked out, past Doc, past the walls of the Can-Can, to a view Doc couldn't see. "There's strength in things. In the ground, even. It's like food to me. That's what I could feel in my family, at first. Now I feel it everywhere."

"That's it? You *feel* things?"

Wyatt huffed out through his nose. "Feeling's no

damned good unless it leads to doing. I've found there's ways to help my dealings along, make 'em come out right."

"And you employ those ways."

Wyatt's gaze came back to Doc's face, but for a moment Doc wasn't sure Wyatt recognized him. "Does God give a man his senses so he won't use them?"

"So you have no doubt of the identity of the giver?"

Wyatt focused on him and smiled a little. "I can't send this back, can I? Until I know otherwise, I'll assume the best."

They were at the back of the room, but even so Doc could hear a faint clamor of voices from the street, the knocking of boots on the sidewalk. Wyatt's head came up, like a dog testing the air.

"What do your senses tell you now?" Doc asked. But Wyatt was already up and heading toward the door.

Doc dropped his napkin over the congealing mess on his plate, pushed back from the table, and followed Wyatt.

The stationer's clerk wrapped and tied Mildred's box of paper, then cast a sullen look out the window onto Allen Street. "This won't keep off rain," he grumbled, poking the bundle.

"It's fine. The box can get water spots; I don't mind."

She might as well not have spoken. The clerk, muttering under his breath, trotted into the back room.

Mildred sighed, picked up the box, and headed for the door.

As she reached it, three men hurried past toward Fifth Street. Then two more. A gig stopped in the middle of the street, its driver staring toward Fifth. She heard a low-key hubbub of voices, hooves, and footfalls.

"Here, missus!" the clerk called behind her. But she stepped out the door.

The rain had settled to a sullen, heavy mist. Near the corner of Fifth and Allen a crowd grew, blocking traffic in the muddy street. Her first thought was for the president; but news of him would come through the telegraph office, and that was behind her.

At the center of the crowd was a buckboard with two men on the seat, drovers in work clothes. The two mules between the shafts laid their ears back as people pressed too close.

The driver was thick-bodied, bearded, and dour. Beside him sat a much younger man, small, with a light-colored moustache. There was a bandage around his head, just showing beneath his hat, and he sat hunched as if his stomach troubled him. He was sweating and white-faced.

As Mildred came in hearing range, the young man shook his head at something someone asked him.

"It was Mexicans," he said. "I saw 'em close."

"Smugglers?" called a voice near the buckboard.

"Hell, no. Mexican army regulars. And they could hit what they aimed at, all right." At that the young man shivered. "My God, we were sleeping, most of us. We were sleeping."

"What happened?" Mildred asked a dark-skinned drover beside her. He shook his head and leaned toward the buckboard.

Mildred tucked her parcel and her umbrella tighter under her elbow and squeezed sideways through the crowd. She got to within a few yards of the wagon before the gapers were too tightly packed to pass.

Ike Clanton shoved up to the buckboard on the other side. His absurd cherub-curled rusty hair was flattened with damp, and beads of moisture hung from the ends of his upturned moustache and the waxed point of his imperial. He was pale except for a patch of red on each cheek.

He clenched both hands on the wagon's footboard. "This is our wagon," Clanton said. "My pa was driving it."

"So I brung it back," the young man answered. "You take it as it suits you." He sounded as if ownership of the buckboard and the rest of daily life were far from his thoughts.

Clanton thumped the side of the wagon with his palm. "Why didn't my pa bring it back? Where is he?"

"Jesus goddamn," said someone off to Mildred's right. "Look at this."

"There's dozens of 'em," said another voice.

The young man peered into Clanton's face, then around the street, as if wondering where it came from. "Gray's ranch, with the rest of 'em. Except Earnshaw. He didn't get a scratch."

"Why didn't he come in with the wagon?"

"Earnshaw?"

"No, damn you! My pa! Old Man Clanton!"

The young man frowned. "They're all shot dead. Buried at Gray's ranch. Will Lang, Dixie Gray, Charley Snow, Jim Crane, and your pa." He scrubbed a trembling hand over his face. "No, that ain't right. They buried Charley there in Guadalupe Canyon. He was too far gone to move."

Jim Crane. Five men, and one of them Crane. Where was Jesse Fox, and what had he done?

"You're lying," Clanton croaked. "It's a lie."

The crowd around Mildred shifted, and she saw the side panels of the buckboard. She thought she saw light reflected off drops of water or bright new nailheads. The crowd closed again.

It was only from the afterimage that she realized what it was. Light through a score of bullet holes.

Not one man with a gun. The drover said it was Mexican soldiers. Mexico had made official protests about Arizona rustlers raiding over the border; the Mexican government might have sent a troop to search them out.

Had Jesse not found Crane, then? Jesse Fox wasn't in the list of dead. But they might not have recognized him.

Old Man Clanton was rumored to deal in stolen stock, but not in men's lives. Will Lang raised cattle near the New Mexico line and was well thought of. Dixie Gray, barely grown, with his game leg; had he gone with the party as a lark? They weren't gunmen or thieves. They were ordinary men, working for a living. Their capital crime was to share a camp with Jim Crane, last of the men who could say for sure who had stopped the Benson stage.

Clanton grabbed the side of the bench seat, as if he meant to tear it and the men out of the wagon. The young drover winced and pressed an arm against his middle. The driver jerked the reins. The mules balked and fussed, and the onlookers pressed backward.

A man caught Clanton's shoulder from behind. For an instant Mildred didn't know him—hatless, pale, unshaven, a gash and a purpling bruise on one cheek, shadows under and in his eyes. It was Jesse.

He seemed to be wearing someone else's waistcoat. It hung too wide and too long over his crumpled shirt. As shabby as he'd been when she'd first seen him, it hadn't been a patch on this.

Jesse pulled Clanton back and kept both hands on him as if the man might run away. But the fight had gone out of Clanton. He stared at the wagon as if he just now understood it. Was he seeing the bullet holes and imagining his father's body twitching and jumping in his bedroll under a rain of gunfire, or springing up only to fall and jerk and jerk as the bullets snatched at him—

Mildred squeezed her eyes shut and breathed hard and deep. Harry would use "massacre" in the head. What size type would he order? It would be tomorrow's lead.

There, she wouldn't faint, or be sick.

Someone had finally gathered his wits and cleared the crowd out of the buckboard's path. The driver looked to Clanton for instructions, but Clanton stood working his hands, not meeting his eyes. The driver shrugged, growled at the mules, and the buckboard creaked and splashed down Allen Street.

The clot of onlookers fragmented, spread out like sugar dissolving in tea. Mildred crossed the street.

Jesse hauled Clanton back onto the sidewalk. Mildred could see his fingers digging into the cloth of Clanton's coat.

"Let loose of me," Clanton snapped.

"Where did you get it?" Jesse asked him, almost too soft to hear.

"What?"

"The bag for Crane."

Color rushed into Clanton's face and drained again. "I don't know what—"

"Yes, you do. Who gave it to you?"

Clanton peered into Jesse's face as if it were much farther away than it was. His expression changed, crumbled. "Wyatt Earp," he said. Jesse let go of him.

Mildred knew neither of them had seen her. She stepped back into the doorway of the cigar store.

As if Clanton had conjured him, Wyatt Earp pressed forward out of the dwindling crowd. Doc Holliday followed after.

Earp looked down at Clanton, his face flinty. "I'm sorry about your pa."

Clanton frowned. "You're sorry."

Earp nodded. "For your loss."

"You're sorry. Jesus," he asked mildly, "d'you think I'm a half-wit? That I don't know what you done?" Clanton paused for breath, and to squint into Earp's face. It might have been hewed from rock.

Clanton stepped back, almost tripping over Jesse, and raised his voice. "I'm gonna make you god-damned sorry before I'm done. I'm gonna send you to hell. I'm gonna send all you God-damned Earps straight to hell." He flushed an unpleasant purple and clamped his mouth shut. Then he flung himself away and half ran up the street after the buckboard.

"Good day, Mr. Earp, Dr. Holliday." Jesse's voice was steady and cool, his face almost as impassive as Earp's. But Mildred saw a flash of light in Jesse's eye, as if reflected off something that wasn't there.

"Mr. Fox," said Earp. There was no warmth in his voice, not as there had been in the ice cream saloon. Holliday settled for a nod and a raised eyebrow.

"What a dangerous place this has become," Jesse said.

"Decent folk have nothing to fear in Tombstone."

Jesse laughed, a sound like a blacksmith's hammer striking steel. "Even God Almighty doesn't make that kind of guarantee. He didn't make it to those men in Guadalupe Canyon."

Earp's jaw shifted, clenched. "Fellows who take other men's cattle can't expect to die in bed."

"They were stealing cattle?"

"The Mexicans wouldn't have been there other-wise."

"Ah. Is that why *I* was there?"

Earp said nothing. Mildred thought the muscles around his eyes tensed; that was all.

Dr. Holliday watched them warily. Could Holliday

feel it, too—the pressure of air and stillness around Earp and Jesse, like a container for some dangerous experiment? The street noises seemed muffled, but the shift of Earp's boot on the sidewalk, the rub of Jesse's sleeve, their breathing, were almost painfully clear.

"You'd know best what took you into the company of outlaws."

"What took me was a grudge against Jim Crane. I meant to kill him. But unlike you, I meant to do it face-to-face. And unlike you, I wasn't prepared to murder four innocent men to see it done."

Earp closed his eyes. Such a small thing . . . but it was like stone splitting away from a cliff face. "But that's just what you did."

"Is that what you'll tell yourself, when you wake up from a sound sleep in the dark of night? That I spoiled your aim? You can try that."

I missed something, Mildred thought. *Something big*. Earp blamed Jesse for the massacre. Jesse was blaming Earp—but Earp hadn't been there.

Earp stepped closer. His face, no longer controlled, was twisted with rage. "You no-account drifter. This ain't a thing that ever crossed your mind, but it's what I live by: I will protect my family any way I have to. If I die with a few souls on my conscience, that's how it is. You cow-boy leeches, living off other men and caring for nobody, maybe that ain't the way you think. But I am prepared to do what I've done and more, to see my family right."

Jesse lifted his chin, looked past Earp's shoulder. "Shall we ask Dr. Holliday about those who live off other men?"

Holliday flushed. "I suggest you have your quarrel without my help." He turned to go.

"Stay." Earp's voice was like a slap. "I want Mr. Fox to hear this in front of witnesses." He smiled. "You might want to hunt out less crowded parts, Mr. Fox. Tell your cow-boy friends to do the same. I don't doubt you've got sand; but we fight bigger dogs 'round here."

"And use the smaller ones to hunt the rats?" Jesse cocked his head inquiringly at Earp. "Do you know, a lot of blood soaked into the earth in Guadalupe Canyon. Five men's life blood, spilled where they died." A faint cold smile touched his face. "I left a good deal of my own there, too."

Earp went pale.

"That gave me . . . a say in the matter, you might call it." Jesse raised his eyebrows and waited. Earp didn't speak. "So I did what I felt you'd given me the right to do."

Earp shook his head. Sweat trickled into his trimmed moustache, his shining white collar.

"I'm glad we have witnesses." Jesse turned his head a little, toward Holliday, toward Mildred. "If you forget what I'm about to say, they can remind you. But I doubt you will."

Something changed; the air was cold and moist and smelled like the exhalation of an abandoned mine. Mildred shivered and clutched her arms, even as she thought, *He knew all along I was here.* She couldn't hear Earp breathe now. She couldn't hear herself.

But she heard Jesse's voice, relentless and soft. "Never again on this ground will you kill a man at a distance. That power is sealed from you."

A sort of binding, Jesse had said. A blood sacrifice.

"Nothing made of earth or air will do that work for you."

The lock surrounded them, open, waiting like an in-held breath for the key to turn. Earp clenched his jaw and shut his eyes like a man in pain.

"No matter what weapon you bring, unless you can

look in a man's face when you strike, he is safe from you."

The key turned. Mildred swayed with the force of it and clutched the door frame.

Earp raised a hand. Mildred was shocked to see it tremble. "You're crazy."

"You know I'm not," Jesse whispered.

Holliday stared at Jesse in horror, in fascination. Then he looked to Earp. He opened his mouth, closed it, swallowed, and opened it again to laugh hollowly. "It is just possible that we have all, in our separate ways, underestimated Mr. Fox."

Earp began, "I will still do—"

"—whatever it takes," Jesse said. "But not like that. Not again."

Earp made a fist of his raised hand. He looked at it as if it surprised him, as if he could command it with his eyes not to betray him. But it still shook. He let it fall, turned on his heel, and strode across the street and into the Oriental.

"So you're another of them," Holliday said. As one might say, "So you went to my college."

Jesse closed his eyes and let out a long breath. "I am."

"Well, don't let it carry you away. He will do what he says; one of Wyatt's great virtues. And when he does, I will back his play." Holliday smiled. "Though I've a notion any sane man would take to his heels. But Wyatt does not share, Mr. Fox. Keep it in mind." He touched his hat brim and followed Earp into the saloon.

Mildred left her doorway shelter and came to stand at Jesse's elbow. "I hope I didn't distract you."

"If you had, I don't think I could have done it." The bruise stood out appallingly against his pallor.

The atmospheric oddities were gone; it was just rain, just air, just Allen Street.

"I set out to kill him," Jesse said apologetically.

"Crane?"

He nodded. "I couldn't do it. He was bad straight through. But he was also ignorant and scared nearly out of his wits. You were right, it was the law's business." His head drooped, but with a visible effort, he raised it again to meet her eyes. "Just for a moment, you were afraid I'd done it. I wanted you to know it was a reasonable moment's doubt."

"Very thoughtful of you," she said, though her voice quavered. "I think you ought to be in your bed." She looked down the street and felt a jolt of alarm. "Where's your horse?"

"Taking his ease at Gray's ranch. It was a long, hard ride."

"But he's all right? Otherwise, I don't think you can face Chu and live."

"I need to say 'You were right' to Chu, as well."

"Then you have a mortifying day ahead of you. Perhaps you should rest up for it."

"All right, all right." Jesse laughed weakly. "You need me to be quiet and go away, so you can piece together everything that just happened."

"I need you to not fall down in the street." But he was right; even she hadn't known it until she heard it from his lips. Mildred shivered and thought, *I have a friend who will always know more of me than I do of him. Can I be comfortable with that?*

No, not comfortable. But she thought she could learn to accept it. She held out her arm. "Feel free to lean, if you need it."

He gave her an odd, penetrating look, as if she'd said more than she knew. Then he put his hand under her elbow. "The same to you. Anytime."

* * *

Mildred stood at the edge of the cemetery, looking out over the valley to the mountains beyond. The rain had stopped, and the sun burned like wildfire on the western edge of the sky, washing the Dragoons in an unlikely candy-pink light. She heard the wash at the foot of the flats churning and bubbling in the blue shadows yards below her feet. A month's rain had sprouted the seeds in the rocky soil, and grass fringed the paths and colored the plain like a vegetable blush. The land's bones were just as they'd been on Decoration Day, but the skin over them was new and strange.

No, not strange. This was what the earth did, whenever there was rain enough.

She'd half expected everything to be different. If Wyatt Earp and Jesse Fox were nature's laws overthrown, nature should be changed by it. But nature ran in its same unmanageable course. So perhaps they weren't unnatural after all.

She walked back to David's grave and crouched at its foot. "Well," she said to his marker, and found that a dozen different thoughts had jostled each other aside on the way to her tongue. "He ought to be frightening," she said finally. "I don't know why he isn't. If I put him in a story, he'd be downright hair-raising."

Mildred grinned, imagining Jesse's reaction to that. Maybe she'd tell him about M. E. Benjamin. Or maybe she'd just write the story and let the revelations fall where they might.

Revelations—oh, heavens, he still didn't know about Chu, did he? He was going to find out that Mildred had known, and hadn't told him. He'd probably like that less than being cast as a sorcerer in a frontier Gothic. She found she looked forward to the argument.

Fire, floods, Apaches, and rustlers; robbery, land swindles, and political feuds. Tombstone teetered between death and riches, and its people fought each other for every advantage. Some of them did it with a power that turned stone and blood into a weapon. And Mildred was in the middle of it, thanks to the *Nugget* and her own curiosity.

The warm and slightly quivery feeling in her chest was happiness. What would Jesse think of that when she told him?

When. She felt the heat rise in her face. She stood up, shook out her skirts, and smiled down at David's marker. "I'll be all right. I promise."

Water had welled up or trickled down from somewhere to form a still oval at her feet, like a miniature bowl of evening sky. She didn't think it had been there when she walked up. That was water in Arizona Territory: appearing from nowhere, disappearing like a conjuring trick. Improbable, but not unnatural.

The sunset was over. She turned and started back to town.